D0062823

Angela Thirkell

Angela Thirkell, granddaughter of Edward Burne-Jones, was born in London in 1890. At the age of twenty-eight she moved to Melbourne, Australia where she became involved in broadcasting and was a frequent contributor to the British periodicals. Mrs. Thirkell did not begin writing novels until her return to Britain in 1930; then, for the rest of her life, she produced a new book almost every year. Her stylish prose and deft portrayal of the human comedy in the imaginary county of Barsetshire have amused readers for decades. She died in 1961, just before her seventy-first birthday.

"[Thirkell's] satire is always just, apt, kindly, and pleasantly rambly. Blended in with the satire, too, are all the pleasures of an escapist romance."
— *New York Herald Tribune*

"The happy outcome of her tale is secondary to the crisp, often quaint amusement one derives from discovering how deftly Angela Thirkell makes the most unexciting incident appear important ."
— *Saturday Review of Literature*

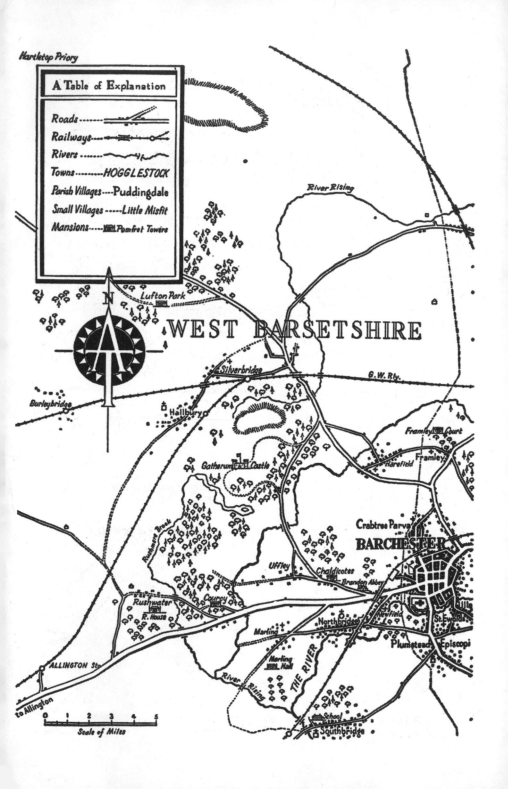

Hartletop Priory

A Table of Explanation

Roads ……
Railways……
Rivers ……
Towns ……… HOGGLESTOCK
Parish Villages …… Puddingdale
Small Villages …… Little Misfit
Mansions …… Pomfret Towers

N

WEST BARSETSHIRE

River Rising

Lufton Park

Silverbridge

G. W. Rly.

Burleybridge

Hailbury

Framley Court

Gatherum Castle

Framley

Harefield

Rushwater Brook

Crabtree Parva

BARCHESTER

Uffley

Chaldicotes

Brandon Abbey

Rushwater

Courcy

R. House

Newfield

St. Ewold's

Northbridge

Marling

Plumstead Episcopi

ALLINGTON St.

Marling Hall

THE RIVER

River Rising

School

to Allington

0   1   2   3   4   5

Scale of Miles

Southbridge

A Map of the County of

BARSETSHIRE

Shewing the Situations of the
various great Estates and Seats

ENTER SIR ROBERT

A Novel by

Angela Thirkell

MOYER BELL
Wakefield, Rhode Island & London

Published by Moyer Bell
This Edition 2000

LIBRARY OF CONGRESS
CATALOGING-IN-PUBLICATION DATA

Thirkell, Angela Mackail, 1890–1961.
    Enter Sir Robert / by Angela Thirkell. — 1st ed.
    p.   cm.
    ISBN 1-55921-236-5
    I. Title.
    PR6039.H43E58   1999
    823'.912—dc21   98-53771
                                     CIP

Cover illustration: Jacques-Émile Blanche, *Igor Stravinski*.

Printed in the United States of America
Distributed in North America by Publishers Group West, P.O. Box 8843,
Emeryville CA 94662, 800-788-3123 (in California 510-658-3453).

CHAPTER I

As it is some time since we were at Hatch End, we will take this opportunity of reminding our Reader (the one who says our books are so nice because it doesn't matter which you read or where you open it as they are all exactly the same—as indeed they are, with a difference) that it is a small village in the valley of the Rising, which here flows through water-meadows. Hatch House, since 1721 the seat of the Hallidays, local land-owners or Squires, is a pleasant red-brick building sheltered by the downs at the back. In front of it is a lawn, bounded by a low red-brick wall with a stone coping and an eight foot drop on its riverward side to the old Barchester Road, beyond which lie the water-meadows and the Rising. The village of Hatch End, on the other side of the river, is reached by a narrow road, carried high on stone arches, spanning the water-meadows above the reach of floods, built by the sixth Earl of Pomfret at his own expense after the great flood of 1863 when the two banks of the river were completely cut off from one another for seven or eight miles and a jackass was found in a willow tree, unhurt, but extremely difficult to extricate. The valley is still mildly flooded from time to time, when carts have to splash axle-deep and cars either go round the long way by a bridge two miles lower down or, tempting the flood, expire with shrieks and hissings and have to be pulled out by any cart horse who happens to be at leisure; and as nearly all the cart horses are now tractors, forbidden to use the bridge because of their weight, the car has time to sit there with wet feet and repent its sins.

The village itself had been, up till the end of the war, the usual Barsetshire type, with one or two small gentry stone houses, some pleasant red-brick houses and a number of cottages with white-washed fronts (if anyone remembered to white-wash them), thatched roofs with bits of wire netting supposed to keep birds off and now mostly so covered with moss that the netting was invisible, and garden walls consisting largely of mud or clay, some of them still with a thatched top to prevent their total disintegredation (as Mr. Geo. Panter, licensee of the Mellings Arms put it), others hideously, though utilitarianly, with a corrugated iron cover like half a drain pipe split lengthways, if we make ourselves clear.

Owing to a totalitarian war in which many thousands of lives were lost and a generation sorely depleted, the population of England was larger than ever. Where it all came from, Hatch End did not know, nor do we. Perhaps some kind of explanation lies in the fact that far too many people, having tasted the sweets of freedom at our expense, preferred to go on doing so; also that the children of Dark Rosaleen (we allude to what we still call Ireland as no one knows quite how to pronounce the native name which is written in Cunic, or Ogham, or perhaps Runic characters on its stamps), found good wages under the Saxon oppressor well worth an exile from Erin; that our dusky brethren from Africa and the West Indies and elsewhere prefer our climate and our increasing bureaucratic tyranny to their own; that we are, in fact, what Imperial Rome was, and if the Orontes does not flow into the Tiber here, rivers from every less agreeable part of the world are flowing like anything into the Thames, the Forth, and even the Rising. Saxon and Norman and Dane are we, as Lord Tennyson writes, and a good deal besides: and as Mrs. Morland the popular writer of the Madame Koska thrillers said, after a visit to friends in Riverside, London, S.W.3, it is disconcerting if you are coming back from a friend's house after dark to meet two or three people with no faces, only white collars and the whites of their eyes; it made one think of Othello and wonder if they would strangle one, only of course he was really only *brown*, she understood. At which point her old friend George Knox, the still very successful writer of historical novels, said Laura's foolishness was passing the foolishness of woman, and Mrs. Morland said, without heat, *man* he meant, and Mrs. Knox laughed at them both. But, having by-passed this divagation, what we meant to say, though the telling gives us no pleasure at all, is that as a result of the general overcrowding of our little island cheap houses were being built everywhere and nearly always on the best agricultural land. Hatch End had not escaped. A large suburb of depressed semi-detached houses had been begun on its outskirts and was rapidly growing, to house some of the overflow from Barchester. For with the growth of Mr. Adams's works and Mr. Pilward's brewery (including the by-products of brewing which we shall not particularise as we do not know what they are) and Mr. Macfadyen's Agricultural Laboratory which had begun after the war in a modest way but was yearly becoming bigger and better, a large population of foreigners (by which Barsetshire merely meant people who lived outside the county) had come in and they had to be housed. West Barsetshire had fought manfully against a satellite town, but one cannot stem the tide of so-called progress. The only redeeming feature of this revolting new suburb was that it lay on the Barchester side, well away from the village and Sir Robert Graham's estate, and did most of its shopping and all its cinema-going in Barchester.

Three or four miles above Hatch End is the still fairly unspoilt village of Little Misfit, past whose lower end the Rising takes its course. Here, just off the main road, lies Holdings, the ancestral property for at least two hundred years of well to do landowners called Graham, the present owner being Sir Robert Graham, K.C.M.G. and a good many other letters, who had been a professional soldier and served with high distinction in the last World War to End War; 1939–1945 nominally, but thanks to the more repulsive of those nations who took part in it, still going on, or being just about to blow up again in every part of the world, with the cordial cooperation of many unpleasant powers or dependent states, large and small, who felt that having avoided fighting themselves it would now be a good plan to throw their weight about and demand Self-Government. Self-Determination, Ambassadorial Status, large gifts of money and arms and complete freedom to be as nasty as they wished to everyone, while no nation—under pain of expulsion from a number of Leagues or Pacts known only by their initials though most people had not the faintest idea what words the initials represented—was to be allowed to defend its own frontier, protect its own nationals, or publish any newspaper article in any way depreciatory of its grasping ill-wishers. All of which was called the Free United Nations Kinship (whose initials, we may say, gave considerable pleasure to the large number of those who did not believe in it nor trust it).

But we must leave this golden dream of permanent war on earth and universal bad will to men, and return to Holdings whose owner, owing to his multifarious occupations, has never been in residence when we were about. For this his wife made full amends, keeping open house for friends and neighbours and such young people as were within easy distance. But not so many of these now, for all our dear young are in jobs, the better to be among their contemporaries. And very nice they are; hard-working and taking their fun when they get it and altogether, from their point of view, having a good time. And when they get married, if they do have their kitchen like the beach after a fine Whit Monday and are—to our eyes—sluttish and slatternly, they have quite delightful grandchildren for us who are turned out like princes and princesses when they go to each other's parties, even if they are like Darkest London at home.

Now, with her three sons professional soldiers as their father had been, her two elder daughters happily married and only

Edith at home, Lady Graham had for the first time in her life felt a little lonely. But being with all her appearance of elegant fragility remarkably strong, and though she seemed vague really very practical, she had taken on the organising of local branches of such worthy bodies as the Barsetshire Archaeological Society, the Friends of Barchester Cathedral, and the Friends of Beliers Priory, a monastic building whose remains consisted entirely of one end wall of a barn popularly supposed to have been a Refectory, or an Ambulatory, or a Scriptorium, and a chain of picturesque almost stagnant pools known as the Dipping Ponds, fed by a streamlet, tributary to the Woolram, where The Monks were supposed to have Kept Carp in The Olden Times. As there was no proof of this, nor of anything else, the Barsetshire Archaeological Society had organised an Outing in July, but owing to the weather it had to be abandoned, so that everyone's opinion remained unchanged, as indeed it would have been in any case. There were also the less spectacular but really useful societies such as the St. John and Red Cross Hospital Libraries, the Friends of Barchester General Hospital, the Women's Institutes and several smaller local bodies, for all of which her ladyship did good work, never promising to do anything she could not do well and lending her large beautiful room, known as the Saloon, for meetings; in all of which worthy works Edith helped her mother very efficiently and kindly. Also, being animal-minded as most Leslies were, Edith had, after the marriage of her sister Emmy, taken a practical interest in her father's farm and was considered by Goble, the bailiff, as a young lady who did understand pigs. He wouldn't say cows. Now Miss Emmy, she as married young Mr. Grantly, she knew a cow when she saw one and a bull; and 'tother one too, Goble was apt to add, with a fine lewd Saxon chuckle. But Miss Edith, he said—and far too often his friends at the Mellings Arms held— now there was a young lady as *did* know a silk purse from a sow's ear and he wouldn't be surprised if Holdings Blunderbore got the Barsetshire Agricultural's Challenge Cup this year, the way his father, Holdings Goliath, did in '47.

Whether Edith had other immortal longings in her we do not know, for she has grown in the years of peace from the child we knew to a young lady whom as yet we do not quite know. Not so fair nor so overpowering as her sister Emmy, Mrs. Tom Grantly; no dainty rogue in porcelain like her difficult sister Clarissa Belton; but with a mixture of Pomfret and Leslie which was very attractive. Could old Lord Pomfret, the seventh Earl and her great-uncle have seen his great-niece, he would have been grimly pleased to recognise in her the Foster strain, taken her riding about the place to be talked to by the old tenants and working people, appreciated her card-sense and liked her looks. Had her grandfather, Lady Emily Leslie's husband, lived to see her grown-up, he would have found in her a charming friend with good manners to her elders, a sound grasp of the essentials of cow-breeding, a working knowledge of how a small farm is run and an unusual gift with pigs.

With love she was not particularly acquainted. In her salad and rather stout days, she had made eyes at most of her elder sisters' and her brothers' friends, but though at seven or eight she behaved like a finished coquette, her heart had not been affected then, or later. Two or three years ago, at the dance in the elegant Assembly Room of the Nabob's Arms at Harefield she had flirted wildly, but always with married gentlemen who, though still fairly young, could at a pinch have been her father. That a daughter of hers, still under twenty, should not have been in love at least with a curate, or a film star, would have seemed unusual to Lady Graham, but though her ladyship had an uncommonly good world sense as a rule, she had little clue to her youngest daughter, part romping hoyden, part a sound pig-fancier, part a poetical improvisatoressa, if we may coin such a word. Perhaps there is a real one, but our Italian dictionary is downstairs. And also, to go back to what we were saying, a very affectionate and easy person to live with.

*   *   *

On this particular morning Lady Graham and Edith were in the village doing odds and ends of shopping which included fish. In spite of the march of civilisation Hatch End, unless it had the means and the time to go to Barchester, still had to depend for its fish on Vidler's van which called at The Shop twice a week. Here regular customers could leave their orders on a Monday and Thursday, which orders Vidler would carry out on Tuesday and Friday, provided he had the right fish in his van. For, as he truly said, it stood to reason a man might know what kind of fish his customers wanted but a man couldn't guess what kind fish would be in the market. But it all worked pretty well.

So they walked down to The Shop, where the proprietress, old Mrs. Hubback, cousin of the Hallidays' faithful maid, had a large damp parcel wrapped in an insufficient amount of newspaper waiting for them.

"Good-morning, my lady," said Mrs. Hubback. "It's cod again, but I saw some lemon soles out of the corner of my eye and I said to Vidler, fridge or no fridge, I said, cod's not the stuff for her ladyship. And if you don't mind your business better, I said, her ladyship's going to get her fish in Barchester."

"How kind of you, Mrs. Hubback," said her ladyship. "Did he believe you?"

"I couldn't say, my lady," said Mrs. Hubback, "but he looked a great fool, as he is and all them Vidlers are. A gypsy lot, that's what they are and I ought to know seeing my auntie married one. Beat her proper he did."

"How unfortunate," said Lady Graham, assuming a sympathy she did not feel. And this, I may add, is what we all do now. A kind of blackmail in which no money passes but the blackmail is exacted to the utmost farthing's worth by the amount of listening and sympathising we have to do with people whose time appears to be of no value to them and whose affairs are of no interest to us. To one's maid (if one has one), to the milk, the bread, the butcher, the grocer, the fish; to everyone up and down the village street, or the shopping road in London. To the taxi driver we have overtipped, to the baker's head assistant who expects one to ask after her old mother whenever one comes into the shop, to all of these and hundreds more we pay ceaseless toll. Perhaps it promotes human fellowship, but sometimes one would like to tie them all up in a row and gag them and do the talking oneself. Or, better still, just leave them there gagged and walk away.

"Black and blue she was, as the saying is," Mrs. Hubback added, as she wrapped the fish parcel in a large and fairly clean newspaper. "Still it takes all sorts to make a world," and as this remark, though very true, did not appear to have any particular bearing on the subject, Lady Graham managed to say "Good-morning" and go out.

"Now, what next?" said Lady Graham to her daughter. "I must see Mr. Choyce about a little service for darling Gran's anniversary. I mean of the day she died. It seems so long ago. It is six years."

"I'm so sorry, mother," said Edith. "Gran was so darling and I remember that day because we were talking about how kind our American friends were, because they sent us food in the war and then when the war stopped they still sent it and I made a poem about it. But Gran was in the little drawing-room and didn't hear it and then Martin came in to tell us. *Darling* Gran," and her eyes misted a little. "When is the service to be?"

Lady Graham said on Thursday afternoon if it suited every-one, and only the family or any old friends who liked to come.

"I wish we could have had Mr. Bostock," she said, "because darling Mamma is buried at Rushwater, but then it would be Martin's business and he has so much to do. In any case our little service is only a sort of private one, because Gran died here, though she was buried at Rushwater. Just for all the people here who loved her. And it will please Mr. Choyce *so* much," at which moment the vicar came past and stopped to speak to them.

"You are the very person I wanted to see," said Lady Graham. "About darling Mamma's funeral."

Mr. Choyce, surprised by her ladyship's way of putting it, wondered if there was some difficulty at Rushwater and Lady Emily Leslie would have to be exhumed and buried again and if so why and by whom.

"Because, Thursday is her anniversary," Lady Graham went on, not noticing Mr. Choyce's agitation. "I mean the day she died, not her birthday. Though of course we have to believe that it is all much the same thing, haven't we? I mean when one is dead it probably feels like being born again, only as one doesn't remember being born it would be a little difficult to get it right the first time," by which religious-philosophical thesis Mr. Choyce was considerably exercised and wondered what on earth her ladyship meant; though he admired, nay adored her too much to say so.

"So I thought if we could have a little service of Remembrance for her, with some prayers and something out of the Bible," her ladyship went on, "darling Mamma would like it so much, and after all if one is in heaven I cannot think that it matters much if the service is at Rushwater or Hatch End. They must look exactly alike from there."

Mr. Choyce, an old friend of Mr. Halliday's, a gentleman, extremely kind-hearted, and a Christian in the best and happiest sense of the word, was overcome with compassion for Lady Graham who bore her sorrow so angelically and said he would feel it a privilege to do anything for Lady Graham.

"Oh, but it's not for me," said Lady Graham, "it's for my mother," at which words poor Mr. Choyce fell into a kind of religious melancholia at the thought of having made such a floater (for his slang was a little out of date) and perhaps wounded the tender heart of a woman mourning a beloved mother.

"If you are not busy, Mr. Choyce, do let us go into the church for a moment," said Lady Graham, "and then I can show you *everything,*" which made the vicar even more nervous, but he remembered that he was not only a clerk in Holy Orders but quite as old as Lady Graham, if not older, and braced himself to accompany her ladyship.

"We have had some quite dreadful men here," said Lady Graham.

"Not the gang that broke into Lord Aberfordbury's house and stole all the whiskey!" said Mr. Choyce, alarmed for Lady Graham's safety.

"I meant in the *church,*" said Lady Graham in a religious voice.

The vicar said he always kept the church plate, not that there was much of it, in the locked cupboard under the organ to put thieves off the scent, and had fixed an alarm which was connected with the vicarage, so that if it went off he could get his gun and go straight down to the vestry.

"How *very* clever of you," said Lady Graham admiringly. "You must let me see it," at which the vicar's heart beat quite uncontrollably for a few seconds. "But I wasn't talking about burglars, Mr. Choyce. I meant we had some dreadful vicars. *Long* before you came of course. When my husband was a boy there was a vicar who used to pray by name for everyone he didn't like. And there was another one who shot a fox in the churchyard."

Mr. Choyce, not quite certain whether the sin lay in shooting the fox or doing it in the churchyard, said If we had no sins we deceived ourselves and then wondered if that was what he meant.

"And the man who stole socks," said Lady Graham. "You could trust him with the collection or *anything*, but if he saw socks on a line he always took them. He did not stay long and I believe he was sent to a nudist colony, because they had nothing on that he could steal. So I think just a few prayers and something out of the Bible. Her children *do* rise up and call her blessed, Mr. Choyce. Shall I come back to the Vicarage with you and we could choose something?"

Torn between his respectful adoration for Lady Graham and his uncertainty as to what she might say next, Mr. Choyce took her ladyship and her daughter through the side gate, along the short and depressing drive overshadowed and encroached on by evergreens, across the lawn where a gigantic monkey-puzzle blocked the light from at least three windows, and so through the encaustic tiled little hall (or lobby, horrid word) into his study, which was so exactly like a study that words are not needed. If we say that there were coloured Arundel prints on the wall, framed in what is known as an Oxford frame (and is so hideous that we feel the name must have been given to it at The Other Place) and a hockey stick over the mantelpiece, we shall have said quite enough. Edith, who knew by experience that when her mother had decided on a course it was impossible to stop her, unless by physical force, sat in a comfortable chair and read a back number of the Guardian, that excellent church weekly with its equally good secular side now, to the dishonour of the reading public and more especially the active church-goers among it, dead for want of support, leaving not a wrack behind.

"Only something very simple," said Lady Graham, "because darling Mamma could not bear a long service on account of her arthritis. And perhaps you would let my husband read something out of the Bible if he is down here. If not we might ask George Halliday because his father was a churchwarden and feels so out of it now he is an invalid. Only we must be careful about the Bible reading because you never know *what* you will find. Perhaps just the words about her children rising up and calling her blessed."

"Proverbs, chapter thirty-one, verse twenty-eight," said Mr. Choyce.

"How *did* you know that?" said Lady Graham, with frank admiration.

"It is part of my job," said Mr. Choyce. "And I would like to remember verse twenty-nine as well: 'Many daughters have

done virtuously, but thou excellest them all,'" and then he
wondered if Lady Graham would say, "Unhand me villain" and
have him excommunicated.

"*How* true," said Lady Graham, her lovely eyes a little misty.
"She did excel everyone. *Thank* you, Mr. Choyce," at which
Edith, who had listened with composed interest, suddenly realised for the first time that her mother was not only her mother,
to love, to be loved by, to laugh at sometimes though always
affectionately, but that real grown-up people found a rare and
precious quality in her. Which discovery was very good for the
rather spoilt youngest child and though the immediate impression passed, it will leave some mark in her and strengthen her
affection.

"And now, as we are here," said Lady Graham to the Vicar,
"will you be kind enough to show Edith and me your burglar
alarm?"

Mr. Choyce was more than willing. Edith suggested that she
should go back to the church and try to open the safe and see
what happened. Mr. Choyce took the key off his chain and gave
it to her. When a minute or so had passed a bell began to ring
stridently and violently.

"There!" said Mr. Choyce, with unfeigned pride. "The bell is
hidden behind those two volumes of Paley's Evidences. They
are dummies of course. And once it has started the burglar can't
stop it," and he pressed a knob on the shelf where the books
stood. The bell stopped. Lady Graham could not contain her
admiration of his ingenuity.

"I'm so glad you like it," said Mr. Choyce. "I invented it, and
my only disappointment is that no one has used it. I mean
professionally. If it rang in the night I should of course ring up
the police at once and not do anything till they come. I make
gadgets like this when I have any spare time. I have another one
that may interest you. You know I have a fine tabby cat who is
kind enough to like living here?"

Lady Graham said she had seen it and admired it.

"Well, he is a good mouser and often out at night," said Mr. Choyce, "and I used to get rather worried about him. So I gave my mind to it. You see the big chair by the fireplace where I usually sit at night? Well, my cat has a basket in the kitchen where he sleeps. I made a little door for him in the kitchen wall just by his basket and he opens it by pushing his head against it and it shuts behind him with a spring. And the spring releases a catch—but if you will wait here for a moment by the bookcase I will show you."

He left the room. In a couple of minutes Lady Graham heard a click and a small flap fell down from the wall, disclosing a photograph of a cat curled up in its basket.

"There!" said Mr. Choyce coming back with Edith in triumph. "Then I know pussy is safely in bed."

Lady Graham and Edith were loud in their applause of his ingenuity, but this was not all, for there was a burglar-alarm which played Home Sweet Home on a chime of tubular bells if anyone tried to force a ground-floor window and several other inventions no less ingenious.

"And now I think we have arranged everything," said Lady Graham, who always knew the exact moment at which she would be bored and if possible anticipated it. "The service on Thursday, which is early closing so that the village can come if it likes. Just very simple as darling Mamma would have liked it. And one thing I want to ask you *particularly*, Mr. Choyce."

Mr. Choyce said, rather nervously, for much as he admired Lady Graham he never knew where her ladyship might break out next, that he would be delighted if he could be of help.

"It is only," said Lady Graham, looking at him with what he felt to be the pure friendship of an attractive and gifted woman though it really expressed nothing at all, "that bit of the carpet in the aisle where the hole is. I am always afraid someone may trip up on it. I am sure old Caxton, Mr. Halliday's carpenter could mend it. He can do *anything*. Could you ask him? It is no use asking the Women's Institute because they are all making jam. Or I could ask Caxton for you. After all he *is* the organist."

At this moment Mr. Choyce felt a sudden drop in the thermometer of his respectful adoration of Lady Graham. Her ladyship's interest in the church had moved him considerably. Her appreciation of his various cat and burglar gadgets had almost puffed him up with unseemly pride. But somehow the question of the carpet in the aisle—*his* aisle if it came to that so long as he was vicar—didn't please him. And, though he knew it was done in kindness, her suggestion that she should approach Caxton about the carpet—one could tolerate much from a beautiful and charming woman, but there *were* chords in the human mind—and then somehow the remembrance of Mr. Guppy in Bleak House and the great writer whom we have read from our earliest years and hope to read till our last days, made him feel charitably disposed to everyone.

"I know exactly what you feel," said Lady Graham, whose flashes of insight often surprised her friends. "I am a meddling old woman. Oh indeed I am," she repeated, laying her hand on the sleeve of Mr. Choyce's rather horrid grey alpaca jacket which he only wore to save his priestly blacks, for clothes are a heavy charge upon a clergyman, even if he has, as Mr. Choyce had, a small private income. "Of *course* as Caxton plays the organ he comes under your jurisdiction," and her ladyship looked at the Vicar with a learned expression.

Mr. Choyce's slight resentment melted like lard in a frying pan. Here was Lady Graham trying to help the church, and who was he to disapprove of her kindness? Did he not owe the living to his friend Halliday, who had rescued him from a Liverpool parish where practically all his parishioners were Dissenters or total abstainers from any form of religion. And what would Halliday think—poor fellow, never in good health now—if he knew that the incumbent of his choice had let the side down. With which very mixed thoughts he came to—so quickly do our strange minds travel—before any pause was noticeable to Lady

Graham, and said the suggestion was an excellent one and it would be more than kind of her to suggest it; at which point the word tautology somehow floated into his mind and he wished he had never taken orders.

"Then that is all settled," said Lady Graham, by which we think her ladyship meant that she had settled everything as she wished it. "Good-bye, Mr. Choyce, and thank you so much. I always feel better for seeing you," with which words her ladyship, quite unconsciously, lifted her still lovely eyes to Mr. Choyce like a repentant Magdalen, thus upsetting him considerably, pressed his hand and went away with her daughter.

It was a principle with Lady Graham—though we doubt whether she would have recognised it as such—never to put off till tomorrow anything that it would be more convenient to do today. Today was Tuesday. Thursday was the day for the little Memorial Service, which meant that if the hole in the carpet was to be mended it must be done soon. It would have been easy to ring up Mrs. Halliday and ask if Caxton, the estate carpenter, could come down, but to Lady Graham it seemed more friendly to go over and see for herself how Mr. Halliday was and so draw to a point. In this we think she was quite unconsciously imitating her delightful and maddening mother, Lady Emily Leslie, whose intromissions (as the old agent at Rushwater, Mr. Macpherson, used to call them) were famous in the family and indeed in her whole circle of friends, for Lady Emily so long as she had the strength to get about enjoyed nothing more than paying unexpected visits to her relations and friends with the express purpose of interfering with whatever work or play they had on hand. Accordingly Lady Graham rang up Mrs. Halliday, saying nothing about Caxton, and asked if she would find her at home. Mrs. Halliday said she would certainly be in and it would do Leonard so much good to see an old friend as he got about very little now, and would she bring Edith whom her husband was very fond of. So about four o'clock of a nasty, cold, grey, windy summer day Edith drove her mother down to Hatch End, whence Lady Graham proposed to walk across the river while Edith went to the Friends of Barchester General Hospital sewing party to cut out nightgowns, and would follow her mother later.

It was usually thought by those who did not know Lady Graham well that she probably could not walk, so helpless and elegant did she look, but they deceived themselves, for her apparent helplessness and frailty meant nothing at all. In her youth many a dancing partner had figuratively had his shoes danced to pieces by her soft energy; strong men had, on the moors in Scotland, wilted while she remained cool and fresh. Even Mr. Wickham the Noel Mertons' agent, as tough a customer as any in Barsetshire, had to admit that Lady Graham could give him points when it came to an endurance test. No one, he said, without pride and as one stating a simple fact, could give him points when it came to punishing the rum, or downing the beer, but he would back Lady Graham against any of his acquaintance for general toughness. He was not going to forget in a hurry, he said, that weekend at The Towers one New Year's Eve in old Lord Pomfret's time when Mrs. Graham, as she was then, had walked to the meet, followed the hounds, attended the later stages of a point to point on foot, taken part in a paper chase with a trail all over the Towers from the nurseries on the top floor to the boot-room at the extremity of the kitchen wing, danced all evening, attended a watch-night service in the chapel of the Towers and been out with the guns next morning. And all the time with not a hair out of order, nor a feather out of place, he added, as he drank her health in absentia.

Perhaps Mr. Wickham exaggerated. In fact we are sure he did, but the fact remains that under Lady Graham's appealing and apparently helpless exterior the blood of Fosters and Leslies was strong and she had transmitted it to her own children. She left Edith and the car at the working party and walked down the village street, and so to the right along the causeway that led, gradually rising, to the bridge. It was a pleasant afternoon so far as this summer allowed. That is to say it was not raining though it obviously would before long; the wind though very boisterous was blowing across the water-meadows which was much better than when it came raging and whistling down the valley, driving the rushes and the reeds almost horizontal, making foot-passengers stagger and grab at their hats. At the further end of the bridge the well-known Hatch End artist, Mr. Scatcherd, was seated on a camp stool, his feet on a bit of linoleum, busily making one of his well-known Sketches of the Rising Valley, which sold very well in Hatch End and even in Barchester during the summer season. Anyone who saw him would have known at once that he was an artist, for no one else would have been wearing a Norfolk jacket with a belt, knicker-bockers buttoning below the knee and a deerstalker hat with several unconvincing flies stuck in it; nor would anyone today, we think, have a drooping walrus moustache. Those lucky enough to have known the palmy days of the Strand Magazine and Sydney Paget's illustrations to Sherlock Holmes in each monthly number, would have been overcome by nostalgia on seeing Mr. Scatcherd; of which we think he was quite aware, as he took the position of Artist very seriously, dressing the part as it had been played in his extreme youth and even boasting about the week he had once spent in nervous sin at a cheap hotel in Boulogne. Unfortunately no one believed this story, though it was quite true.

On seeing Lady Graham, Mr. Scatcherd unwrapped his legs from a shepherd's plaid shawl, got up and bowed.

"Oh, *don't* get up, Mr. Scatcherd," said Lady Graham.

Mr. Scatcherd said gallantly that he always rose for the ladies.

"So did an uncle of my father's," said Lady Graham. "He had a false leg and he always had to click it into position before he could stand. And before he could sit," she added. "How is your niece, Mr. Scatcherd?"

The artist, who thought but poorly of his maiden niece who

kept house for him, took any money he earned, made him a weekly allowance from it, and fed him, said she was much the same. To avoid any further discussion of this painful subject he tilted his camp stool, threw his head back, stretched out his right arm and did what looked like a kind of amateur surveying by means of a pencil held between two fingers and a thumb.

"Michael Angelo would have seen *nothing* in this," said Mr. Scatcherd, indicating the whole circle of river, valley and downs.

Lady Graham said he might have seen it, but of course he wouldn't be able to explain it, as he was an Italian; hoping, in a rather cowardly way, thus to placate the artist.

"AH," said Mr. Scatcherd. "That is just where your ladyship hits the crux. All them Italians," said Mr. Scatcherd, dropping to the level of everyday's most common speech, "they may be well enough, but do they get the idea *behind?*" to which Lady Graham replied, with great truth, that she had not the faintest idea.

"Well, let me put it clearer to your ladyship," said Mr. Scatcherd. "They had a good general idear of painting. Charosskoorer and the rest," by which Lady Graham dimly apprehended him to be thinking of chiaroscuro. "Ah! but had they the Mental Conception? It's not so much what I put onto the paper as the mental conception of what I am driving at."

Lady Graham rather basely said that foreigners were different.

"Your ladyship has driven the nail home!" said Mr. Scatcherd. "They are different and they KNOW it. That is where we differ from them. We are NOT different."

Lady Graham said How true and asked after his brother, who was Mr. Scatcherd at Northbridge, the present proprietor of Scatcherds' Stores, Est: 1824, and had bought for his ne'er-do-weel brother (for anyone who prefers messing about with paints to a well established business must be a ne'er-do-weel or a fool and Mr. Scatcherd had quite good premises for his conclusion) a small uncomfortable house called Rokeby and had sent his eldest daughter Hettie, who had the worst temper in Northbridge, to keep house for her uncle.

There was a chill silence and then Mr. Scatcherd said his brother went his way and so did he, leastways he went his *own* way if Lady Graham saw what he meant. But it was cold and blustery on the bridge, so Lady Graham said she must be going on.

"If your ladyship would like to look in at Rokeby on your way back," said Mr. Scatcherd, "I have something that would interest you. Something out of the Dear, Dead Days beyond Recall."

Lady Graham did not answer for a moment. The song which began with those words, a song called Just a Song at Twilight, had been one of the joys of her nursery days, sung to her when she was a very little girl by the Nanny of the time on winter evenings after tea, sitting before a comfortable coal fire on a hassock while she worked at her first piece of needlework; a piece of canvas about eight inches square with the outline of a kettle drawn on it. Nanny had embroidered the kettle in purple wool as it was rather difficult for a little girl of five and little Agnes had filled in the background with red wool. Nanny had then backed the canvas with a material called mysteriously Domett, though not, we presume, after the original of Browning's Waring, and over that a piece of blue Chinese silk, left over from one of Lady Emily Leslie's gowns (as we called them then). On this Agnes, with small unaccustomed hands, had embroidered in large sprawling letters the words TO DARLING MOTHER WITH LOVE FROM ANGES; which work had taken her quite a week and Lady Emily, deeply touched by the tribute, had not allowed Nanny to correct the spelling.

"If I have time, I should like to look in, Mr. Scatcherd," she said, and went on her way.

In the drawing-room at Hatch House there was a roaring fire, eminently suitable for a late summer afternoon, and Mr. Halliday was sitting beside it doing the Times Cross-Word Puzzle.

"Now please don't get up, Mr. Halliday," said Agnes, coming
with swift elegance across the room to him. "How deliciously
warm you are here. Mr. Scatcherd stopped me on the bridge and
the wind was bitter." And as she talked one part of her mind was
appraising her host, a kindly neighbour ever since she had come
as a bride to Holdings, a newcomer in a strange land. For in
Barsetshire, in spite of motors and telephones, one still is apt to
regard anyone from a neighbouring town or village as a foreigner
till he has proved himself or in this case herself. That was now
thirty years ago. How time went—and where did it go?

"Is that impostor still at it?" said Mr. Halliday, amused, and
then Lady Graham went on to tell him various bits of local
gossip which he enjoyed. His wife, seeing her husband happily
engaged, smiled to her guest and went away, saying she would
be there as soon as tea came in. Lady Graham was not shocked
by her host's appearance, for her mind, eminently reasonable
under her apparent vagueness or even foolishness, was the mind
of a country dweller and, even to those who live on the land
rather than by it, the cycles of birth and life and death often
come more easily than they do to the town-dweller. She had
seen her father gradually decaying till his death early in the war.
She had watched her brilliant, exasperating, adored mother
travelling down that slope till she too crossed that river, and had
felt deep sorrow for that parting; but no bitterness, hardly even
a regret, for when the appointed time has come we have to go
and the willingness is all. Leonard Halliday had done his duty as
well as most of us do, indeed better, and now he too must go
through the door.

Mr. Halliday liked to hear any village gossip, so Lady Graham
told him how she was planning a little service of remembrance
for Lady Emily and made him laugh by her account of the
Vicar's mechanical contraptions.

"Choyce is a good fellow," he said. "I knew him when we were
at school. He was younger than I was then, now he feels the

same age. All time gets very close together as you get older, Lady
Graham."

"I know," said she. "At least I am beginning to know. And
when darling Mamma died, at Holdings, she had slipped into
the past. Martin was there and she thought he was his father
who was killed in the first war. Martin was only two then and
now he is a married man with a family. And all our children are
getting married. It is most confusing."

"But we *are* confused here," said Mr. Halliday. "More and
more so. Tell me how Sylvia looked. She comes as often as she
can, bless her, but Rushwater doesn't let go very easily," and
Lady Graham said that whenever she went over to Rushwater it
was like a dream of old times and sometimes she felt that she was
her mother and sometimes that she was still a little girl in the
nursery, being teased by her elder brothers.

"And we did all so enjoy having George there," she said,
"What a very nice boy he is. And that," she added with a smile of
mischief very like her mother's, "just shows you how old we get.
Here am I calling George a boy, and he is a very nice grown-up
man."

"He is a good boy," said Mr. Halliday. "I think he would have
liked to make the army his profession after the war, but he came
back to Hatch End and took on the place bit by bit. We had our
differences. There was one real row when George wanted to put
a bit of that land up towards Gundric's Fossway under wheat
and I told him he knew nothing and he went straight out of the
house. But he came back next day and said he had been over to
see Mr. Gresham in East Barsetshire who has farmed all his life
and his father's before him, and Mr. Gresham told him he was a
young fool and the land was too poor for wheat, but with some
good fertiliser it would be all right for other crops. So it was.
And I learnt my lesson and didn't try to teach George to suck
eggs. Well, well."

"And George listened to you after that?" said Lady Graham.

"He listened to me and I listened to him and we worked

together and the property is doing very well—as well as the
times will allow," said Mr. Halliday, with the proper farmer's
grumble which is sometimes, perhaps, some dim atavistic yearning
to propitiate the gods of blight and mildew and the bots and the
strangles and all such pastoral joys. But the modern farmers, not
having the old helpers, Furrina, Robigus and the other lost
deities to worship or to propitiate, have substituted chemical
products, and perhaps do as well; or worse, or better. But no
deity has been found to give the farmer the weather he wants, so
perhaps a supreme deity is really doing his best and better than
we know, though our human frames feel heat and damp and
cold more (we think) than do the corn and the animals; which is
manifestly unfair.

As Mr. Halliday finished speaking there was a knock at the
door.

"That's Caxton," he said. "It looks as if Ellie were out, or he
wouldn't dare to come into the house unless it were the estate
room, but I don't get there much now. Come in!" and in came
the old estate carpenter. Caxton was a spare elderly man who
had worked, as he often said, being a man of few words and
those far too often repeated, father and son at Hatch House this
many a year, though as his father had been a gamekeeper on the
Pomfret estate and he was unmarried and as far as he knew
childless, this description can only be considered as a figure of
speech specially invented to lure half-crowns from visitors to
Hatch House or tourists at the Mellings Arms. The further to
impress his hereditary carpentership upon a credulous world, he
still wore when working a kind of square paper hat, rather like a
strawberry punnet upside down, as we remember it on Mr.
Chips the Carpenter when we played Happy Families in the
nursery. The game, we believe, still exists, but alas! the pictures
on the cards have been brought up to date by—we think—the
same artist who does the odious illustrations for those revolting
little Kiddy-Books about Hobo-Gobo and the Fairy Joybell.
Undoubtedly we are seeing the end of a civilisation.

Caxton, who we think had deliberately chosen this moment because he had seen Mrs. Halliday on her knees weeding a flower-bed, came in, touched his paper hat to Lady Graham and said nothing.

"Shut the door and come in, Caxton," said Mr. Halliday. "Lady Graham has come to see me," which Caxton knew perfectly well and indeed it was the reason of his visit. And if he did not pull his forelock, it was because he did not wish to remove the paper hat, insignia of his craft (and here we may say that we believe insigne would be more correct as being the singular, but as the plural has become Modern English Usage, it might be pedantic and would undoubtedly be showing off).

"Well, Caxton, what is it?" said Mr. Halliday, who knew that only a matter of life and death, or to put it less vaguely something connected with his work, would bring the carpenter into the drawing-room.

"Well, sir, it's this-a-way," Caxton began, which is barely credible except that Lady Graham was witness to it and as her ladyship was very truthful and certainly would not have exerted herself to invent a lie it must have been so. "I was thinking, sir, when I was mending that fence on the other side of the pig-yard that we did ought to have a bit of a drain on the far side. She'll never drain that old yard won't unless we lend a hand. Give her a hand, I say, and she'll do nicely."

"I can't do much about it, Caxton," said Mr. Halliday good-humouredly. "Here I am, being a nuisance to everyone. You ask Master George."

"That's just it, sir," said Caxton. "Master George is willing and he's a rare one with the farm, but drains are drains."

"Well, what *do* you want?" said Mr. Halliday, with perfect good-temper, but Agnes saw him growing tired under her eyes.

"Now Mr. Goble, over at Holdings, *he's* got some good drains," said Caxton, addressing an invisible audience above one of the long windows. "Good quality drain-pipes, he has. Last a century those will."

"Good lord, Caxton!" said Mr. Halliday, roused in a way that Lady Graham felt could not be good for him. "Do you expect me to ask Sir Robert for his drain-pipes?"

"Oh no, sir," said Caxton, shocked. "Only seeing as her ladyship was here I thought now's the time to mention it," at which words Agnes really felt that Mr. Halliday might be disturbed beyond reason by his carpenter's diplomacy.

"Now, please Mr. Halliday, may I ask for something too?" she said. "You know we are having a little memorial service for darling Mamma on Thursday and there are some nasty holes in that horrid bit of red carpet in the aisle and if anyone tripped over them it would be really quite awkward. If Caxton could come over to Holdings on Thursday morning and see Goble about the drains, he could mend the carpet on his way back," said her ladyship, rather as though the church aisle were the direct road from Holdings to Hatch House. "You will only need," she went on, addressing the carpenter, "one of those things sailors use on their hands instead of a thimble because if you try to get a carpet-needle through that carpet you can't."

Caxton, whose face had at first darkened, now resumed his normal tone. There was, he remarked, something in what her ladyship said and he wouldn't be surprised if he hadn't got a bit of that old carpet in his shop. And a carpet-needle too, he added. Many was the carpet, he continued, as he'd mended at Hatch House since he come there he couldn't say how many year ago. Mr. Halliday who, as Lady Graham did not fail to observe, was looking much more himself since the conversation took this friendly turn, said it must be a matter of forty years or more.

"Forty year, sir? Nearer forty-three," said Caxton indignantly. "Mrs. Fothergill was in the kitchen when first I come here, sir, scullery-maid she was then, and she'll tell you. *She's* not the woman she was," he concluded with the relish we all feel for the decay of our co-evals, knowing that we ourselves look far younger and are probably immortal.

"Well, that's all right and never mind about Mrs. Fothergill," said Mr. Halliday who, as Lady Graham did not fail to notice, was now looking more tired every moment.

"I don't mind about her, sir, no more than I don't about Miss Hubback neither," said Caxton, but at a most unfortunate moment, for Hubback who was bringing tea in heard him and managed to exude such an aura of resentment, scorn and determination to have it out with him later, as made Mr. Halliday sink back in his chair.

Lady Graham, despite her helpless appearance, had a great deal of courage and at once came to the rescue.

"Thank you, Caxton, that will do," she said. "I will tell Goble you are coming over tomorrow and he will look after you. And don't forget to bring that piece of carpet and a proper needle and thread and something to push the needle through with. I want the church to look *really* nice for the service. You remember my mother, Caxton; Lady Emily Leslie. I am having a little service on the anniversary of her death and it would be so uncomfortable if anyone fell over the carpet" and though her ladyship did not say in so many words, "and you can go now," the carpenter made a kind of bow and went away.

Hubback, rather resentful at having been done out of a row, or scene, laid the tea-table in a grim silence which had no effect upon her employer or his guest but satisfied her amour propre. Then Mrs. Halliday came in with Edith, who had found her weeding and offered to help.

"Another cup for Miss Edith, please, Hubback," she said.

"There's only the four left of this service," said Hubback with gloomy satisfaction.

"Then we'll have to use the other service," said Mrs. Halliday. "I think there are five cups and seven saucers left of it."

"I'm sure I couldn't say, madam," said Hubback, seeing an opportunity for putting it in an unkind word about old Mrs. Fothergill the cook, who was feeling her age and her legs and was always having a nice cup of tea or a quiet lay down, but was faithful and honest and never went out, which meant that Mrs. Halliday could always leave her husband and go out herself without any need to worry. "Them cups and saucers are in the cupboard in Mrs. Fothergill's room, madam."

"Then that's all right," said Mrs. Halliday cheerfully. "Bring Mr. Halliday's big cup and I'll ring if we want more hot water."

"You needn't," said the devoted old servant. "The kettle's by the fire there," and she left the room with mutterings that boded no good to Caxton, returning however with some more cups and saucers and plates and a large copper kettle of boiling water, which she put down on the open hearth, and with a last severe look at the party, implying that she hoped they were happy now, she left the room.

By a kind of tacit consent no allusion was made to this Scene from Domestic Life. Mr. Halliday began to revive under the influence of hot tea and listened with amusement to the ladies' conversation which was largely parochial. Presently loud clumpings were heard outside, followed by a short silence and then by George Halliday in his farming clothes of old khaki shirt with a shabby tweed jacket, corduroy breeches, thick stockings and heavy boots; but he always came in by the back way and used first the door-scraper by the scullery door and then the well-worn mat.

"How do you do, Lady Graham," said George. "Hullo, Edith, I'd have washed my hands again if I'd known you were here. I say, father——" and he sat down by his father and began to talk about a sow who, so he said, was so late with her litter that he thought she must have made a mistake and was really an elephant.

Lady Graham, distracted from her hostess by hearing these words, asked why an elephant.

"Don't elephants take about two years or something to have an Elephant's Child?" said George, which impressed all his hearers very much. His father questioned the veracity of this statement, but as he had no supporting evidence for his opinion, that part of the talk came to an end. The telephone rang. George went to it.

"Oh, it's *you*," he said. "I thought you were the people about the tractor. They promised to ring up about that missing part. Lady Graham's here and Edith. Wait a minute and I'll get mother. It's Sylvia," he said turning to the tea-table. "She wants to talk to you, mother," so Mrs. Halliday took the telephone and George sat down to his tea again. Politeness made Lady Graham and Edith talk in lowered voices that they might not disturb Mrs. Halliday's talk, but as it appeared to have no end they gradually rose to a normal tone. Then she hung up the receiver and came back.

"It was only about coming here for a few days," she said, "so I told her about the service for Lady Emily and she said she would come over that morning so that she can go to it," by which plan her ladyship seemed gratified. "She said would it matter if she came as she was."

Lady Graham said it always seemed stupid to wear mourning in the country, though she did not know why, and she was certainly coming just as she was, a sentiment which made her audience feel vaguely religious.

George said she must be thinking of that hymn that begins "Just as I am without one plea" and at his prep. school they—

"Of course they did, darling," said his mother firmly.

Lady Graham asked who did what.

"George is being very silly," said his mother, who privately did not think so, but did not wish her son to lose caste before Lady Graham.

"I know *exactly* what you said," said Lady Graham, her still lovely face alive with interest. "You said 'without one flea.' So did David and I, and Mademoiselle—or perhaps it was Fräulein—scolded us dreadfully. We were staying at The Towers then. I remember it because David dropped his three-penny piece for the collection down the hot air grating in the chapel. I was in love with the curate and I tried to fast in Lent but Nurse wouldn't let me. She said young ladies didn't do that sort of thing," at which, we regret to say, George guffawed, at least to put it more elegantly he suddenly exploded into his tea-cup and apologised.

Lady Graham had not lived with an elderly invalid (if either of those words can be used about Lady Emily Leslie) in her house for several years for nothing. She saw that Mr. Halliday, though liking the party, was getting very tired and told Edith they must go home. While good-byes were being said Mrs. Halliday took Lady Graham to the far end of the room to show her a very good engraving which she had lately picked up in Barchester of Hatch House as it was in 1721, the year of its building by Wm. Halliday, Gent.

"I wonder, Lady Graham," she said, "if Edith could come to us for a few days while Sylvia is here. I am rather tied in some ways" she went on, lowering her voice, "and it will be such pleasant company for Sylvia when George is down at the farm."

Lady Graham said she was sure Edith would love it and called to her daughter to join her. Edith was delighted by the plan and thanked Mrs. Halliday very prettily. Then everyone said good-bye and the Graham ladies got into the Holdings car and drove away. As they crossed the bridge Lady Graham remembered her talk with Mr. Scatcherd earlier in the afternoon and the conditional promise she had made to him and asked her daughter to go to Rokeby.

Rokeby, Mr. Scatcherd's house, stood on a little hillock at the far end of the village. It had been built by a Barchester contractor to house his old mother and it was his boast that the bricks were a bargain, as they doubtless were, but they could not have been uglier, being a purplish-red colour with flecks of black. The woodwork, which was of the fretsaw type, was chocolate re-lieved with coffee; the slate roof was at an abominable pitch and the box staircase which led to the upper floor was almost directly inside the front door, so that it was almost impossible to squeeze into the sitting room. On the front door-step lay a woven wire mat in which white marbles were embedded, originally forming the word ROKEBY. Owing to a heavy piece of furniture having been dropped on it when Mr. Scatcherd and his niece were moving in, and the loosened marbles having been extracted by the careful fingers of the Hatch End school children, this had during the war dwindled to POKFRY and since Peace had brought her blessings to this favoured Isle the children in the new suburb had so improved on this that the name now stood as IOKIPY. So has Babylon vanished, so Palmyra and the Cities of the Plain and Angkor Wat (whose name was doubtless far more like a real name before the dear little kiddies got to work on it).

Edith knocked at the door which was opened by Hettie, Mr. Scatcherd's niece, a middle-aged woman on the wrong side of the middle who might have been not ill-looking if she had not cut her hair short with the kitchen scissors and refused to have false teeth, owing to some religious confusion about graven images.

"WELL, Uncle," said Miss Scatcherd, addressing over her shoulder what was evidently Mr. Scatcherd in the background, "and a nice state I'm in for her ladyship and Miss Edith to see with the sitting-room floor still wet where I've been washing it and your room all anyhow and the fish not come you'd better take her ladyship into your studio though goodness knows there's not a chair fit to sit on leaving all your paints and things about the way you do good GRACIOUS do you think I've got two pairs of hands like an octopus and your paints and rubbish all over the place and of course my washing has to be out on the line and goodness knows where I'm going to put it all damp come in your ladyship," and she led Lady Graham and Edith through the little sitting-room into what had evidently once been a lean-to washhouse and was now, just as evidently, Mr. Scatcherd's studio or atterleer, as he preferred to call it, though it bore an uncommonly close resemblance to Mr. Krook's Rag and Bottle Warehouse near Lincoln's Inn.

"Now," said Mr. Scatcherd, moving an armful of paper and

two broken picture frames and a bottle of Linseed Oil from two chairs to the floor, "if you ladies will take a seat, I will show you the Object we had words about earlier in the day. Not that I mean words in the sense some people might take it if you see my meaning, but our little conversation when your ladyship surprised me painting on the bridge."

With her usual composure Lady Graham sat down upon the chair which seemed the safest and at least had its complement of legs, while Edith perched on an old leather trunk whose straps had rotted, whose lid had rusted from the hinges. Luckily it was full of dilapidated curtains which Mr. Scatcherd had bought at sales to use as properties and so made a quite safe and not too uncomfortable seat.

"Just one moment, your ladyship," said Mr. Scatcherd, who was rummaging in another and even shabbier trunk. "Do you remember the Bring and Buy Sale at Holdings by your kind permission just when Peace broke out? Her ladyship Lady Emily Leslie was living with you then, my lady, but did not come to the Sale it being considered, so I understand, too exciting for her ladyship."

"Dear Mamma," said Lady Graham. "I remember it quite well, Mr. Scatcherd. My daughter, who is Mrs. Belton now, painted some bulrushes on a vase—I mean they *were* painted on the vase, so she painted them with some gold and silver paint to make it look more attractive. Lord Stoke won it in a raffle and Mrs. John Leslie's elder boys broke it, so everyone was pleased."

"But there was another Objy Dar which was *not* broken," said Mr. Scatcherd in an imposing voice. "It was My Picture of the spire of Barchester Cathedral as seen from the bridge; the very bridge where your ladyship saw me today and—"

"—and I was fool enough to spend sixpence on tickets for the raffle seeing it was for a good cause, my lady," said Mr. Scatcherd's niece who had come back to see that her uncle did not disgrace himself in public, "and there it was, back on our hands as if there wasn't enough of Uncle's rubbishy stuff about the place without *that.*"

"How dreadful," said Lady Graham, entirely unmoved by this story. "But I remember that I bought it back and gave it to that nice woman who taught at the Infant School and she said she would hang it in the dark corner where the children hung their coats to brighten it up."

"And so she did, my lady, and of all the impertinence she put it up for a raffle when your ladyship was abroad. When I see that picture being raffled, my lady, my mind nearly deserted me. I couldn't hardly hold a pencil, let alone a brush," said Mr. Scatcherd, the just wrath of the artist boiling in him. "When I think of the Work that went into that sketch, my lady, I haven't the words to put it into."

"So what did uncle have to do," said his niece, directing a look of scorn at Mr. Scatcherd, "but buy that picture back! Three and sixpence he gave for it and what teacher did with it I couldn't say. Cheap lipstick at Sheepshanks or Gaiters if you ask me. But there's plenty in the Bible for them as can read about those that paint their faces and—"

Lady Graham, realising that if not checked Miss Scatcherd would give them some fine, full-blooded Jacobean words about opening one's feet to everyone who passed by and multiplying one's whoredoms, said she must get back to Holdings but did so want to see the picture before she went.

"This," said Mr. Scatcherd, dexterously producing the picture from a pile of odds and ends in a corner, "is the shayderve to which I was reluding to to your ladyship."

Though his prepositions were overdone by excess of zeal his meaning was clear. He laid the drawing on the table, dusted it with an old silk muffler and stood back to observe its effect.

"That is very nice," said Lady Graham placidly. "That's the Rising, I can see quite well. And some bulrushes," she added with a voice of admiration that would not have deceived any of her own family. "Do the bulrushes really grow as tall as that?"

she added, pointing to the centre background of the picture. "I have never measured one," at which words Edith nearly laughed.

"Ah, it takes a Lifetime to understand the Artist," said Mr. Scatcherd. "If your ladyship were to look again now."

Lady Graham looked again. So did Edith.

"I know," said Edith. "It's the spire of the cathedral. Only one can't see it from the bridge," she added rather smugly.

"That's where Art comes in, miss," said Mr. Scatcherd. "What the Eye doesn't see the Imagination can imagine. Composition is the word. Look at Michael Angelo and all the Old Masters. *They* never sat on a bridge for hours at a time with a nasty east wind coming down the river. And why?"

This question was so obviously rhetorical that none of his audience tried to answer it. His niece said More fools they if they did and went into the back garden to collect the washing from the line.

"And well you may say Why," Mr. Scatcherd continued, though no one had said it. "They had studied Composition, same as I did. Say an Old Master wanted to paint a landscape in his background, for landscape *as* landscape if you follow me was not in their line nor did they wish it to be. They took a bit here and a bit there same as I do. And they were Old Masters."

"And I am sure you will be one some day, Mr. Scatcherd," said Lady Graham getting up. "And if you will let me buy the drawing back it will be taken great care of."

"If I LIVE," said Mr. Scatcherd, "this little effort is what I shall live by."

Miss Scatcherd, who had come in with a bundle of washing from the line, shoved her uncle's pictures to one end of the table and began spreading and rolling the washing preparatory to ironing it.

"Eleven shillings' worth of tickets were taken for that Thing of uncle's at the raffle, your ladyship," she said. "All in sixpences and one of them was mine. Born a fool, die a fool, as the saying is," and she looked darkly at her uncle, though whether she was applying the word fool to him or to herself was not quite clear.

"Then suppose I give you eleven shillings, Mr. Scatcherd," said Lady Graham, opening her bag and finding a ten shilling note and two sixpences which she laid on the table.

"All right, uncle, I'll look after it for you," said Miss Scatcherd, dexterously appropriating the money before her uncle could take it. "I'm sure uncle's much obliged to you, my lady," and she rolled up her bundle of linen, slapped it, put it at the far end of the table, opened a drawer, took out an old blanket with many marks of scorching on it and prepared to start work.

Lady Graham did not know fear. Partly because—apart from her husband's absence during the war—she had never had real occasion to feel it, partly because in spite of her vagueness and the air of frailty that made people feel she must be protected she was extremely practical and saw no reason for being afraid until there was something to be afraid of. But at this moment, with Miss Scatcherd coming out of the kitchen with an iron which she spat upon to test its heat and set down on a small gridiron to cool, she felt she had seen enough of Rokeby and wafted herself and her daughter away.

CHAPTER 2

Thursday dawned bright and fair, but shortly after breakfast changed its mind. Luckily Edith had cut all the flowers for the church the night before and put them up to their collars in water. Mrs. Halliday rang up from Hatch House to say that Caxton would be at Holdings about ten o'clock if Lady Graham wanted to see him and would mend the church carpet on his way home. Shortly after ten Aggie Hubback, great-niece of Mrs. Hubback at The Shop and now on approval at Holdings, came into Lady Graham's sitting-room and said Please it was Mr. Caxton and would her ladyship wish to see him; for her great-aunt had instructed her in the right way to address the quality before she went to Holdings and Aggie (christened Agnes by kind permission of Lady Graham though her mother never allowed the name to be used lest folk should think her proud) was a zealous pupil. So Caxton was brought in, made a kind of token gesture of wiping his boots (which were perfectly clean) on the threshold, and stood with his cap in his hand. Lady Graham asked after Mr. Halliday. Caxton said the Squire was about the same. He would not, he said, take his Bible oath that the Squire was better, because the days of man were three score years and ten, which was a sight too much for *some* people, he added darkly.

Lady Graham, who knew West Barsetshire ways too well to

be side-tracked by this hint, said Goble was looking forward to seeing him and could quite well spare some drain pipes.

"How will you get them back?" said her ladyship. "Our farm lorry had to go to Barchester today."

"Cart and horse, my lady," said Caxton. "There's always been carts and horses at Hatch House and will be as long as I'm alive. If the Squire likes to have a motor lorry and Master George likes to have a motor tractor, well I say let them *have* one. But as long as I'm working at Hatch House I'll have a cart and horse. And a good horse he is. Master of—" and he mentioned the considerable weight that the horse could pull, starting from a stationary loaded waggon or cart. Owing to tractors that fine expression is not common now and may vanish with Nineveh and Tyre, but it can still be seen in the country on posters about sales of stock. "And I've brought the bit of carpet, my lady. And a proper thimble" which last word he evidently considered a good joke, pulling from a side pocket that leather contraption of whose true name we regret to say we are ignorant. Then Lady Graham dismissed Caxton to the farm, whither we shall not attempt to follow him, as he and Goble were discussing high matters of policy in the slow West Saxon speech which—we are glad to say—still holds many archaisms and turns of speech untouched by education and genteelism.

Later in the morning Lady Graham went down to the church with Edith and all the flowers the garden could give. Late August is a dull time for flowers with nearly everything yellow, but Edith had done her best, though she and her mother both lamented the absence of Clarissa with her genius for turning anything she touched to favour and to prettiness. Mr. Choyce was already in the church when they came, with some tall lilies from his own garden. Various village woman brought cottage garden bouquets, very compact, their stalks tightly bound with coloured plastic tape. So does the old order change—and there is a good deal to be said for these strange, lifeless products of the Brave New World, made for the moment, not for endurance.

"Now, Mr. Choyce, the *really* important thing is the pulpit," said Lady Graham. "I did think blue delphiniums, but of course if you are there they might be in your way. Once at home, long ago, our vicar Mr. Banister, only he is Canon Banister now and there is a delightful clergyman called Bostock at Rushwater, had so many flowers on the pulpit at the Harvest Festival that he could hardly see over them and he said the pumpkins made it very difficult to get up the steps, especially as an ear of barley had somehow got loose in one of his trouser legs and you know how they work their way up. I always think barley is rather like spiders."

Mr. Choyce said he was sure they were if Lady Graham said so, but did not quite see why.

"But it is in the Bible, Mr. Choyce," said Lady Graham. "Where it says the spider lays hold with her hands; *exactly* like barley," and she looked at him so appealingly that he felt inclined to say "God bless you, Lady Graham." But being in church he refrained. Women came in and out with brooms, or dusters, for the whole village had adored Lady Emily and each wanted to be able to say she had done something for her ladyship's service. Mrs. Hubback at The Shop brought a large teapot, tea, milk and sugar and by permission of Mr. Choyce boiled a kettle on the little gas-ring in the vestry and had a kind of religious canteen. Very luckily there was a tap just outside to refill the kettle and seldom had the village had a happier morning. By the time they had finished their elevenses which were pretty well twelveses, or luncheons, by then, Caxton drove up the little lane by the church, told his horse to stay there, and came in with a proper carpenter's bag full of tools of trade many of whose names are vanishing now.

"Thank you very much, my lady, I'm sure," said Caxton to Lady Graham. "Goble he's got a fine lot of pipes up there. Good glaze and all."

Lady Graham said she hoped he had got what he wanted. Caxton said he had got a nice little lot, just what was needed and give a man the proper tools and he would do anything. But give a man cast-iron pipes, he said, and a man couldn't swear to give satisfaction with the work. Cast-iron was cast-iron, he said, and so was galvanised iron, leastways it was galvanised iron, but give him proper drain-pipes with a nice glaze, have a nice trench dug and lay them even, you'd never repent it. Then he betook himself to the aisle where he took up part of the carpet. A cloud of dust rose and several spiders ran about shrieking for help because the atom bomb had been dropped.

"Pity I didn't bring down Miss Hubback's Hoover," said Caxton, after the custom of his kind calling any tool of trade after the user rather than the owner. "They say it's unlucky to kill spiders, but I can get all the bad luck I want without troubling the spiders" and he hit with a ball of strong twine at a spider who had come out to see if it was the atom bomb, but she nimbly avoided it and went down into the basement again. Caxton settled himself cross-legged on the floor of the aisle, girded his hand with the needle-pusher, and made a very satisfactory patch. By this time the helpers had finished their work and gone home. Lady Graham said good-bye to Mr. Choyce.

"But not really good-bye," she said, "because we shall meet again at half past two for darling Mamma's service. *How* she would have loved it. And she always loved Caxton's playing," for Caxton was the organist as well as the estate carpenter and being a proper man of his hands could do minor repairs and we believe could have taken the organ to pieces and re-assembled it. Then she took Edith away. Mr. Choyce went back to the Vicarage. The church, swept clear of spiders, garnished with flowers, its carpet neatly patched, was quiet again, waiting for the afternoon.

As the little service for Lady Emily Leslie at Hatch End was really for those who had loved her in the last years of her life, Lady Graham had not invited anyone from outside the village except her cousins the Pomfrets. The link between Rushwater and Pomfret Towers had lost much of its strength since Lady

Emily's death and though the families were on most amicable terms there was not the visiting there used to be. Martin Leslie and his wife were up to their eyes in the estate, the people on the estate and the important business they did with their prize bulls. Both Lord and Lady Pomfret were up to their eyes in the estate, the people on the estate and every possible county activity, Lord Pomfret being, as a side line, Lord Lieutenant. Martin and Lord Pomfret met at The Club in Barchester and on various boards. Sylvia and Lady Pomfret supported each other loyally on county committees, but the easy coming and going of old days had gone; stifled by a new way of living which hardly allows for much ease of intercourse. A big business concern like Amalgamated Vedge can be left for a time, or Mr. Macfadyen would not have been able to take his honeymoon. The Hogglestock Rolling Mills can run themselves for quite four weeks without needing Mr. Adams's eye on them. Mr. Pilward's Brewery can also go on calmly and well if Mr. Pilward takes a month off and goes to America with his son and his daughter-in-law who was Heather Adams, charging everything as expenses against the Income Tax people. But cows and bulls and grass and corn do not like to be left and Martin took to heart the old words that the master's boots are the best muck.

So Lady Graham had asked the Pomfrets to lunch and to bring the children if possible: Lord Mellings, now at Sandhurst and to proceed, all being well, to the Brigade of Guards; Lady Emily Foster, a roistering schoolgirl and a country-woman to the tips of her capable fingers; and the Honourable Giles Foster who was so like an English schoolboy that he obviously was one and would go through life succeeding in whatever he did by sheer bluff, good-looks and, we may add, the quite appalling self-confidence which his father so completely lacked.

Lady Graham's cook who had been with her for many years was very dependable and knew how the gentry should be fed. Like all good country cooks she lived in a permanent state of guerilla warfare with Goble the bailiff and with the gardener and had under her a series of local kitchen maids who lived in considerable terror of her rule which though just did not let any mistake or forgetfulness pass unnoticed. They had all gone on to good places where they were able in their turn to bully their less fortunate fellow workers and boast of the glories of the Holdings kitchen. The present acting kitchen maid was Odeena Panter, one of the large family of Mr. Halliday's carter George Panter who lived in the village at 6, Clarence Cottages. She was so called by her film-smitten mother after the Barchester Odeon where she had sat every Saturday during a long courtship, holding Mr. Panter's hand. Odeena was a nice girl and, apart from a kind of savage's fear of all callers previously unknown to her, was almost normal.

"Now Aggie," said cook, to the so-called parlour-maid, "you mind out not to forget the company's names. There's Lord and Lady Pomfret and Lord Mellings and Lady Emily and Master Giles and mind you say my lord to his lordship and Lord Mellings and my lady to Lady Pomfret—same as you say my lady to Lady Graham, see? And my lady to the young lady and sir to Master Giles. He's only a honourable."

"Why?" said Aggie, but cook said to get on with the potatoes and not ask all them questions and to say "sir" to Master Giles, the way she said, after which excursion into Debrett, Aggie's mind, if one can call it that, went back into its accustomed vacancy.

At a few minutes before one the Pomfrets drove up to the front door which, after the pleasant country fashion, was usually left open during the summer with a glass inner door to keep out the icy blasts of that season. As cousins the Pomfrets could have gone straight in, but Lady Pomfret who was not a cousin felt it would be more becoming to ring. Nothing happened. So she rang again. Aggie, who had been detained by cook to wash them hands of yours, my girl, and take that stuff off your lips you won't see Miss Edith looking like that, opened the door.

"You're Aggie, aren't you?" said Lady Pomfret.

Aggie looked at her in terror.

"Please miss, I'm under cook," she said in a hoarse whisper.

"A very good person to be under," said Lady Pomfret, adding kindly, "I hope you are getting on nicely," but this was beyond Aggie's power of comprehension.

"Cook said to take you in the sitting-room, miss," she said.

Lady Pomfret said there was no need to trouble, but Aggie with the ever-present fear of cook in her mind, said to please come this way and led the party to Lady Graham's sitting-room. Here her wits completely deserted her and—rather like Guster when she announced the Chadbands to Mrs. Snagsby as "Mr. and Mrs. Cheeseming least which I meantersay, whatsername,"—she uttered in a strangled voice the words "Please your ladyship it's the Lord" and retired to the kitchen where she at once burst into tears and was told by cook to stop that noise and go and wash her face at once and get those plates down and not to drop none of them. All those girls were the same, said cook darkly. There was that girl as had the nerve to talk to Lord Stoke the time his lordship came in by the back door the way he always did.

"Did he come in *your* back door, cook?" said Odeena, wondering that even a real lord should so far presume, but cook, feeling that her minion had had quite enough rope, told Aggie to take the potatoes in and tell her ladyship lunch was ready.

"And remember, my girl," said cook, "that it's all on your account her ladyship's having cold lunch except the potatoes, so as you wouldn't act silly in front of company," and thrusting the dish of potatoes into Aggie's hands she went back to see that the ice pudding was doing nicely in the fridge.

Aggie, nerved by desperation, put the potatoes on the table, went to Lady Graham's sitting-room, and (as she had repeatedly been told by cook not to do as Lady Graham and her guests wouldn't be doing anything that the Queen herself couldn't look at) knocked at the door. A voice said "Come in" and Aggie opened the door onto the party all talking family at the tops of their voices except Lord Pomfret who, as usual, kept a little apart, though quite at his ease.

"Please, my lady, cook says your dinner's ready," said Aggie, backing out of the room as she spoke and retreating to her post in the dining-room. Lady Graham and her guests followed, there was the usual muddle about seating like a kind of dining-room musical chairs and the lunch began.

"You needn't wait, Aggie," said her ladyship. "I will ring when we are ready for the ice." Aggie backed out of the room, shut the door far too hard so that it opened itself again and fled to the kitchen where she incurred cook's scorn by not remembering what Lady Pomfret was wearing.

"And how is Sandhurst, dear boy?" said his Aunt Agnes to Lord Mellings, though only Aunt by courtesy as she was of an older generation and really a cousin of sorts.

Lord Mellings, who we are glad to say has stopped growing since we last met him and has put on nearly a stone, said oh it wasn't bad and he and some of the chaps had been to Aubrey Clover's first night of "Pigs in Clover," his new comedy, and had supper with Aubrey and Jessica Dean his wife afterwards in their flat.

"It really was fun, Cousin Agnes," he said. "And Aubrey has had the flat above his made into nurseries for the children and a special staircase put in. I can't think how they got the landlord to do it. We were allowed to go up, very quietly, and see the children asleep. Aubrey says he'll always have a job for me if the Brigade of Guards won't have me," but he laughed as he said it and his cousin Agnes thought how the boy had come on.

"I'm going to farm like Uncle Roddy," said the Honourable Giles, who had been filling himself with food as only a healthy schoolboy can. "I'll get father to give me a cottage somewhere on the place and have a whale of a time. You can come and stay with me, Edith, I'll shoot the rabbits and you can cook them," but his cousin had grown up suddenly since he had last seen her, as young girls do, and showed no enthusiasm for his plans.

> "To shoot at a rabbit
> Is not a good habit.
> I'd walk for ten miles
> With plenty of smiles,
> But *not* with that Giles"

said Edith.

"That is quite enough, Edith," said Lady Graham and Edith subsided and attached herself to young Lord Mellings who was almost exactly her age, but, unlike most boys, fully as old mentally and socially as she was. Whether it was Eton, or Sandhurst, or his parents we do not know; more probably all and—for we must be fair to the strange uncharted person within us—also himself.

"I wish I had known Aunt Emily more," said Lord Mellings to Edith. "You knew her very well, didn't you? I do remember when she came to the Towers when I was quite small and I thought she was a magic person in disguise."

"I think she probably was," said Edith. "But I wasn't quite old enough then to understand. Clarissa was the one who understood. You see, Ludo, I'm a bit out of it. I mean the boys are always away because of the army and Emmy and Clarissa are married and I expect I'll be an old maid."

Rather embarrassed by this confession in the middle of a family lunch-party, Lord Mellings wondered if his cousin Edith was right, or if she was only inventing a romance for herself. He felt sorry for her, but with real kindness and, we may say, an understanding beyond his years, he felt that sympathy would probably only encourage her to be misunderstood. Then his naturally kind heart smote him and he said firmly that none of the Pomfret blood had ever been old maids.

"There was darling Gran's sister Agnes, the one mother was called after," said Edith. "She was never married."

"And for why?" said Lord Mellings. "You only have to look at those ghastly old photographs in the housekeeper's room at

Rushwater to see that she must have been dotty. In fact I believe she was engaged once, hundreds of years ago, to one of the Pallisers, but old Uncle Giles made a frightful fuss because he said the Omniums were rich parvenus and nearly as bad as the Hartletops, so it didn't come off. I think she took to curates and church embroidery and was a bit of a nuisance. You're all right, Edith."

"Yes, I suppose I am," said Edith "and you're a good old Ludo. But don't be kind and understanding to *too* many people. It makes men a bit soft and they never get married, like that old Lord Algernon Palliser, the Duke's youngest brother, who still thinks he's a lady-killer. *Horrid* old man!"

"Did he try to make love to you?" said Lord Mellings, almost unconsciously (impelled thereto by the subconscious we suppose, which makes a horrid Trinity of I, non-I and sub-I).

"Not exactly," said Edith. "At least," she went on, her eyes on the tablecloth and the ice-cream she was eating, "he said I was an ice-maiden and some day the prince would come," and then she began to giggle in a highly unladylike way and her cousin Mellings laughed too and they made so much noise that their respective mothers apologised to one another for the bad manners of their offspring.

"What is it, Edith?" said Lady Graham, entirely uncurious, but wondering what on earth had made them so noisy, to which Edith's natural answer was "Nothing, mother, only Ludo and I were being silly," which appeared to satisfy both ladies who returned to their own talk.

"I know what mother is saying," said Lord Mellings. Edith asked what.

> "'Well, if it prove a girl, the boy
> Will have plenty: so let it be!'"

said Lord Mellings and then wondered (a) if his young cousin could place the allusion and (b) if he had gone too far in making it.

Edith asked what he was talking about.

"Tennyson, my girl," said Lord Mellings loftily. "I've read an awful lot of him lately. It's out of Maud where the man who tells the story's father is talking to another fellow about their children getting married if the other one's a girl. Mother is always match-making for me in her mind, but of course I don't let her know I know," which remark shows us how far Lord Mellings has travelled in the last year, from a rather awkward schoolboy with dreams to a very nice young embryo Guardsman with a taste for reading and quite a good deal of common sense.

"How awful," said Edith. "Thank goodness mother never worries. Emmy and Clarissa got married quite on their own and I expect I shall. Only no one's asked me yet" she added cheerfully.

"Come, come, my girl, you've plenty of time," said Lord Mellings.

"Come, come, my boy, so have you," said Edith, with cousinly frankness. "Your birthday comes a month after mine," but a month or so between them in whatever direction did not matter much and they continued a very pleasant conversation till Lady Graham said they ought to be going because it would be so dreadful for Mr. Choyce if they were late as he couldn't very well start without them. Lord Pomfret took Lady Graham and his wife. The young people got into the small Holdings car into which Edith had already put a suitcase for her visit to Hatch House after the service. There were very few cars outside the church except the Hallidays' and one or two local friends, though not intimates, to whom Lady Emily had shown kindness—and when did she not, to whom did she not? Caxton was at the door.

"Could I speak to you a moment, my lady?" he said to Agnes.

It speaks volumes for Lady Graham's character that instead of immediately inventing for herself, as most of us would, such social problems as the arrival of Lady Norton, or practical difficulties such as the collapse of the church tower, or the brass eagle having fallen off the lectern, she merely asked what it was.

"It's Sir Edmund Pridham, my lady," said Caxton, who in the surplice that he wore as organist looked like a figure from a missal or a fifteenth century church statue, so does the type of face and figure continue in the deep country. "I put him in your pew my lady. I hope I did right."

"Of course you did, Caxton," said Lady Graham, "how good of you," and she led her guests to the Graham pews, where Sir Edmund, in his neat, old fashioned blacks with rather tight trousers was kneeling. Lady Graham, with a half laughing, half crying look of apology, held her party at bay till Sir Edmund heaved himself up, dusted his knees and saw her.

"*Dear* Sir Edmund, how good of you," said Lady Graham, "and *how* pleased darling Mamma would be. She always said of Papa that he was the most just and the most generous of men and we may say the same of you. I have brought the Pomfrets. Sally, will you go in and sit on the other side of Sir Edmund and then I will come and dear Gillie next to me and the others can go in the pew behind. We have always had these two front pews," her ladyship went on in a clear soft voice, "and it was the same at Rushwater. When there were a lot of us in the nursery and two nurses we used to overflow into the upper servants' pew at the back which we *much* preferred. Darling David always sat there playing noughts and crosses with himself quite quietly when he was little."

By this time her ladyship had got herself into the pew beside Sir Edmund and composed herself to the silent prayer which is the beginning of the service—and, we may add, perhaps the most difficult part, for in the service itself the glorious words are set down for us in golden English, while left to ourselves we are very apt to get muddled among our various devices and desires and sometimes, like Man Friday, only able to say "O." But on this day there was only one thought in her mind, not of her loss, but of her mother still alive, somewhere, her youth and her age all as one; something so impossible to explain, so possible to feel.

There was not a printed order of the ceremony. Mr. Choyce had made a short service with some prayers, the latter part of the thirty-first psalm and a hymn. And will anyone who reads this think it is the hymn that she feels it would have been most suitable to sing; for not all are and there are a great many newish ones that are not only works of supererogation, but set the teeth on edge, not to speak of their great dullness. Then Mr. Choyce gave the blessing and all was over. Out of God's blessing into the warm sun came the little congregation and Lady Graham held a kind of reception in the churchyard, just as her mother would have done.

"And here is Sylvia, Sally," said Lady Graham to Lady Pomfret. "Martin couldn't come because of the farm, so Sylvia came and Edith is going back to Hatch House with her for a few days." Mr. Choyce then came into the churchyard, clothed and in his right mind as Lord Mellings irreverently said, and asked if they would all come into the Vicarage for a few moments. Lady Graham and Lady Pomfret excused themselves and went away with some of their party; while Lord Pomfret with Giles followed the Vicar up the depressing drive to where the monkey-puzzle blighted house and lawn.

"I say, what a ripping tree," said Giles. "I say, father, I wish Minor was here. I bet he couldn't climb that one. I mean," he added, turning to Mr. Choyce with a kind of formal courtesy as from one gentleman to another, "if you'd let him, sir. He's my cousin, you know. Uncle John has three sons, but Minor's the best at trees. He climbed the Mertons' monkey puzzle at Northbridge, but yours is a whopper, sir," to which Mr. Choyce, who had always got on with boys, even in his dreadful northern exile, replied he would be delighted to see him. "What did you say his name was?" he added.

"Minor, sir. Like the cigarette adverstisements," said Giles. "It's because there are three of them and at school they were Major and Minor and Minimus and the names stuck. In fact most people don't know they've got any names. A bit like savages," and he looked with the innocent eyes of a lower-form boy (exactly how innocent their masters well know) to see how Mr. Choyce was taking it, but that gentleman took the wind completely out of his sails by saying he had better read Warde Fowler's *Religious Experiences of the Roman People*, also his *Roman Festivals of the Period of the Republic*, after which Giles did not utter for some time and drifted quietly away to consider future tree-climbing.

"Thank you, Vicar," said Lord Pomfret. "Exactly what that boy of mine needs. I must apologise for him."

"Indeed not," said Mr. Choyce. "When I had a living in the poor parts of Liverpool I learnt everything there is to know about boys. Nice animals, but like all animals they need a master. I like them."

"You wouldn't consider giving this boy of mine some holiday coaching I suppose," said Lord Pomfret. "His classics are frightfully weak and I do want him to get on. Mr. Fanshawe of Paul's who married the eldest daughter of Dean, the big engineer at Winter Overcotes, told me you were a first-rate scholar."

"This is so sudden," said Mr. Choyce, violently balancing pros and cons in his mind. "Fanshawe was really too kind."

"I mean seriously," said Lord Pomfret. "As a boarder for a few weeks at Christmas. My wife and I shall be abroad and the two elder children are going to a Swiss hotel with a gang of friends. If you felt like taking Giles it would really be doing us a favour. If he is troublesome my cousin Lady Graham would deal with it, and you can pack him off to Holdings whenever you get tired of him."

"I would like to have your boy, Lord Pomfret," said Mr. Choyce. "I did take a first in Literae Humaniores in my time and it will be a pleasure to rub up my Latin. And I do not think I shall find him troublesome. After the lads I had to deal with in a Liverpool parish down near the docks any average high-spirited boy is as easy as—well as a sofa cushion. If I have any trouble I'll set him to climb the monkey-puzzle. And I hope he will come with some very old clothes as he is bound to tear anything he wears to tatters."

"That's a weight off my mind," said Lord Pomfret, "and I can assure you that my wife will be delighted. May I write to you about terms? Or if you will say what you think suitable, I am sure I will agree," and the two men felt each a liking and some respect for the other.

"I wonder," said Mr. Choyce, "if you would have a word with the organist. Caxton is his name, and he works for Squire Halliday. A carpenter by trade but an unusual man. And, I may add, sometimes a thorn in the flesh. He would appreciate it."

Lord Pomfret, who made it a rule never to shirk a duty and never to refuse a request unless it was obviously unreasonable, said in his tired courteous way that he would be delighted. Mr. Choyce, going to the low wall that divided the vicarage garden from the churchyard, called to Caxton, who had studiously not been trying to hear what they said. He was wearing his Sunday blacks from respect for Lady Emily, but even these, ill-fitting and hideous though they were, could not altogether hide his individuality.

"Good-afternoon, Craxton," said Lord Pomfret. "I must congratulate you on the organ. It was a fine performance and I am sure Lady Emily would have liked it if she had been here."

Caxton turned his Sunday hat round and round and said he was sure he must thank his lordship.

"I suppose you know a bit about the construction of an organ," said Lord Pomfret, seeking, as always, something which might give pleasure to others.

"Ah, that's a question I can answer, your lordship," said Caxton. "That organ, I've taken her to pieces and I've put her together again till I fairly got the hang of it. There were times, my lord, when the old devil, saving Mr. Choyce's presence, got the better of me. But it stands to reason a man as is a carpenter, a master-carpenter I might say, your lordship, well, if that man can't get the hang of a bit of work that man isn't worth his wages.

So long as there's a boy that will blow her proper and I'm at the other end, she's all right, my lord."

"Well done," said Lord Pomfret. "I am sure Lady Emily would have appreciated your playing. She was my cousin you know. I should like you to have this to celebrate the memorial service," and he put a green note into the carpenter's hand.

"I'm sure it's very good of your lordship," said Caxton, making a kind of gesture of pulling his forelock. "I've met your lordship's estate carpenter once or twice and he knows what he's about. If it's not presuming, would your lordship tell him that I've got just the bit of wood he wants, best walnut seven by three and a half and a lovely close grain," which Lord Pomfret promised to do and shook hands with the carpenter who went away.

"I can't thank you enough, Lord Pomfret," said the Vicar. "That will put him in a good temper till Christmas," and Lord Pomfret laughed and said he must be going or Lady Pomfret would wonder where he was. So he took Giles back to Holdings where Lady Graham and Lady Pomfret were talking about joining forces for a week or so in London during the autumn, to buy some clothes.

"If we made it at the children's half-term holiday," said Lady Pomfret, "perhaps Ludo could get leave from Sandhurst and we could all go to a play," at which Emily and Giles shrieked with delight. "And you will bring Edith, won't you? Where is she?"

"Oh, the *dreadful* girl," said Lady Graham, in just the same voice of proud deprecation, or deprecating pride if that is any clearer, that she had used about her eldest daughter some twenty years ago, when—as her brother David Leslie said—to hear Agnes saying "Wicked one! wicked one!" was like hearing the Commination Service read backwards. "Didn't she say good-bye? She went back with Sylvia to Hatch House. Sylvia has deserted Martin for a few days to stay with her father and mother. Mr. Halliday is very much of an invalid now and Mrs. Halliday asked Edith to come too. It is a change for her. You know, Gillie," said Lady Graham, addressing her cousin Pomfret not because she cared less for his wife, but because of the peculiar and indefinable bond between all the ramifications of Fosters and Leslies which made them, whenever they met, however amusing or glamorous the party of which they were partaking, or the person to whom they were talking, leave all others and cleave to their own near kin, "I sometimes feel I haven't done enough for Edith."

"I can't imagine that anyone else thinks so," said Lord Pomfret. "You have given her a perfect home and a great deal of love, and what is even cleverer of you, Agnes, a great deal of freedom. So many girls who live at home become shadows of their mothers, like that poor girl of the Hartletops'; or else they turn into managing viragos. Edith isn't a shadow of you. What that young women is at bottom I have not the faintest idea, but she is a person in her own right."

"I am so glad you think that, dear Gillie," said Lady Graham. "Sometimes I wonder if life hasn't been too easy for me and whether I have done enough for the children," upon which Lord and Lady Pomfret fell upon Lady Graham, telling her not to be so foolish and what better children could anyone have than hers; three boys doing very well in the army, two girls very happily married and a third who in time obviously would be. Under these kind and, we may say, well deserved praises Lady Graham's spirits at once rose. With feathers preened and glittering eye she said she was a silly old woman; which provocative words were at once taken up by the Pomfrets who poured flattering contradiction on her.

"It is *most* sweet of you, dear Sally," she said, "and when Robert rings up this evening I shall tell him how kind you have been. He *did* so hope to get down for the service, but that tiresome War Office wanted him. I sometimes wonder *what* the War Office think about," said her ladyship in a kind of mild Sibylline abstraction. "When Robert retires I shall ask General Platfield to come down for a weekend and I shall scold him. You must know him? He is only the second Earl but a charming man and his son, Lord Humberton, married Phoebe Rivers whose mother is that *dreadful* woman that writes those books where middle-aged women fall in love with young men and Uncle Giles—*your* uncle, Gillie," said her ladyship accusingly, "couldn't abide her, but she was always asked to The Towers once a year because her husband, poor George Rivers, is a cousin."

These excursions by her ladyship into family ramifications were apt to leave her less well-connected audiences bewildered and almost senseless, but today both her hearers—though Lady Pomfret was simply good county stock and Lord Pomfret, as we know, was only an Earl because the young heir whose name Ludovic now bore had been killed in a frontier skirmish, so many years ago now—knew perfectly well what she was talking about and both shared, as indeed did most people, her dislike of Mrs. George Rivers and her entire want of interest in that gifted writer's books.

"If it comes to that," said Lord Pomfret with some spirit, "he was your uncle too, Agnes. At least he was your mother's brother. And if we are to be accurate, which I find extremely difficult, he wasn't my uncle. My father was a cousin and a second cousin at that and Uncle Giles loathed him. What that makes me, I really don't know. A cousin-germane, perhaps, whatever that is."

Lady Graham said it sounded like Shakespeare and then Lady Pomfret got up and everyone said good-bye. The house felt empty when the guests had gone. Lady Graham almost wished that the Hallidays had chosen some other time to invite Edith. Holdings had been so filled with life, even though her husband was so often kept in London. Now all the boys were in the army; Emmy was married, Clarissa was married. Only Edith was left. Of course Edith must marry sometime and her ladyship would have thought very poorly of herself if she had a spinster daughter. More than once had she been gently sorry for the Dowager Lady Lufton when Maria Lufton remained, far too long, a dog-fancying spinster; but Maria was now the Honourable Mrs. Oliver Marling and had two children. Then she thought of Clarissa and the approaching baby and felt cheered. By long habit she went to look at the Saloon; the handsome drawing-room that was now only used in summer because it was so difficult to heat properly in the rest of the year; the room where her mother, Lady Emily Leslie, had so often sat in the last years of her life, the joy and the distraction of all who came within her orbit. All now an old story. She went back to her own sitting-room, rang up Rushwater, and in the pleasure of a long gossip with her daughter Emmy Grantly forgot her nostalgia.

When the service of remembrance was over, Edith and her luggage, which she had parked in the vestry by Caxton's permission, were taken aboard the Hatch House car and she and Sylvia Leslie drove across the river to Hatch House. Sylvia could not easily get away from Rushwater owing to her children and the house and the farm and the prize winning cattle, but Martin seeing, or thinking that he saw, that she was anxious about her father, had strongly supported the plan. Nurse was perfectly competent to look after Miss Eleanor and Master George (called after Sylvia's mother and her brother). Martin would of course miss her, but he had plenty of work on hand both outdoors and in the estate office and his cousin Emmy Grantly and her husband would come in the evening, or he could go to them. So she had very wisely decided to forget them as much as she could and enjoy her holiday. She liked her young cousin-by-marriage and was glad to have her at Hatch House, for fond as she was of her parents her brother George was her particular friend and if her father liked Edith, as he was bound to do, it would leave her all the more free to go about with George and see the improvements and talk to the people on the place.

Sylvia had to call at The Shop and the Mellings Arms, on instructions from her mother. Edith, a not unobservant young woman, felt the difference between the greetings to her mother and the greetings to Sylvia. Not but what the village liked Lady

Graham and even trusted her, but her ladyship was a foreigner from Rushwater and even Sir Robert Graham, though his family were long-established in those parts, was still at Hatch End (though accepted by now at Little Misfit) what in the North is called an off-come. Another two hundred years and the Grahams would be part of life—if they were allowed to exist. Meanwhile the Vidlers, the Hubbacks, the Caxtons, the Panters were the real life and—as must always have happened in the country since Britons (whoever they were) lived in horrid huts above the reed-choked marshes of the Rising (whatever it was then called)—they led that life very much as their ancestors had led theirs, allowing for the March of Progress, with on the whole a matriarchal rule. As in the case of Mrs. Panter, who during the war did the proxy voting for her son Fred Panter somewhere abroad with H.M. Forces and, disregarding any wishes expressed by him, very properly voted for Mr. Gresham. And as Sylvia Leslie (then Sylvia Halliday) had said, it wouldn't be a bad idea to give mothers a vote for each of their children till the children were married and had children of their own and could see life straight.

As usual there were parcels to be collected; some washing from Mrs. Panter, some groceries at The Shop. Here Mrs. Hubback handed them an untidy bundle of washing for her daughter and then they stopped again at the Mellings Arms to pick up some beer and some gin and a couple of rabbits about which it was better to ask no questions.

Edith, living at Holdings where the cook had sources of supply from Barchester and through Lady Graham from London, had never quite realised what the village could do and expressed the same to Sylvia.

"Oh, that's all right," said Sylvia. "They expect *you* to get some of your stuff in London. You see Lady Graham is really Little Misfit, so they don't expect her to know about Hatch End. But we do really know it. We've been here since 1721. At least William Halliday, Gent., built this house then, but the Hallidays had been here since goodness knows when. We don't know much about them except that George Halliday was in trouble after the Battle of Bosworth. But it blew over and here we are." And indeed they were; across the river, along the river road for a few yards and a sharp turn uphill into the front garden where Mrs. Halliday, as her children had so often found her, was digging up a flower-bed, preparatory to re-planting from a kind of nursery which lived away behind the house and outbuildings.

"Mother *darling*," said Sylvia, bursting out of the car into her mother's arms. "And here's Edith," whom Mrs. Halliday kissed very kindly. "I've heaps to tell you. Eleanor can talk so well now and George is getting on like anything and I and Number Three are on top of the world."

"Well, don't overbalance," said Mrs. Halliday in a Gampish way. "Your father is in the drawing-room and we'll have tea. Is that all your luggage, Edith? Good girl. Do you remember, Sylvia, when Captain and Mrs. Fairweather came here for the night, when he was speaking for our Navy League Branch, and all the suitcases she had? Dreadful girl!"

"But *so* lovely, mother," said Sylvia, who had all a good-looking woman's admiration for another handsome woman.

Mrs. Halliday said Lovely was as lovely did, and the mess in the bedroom when the Fairweathers had gone was indescribable and she had to get Mrs. Panter to wash some of the towels before she could send them to the laundry, because she was so ashamed of them.

"Take Edith upstairs, darling," said Mrs. Halliday to Sylvia. "She is in the Little Tulip Room. I have put you in your old room."

So the two girls—perhaps Sylvia is now more than a girl, but we cannot say the two women, for Edith is young for her age—went up the solid wooden staircase to the first floor where each door had a name written on it. Outside a door marked Tulip Room Sylvia stopped.

"This is me," said Sylvia ungrammatically as she opened the

door. "I had this room from when I was eight and nanny left us, till I married. Come in."

Edith followed her. The white-panelled room was full of the late afternoon across the water-meadows. A four-poster bed had faded chintz curtains at the head with a large sprawling pattern of tulips on them. The two sash windows had curtains of the same. Everything was faded, but very comfortably, as if the sun had warmed it for many years—as indeed it had. On the wall were flower-pictures from some old book, elegantly engraved and coloured by hand. A rather tattered bell-pull of linen embroidered with tulips hung by the fireplace which was of good design. The furniture was a mixture of good and bad.

"I *do* like this," said Edith. "It's so awful when everything is too period."

"I like it too," said Sylvia. "Those arm chairs look pretty awful, but mother had the seats re-sprung. I adore the washing stand," and so did Edith when she turned and saw the bedroom china all with sprawling tulips on it and, sitting beside the large jug and basin, that little jug and basin which has always fascinated us.

"I suppose people did use it just for cleaning their teeth," she said, "but I'm sure I never could remember."

"And now your room," said Sylvia and opened what Edith had thought was a cupboard door. And rather like a cupboard it was, with a space between it and another door which opened into the Little Tulip Room, smaller than Sylvia's, but with the same wallpaper and curtains and much the same furniture.

"We did think of turning this little bit between the doors into a hanging cupboard," said Sylvia, "but I think it's more fun like this. Would you like Hubback to unpack for you?" but Edith said Please not, because she knew she would never find anything again and then Sylvia said tea would be in a few minutes and left her. Edith unpacked her suitcase, put her belongings away and then, kneeling on the window seat, looked over the valley. Below her was the front lawn with its flower beds. Then came the low wall with its high drop to the road, and beyond it the water-meadows and the winding course of the Rising with the afternoon sunlight over all. Edith felt it was very romantic, as indeed it was, but it did not occur to her that from Holdings one also saw the river, and the bank where her sister Clarissa had observed their Uncle David proposing to Rose Bingham and being accepted by her. Things one sees at home are just things one sees at home; what one sees in other people's houses has something of the magic of the unknown. Here was the Rising valley which she had known all her life—her long life of eighteen years. But because she saw it from a bedroom with old furniture and faded chintz with tulips on it, it became a magic casement. It would be fun, she thought, if a Cavalier with becoming love-locks, a plumed hat and a lace cravat, suddenly reined up his horse under the window and threw up a rope-ladder so that she could fasten it to the bedpost and go down it and be carried away on his horse, but Sylvia knocked at the door between their rooms and said tea was ready.

"Here's the bathroom," said Sylvia as they went along the passage. "It hasn't got much of a view, but it's always warm because it's over the kitchen. The parents have been meaning to have a new bath for twenty years or so, bless them."

She opened the door and Edith saw a kind of grandfather of baths with a wooden ledge wide enough to walk on round it and two immense brass taps below which were two deep brown rusty streaks.

"It's the water here," said Sylvia. "We're on the mains for drinking water and the kitchen, but the bath water still comes from the spring up the hill. Something to do with a row father had with the Barchester Water Supply Company. It's so soft that it's like having a bath in warm treacle and heavenly for one's hair and stockings and things. Come on. Father doesn't like waiting for his tea," which Edith thought a little unjust as it was Sylvia who had caused the delay, and they went down the wide slippery staircase of some dark hued wood to the drawing-room.

Here tea was laid properly on a table with a cloth and Mrs. Halliday pouring out tea for her husband, who had a special very large cup with a view of the Eddystone Lighthouse on one side and Rule Britannia in elaborate golden lettering on the other.

"Oh, *what* a lovely cup," said Edith as she sat down.

"I'm glad you like it," said Mr. Halliday. "I've had this cup ever since I was a child. My old nurse gave it to me. What I can't stand is these drawing-room cups with rims that turn out and over."

"I know the sort you mean," said Edith. "The tea runs down both sides of your face if you aren't careful. And who is the other big cup for?"

"That is for George in case he comes in," said Mrs. Halliday. "But it depends what he is doing. If he's up in the top field I don't suppose we'll see him till supper time."

"What are they doing up there?" asked Edith, who had often been talked to by Goble the bailiff; a delicate distinction, for very few people had succeeded in talking with him, owing to his habit of either monopolising the whole conversation when he knew the subject well, or, if it was something in which he was not an expert, such as sugar beet which had been tried in Barsetshire and not succeeded, asking very intelligent and piercing questions, and further disconcerting his victim by making no comment whatever on the reply. Though there were those who maintained that the habit of old Mr. Macpherson who was the Leslies' faithful servant till the day of his death, namely of saying little but Imphm, into which dissyllable he could put a powerful and often disconcerting amount of meaning, was perhaps the most effective.

Mr. Halliday told Edith what George and the men were doing, but we shall not repeat his words lest our reader should be confirmed in what she has long suspected, namely our total ignorance of the farming on which so much depends. We can only say that whatever George Halliday was doing would be well and conscientiously done, as all work done by Hallidays has

been since Wm. Halliday, Gent. 1721; and probably by his
ancestors for several hundred years before that. And so deep
were they in their conversation that Mrs. Halliday was able to
take Sylvia away to have a nice Gampish talk about Number
Three in the course of which it was decided that if a boy it
should be Leonard Martin—Leonard being Mr. Halliday's
name—and if a girl Emily after Lady Emily Leslie, and probably another name as well, to be decided later, for Mrs. Halliday's own name Eleanor had already been used. All of which
Mrs. Halliday approved and they had another delightful talk
about what fun the new baby would be and would stop Master
George Leslie from being too spoilt.

"Though one can't go on having another baby for ever," said
Sylvia, "just to make the one before the last not be spoilt," which
is perfectly true and we do not see any answer to it, nor did Mrs.
Halliday.

"I think George is rather a beast not to come and welcome
me, mother," said Sylvia. "Let's go and welcome him instead. Or
supposing I take father up in the car—if it's all right," she
added, for she knew little about illness or a heart and had a
sudden vision of her father dead by her hand—or at least by her
deed—his eyes fixed and glassy, the death-rattle in his throat.

Mrs. Halliday saw no reason against it, so they went back to
the drawing-room where her husband was still telling Edith
what it was the men were doing up there. There was, quite a
long time ago when we were young, a book called "Listener's
Lure" in which the heroine won a very good husband and made
many friends simply because, being too shy to talk, she listened.
We would by no means insinuate that Edith Graham was like
this heroine, for shyness was not in her; but she had been well
brought up to be polite to older people and being a good-
humoured girl—child we had almost said, but one cannot be
called a child now at nearly eighteen—she was honestly doing
her best to make Mr. Halliday feel that what he was saying
interested her.

"I was thinking, Leonard," said Mrs. Halliday, "that if you felt like a drive we might go up as far as the three-acre and see how George is getting on. They are supposed to be carrying this afternoon."

We must say that Mr. Halliday deserved full marks for his behaviour as an invalid. An active man all his life till the last few years, he had at first resented bitterly his state of semi-invalidism and dependence. His children took it for granted that when people got older and were not well they would not want to do the things that were forbidden and to Mr. Halliday's eternal credit it can be said that never had he let them suspect that his spirit, imprisoned in a body from which death was the only release, was chafing and beating its wings against the bars. His wife saw more, for she knew him better and with a more understanding love, but even she was unable, thanks to his unselfish self-discipline, to believe that he kicked ceaselessly against the pricks and that the sword might out-wear the sheath.

"It would be very pleasant," said Mr. Halliday, so Sylvia brought her car round to the door and Mr. Halliday got slowly into it beside her. Mrs. Halliday and Edith took the back seat and Sylvia drove, very carefully and slow, up the lane that skirted Mr. Halliday's property, but before they reached Bolder's Knob (a steep green lump possibly once dedicated to Baldur, or just as probably not) she turned off to the right along a rutty track which petered out as they came to the field where George Halliday and a couple of farm hands were at work. The tractor was banging and panting and sending out vibrations that must have gone right round the world and come back again so loud they were, so resonant in the clear air of the late afternoon. As Sylvia pulled up, the tractor came to a standstill near them, gave some last convulsive pants and became silent. George Halliday in an old army shirt, an old pair of army breeches and very disgraceful boots, dismounted from it, his manly face—and we may add, his manly and rather hairy chest which his open khaki shirt showed off to the best advantage—bedewed with honest sweat.

"Hullo, Sylvia," said he, wiping his forehead with the back of his hand. "I won't kiss you just yet. How are you, old girl?"

Sylvia said Both quite well, thank you, which made her brother first stare in bewilderment and then burst out laughing—though very kindly and affectionately.

"And here's Edith," said Mrs. Halliday.

As he knew she was coming and had after all known the kid ever since she was born, for this was, we regret to say, the rather lofty way he put it to himself, he merely smiled at her and Edith smiled back.

"Look here, mother," he said. "If the girls get out I'll drive you and father round the field. We want a bit of advice from you, father," which words did not in the least impress Mr. Halliday who knew that George and the farm hands were every bit as competent as he was now.

"Don't get out, Edith," said Mrs. Halliday, "and you stay there too, Sylvia. I want to have a word with Fred about his grandson, the one that's got a scholarship or something. Scholarships are all very well, but there are clothes to consider."

"Oh, Jimmy!" said Sylvia. "Do you remember the time, just before the end of the war, when he borrowed some other boy's bicycle and rode down that steep hill to Nether Hatch without a brake and put his nailed boots on the tyre of the front wheel and ripped the tyre to pieces. Fred gave him a good thrashing for it."

Mr. Halliday, somehow taking this anecdote of his carter as a compliment to himself, said Fred Panter could still handle a horse as well as any man in those parts, even if he did leave an arm in the Ypres salient. Mrs. Halliday said it was hard luck when a man had to thrash his small grandson just because the Germans had killed the boy's father in the Second World War to End War.

"And thank goodness there's no one here to say the Germans have fathers just like us," said Sylvia Leslie with some violence.

"I wish all *their* fathers had had their foot blown to pieces at
Anzio like Martin, or been killed like Martin's father in the first
war," which outburst was not like her, but there *are* chords in the
human mind, as a greater writer than all of us put down
immortally on paper.

No one answered this, but there was a kind of affirmative
murmur, rather like the crowd during Mark Antony's oration
saying "Rhubarber, rhubarber" as we have been brought up to
believe they do. Then Mrs. Halliday and the girls got out saying
they would walk back and George Halliday got in and drove
slowly across the stubble, talking with his father.

"Lucky we've had a few dry days," said Mr. Halliday, "or you
couldn't have driven on this ground. But it's well drained. My
grandfather saw to that. 'You mind the drains and the ground
will look after itself,' he used to say."

"I expect you got a bit sick of hearing it, father," said George,
skilfully by-passing a partridge who was madly considering a
nest in the stubble; not that she had, so far as we know, anything
to lay in it, but one can hardly expect people who have eyes on
each side of their head instead of in the middle to think as we do.
Much the same thought must have struck George, who said to
his father that all those hen-birds were fools, adding that he
wondered what on earth they saw when they looked two ways at
once. His father, being more experienced in the ways of the
world said If it came to that, what about horses, who somehow
managed to see where they were going.

"Which is almost more than I can," said George, "with all
these bumps. Are you all right, father?" for the car was making
heavy weather across the furrows. "I'd forgotten it isn't the
tractor."

His father only laughed and said once he was on the downs he
could stand anything and we rather agree with him for there is,
up on those great whale-backed monsters, whether in Sussex or
in Barsetshire, an air that sweetly recommends itself; and many
a Barsetshire man on foreign service must have remembered

those windy heights from the trenches, from the desert, from forest land, from the sea, and said—or felt—according to his upbringing and his reading, "Into my heart an air that kills From yon far country blows."

As they went Mr. Halliday with his farmer's eye noted what had been done and George hoped, not very hopefully, that his father would not notice the things that had been wrongly done, or left undone. Through a gate at the end of the field they went out onto an enclosed piece of grass-land where sheep were gently grazing, their bells tinkling in the metallic cadence so nostalgic to the Barsetshire ear. Mr. Halliday said he would like to get out and walk a bit, so George helped his father out of the car, noticing afresh how small his father had become, his very bones frail to the touch through his clothes. The downhill journey had been long and slow, and living at home, seeing his father day by day, George became used to the change as it came. But here, alone on the windy pasture-land, the arm that was put through his suddenly felt as light as a sapless branch in winter. One sometimes wonders whether, if death forgot to claim an aging person, he would in time grow so light, so little bound to the earth, that a gust would whirl him away; or sink to the ground, becoming one with it.

"Ever read Meredith, George?" said his father.

George said he thought not.

"You don't think; you must know whether you have or not," said his father, almost sharply. "There's a lot of him that one could do without, but he was a poet and he knew a thing or two. I often think of a line of his when I'm feeling my age—and not being able to get about alone," he added, giving George's arm a friendly pressure; by which simple act of affection half of George was moved to wish that father would come off it as it made a fellow so uncomfortable, while the other half found a slight difficulty in speaking. "'Into the breast that gave the rose,'" Mr. Halliday went on, saying the lines aloud to himself, "'Shall I with shuddering fall?'" at which point George very nearly shook himself loose from his father to go off and re-enlist; for when our elders make an appeal, even unconsciously, to our emotions, we are apt to rationalise (which horrid jargon has apparently come to stay, so we might as well use it) them and feel outraged that a person can't make a remark without other people saying something that makes one feel uncomfortable. But his better self coming to the rescue said one must remember that father was a bit of a crock, and how thin his bones felt when one took his arm—like a bird's—so he tried another subject.

"It's bad luck that the summer's nearly over, father," he said, "and a rotten summer too. But we may have a good autumn," and though he said this cheerfully he said it without conviction, for it is quite obvious that what with the Germans and the Russians and India and the Far East and the Atom Bomb and Crashing the Sound Barrier (or whatever it is) and the general March of Progress, the weather is going to be worse and worse for ever and ever.

"Well, whom the Lord loveth He chasteneth," said Mr. Halliday. "At least so we are told, but it isn't the way I would behave to *my* children."

"Oh, come off it, father," said George, rather glad of any excuse to get away from what threatened to be embarrassing emotion. "You've always been awfully decent to us. You did give me one or two pretty good whackings when I was a kid, but I deserved them."

"So you did," said Mr. Halliday, apparently much cheered by this remark, and then he asked George several very pertinent questions about the farm, all of which George most patiently answered and apparently his answers gave satisfaction.

The position of a grown-up son at home who does all the work, yet is not the ultimate authority, is not always easy, but we think George Halliday had made a pretty good job of it. Perhaps partly that his army training had accustomed him over a period of years not only to do as he was told, but also to take things as they came and never to give lip to his superior officers, or be impatient with the men for whom he was responsible. In this case his father surprised in himself, as Count Smalltork so well put it, both positions. As George's father, the owner of the land and a farmer of long experience, he had every right to dictate and knew it. As a man failing in health, unable to get about the estate and see what the men were up to, it was obvious that much must be delegated to George and this, we think, was harder for George than for his father.

"I sometimes wonder if I ought to have made the place over to you after the war," said Mr. Halliday, looking away across the fields to Bolder's Knob, standing out against the grey summer sky.

"What for, father?" said George. "I'd only have been run over, or fallen off a mountain in Switzerland, or even cracked my head once too often on that beam in the corner of my room, and then you'd have been *my* heir and whacking death duties. They've got you whichever way," said George cheerfully, "and no more nonsense about making it over to me, father. I might marry a female native and go to live in Mngangaland, and then where would you be?"

"Well, don't marry her while *I'm* alive," said his father, with nearly all his wonted fire and George made a mental note that next time his father got down in the mouth he would say he was going to marry a female Labour M.P., which ought to pep the old man up like anything.

They were now on the highest part of the farm where the arable land gives way to downland. The chalk track known as Gundric's Fossway, which skirts Mr. Halliday's property, here mounts the downs to where the steep green hump, possibly once dedicated to Baldur (which question has rent the Barsetshire Archaeological from top to bottom more than once and as there is no way of deciding it will doubtless continue to do so), rises abruptly. Mr. Halliday stopped and looked round him, where Barsetshire lay at his feet like a map, as lovely a county as any. To the north and east the downs encircled them and protected the valley from the more cruel winds; Humpback Ridge, the Great Hump, Fish Hill with its clump of stone pines; the Plumstead water tower (a hideous great cylinder on open-work iron legs) was looking romantic in the distance. To the south and west the downs melted into river-valleys, water-meadows, cornland and the low pasture lands, with the most beautiful spire in England pointing heavenwards, white or grey as sun or cloud-shadow moved over it. A group of pylons far away looked like minarets.

Mr. Halliday drew a deep breath of satisfaction and George, his temporary irritation with his father forgotten, said, "By Jove" softly. Up the Rising valley came five notes from a bell.

"What's happened to the cathedral clock?" said Mr. Halliday. "It must be all of six o'clock by now."

"It's all that blasted Summer Time, father," said George, with a good conservative farmer's dislike for any changes within the span of his own life. "If you remember there was a row about it when Double Summer Time came. Old Canon Thorne who knows the clock better than anyone said if they tried to alter it, it would burst. The Bishop wanted to let it run down for Summer Time and set it going again for the right time—I mean the wrong time—so of course the Dean said it was impossible and he couldn't allow it. So it goes on telling the right time."

"But it isn't the right time," said Mr. Halliday rather peevishly. "It struck five and it's six now. Oh, I see what you mean. It's right by the *right* time."

George was divided between amusement and irritation, but when he saw that his father was tired, his kind, practical nature took charge and he persuaded him, not altogether unwilling to be persuaded, to sit on the grass bank that bordered the road while with long strides he went over the field, fetched the car, brought it up the track and helped his father in. The drive back was uneventful. Mr. Halliday did not suddenly die in the car, his face irradiated with a wonderful look of peace; nor was he smitten with paralysis so that George had to lift him reverently from the car. All he did was to sit quiet while George drove carefully downhill and into the yard, to get out with a little effort and say he had enjoyed the outing.

"There's only one thing George," he said, standing with a hand on the door of the car, rather to his son's annoyance who wanted to put it away and change his boots and if possible have a bath before taking sherry with the ladies, "when I am dead, I will *not* have char-à-bancs driving up the Fossway. It is my private property and those things tear a chalk road to pieces."

"All right, father," said George, with great presence of mind. "I'll mine the road and put a pill-box with a nice little gun inside the gate. Don't worry, father" and he drove the car away to the garage at the back, where he found Caxton.

"Hullo, Caxton," he said, "I thought you'd gone."

"So I have, Mr. George," said Caxton, "but I thought I'd wait."

"Well, what is it?" said George, sitting himself on an empty packing-case. "Not the lathe again?" for the little motor in Caxton's workshop had been giving trouble.

"It's not that, Mr. George," said Caxton. "It's Squire," which now alas rather outmoded way of address Caxton had firmly stuck to.

"What's he been up to now?" said George, knowing that his father did sometimes give contradictory orders without realising it.

"It's not what he's up to, Mr. George," said Caxton. "It's what's coming to him? I don't like it."

"All right, Caxton, I know what you mean and I don't like it either," said George. "Carry on," and with the old habit of obedience to an officer, learnt in the trenches before George was born, Caxton made a gesture between saluting and pulling his forelock and went home for his tea.

"Well, sitting on a packing-case gets one nowhere," said George aloud to himself and went indoors to have a bath before dinner. The bathroom door was locked so he banged on it, and called, "Time's up."

"Who is it?" said a voice.

"Oh, I'm sorry," said George, retreating a step or two from the locked door in his agitation. "I thought it was Sylvia."

"It's only me," said Edith. "I'll be as quick as I can, but the bath's so slippery I can't get out. Your water is so soft and I used too much soap. I shan't be long" and a sound of splashing told George that the guest was keeping her word and he went back to his room feeling himself a Tarquin unmasked.

"All clear now," said Edith's voice in the passage, as she went to her room.

George went across to the bathroom, noted with vague approval that everything was tidy and the window opened, so he shut the window and turned on the hot tap. He had lazily thought of simply having a good wash, say up to the elbows and well round the neck and the ears, but his better self said to him that wasn't the way to behave when there was company. Edith Graham, George then said quite firmly to his better self, was not company. He had known her parents and her elder brothers and sisters ever since he could remember; before there was any Edith at all in fact, and he was not going to have a bath to please anyone. Without thinking he undid the neck of his shirt—one could at least wash round one's ears after a day in the farm—but to his own great surprise he found he had undressed and was getting into the steamy soft-water bath. Being there, one might as well luxuriate and wallow, so he did both. But all is Vanity, and when he had dried himself he remembered he had not brought a dressing gown. To hurl himself across the corridor, draped in a towel, would be easy enough, but he had not brought his own bath towel and there were only face towels on the towel-horse. There had once been a bell in the bathroom so that anyone in distress could summon a menial, connecting with one of those enchanting bell-boards in the basement where each bell has its own name above it, as though it were a horse in a good stable, but that had gone years ago, during the 1914 war. A man must do something. A man cannot stay all night in a bath which is rapidly getting cooler. With a good flow of army language he picked up the soft bath mat which was a good deal larger than the towels, wound it round him, and opened the door to get across to his room, when Edith's door opened and out she came, suitably dressed for a summer evening in a light woollen dress and holding a large bath towel.

"Hullo! have you finished your bath?" she asked.

"Well, I have," said George, "but I forgot my bath towel."

"Well, take mine," said Edith, who owing to three elder brothers was well used to young gentlemen in every stage of déshabille. "I was just going to put it in that hot cupboard to dry, so you can put it there when you've used it. Does the water always stick in the hot tap and suddenly come out with a thump?"

George felt this was not the moment to discuss the Hatch House plumbing, so thanking Edith he retreated into the bathroom, turned on the hot tap again, and had what their Nurse used to call a good lay in the rich, soft, soapy water, so that he would be nice and wet to dry himself. Then he went downstairs and they had supper and as everyone was sleepy they went to bed early. Edith, who did not know what a bad night meant, did not wake till Hubback came in to call her next morning. For a moment she did not know where she was. Then, everything fell into its place and she got up and looked out of the window. As usual it was a nasty chill grey day, but she did not particularly notice it and thought everything was rather fun.

CHAPTER 3

Over at Greshamsbury Mr. and Mrs. John Leslie had decided not to go away during the school holidays. The weather was being unpleasant all over the world. Postcards from friends who had gone to Sunny Spain, Sunny Italy, Sunny Majorca and a great many other Sunny Places, announced that it was very cold, very wet, and there was no central heating and—in many cases—nothing to do; also that every hotel was full of English, a fact always resented with peculiar venom by Us when abroad. So John and Mary Leslie felt gladder and gladder that they were not there, and their boys were delighted to be at home. For if one is away at school and does not see one's home in term-time and if your kind parents take you away for the holidays you can never do the really important things like digging out that badger near Hamaker's Spinney, the one no one had managed to dig out yet, with your Pomfret cousins (Major); or going on the cathedral roof with George Halliday if he remembered to ask you and perhaps having a go at that big tulip tree in the Palace Garden again, which he knew old Tomkins the gardener would let him do, if only to annoy the Bishop (Minor); and going to the Barchester Odeon every day as long as your pocket money lasted to see Glamora Tudor in a revival of "Burning Flesh" re-filmed at great expense in Glorious Technicolour and a Three Dimensional Screen with her new co-star Washington Swop (Minimus). So far the Leslie boys had not told their parents what they intended to do; for parents are notoriously allergic to Good Ideas and the boys felt it would be both kind and polite to keep them in ignorance.

There was also, as we know, a cricket-match at Southbridge of Old Boys versus The Rest, which latter team was being with some difficulty recruited, but had a strong core of the Vicar, Colonel Crofts (as he still liked to call himself), his excellent butler Bateman who had so confusingly been his batman and the two assistant masters who were remaining at home, Mr. Feeder and Mr. Traill. Leslie Major, who was much attached to his cousin Edith and patronised her quite abominably, had said something about her coming to see him make a hundred runs, which treat she had accepted with pleasure before her visit to Hatch House and she now felt a certain diffidence in asking Mrs. Halliday if she could take a day off, as it were, and had several arguments with her social conscience. These, however, were solved for her when Major rang up Hatch House after dinner and asked to speak to his cousin Edith.

"Oh, hullo Edith," said Major, "I say, I rang up Aunt Agnes but she said you were at the Hallidays'. Look here, you know it's our great cricket do on Saturday. Can't you come? Get George Halliday or someone to drive you over, and bring Sylvia."

This put Edith in a social quandary. She much wanted to go to Southbridge and see her cousin Major make a hundred runs, but she had been well trained in the politeness one should show as a guest, as well as a hostess. George was busy on the farm. Sylvia might be able to go, but she thought Sylvia wouldn't want to leave her parents in the middle of her all too short visit. Luckily Mrs. Halliday was writing letters at the other end of the drawing-room so Edith very sensibly asked Major to hang on a minute while she asked her hostess.

Mrs. Halliday was one of the many quiet women who do everything very competently and with a minimum of fuss, rather like Mother Carey in the Waterbabies. She laid down her pen, the better to give her full attention to Edith, who explained Major's invitation.

"I think George had better take you," said Mrs. Halliday, which suddenly made everything quite clear and simple. "Sylvia won't want to go; she likes to be with her father while she is here," and if there was an undercurrent of anxiety in these words Edith did not recognise it; nor would her hostess have wished her to. "They will probably have finished on the farm by Saturday so long as the weather keeps fine for the next two or three days. Yes; you and George go. It will be so good for him to get away from us," which she said with no kind of emotion, but rather as a wise hen-wife might think those young cockerels would be better in that run down beyond the asparagus beds. So Edith thanked her hostess and went back to the telephone with the good news.

"Good girl," said Major's voice approvingly. "And there's to be a kind of do afterwards at Wiple Terrace and everybody's going, so tell George. And tell him he'd better bring a bottle of something. How are you enjoying it?"

Edith hoped this question would not reach her hostess, Major's voice being none of the softest, but luckily she could say with complete truth that she was having a lovely time and had been up to Bolder's Knob, to which her cousin replied loftily that she could keep it and when each had sent polite love to the parents of the other the talk came to an end.

"Thank you so much, Mrs. Halliday," said Edith. Her hostess, who was used (as most of our generation are now) to benefits forgot even as they are given, looked up from her letters and smiled. Not so pretty as her sister Clarissa, Mrs. Halliday thought, with that peculiar divided mind that allows us to think of two things at once, yet independently, so long as we are unconscious of it—and then slams the door if we begin to think what we have been thinking about. And if this sounds unreasonable, so would most of our thoughts if they could be recorded as we think them, but thank goodness they can't, for a more worthless bundle of rubbish it would not be easy to find. Memory Muddle-the-Door, in fact. It is not given to us all to have the equal mind of Hold-the-Door.

As Mrs. Halliday was busy and Sylvia was telling her father about her children, their beauty, charm and intelligence, and how Martin and Tom Grantly were hoping to do well at the Bath and West Show with their pedigree Rushwater bulls, Edith went into the garden and round to the back where Hubback was having Words with Vidler's young man about the fish. Fearful of being drawn into the controversy, she went on to the old carpenter's shop where Caxton was reading the Barsetshire Free Press while he ate his elevenses, namely some cold sausages and a large tin of hot tea made with condensed milk and liberally sweetened, which he was hotting up on a kind of small electric gridiron, installed by him for his greater comfort. Here also was George Halliday, doing something to his gun.

"Hullo, Edith," said George. "Come and help me to get some rabbits up the Four-Acre. There's a nice bank where they sit in the sun and wash their faces. Have a look at her now, Caxton," and he handed the gun to the carpenter, who put it to his shoulder, looked along it, broke it (we think this is the correct expression but accept no responsibility for same), looked at whatever lives inside, shut it up again and said he'd seen worse jobs. George, almost unmanned by this praise, tucked his gun under his arm and went out, Edith obediently by his side.

Though it could not by any stretch of imagination have been called warm up on the hillside, it might have been worse and indeed usually was in that odious summer. George, with unusual thoughtfulness, suggested a sheltering bank to Edith, under which she might sit and watch him, possibly with a view of getting her out of the way. But Edith had not been brought up by three elder brothers for nothing and was a very good audience, showing a quiet appreciation of his marksmanship but falling into mocking laughter when a large buck rabbit, who though not old in years by our reckoning was an Elder Statesman in rabbit circles, turned head over heels three times at the sound of the gun and then rushed down his hole warning everyone that the Russians were coming.

"Blast that fellow," said George, though fellow was not the word he used. Edith, accustomed to her brothers' freedom of speech, did not appear to notice it, which raised her in George's estimation. He then wondered vaguely if it was ignorance or tact, but decided not to bother about it. One of the dogs who had thought it his duty to chaperon Mr. George, came lolloping up and sat down by the rabbit-hole, panting loudly with its tongue hanging out, and so letting the young Squire know that it would sit there on and off for days and days if required.

"No need to, old fellow," said George, who quite understood it. "I'm taking my rabbits home in my pockets," so the dog got up and pretended it had never seen or thought of rabbits. When George had got a couple more he said that was enough and they might leave Pincher on guard with the rabbits, go for a bit of a walk, and pick up dog and rabbits on the way home, all of which they did, skirting the hill and coming up Bolder's Knob from the far side, talking all the time, mostly about the estate. Edith rather impressed George by the sense of some of her remarks, and he told her so when they sat in the lee of the Knob for a rest.

"Oh, it's only things that father says," said Edith. "I usually go round the place with him on Sunday afternoons when he's at home. When he retires we are going to do a lot together. Goble—that's our bailiff you know—is getting on a bit and he says his heart's in the pigsties. You know father's pigs do awfully well at all the shows. His Holdings Goliath was runner-up for the Challenge Cup the year we had the Pig-Breeders' Association show at the Conservative Rally and he beat everyone at the Barsetshire Agricultural in 1947. Of course I don't really know pigs as well as Emmy knows bulls, but I'm not bad. And father's White Porkminsters are the best in England."

George, amused and also not a little impressed by Edith's knowledge, asked what her father thought.

"Oh, father says it will be a great help," said Edith, not puffed-up but as one who announces a fact. "And so does Goble and he *really* knows. Goble says the farmer's boots are the best muck, and it's the same for pigs. If you visit them regularly they fatten much better," all of which farming lore, coming from Edith in her pleasant voice and her slightly didactic air, amused George a good deal and his respect for a girl who could be so pig-minded and yet not throw her weight about went up considerably.

"Why don't you have proper pigs here?" said Edith.

On hearing these words George realised that all his farming knowledge, absorbed when he was a boy without his knowing it, studied with a kind of dogged enthusiasm when he came back from the war, was as nothing compared with a true knowledge of pigs. Horses he knew pretty well, to ride, to drive and to work on the farm. Tractors were his washpot and over potato-spinners he cast out his shoe. But pigs—

His silence was prolonged till Edith wondered if he had listened to what she was saying. She knew that while really good farmers like Martin Leslie and Goble could teach her a great deal, she already knew quite as much as her father—though this she admitted to herself was not quite fair, because father had to be away so much on his various boards and military missions. The blood of Pomfrets and Leslies pulsed hotly within her as she repeated to George, "Well! why *don't* you have some good pigs here?"

There was a short silence, during which she began to wonder if she had gone too far. Oh well, if she had, she would go back again.

"You know, that *is* an idea," said George. "Of course I'd have to see what father thinks. But look here Edith, when Sir Robert is down sometime, could I come over and have a talk with him and with your man? I think a few good pigs might cheer father up a lot. He gets too tired if he goes up to the fields, even in the car. But if I could have one really good sow, it would be something for him to think about. Our pigs are quite all right as pigs go, but not in the Porkminster class. We've got a Norfolk Nobbler sow, and Lord Bond sent his Cropbacked Cruncher prize boar over here one year. But I've an idea that we might do with some White Porkminsters."

Not more astonished was Aladdin when the Jinn came out of the brass bottle he had been rubbing than was Edith by George's words. That George, a *real* farmer who worked with the men and had hard hands and was sunburnt almost to the waist (as her quick eye had noticed with some interest during the bathroom interlude of the previous evening) should not know the difference between pigs and Champion Pigs almost shocked her. Then, being a fair-minded young person, she began to think of all the things that she didn't know, like Land Acts and County Council Regulations and Board of Agriculture Regulations and Swine Fever Regulations, or even how to make a tasty if superficially revolting mash for a sow with sixteen or seventeen children all the same age, and felt rather depressed.

"And now I've got those drain-pipes we could make a really good thing of the pig-yard," said George, "and I might get father to let me recondition the old barn, the smaller one. We hardly ever use it now. If I got a good man to concrete all the floor, with drains everywhere, and see to the roof—and of course put windows along one side and it would be easy to lay a pipe from the spring up the hill."

"Constant hot water," said Edith, but George, in a golden pig-dream did not notice her. "And," he went on, "supply a trough for each sow. And we could get plenty of litter if we cut the ferns up on that poor bit of land and—"

It began to appear to Edith that she had let loose an even larger and more powerful Jinn than she had bargained for—even as Aladdin had. However she was not a worrier and having sown her seed, she would be content if some the birds devoured and some the season marred, and could wait quite patiently, as the daughter of generations of landowners should do, till in the fullness of time there might flower the solitary stars. A really good pig-establishment at Hatch House; what fun it would be and George would get hundreds of prizes and it would cheer Mr. Halliday up.

"Well, I must think about it," said George, rising to his feet in one easy gesture.

"I wish I could do that," said Edith, frankly envious.

"Sylvia's better than I am," said George, not without pride in his sister's achievements. "She can sit down on the floor with her legs beside her."

"How?" said Edith. "It sounds as if she had false ones and took them off."

"Well, it's rather difficult to explain," said George. "You stand up with your legs together and you sit down on the floor quite slowly and make the bottom part of your leg—I mean the calf and all that—lie alongside the upper part of your legs. It looks awfully easy when Sylvia does it, but Lord! how it hurts when you try."

Edith said she must have a try anyway, stood up, took a deep breath and began to sink to the ground, bending her knees as she did so. Just at the point where the lower part of each leg should lay itself, neatly doubled up, on the carpet alongside its upper part, she fell over sideways. George pulled her up and they both laughed consumedly. Then they walked back to collect the rabbits and relieve Pincher from sentry-go and so homewards, making plans to join a circus and be the people who do everything wrong so that the star performers may shine the more brightly in contrast.

All being settled for the jaunt to Southbridge, Edith had only to enjoy herself and to her credit it must be said that she managed to enjoy talking with Mr. Halliday, thus releasing Mrs. Halliday to her own house and village occupations and giving her a chance to have her daughter Sylvia to herself a good deal for delightful Gampish talks. Sylvia, accustomed as the ruler of

Rushwater to consider the interests of everyone on the estate, from Martin when his leg hurt him to Aggie Propett who never quite knew whether she was in trouble or not, nor as a rule by whom, took a lively interest in Hatch End doings and she it was who finally bullied Mrs. Vidler into going to the Barchester General Hospital and having a Nasty Finger properly treated, though Mrs. Vidler stoutly maintained that it was really the application of dandelion tea, boiling hot, with a bit of lard in it that effected the cure. Possibly both were efficacious; we do not know.

Mr. Halliday for his part, much as he adored his wife and his daughter, was not displeased to have a pretty child to talk to for a change, especially when he found that Edith had an insatiable curiosity about Hatch End and its history and Bolder's Knob. And we may say that her interest—though she did exaggerate it with the laudable motive of giving pleasure to her host—was quite real.

"Have they ever excavated Bolder's Knob?" she enquired.

"They have," said Mr. Halliday. "About fifty years ago, when I was a youngster. The Barsetshire Archaeological had a field-day here and got permission to drive a kind of tunnel into the side of the mound. Lord Stoke was at the bottom of it all—do you know him?"

Edith said he came over to Holdings to talk with Goble about pigs sometimes and had once shocked cook by coming in by the kitchen entrance and the kitchen maid had nearly had hysterics because he was a Lord and Lords didn't ought to act like that, which made Mr. Halliday laugh. And when Mr. Halliday laughed it may have tired him, but it also did him good and his wife was pleased to hear the two together.

"But what happened about the excavating, Mr. Halliday?" said Edith.

"They tunnelled into the mound for about twenty feet," said Mr. Halliday. "First it was open-cut and then they put some timber in to hold it up. In the end they came to some bones."

"Were they Ancient Britons," said Edith.

"Stoke thought they were," said Mr. Halliday, "or at any rate he wanted to think they were; much the same thing. But one of the men on the place—Caxton's great-uncle I think it was—said there used to be a kind of natural spring at the top of the hill and in his young days there was an opening from the top and if you let a bucket down on a rope you got quite good water, but it got choked-up like and the boys they threw rabbits and things down. If I had a bit of money to spare I'd like to do something about that spring. The place where they dug the tunnel is on my land."

"But, Mr. Halliday," said Edith, "you couldn't have a spring on the top of a hill."

"Couldn't you!" said Mr. Halliday. "When I was a young man I used to do a good bit of walking in the Lake Country and there, the higher you go the more water. There was quite a dangerous boggy patch on the high ground between Thirlestone and Watendlath—may be still for all I know. And there's a spring bubbling out at the top of Coniston Old Man—or is it Wetherlam? It's so long since I was up there that I forget. I'll never go up there again," and he was silent. Edith rather wished she had not begun the conversation and did not know what to say.

"Don't worry," said Mr. Halliday. "We old people do talk like that. But to go back to what we were saying, the water's still there all right. If one had nothing else to do and plenty of money to do it with, one could unchoke the spring and get a permanent supply of water for the farm. But we shan't get that done now. The Archaeological think the Knob was a British camp and the tribe who used it knew all about the water. I don't know," and as he seemed tired Edith offered to read aloud to him which she did very nicely, with no affectation and pronouncing the words properly. The book she was reading was Bleak House and Edith had to stop occasionally to say how horrid and affected Esther Summerson was with her fussing ways.

"If you live long enough," said Mr. Halliday, "you will find that Dickens is always right. I used to think as you do that she was an affected little bore. Now I see her as she really was. It is a great help to have your Dickens with the original illustrations. They show you what Dickens meant" and Edith had to admit that in the pictures Esther did look very pretty and rather a darling.

"I expect he told the artist about her," said Mr. Halliday "and the artist drew what Dickens had only seen in his mind. I have always hoped," said Mr. Halliday, more to himself than to Edith, "that those illustrations to Edwin Drood by Luke Fildes held the secret. We know that he discussed them with Dickens. Every time I look at them I hope I will see the clue. But I never have," and he sounded so discouraged that Edith told him how she and George were going to the cricket match at Southbridge and how her Leslie cousins were going and how Major was playing because he was an Old Boy now, but Minor and Minimus weren't in the team. Mr. Halliday, who had played village cricket a good deal in his time and had just not got into the West Barsetshire eleven as a young man, took considerable interest in the match, remembering the names of the second and even third generations of old Southbridgians whose people he had known.

"And how are you going?" he asked.

Edith said George wasn't very busy that afternoon, so he was going to take her, and Mr. Halliday thought the young woman was very sensible and it would do George good if he got away more often. It did then occur to him—for parents are not always as dull as their children think they are—that George led rather an isolated life now, farming late and early, doing his best to take his father's place in that part of West Barsetshire. But of this he did not speak to Edith, for it was not her business and he did not wish in any way to dull her pleasure in the treat.

Saturday dawned bright and fair and a cold wind and heavy clouds coming up from the west. Edith, looking out of her bedroom window before breakfast saw Caxton in the garden and called a Good-morning to him.

"Good-morning, Miss Edith," said the carpenter, more or less pulling a non-existent forelock. "I've been about the place since six. Got a couple of nice young rabbits as'll never see *their* homes again. Saw them cleaning their whiskers, same as like a cat, so I got them sitting."

"Wasn't that a bit mean, Caxton?" said Edith who, though as a country bred girl she took it for granted that one shot things, felt one ought to give them a sporting chance.

"All depends what you mean by mean, miss," said Caxton. "If I go out of a morning and I see rabbits cleaning their whiskers I say to myself, What's their game? Now, if it was, say, some kind of a do over at Lord Aberfordbury's place, well I'd say to those rabbits, Go on, my fine fellows, I'll get you another day. But with us carrying the last of the top field this morning and you and Mr. George going to see the Southbridge young gentlemen's cricket match, miss, Fred Caxton doesn't take no chances. So I got both my young fellows with the one shot and they'll make a nice tea for me and my old woman on Sunday. She's rising seventy but she's got every tooth in her head," and Caxton continued his way to his cottage.

It was rather damping to know that Caxton predicted bad weather, for in Edith's experience the older countrymen were nearly always right. Some went by cats or rabbits washing their faces. Old Mrs. Hubback at The Shop knew by the tea-leaves in her first cup of tea. Mrs. Panter who took in washing said you could always tell by the clothes-line and it stood to reason if you left it out all night, nice and slack, it was bound to get the inference; which word coming to the knowledge of Lord Stoke, he had invited himself to tea with Mrs. Panter, talked with her as with an equal about country matters and signs and portents, and come away with the certainty that she was really saying the Influence and it went right back to the Dark Ages and astrology, not to speak of a bit of demonology and spirit-raising. Whether his lordship was right or wrong we cannot say, but undoubtedly Mrs. Panter's clothes-line had foretold bad weather for the

Coronation in the previous year and would probably have been burnt for sorcery, together with its owner, in more enlightened times. But now most of us listen to the seven or eight o'clock weather bulletin on the wireless instead of to the dreamer Merlin and his prophecies as described by that brilliant talker Harry Hotspur; and are little the wiser.

Still, one more wet day or less in that most distressful summer was not going to stop the cricket match, if human power could hinder it. The pitch had been covered, there was even talk of coconut matting for batters and bowlers; perhaps not quite like Lords or the Oval, but a one-day match must do the best it can, and while Hatch House was having its breakfast the experts were out on the School cricket ground and decided that barring a cloud-burst, or six hours' soaking rain before two o'clock, it would do. And the nasty northeast wind which was blowing from all directions—a description which anyone who has lived in river valleys with their twists and turns will at once understand—was at least drying the pitch.

It is now so long since the older generation we knew at Southbridge had dispersed to war, to work, the marriage, some-times to failure, that we are a little confused. Tony Morland, the inscrutable master-baiter, he who had driven to junior classical master Philip Winter to frenzy by his deliberately calm gaze; Eric Swan, who had further exacerbated Mr. Winter by looking at him through his spectacles; Hacker who kept a tame chame-leon and was the head classical master's secret pride and had let his bath overflow till the water went through into the kitchen quarters; Featherstonehaugh the Captain of Rowing who went into the Nigerian Police; all these had gone their ways. Tony to a good Civil Service job, with a delightful wife and several children; Eric Swan, who had what are called private means, to an undermaster's post in Philip Winter's preparatory school at Harefield and a marriage of love with Justinia Lufton, Lord Lufton's sister; Hacker to rise to Senior Classical tutor at Red-brick University and publish (through the courtesy and gener-

osity of the Oxbridge Press) several works on classical subjects
highly thought of by such as were qualified to understand them;
Featherstonehaugh, coming home on leave, to be torpedoed in
the Lancashire; the list might go on for ever. But there were still
boys of the same name as their fathers, uncles, cousins.

Mr. Birkett, Headmaster before and during part of the war,
had retired some years previously and was now engaged in his
great edition of The Analects of Procrastinator with Critical
Notes, while the second master, Everard Carter, was now Headmaster and a very good job he was making of it, and liked by the
younger masters. Matron, still ruling the Upper School Board-
ers' House, with the hideous housemaid Jessie under her, was as
capable and cheerful as ever, and talking even more. Whether
George Halliday had been at Southbridge we are not quite sure;
but we rather think not. For two reasons, (a) that we do not
remember him there and (b) that, not knowing his past we
cannot be troubled to invent it.

"Well, that's pretty well all right," said George, coming into
the drawing room about eleven o'clock. "Even if it rains today or
tomorrow it can't do much harm to us now." "I'm sorry," said his
mother "but it can. They have had a cloudburst at Southbridge
and the pitch is flooded. Minor rang up to tell you."

"Then," said George, "I'll take Edith to lunch at the White
Hart in Barchester for a treat. It makes more of an outing and
less work for Hubback."

"Just what I was going to suggest to you this morning if you
hadn't gone off without my seeing you," said his mother, but
with complete absence of rancour, as one who states an ineluctable fact.

"All right, mother, you win," said George. "Sorry. I wanted to
get that last load into the barn. I had a talk with father about pigs
last night and he seemed quite pleased with the idea."

"He will be pleased with anything you suggest," said Mrs.
Halliday, looking among some papers on the table where she
was sitting with her back to the window. "In fact the more you

suggest, the better. He likes to think about it even if he can't do much."

"I say—I mean I didn't think—I mean I think it's awfully decent," George began, not very intelligibly, but his mother said that was very nice and not to bother about being late, on hearing which George expressed real gratitude, for to have to come back by a given time is always a bother in summer, even if the longer evenings are grey and chill.

"Well, I would do more than that for you," said his mother, with the detached but very real affection that she felt for her only son, her first born. "And if anyone asks you to stay to dinner, do. Only don't let Edith get too tired," to which George unchivalrously answered that she was more likely to exhaust him than the other way round.

"By the way, George," said his mother, who had been looking through some letters, "the lease of the Old Manor House comes to an end this year. I didn't know it was so soon."

"You mean where the bank is?" said George. "Lord! I'd forgotten all about it."

"Considering it is where the Hallidays lived for a long time, before William Halliday, Gent. built this house," said his mother rather coldly, "you might as well remember. The bank don't want to renew the lease as they are building a proper branch in the new housing estate. We have got to consider it. I don't want to bother your father more than I need, but it will have to be settled and I am writing to Mr. Keith to ask his advice about it," for Robert Keith, Lady Merton's brother, was the head of the highly respected firm of Keith and Keith, Solicitors and Commissioners for Oaths, who did most of the Cathedral and Close work and dealt with properties all over the county.

"Of course if I can help you at all, mother, do tell me," said George. "But I don't know much about it. I've never even been inside."

"Then you better had," said his mother, quoting a schoolboy turn of phrase with which the little George had considerably bored his family for the whole of one Easter holiday. "We might take Edith there after church tomorrow. The manager is quite a pleasant sort of man."

George said that would be very nice and wondered in himself at the number of things one doesn't know, or hasn't seen, when they are right under one's eye. But so it was, is, and always shall be. And not till we hear that a gem of small Tudor architecture in the next village, or a bit of fourteenth century church embedded in the wall of St. Going Without in the City, or a rustic cottage in Islington where Milton may (or more probably may not) have had his first inspiration for the Allegro, are to be destroyed in the name of Progress—or more often have been already destroyed before we had heard anything of the impending destruction—not till then (we repeat to make it easier for our reader to follow us) do we hurry to see what is probably by now in the lands of the housebreaker, or the bulldozer, or the electric drill.

"And while I think of it, George," his mother went on. "You know that your father has always read the lessons. I think Sir Robert Graham would rather like to fill that position. But never mind that now."

"It's all a bit sudden, mother," said George, though very kindly.

"It is; it is," said his mother. "Though perhaps not so much sudden as trying to face things. We have had enough of being unprepared" and George knew that she was thinking of the 1914 war when her only brother had been missing, reported killed; and of the later war in which he himself had been in danger for the final years and was liable to be called up again with the Barsetshire Yeomanry in case of national mobilisation.

"But look here, mother," said George, "it's not reasonable. Sir Robert is hardly ever here. I mean it's not his fault if he's a soldier, but dash it, to be a churchwarden you must at least live in your own home on Sundays. And anyway father is vicar's warden so that's that."

"Yes, that is that" said his mother, adding half to herself, "and that for the present *is* that—" and she covered her papers with a silk scarf kept for that purpose and went on with the letters she was writing.

People who have cars differ—as we have observed but not having a car, and being unable to drive one if we had, cannot speak from personal experience—in their ideas of time. Some like to allow a good margin in case of road blocks, traffic diversions, or that brake jamming again. Others put off their start till the last moment and when they and their passengers are in the car suddenly remember that the man said he was coming about the boiler today and by Jove I'd let it slip my memory I'll just run inside and get him on the telephone, by which time of course the man has left the shop to attend to an emergency call at a destination unknown so that no one can't say not rightly where he's likely to be but I dessay he'll be along sometime and I'll tell him to give you a tinkle. Luckily for their Southbridge plans both George and Edith were punctual and left Hatch House at the exact moment George had thought suitable. He drove, carefully, down the steep little drive, hooting lest any traffic should be attacking them from the flank, and then turned to the left instead of going over the bridge.

"Aren't we going to Barchester, George?" said Edith.

"Of course we are," said George, "But I'm not going through Hatch End on a Saturday morning. Half the village would be asking me to do errands for them. We're going by the old road," and he put the car into low gear to climb a very steep uphill bend where the road was sunk between high banks crowned by trees and bushes, and on this grey morning was almost in a twilight.

"How nice," said Edith. "We never use this road because it doesn't go anywhere for us. But the boys used to bicycle to Old Barum and take boards and toboggan down the banks in the summer holidays when the grass was dry. They wouldn't take me because I was too little."

"Were you?" said George, glancing at her as he came to the

top of the hill and the road ran high and fairly level above the valley. "Well, you're not as big as all that now. There's Old Barum" and on their left rose the triple-tiered, grass-grown fortress about which no one really knows very much.

"No good trying to toboggan in this ghastly summer," said George. "One could pretty well go down the banks in a boat. I like going this way with the road above the valley and all the ups and downs," in proof of which he went rather too fast.

"I can't think of a rhyme for Barum," said Edith suddenly, "except silly things like 'wear 'em and tear 'em, good body, good body,'" which quotation from that most excellent collection of English Fairy Tales by Joseph Jacobs with just the right kind of pictures by the artist Batten moved George to say, Do *you* know The Cat and the Mouse?"

"Of *course* I do," said Edith with friendly scorn.

"Well! well! I thought you children only had those rotten stories of Hobo-Gobo and the Fairy Joybell," said George.

"Oh, that was mother," said Edith, with the affectionate contempt we have for the vagaries of our parents. "But Gran read us all the *proper* books like Grimm and Hans Andersen and those books that The Cat and the Mouse is in. Mother has them at Holdings, but Clarissa wants them for her baby, which considering it will be *years* before it can understand them, I think is rather mean. I want them ALL to read to MY children."

George, amused by Edith's Programme for Life, asked how many she was going to have.

"Oh, about six," said Edith, "like mother, and call them *proper* names. Not things like Guenevere or Merlin."

George said he should think not and who on earth would do a silly thing like that.

"Oh, people do," said Edith. "I'll call one after you, if you like," to which George, no whit at a loss, said he would be delighted and would call one of his after her and then they discussed the really *ghastly* names that some children had, and George said he knew a girl who was christened Brynhild but

everyone called her Dicky, and then they invented some silly
names like twins called Lifebuoy and Lux and laughed a great
deal at their own wit till they were in the outskirts of Barchester.
Here George had to attend to the driving, because it was a
peculiarity of the city that whether it was market day or not there
were always some sheep with red splodges on their backs trying
to get up on each other's backs and run along them, or a young
bull-calf being backed into or led out of a van with a kind of
drawbridge. But George was used to Barchester and drove by
back ways behind Barley Street and so to the White Hart (just
by the entrance to the Close) where he was well known to the
old head waiter.

"Table for two please, Burden," he said. "I am giving Miss
Edith Graham lunch."

"There's a nice table for two in the window, sir," said Burden,
"and the liver's nice and tasty today. Really fresh and no thoring-
out required before cooking. I'd have it if I was you sir," to which
George gave a cowardly assent while Edith sat by, amused.

"And Miss Graham too," said Burden, as one stating a fact
with only the slightest inflection of questioning in his voice.
"And some nice sauté potatoes and some spinach, sir? Spinach is
very nice today. And what to drink, sir?"

"Beer," said George, "a large one. Oh, what about you, Edith.
Lemonade?"

"Oh, no *thank* you," said Edith. "A small Dubonnet please,
Burden, and then some plain water," and then the old waiter
went away to give the orders.

"Father says Dubonnet isn't spirits, so it's all right for me,"
said Edith, rather primly. "He says really dry Spanish sherry is
the best, but I don't like it," and she made a face of not-liking
which George thought quite attractive.

The dining-room was now getting fairly full, as a good many
of the country gentry came to Barchester to shop on Saturday
morning and have a holiday from cooking, or in rarer cases to
give cook a holiday. Edith was smiling to several people and

George noticed with approval that she did not wave at them, nor beckon them to come to her table, nor try to talk to them across the rising roar of the well-educated, well-bred middle class having its Saturday lunch. Perhaps rather ill-advisedly, he said much the same to Edith.

"But, my dear, one simply doesn't," she said, reminding him of her elder sister Clarissa whom however she did not resemble in the least, for Clarissa was a dainty rogue in porcelain and Edith—but here George was at a loss for a comparison. As far as he could see she was not particularly like either of her parents. Certainly not like Agnes and, from the few times he had seen Sir Robert Graham, not like him either. Probably a throw-back to someone he had never heard of—possibly to the Pomfret side through her grandmother Lady Emily Leslie. Then their lunch came and Edith showed a very creditable appetite almost amounting to greed, so good was the liver, so tender, without any of those nasty little tubes in it.

"I must just go over to the cathedral," said George, when Burden had been tipped and thanked. "I want to see if the verger is anywhere about and ask him about getting on the roof. I promised that young cousin of yours who is so keen on climbing—" and he hesitated. Edith said Oh, that was Minor, "—to see if I could take him up on the roof" said George. "Do you want to come?"

Edith said she did, so they walked under the grey stone arch into to Close with its immense lawn as green as a bad summer could make it, the handsome red brick houses on either side, beyond them the white cathedral with its high windows of plain glass and the perfect spire pointing to heaven over all. Edith asked where they were going to climb.

"Oh, up there," said George, pointing vaguely upwards.

"Well, don't fall off," said Edith who, though she did not wish to confess it, was terrified of heights and used to have nightmares as a child of going up long flights of stairs that doubled over and crumbled as she trod them.

George said he would like her to see him do it and though he spoke quite kindly Edith felt snubbed. But by now they were in the Cathedral where as usual a few sightseers were wandering about and minor repairs were being done by hereditary masons near the tomb of Mistress Pomphelia Tadstock, widow of a Canon of Barchester, to which matron the Rev. Thos. Bohun, M.A., another Canon, had in the seventeenth century written some highly amatory, nay erotic verses; which verses had, as our older readers may remember, been edited by Oliver Marling who married Lady Lufton's elder daughter; but before he was married. The Verger was standing near it looking slightly remote, but with an eye for parties of Americans who would tip him well.

"Good-afternoon, Tomkins," said George. "How's your father?" adding aside, for Edith's benefit. "He is gardener at the Palace."

"Pleased to see you here, Mr. Halliday," said the Verger. "Father's pretty well, thank you, ever since the new mowing-machine. It seemed to put heart into him, it did."

"Don't tell me the Palace have been spending money on a mowing machine," said George who like all true Barsetshire members of the Church of England took a lively if unloving interest in the Bishop and his affairs.

"You'd have laughed, Mr. Halliday," said the Verger, lowering his voice that the profane might not hear him. "Father was having his holiday, a fortnight it's supposed to be, but he can't be happy away from his work and that's a fact, so of course he must needs go over to the Palace to see how the tomatoes were doing in the glasshouse because of course the heat wasn't on yet, though really, Mr. Halliday, we could have done with a little heat this summer as father said in his joking way—you know he will have his joke. So, as I was saying, father went over to the Palace and into the garden by the little door which of course he has his own key for," said the Verger, eyeing George and Edith as if daring them to disprove this statement, "and he heard a noise and he said to himself Someone's monkeying with the mowing-machine and he's messed it all up. And when I say father said messed" he added with a meaning look at Edith, "you'll understand me, Mr. Halliday," at which George, who could easily have offered at least four very fine Saxon words of daily use in the army, smiled and asked what happened next.

"Well, Mr. Halliday," said the Verger, "not to mince matters his lordship and his chaplain had run the machine over the gravel without raising the blades; and what with the stones and gravel in the works and the blades all off the straight, well you'd have laughed. So father he said to his lordship, for he wouldn't demean himself to talk to the chaplain, the long and the short of it is, a nice motor mower's the thing, my lord. It's no trouble and you just turn a handle and the Reverend could do a bit of mowing when he's got time on his hands. Well, the Reverend he didn't like the idea and said it wasn't his job, so father he said Well Adam was the first gardener and he went away and left them to it. And that Girl at the Palace, for they don't keep a Man, Mr. Halliday, not like our old Bishop did, she told Mr. Tozer that does the refreshments at the Palace Garden Party— and a poor show it is, all done on the cheap, fair gives you the sick Mr. Tozer says, and he can't hardly abear to handle the job except for the look of the thing—that his lordship was going to buy a motor mower and blest if he hasn't. And the best part is," the Verger added in a lower voice "that they say her ladyship, as we call her in our Club, Mr. Halliday, just by way of a joke, fair went off the deep end about it and told the Reverend off good and proper and his lordship too."

George now firmly broke in to say he might be bringing some of Miss Graham's cousins to Barchester, Mr. Leslie's boys over at Greshamsbury, and would it be all right to take them up on the roof. He would stay with them, he added, and slid a gratuity into the Verge's rather ostentatiously unexpectant hand.

"Oh, and please, Mr. Tomkins," said Edith, "if I let you know the day they are coming, could you ask your father if he will be there, because my cousins want to climb the tulip tree if he'll let them."

"If they are anything like the young gentleman as father mentioned to me, he'll be pleased as Punch, miss," said the Verger. "If father's told the story about his finding Old Tinkler in the rubbish heap and the young gentlemen putting it back in its place, he's told it a hundred times. It was Mr. James as washed the bell and gave it a bit of a polish. You tell the young gentlemen, miss, it'll be O.K. I'll pass the word to father," so with a few words of thanks, George and Edith went away.

George asked who on earth Old Tinkler was.

"Oh, it was a bell that used to hang into the water over the edge of the pond in the Palace Garden," said Edith, "and the fish used to ring for their dinner," which George said was impossible, but Edith explained that they butted their heads against it. "And Mr. and Mrs. Bishop felt stingy, so they took the bell away. But mother and I and the boys were at the Garden Party when Tomkins found the bell in the compost heap and James, that's my eldest brother that's a captain now, washed the bell in the pond and polished it with his handkerchief and I made a poem about it."

"I say, do tell me the poem," said George.

Edith said, doubtfully, that it was rather long and oughtn't they to be getting back and George said By Jove, yes.

CHAPTER 4

During that most horrible summer there was, we believe, one warm Sunday, though we were not conscious of it. It will therefore be easier and more truthful to say that the Sunday after the cricket-match that didn't come off, was as nasty as any other Sunday. Sylvia had bicycled down to the early service and was back for breakfast looking horridly well and cheerful, as people do when they have combined a virtuous action with getting church over for the day and the additional pleasure of knowing that their friends and relations still have it before them. Edith and George were down punctually, neither of them a penny the worse for their outing and George showing no signs of his broken night beyond one or two jaw-cracking yawns.

Edith, after some eight hours' solid sleep, was looking very well and—so her hostess thought—very charming. Not at all like her eldest sister Emmy, now Mrs. Tom Grantly, who was pure Leslie, large, blonde, cheerful and masterful; not at all like the next sister Clarissa who since a child had been elegant and neat, with lovely hands whose finger-tips tilted a little upwards, a proud carriage which had caused her elder brothers to call her such names as Princes Puffball and Mass-of-Conceit, and deeper affections than anyone had suspected till Charles Belton wooed, won and subdued her; in which state of subjection, we hasten to add, she was blissfully happy and is, we think, likely to remain so. And now there was Edith, with the dark hair and dark eyes of the true Fosters (though in the men the black sometimes came out as red, just as it does with setters and as it did in old Lord Pomfret, the present Earl's much older cousin, brother to Lady Emily Leslie); not a handsome, fair Amazon like Emmy, not such a rogue in porcelain as Clarissa, but with a peculiar quiet elegance of her own and, we think, more capacity for loving and being loved, also for hurting and being hurt, than her elder sisters. Pure Graham, her mother had sometimes said, but no breed is pure and Graham interplayed with Leslie and Foster. Edith had some of her father's brain; the intelligence that had, with other qualities, brought him to high rank at a comparatively early age and had also served him well with money matters, investments, his property and his pigs—which last, according to the bailiff Goble, were in themselves sufficient proof that Sir Robert he was a Wunner. Edith also had some of the quick, certain movements of mind and of body which had made him, in war and in sport, a man worth watching; or so his superiors had said, though these were now comparatively few in number.

After the horrid rain and cold of Saturday, the weather had decided to take a holiday and was almost warm. Sylvia said hot, but as she had bicycled to church and came back most becomingly pink in the face, her testimony was ruled out. It had been arranged that she should stay with her father and the rest go to church. Mrs. Halliday had once suggested to her husband that he should listen to the service on the wireless. His comments on her suggestion would have been lost to the world but for the lucky chance of Caxton—who had no business in the house at that hour and knew it—coming up to tell the Squire that a sow had spent the night with two piglets as a mattress under her maternal weight, which piglets were now as dead as old Crummles; which statement, inciting Mr. Halliday to probe into the matter, he finally decided that his carpenter was not alluding to a famous actor-manager, but to a brewer from Huntingdonshire, and further provoked him to write to the Barsetshire Folk Lore

Society who at once organised an Outing to interview Caxton who told them every lie he could think of. All of which may be found in the Records of the Society if that particular volume is not still missing since the Bishop borrowed it from a member who had no right to lend it.

The church party were to leave at half-past ten. Not that it took half an hour to get to church, for it only took five minutes when George was driving, but Mrs. Halliday liked to leave a good margin for Mr. Choyce to let off steam and to get her approval of whoever was to read the lessons; for though Mrs. Halliday had of course no say in the matter at all Mr. Choyce, with excess of fine feeling, felt that he must treat her as deposed Royalty, or if not deposed, exiled. When the Hatch House party reached the church George parked the car in the lane beside the churchyard and then went in by the side gate. Mr. Choyce was hovering in his old cassock (looking, as George irreverently said, like an ecclesiastical scarecrow) and waylaid them just outside the porch.

"Can I do anything for you, Mr. Choyce?" said Mrs. Halliday, who as Squire's wife felt a certain amount of responsibility for her priest.

"Well yes, how kind of you, at least I hardly know, I hardly like to trouble you," said Mr. Choyce.

Mrs. Halliday would dearly like to have said, "Well then, DON'T," or, no less truthfully, "I am here to be troubled, so what IS it?" But as Squire's wife she had to deny herself these small pleasures, so she smiled in what she hoped was an encouraging way and asked again what she could do for him, at which moment her eye was attracted by Mr. Scatcherd, for once in normal trousers instead of his knickerbockers and wearing a bowler hat, far less suitable to his walrus moustache than was his usual deerstalker hat, or the battered Panama hat which he affected in the summer.

"Oh, it is really nothing," said Mr. Choyce, leading Mrs.

Halliday to the lee side of a buttress and looking round anxiously.

"Well, it must be *something*," said Mrs. Halliday in a soothing
voice, "and I am sure if you tell me what has happened we can do
something about it. That stop hasn't gone wrong again, has it? I
would have heard if it had," for a year or so ago something had
gone wrong inside the organ, which blockage (attributed by
some to The Birds, by others to Something Must have Got In
the Works) had produced a quite terrifying noise, rather like a
steady pounding of tom-toms varied with a whistle, or even
more terrifying gaps of silence before it began again, combined
with a regular Thumping which made the Vicar fear for safety of
his beloved charge.

"Oh no," said the Vicar, "besides now that we know it was
only an air-lock there would be no cause for alarm. No, it is
this," and he drew Mrs. Halliday a little further on, where the
grave of William Halliday Gent., with its fine carved head-
stone, sheltered them from eavesdroppers (not that there were
any, for to no one in the village would a conversation between
Mrs. Halliday and the Vicar have presented the faintest point of
interest).

"It is only the Lessons," said Mr. Choyce. "Sir Robert was
going to read them and he is so rarely here it would indeed have
been a privilege, but Lady Graham has just rung up to say that
he was detained in London last night and cannot get down in
time. The Sunday train service to Barchester is *disgraceful*," he
added with some warmth. "Really hardly any better than it was
when the line first came down here, in old Bishop Proudie's
time."

Mrs. Halliday said she quite agreed which seemed to soothe
Mr. Choyce; and what could she do for him.

"Of course if your husband could have been here," said Mr.
Choyce with a kind of wistful wishful-thinking.

Mrs. Halliday, who was really keeping her temper very well

under the Vicar's mournful maunderings, said she was sure George would read the lessons if that would be any help.

"Though, if it didn't tire you too much, Mr. Choyce," she added, "I am sure everyone would like to hear *you* read them."

This novel suggestion appeared to deprive the Vicar of the power of speech.

"It isn't forbidden or anything, is it?" said Mrs. Halliday. "One never knows."

"Oh dear no," said Mr. Choyce, "but we have got so used to the Squire reading the lessons. It was your husband Mrs. Halliday, if you remember, who got the eagle tilted just the least little bit for us so that it suited Sir Robert on that Sunday when he read the lessons, and he told me afterwards, your husband I mean told me—not Sir Robert—that it didn't really suit him so well—I mean your husband—but if it suited Sir Robert he was perfectly content."

Mrs. Halliday said Of *course*, in a soothing voice, though really she felt as if she were inside a Kaleidoscope, so manifold were the Vicar's well-meant explanations. The bell now began to give its final warning.

"Then shall I tell George, Mr. Choyce," said Mrs. Halliday, "or will you?" which simple question threw the Vicar into such a paroxysm of indecision that Mrs. Halliday called "George" in a loud clear voice. George answered his mother's call.

"Come here a moment, George," she said. "Sir Robert was to have read the lessons this morning, but he can't get here in time, so you had better do it."

"Oh—well, all right, mother," said George. "Are the book markers in the Bible, Mr. Choyce?"

The Vicar said they were and perhaps George would like to read the passages quickly through to himself in case they presented any difficulties, but George said he thought he could manage, which comforted Mr. Choyce for the loss of Sir Robert and as the bell had just about exhausted itself they all went in, the Vicar to the vestry and the Hallidays to the Squire's pew where Edith was already seated, a little above herself because her mother in the Holdings front pew and Cook and Odeena in the Holdings second-best pew could see her in glory. If her father had been there, everything would have been perfect.

There is no need for us to describe the Morning Service in a village church, for it is part of our life, even if our village is only a country outing or a country visit, and our real home a city. The same words bind country and town. Mr. Choyce had been sorely exercised by changes and shortenings in the service he loved. He loyally did his best to agree with them, blaming himself for spiritual pride that he should presume to criticise his superiors, but on one or two points he had stood firm, especially in the opening words, and read Dearly Beloved from start to finish in a way that did prepare the minds of his hearers for the act of contrition that is to follow. For truly one does need to get oneself into the right frame of mind to be conscious, or even try to be conscious, of one's manifold sins and wickednesses. And how well the Bishops knew the mind of sinful man when they invented that prayer; for however good one has been (or tried to be good which is as much as most of us can do) we do really need to face the fact that when we are gathered together to thank, to praise, to hear the most holy Word, we shall hear it with a little more understanding if we first say what we are and then come to the throne of the heavenly grace which will accept us as what we should wish to be. Nor were the hymn books in the little church up-to-date. Not for want of money, for both Mr. Halliday and Sir Robert Graham were generous and Sir Robert was very comfortably off, but simply because all those concerned liked the familiar hymns of their childhood. To those who have been reared on high-numbered hymns in what we can only call Art Hymn-Books, even to hymn six hundred and sixty-six, foretold in the Apocalypse of St. John, the old book may appear dull and inadequate. To us it is memory, tradition, something even of tears, though not unhappy tears, as we look back to our child-

hood. But there is always a fresh generation that knows not
Joseph—as we in our time did not know him.

It is almost impossible to keep one's thoughts from straying in
church—or indeed anywhere else—and Mrs. Halliday's were
straying all the time to Hatch House and her husband who was
rather better every month, but always less well than he had been
six months ago, which round of hope deferred does make the
heart sick—not ever unto doomsday with eclipse, but quite far
enough, and only to be escaped in sleep. So were Sylvia Leslie's
thoughts abroad, though quite pleasantly, to Rushwater and her
husband and young family, for she was one of the happy people
who can face misfortune with equanimity and courage when it
comes, but do not seek it when it is not there. Mrs. Halliday's
thoughts were not only at home with her husband but—so are
our minds constituted and we cannot do much about it—with
that pair of linen sheets that were so gone and sides-to-middled
(a state too familiar to housewives for us to have to explain it)
that it hardly seemed worth sending them to the laundry again
and she thought she could get enough out of them to make three
or even four pillow slips and the rest could go to the Friends of
Barchester Hospital who could make use of practically everything from an Abacus to an old but unused pot of Zinc Oint-
ment. George Halliday's mind was occupied, not unnaturally,
with the lessons he had to read. He had with great foresight
made quick note of them and was industriously reading the
appointed passages and wondering what they would sound like
when he read them and whether he knew how to pronounce all
the names and if he didn't whether anyone would be aware of it.
And if he thought of other things as well, who are we to blame
him?

Perhaps these were not the thoughts for the Morning Service,
but we think that most of the congregation, while quite seriously
desiring and meaning to concentrate on what they had come to
hear and to share, were engaged in very similar divagations.
Brother Ass can be, as we all know, a sore trial; but Brother

Swallow—if we may so describe our wandering mind which darts hither and thither, now perched on the lectern, now wheeling quietly and surely in the high-pitched roof, now darting with exquisite precision through an open window—can be equally trying. The service went on. The Vicar preached a good, uninspired, adequate sermon to which everyone listened according to his or her capacity; some wondering if they didn't ought to have turned the gas down a bit more in the oven before they started for church; some inventing exactly the words they would say to the foreman, or Bill Vidler, or the Bishop's wife, according to their social status; some wondering if they *had* shut the larder door with that cat about; and Edith, who had got the large very old family prayer-book with the Halliday coat-of-arms tooled in gold on the binding and fine printing with long esses on paper as good as the day it was made except where a worm had eaten its way through it, fell head over heels into the prayer for Charles, King and Martyr and the anathema or commination against Guy Fawkes, both of which were new to her and interested her exceedingly. She had read very quietly and she shut the book very quietly while Mr. Choyce finished his sermon, which he did with a few quite ordinary words about loving one's neighbour.

Edith considered this question with that indescribable speed of our thoughts which no machine could write as swiftly as they pass through our minds, and came to the regrettable conclusion that she ought to like Rose Fairweather. Not that Rose was exactly a neighbour, for Greshamsbury was at a considerable distance from Little Misfit, but probably by Bible standards she would count as one. Mr. Choyce had said what little he had to say so simply and kindly that Edith experienced a highly temporary flash of conversion and said aloud to herself inside—we cannot accurately describe this action or state of mind whichever it is, but doubtless our Reader will understand—"Pray God, help me to like Rose Fairweather." She then screwed her eyes up very tightly, which is somehow an aid to prayer, so that she saw

amusing lights and flashes and kaleidoscopes. When she opened
her eyes everything looked much as before, nor were her feelings
about Rose changed yet. The congregation rose to its feet—
some of it rather stiffly, for in those river-valleys where many of
the cottages are still little more than wattle and daub the damp
penetrates everywhere and does not help the rheumatics. The
collection was taken, the bags were carried up to the altar and
there received on the only piece of plate the church possessed, a
small but handsome golden dish, part of the loot that one of Sir
Robert Graham's forbears had brought back from the Peninsu-
lar War. Mr. Choyce lifted them as an offering before the altar,
a gesture which always made Edith think of the expression,
heave-offerings, though it did not explain the expression wave-
offerings. And if anyone should wonder how Edith came to
be so well educated in these degenerate times, it was because
she was the youngest and therefore the latest to be under the
dominion of Nurse, who firmly read selected portions of the
Bible to her charge. It must in fairness be said that Edith understood at the time very little of what she heard. But the words
stayed with her and may come in very usefully as time goes on.

Then everyone came out of God's blessing into the warm sun,
which proverb must have been invented in some golden age, for
the sun was far from warm and has, to our certain knowledge,
never really done its duty since the incredibly warm and beautiful summer of Dunkirk.

It was Mr. Choyce's pleasant custom to hold a kind of
reception after the service, standing in the church porch and
greeting or shaking hands with all his parishioners. Here Edith
met her mother who enquired with soft solicitude about her
week-end and was gently pleased to hear about life at Hatch
End, the old-fashioned bath and her talks with Mr. Halliday.

"It is exactly what John and David used to do," said Lady
Graham, looking back into her youth when her brothers were
young. "Only they didn't do it because of food, but because of
the black beetles. After dark all the kitchen wing was one mass

of beetles, and John and David used to go there and stamp on them. Siddon tells me there was quite a fuss about it because the odd man said beetles inside the house weren't his business to sweep up, and the third gardener said if it was rats, or even wireworm, he was the man, but black beetles in the house were the butler's business, and the housemaids were afraid and of course Gudgeon would not hear of it. And are you having a nice time, darling?"

Edith said *very* nice and meant it, for in Lady Graham's super-sane atmosphere all doubts, all misgivings were apt to vanish.

"Oh, and mother," said Edith, "who do you think Mrs. Halliday knows? Mrs. Morland! *The* Mrs. Morland, mother, that writes those lovely books about Madam Koska and Mrs. Halliday says she came to Holdings once."

"Of course she did," said Lady Graham, whose social sense never deserted her. "It was just when Peace Broke Out and that nice little Anne Fielding got engaged to old Dr. Dale's son that afternoon," but Edith had been too young then to notice what was happening—nine years ago, a long time when you are barely eighteen. "We must ask her again."

"Oh, *do* mother," said Edith and Lady Graham thought how nice it was to have a daughter with whom one could be on such easy terms. Not that Emmy was ever difficult, bless her; but she was so farm-minded and stock-minded that her family took second place—even her mother. Clarissa had been difficult beyond words. Bless her too; and Lady Graham had often thought, though not in his words, what a great Victorian poet had written about a mother; probably by the poet's strange instinct, not knowing that he knew it,

"Often I think were this wild thing but wedded
Much more love should I have, and far less care."

Agnes could not have put her thought into words, let alone poetry, but many a mother knows that feeling. Nor is it unknown to the mothers of sons. Never, never is one freed from the care, however old the children may be, though one accepts it gladly and rejoices to have it.

When Mrs. Halliday joined them, Lady Graham enquired after Mr. Halliday. Mrs. Halliday said he was up and down and if only there were any warmth and sunshine she felt sure he would improve. But there was no sureness in her voice.

"I know," said Lady Graham, moving a little aside with Mrs. Halliday. "A little better every day and not quite so well at the end of the week. Darling Mamma was just the same. I hope Edith is being good."

Mrs. Halliday, grateful to Lady Graham for her understanding and for not pressing her enquiries, said Edith was a most pleasant guest and Leonard liked her very much. "Which is such a help," she added, "because it leaves me freer to be with Sylvia. Not that I would grudge her to Leonard for a moment, but—" and as she did not go on Lady Graham said something sympathetic and then took herself away.

"Sorry to keep you waiting, mother," said George, coming up to Mrs. Halliday. "Old Caxton caught me, about the Holdings pigs. He seemed to think he oughtn't to talk to Sir Robert's bailiff without father's permission, silly old chump. I told him to go ahead."

Mrs. Halliday said Quite right and the subject of pigs was closed. So Prince Hal was trying on the crown, she thought. And then she blamed herself for being so literary—a weakness of which a nice but rather chuckle-headed admirer had accused her many many years ago—and that made her laugh at herself, aloud.

"It's all right, isn't it, mother?" said George, with a slight note of suspicious anxiety, which made her at once stop laughing and say Of course he was right. And she wondered, as we all do in growing older, why the young were—not to put too fine a point upon it—such a mixture of callousness and intense sensitiveness: though if she was to be fair to herself and her generation (a far more difficult thing than being fair to the young) they had been much the same themselves. The same waves breaking on the same shore without ground gained or ground lost.

"We must go now," she said. "I promised that nice Mr. Cross at the Old Manor House that we would go in on our way home. What about you girls? Would you like to come?"

Girl number one in age and position, namely Sylvia, said she would go back to father, who had been very good and promised not to try to stand on a chair and get that volume of the Gentleman's Magazine down that had a description of the Old Manor House. George asked what it was; a vague question, but his mother was able to answer it and tell him that a gentleman who called himself Peregrinator, had made a tour of Houses and Manors of the Gentry of West Barsetshire some two hundred years ago and published his account of it. And a very pretty account he had given of Hatch House as it was, and it had been of some use to George's grandfather when there was a dispute about Boggler's Pound, which piece of land, reclaimed from the downs about that time, had been a bone of contention between him and the West Barsetshire County Council.

"Now mother's off," said George irreverently, but also with a little envy, for his mother, of good undistinguished county stock herself, knew by tradition and instinct much that he did not know, or had forgotten in the years of war and the years—in some ways even worse—of uneasy peace.

It was hardly worth taking the car to the Old Manor House where the road was narrow and had a kink in it, so they left it near the church and walked up the little lane towards the High Street. At the corner they found Mr. Scatcherd sitting on his camp stool with a drawing pad on his knee. As they approached he was doing that mysterious trick of the trade, namely shutting one eye and holding a pencil at arm's length, sometimes vertically, sometimes horizontally, which is popularly supposed to get the length and width of the object to be drawn more correctly than the unassisted eye can do. We do not feel capable

of judging in this matter and can only say in Sibylline words of
an old nurse "It all de-pends." As the party approached, Mr.
Scatcherd kept up with the endurance of a professional model
this awkward and exhausting attitude, the better to have a
well-simulated attack of surprise when they came up to him.

Mrs. Halliday, whose life as the Squire's wife had taught her
to pretend to suffer fools with self-control, if not gladness, asked
Mr. Scatcherd what he was drawing.

"Ah, Mrs. Halliday," said Mr. Scatcherd, emerging deliberately from an Artist's Dream, "there you impinge upon the
borders of Art."

Mrs. Halliday, said it was quite unintentional and she hoped
Mr. Scatcherd had enjoyed the service.

"Ah, there," said Mr. Scatcherd, "is the Crux."

"Do you mean the stone cross that fell off the West Door and
was broken last winter?" said Mrs. Halliday, which—as Mr.
Scatcherd's extended arm was pointing in that direction—was a
reasonable question. "We are still waiting for it to be put up
again."

"Oh dear no, madam," said Mr. Scatcherd, whose long background of calling his betters by their proper titles often got the
better of the Artist's equality with everyone from Emperors
downwards. "It was not a crux in that sense but in a sense quite
other than it; if you take my meaning."

Mrs. Halliday would dearly have liked to say that she did not
take it, did not know how to and did not wish to; but the sense
of charity and courtesy to fools and chatterers, coming from
centuries of land and serf owning forbears, made her say without
any impatience that perhaps Mr. Scatcherd would explain exactly what was the crux.

"Ah!" said Mr. Scatcherd with as profound a hint of a deeper
meaning as was in Lord Burleigh's nod. "That now *is* a question
that needs a power of thinking. To begin at the beginning, we
artists see quite different to Others. Where you may see a
church, or a tree, we see a Composition, and here, today, setting

on this here camp-stool," said Mr. Scatcherd whose florid speech was apt to disintegrate under stress, "I seen a Composition that will Live. You see that tower, madam?"

George, coming to his mother's rescue, said they all saw it and very nice too.

"Ah, that's what a young gentleman like you *would* say, sir," said Mr. Scatcherd pityingly. "There's nothing nice in Nature; no, nor in Art neither if you take my meaning, and that's where the Artist comes in. Now, that sketch I did of the Rising Valley with the spire of Barchester Cathedral showing in the middle distance, that was a Triumph. Whether you *can* see Barchester spire from that particular viewpoint is entirely beside the question," said Mr. Scatcherd, glaring about him for possible detractors. "But if you ask yourself Is It ART, ah—"

But at this point (and to Mrs. Halliday's relief) his niece came hurrying up the lane from the side gate, talking at the top of her voice all the way.

"Now Uncle how often have I told you not to bother Mrs. Halliday nor no one else neither with all your talk," said Miss Scatcherd. "Art indeed! If you'd been to church Uncle same as I have to chapel and prayed for everyone's sins you wouldn't be sitting here talking all your nonsense to Mrs. Halliday and young Mr. Halliday and Miss Edith when I want those potatoes peeled or I'll never get them done in time for your dinner though much thanks I get for it and it's very kind of you I'm sure Mrs. Halliday to let Uncle go on the way he does enough to try the patience of a graven image now put all those rubbishy things of yours away Uncle and come home with me and goodness knows when I'll get your dinner cooked if you stand talking here and interrupting the ladies and gentlemen," with which words she almost jerked Mr. Scatcherd off his stool, took him into custody and marched him away, her voice audible till she got into the main road.

"And now we had better go on, or we shall be late," said Mrs.

Halliday, whose life as Squiress had taught her the value of self control and calm, for others as well as for herself.

A few moments brought them to the Old Manor House, which was so like many other grey stone Barsetshire houses with a flight of stone steps up to the front door and six stone pineapples on squat pillars along the roof that we need not describe it. Why Wm. Halliday Gent. had left it and built Hatch End we do not know, unless it was to show Robert Graham Armiger (and also Gent.) what was what, when the aforesaid Robert Graham had come into a property over at Little Misfit considerably larger and more valuable than Wm. Halliday's, though the charming and commodious Holdings was not built till the Regency Stucco era.

It is sad to see in many small country towns or large villages, how the more handsome of the houses are having to beg their bread as it were; to accept as lodgers people they would never have tolerated as owners. So it had been with the Old Manor House when its owners migrated to Hatch House. It had at first been empty, then let to various gentlemen who had enriched themselves in India, whether as soldiers of fortune or collectors, then to a quite respectable Barchester tradesman with a wife aspiring to county status and so from one hand to another but never passing out of the Halliday family, and last to two maiden aunts of Mr. Halliday's. Every Halliday had sworn that when he succeeded to the property he would sell the Old Manor House which, what with repairs and rising taxes, hardly paid its way: no Halliday had done so. After the 1914 war Mr. Halliday, hard hit by taxation, had also thought of selling it, going so far as to say that he would blow out his own brains as well. To this last threat no one had paid any attention. Then the Barchester branch of one of the big banks had decided, between the wars, that Barchester was going ahead—as witness the growth of a Mr. Adams's rolling-mills at Hogglestock and the revival of the old brewing firm of Pilward, not to speak of a rising market-gardening business later to be known as Amalgamated Vedge—

and would want trade facilities outside the city. The Old Manor
House could be got at a reasonable rent and the bank opened a
branch there. By a friendly arrangement two spinster Halliday
aunts remained as tenants of the upper floors. Both had died a
year or two ago and after their death the bank had taken over the
tenancy of the upper floors and made a very pleasant bachelor
flat upstairs for the manager, a Mr. Cross, a pleasant young man,
unmarried so far as any one knew, who was done for—to use a
double-meaninged phrase—by one of the village women.

But now, with petrol freed and a better bus service, most
people found it just as easy to do business in Barchester where
they often had to go in any case and the directors thought of
closing the branch. As always happens this produced a storm of
protest from the customers who only used it a dozen or so days
in the year and then to cash cheques for ridiculously small
amounts. Then, with the new housing estate which from a
revolting satellite would soon become a revolting town and
already had two cinemas which were packed nightly and four
churches fighting for the souls of those who hardly ever went to
them, one bank in a village a mile away was not enough and
there was not yet a bus between Hatch End and the housing
estate and the bank, though we fear there soon will be, and it will
mean pulling down one or two cottages which are in a shocking
state of insanitation and disrepair but are loved by their tenants
through long habitation, and also widening the road and so
encouraging a flood of motor traffic through the narrow, winding street. Progress! So word went forth from the directors that
the Old Manor House was to be given up and what business was
absolutely necessary to be transacted on Tuesdays and Fridays at
a room in the High Street. There were still a few years of the Old
Manor House lease to run, but if the bank and Mr. Halliday
agreed, that could be arranged. A few years earlier he would have
tackled the job himself, but though his mind was quite alive
where business was concerned it was clear that Brother Ass, who
hampers us in our youth and in our age, would have resented it:

and Mr. Halliday himself acknowledged this with something of
the simplicity of a long line of gentlemen farmers who had seen
the corn spring and ripen and be cut down; and had in earth's
diurnal course seen and felt the same springtide, ripening and
decay, each in his own case. So now George was to take up the
burden; which he was prepared to do though he realised—and
said so to his mother—that father would be as bad as the
Circumlocution Department about it. And Mrs. Halliday could
not help laughing, partly because it pleased her that George was
so well-read, partly because it was perfectly true.

So they went up the stone steps and rang the well-polished
bell. A middle-aged woman opened the door; one of the many
Vidlers or Panters, who were mostly each other's aunts on one
side and nieces on the other owing to perpetual intermarrying
and the fact that generations are so mixed by now that at least
two Vidler nieces wheel their aunt and their uncle about in
perambulators.

"Good morning, Dorothy," said Mrs. Halliday. "I think Mr.
Cross is expecting me."

Dorothy, who knew her place, did not curtsey but gave a kind
of sketch of the gesture and asked them to come inside if they
didn't mind. As it was exactly what they had come for, they
walked in. To Mrs. Halliday the house was familiar, for she had
often been there to have tea with the aunts and look for the
many-eth time at the old family photographs which were now at
Hatch House. George had also been there a good deal in his
boyhood, but never since it had been a bank. As almost always
happens when we re-visit the haunts of our childhood, everything had shrunk. The hall which had been about the size of the
nave of St. Paul's, paved with black and creamy-white flags, was
little more now than a passage through the house, though an
elegantly proportioned passage. The staircase which he remembered as very large and richly carpeted with the best and most
hideous staircarpet on the market, was now a gentlemanly
staircase but not so wide as the staircase at Hatch House and the

carpet distinctly shabby, not to say worn out. On the right, he remembered, was the drawing-room which ran the whole depth of the house; on the left at the back a dining-room that looked over the garden. The room in front which the aunts called the morning-room and reserved for the small cage-birds who were their pets, was now used as the bank premises. To Edith, though she had probably passed the house a hundred times and more, the inside was unknown and therefore romantic.

"Mr. Cross says will you come in, Mrs. Halliday," said Dorothy. "And mother said I was to enquire most particular after the Squire."

Mrs. Halliday said cheerfully that none of us were getting any younger and Mr. Halliday was very well all things considered, but he didn't get about much now. She then added that he had sent his kind remembrances to Dorothy, which was of course quite untrue. For the noble lie we have little use, for it usually brings annoying complications in its train as all novel-readers will have remarked, though whether anyone has ever told a noble lie in real life we do not know: but the small or common lie can be uncommonly useful.

"And this is Miss Graham," she said, for owing to her two elder sisters' marriage Edith now held this status. "She is paying us a visit."

"Pleased to meet you, miss," said Dorothy. "That Odeena that's under Lady Graham's cook at Holdings she was at my sister-in-law's on Friday and the stuff she had on her face was a caution. 'Just you go in the scullery and wash it off, my girl,' my sister-in-law said, that's Jim's wife not Harry's, the one with the mole on her face though I'm bound to say she's a good wife."

"And what did Odeena do?" said Edith, interested in the Holdings kitchen-maid's fate.

"Well, Miss Edith, she commenced to cry and such a mess as her face was you never saw," said Dorothy, savouring to the full emotion recollected in tranquillity, "so Jim's wife she said, 'It's rabbit pie for tea and if you don't clean that stuff off your face it'll be bread and marge for you, my girl,' so my lady she went off to the scullery and while she was washing young Hubback he came in—he's Jim's wife's nephew and got a job at the Housing Estate, carpenter he is and a good tradesman," which word, now almost forgotten, relic of a day when a man had to learn his trade, when the remembrance of apprenticeship and becoming a member of a Craft, was still alive, gave Mrs. Halliday pleasure. "And he said, 'Anyone here for tea, auntie?' and Jim's wife she said, 'None of your sauce Harry'—that's his name—Harry— 'and none of your tricks neither. There's a young lady having a wash in the scullery and none of your holding hands under the table.'"

"And what happened?" said Mrs. Halliday. Not that she cared in the least, but now that we do not distribute beef and beer to our poor tenants, or portion their pretty daughter because our elder son once kissed her at the Hiring Fair and gave her a sixpenny gingerbread, we pay tribute in a far more trying and exhausting way, by listening to their talk; extremely valueless as a rule.

"Well, Mrs. Halliday, nothing didn't occur, not so far as I know and I'm sure Jim's wife wouldn't have allowed it, chapel though she may be," said Dorothy rather primly. "But Harry he's going to walk out with Odeena, he says, leastways take her to the pictures. There wasn't all them pictures when I was a girl and if there was mother wouldn't have let me go to them."

It appeared to Mrs. Halliday that this conversation might go on for ever. Not that she was bored, for the village was part of her life and the older people still liked to have the approval of the Squire's wife, though the cinema-drugged Odeenas barely knew who she was; but she had come on business. Just then there was the noise of a latch-key trying to get into its home in the keyhole, the front door was opened and Mr. Cross came in, in such a hurry to greet his visitors that the latch-key held onto the door with all its might and almost jerked the snake-chain on which it lived off the trouser button to which the far end was attached.

"I must apologise, Mrs. Halliday," said Mr. Cross, having extricated his key from its predicament, rammed it angrily into his trouser pocket and shut the door. "I went to the Cathedral, allowing plenty of time as their service is beautifully short and I can do it in twenty minutes easily, but the Bishop was preaching."

"I *am* sorry," said Mrs. Halliday. "What was he up to *this* time? Last time I went—and it *will* be the last time if he preaches there—it was about the lion lying down with the lamb."

"Any particular lion?" said Mr. Cross. "Do come into my room," and he took them into what used to be the dining-room, at the back, with french windows onto the garden, most pleasant on the one warm day that makes an English summer; for the rest of the year first class manufacturers and salesmen of draughts. By arrangement with Mr. Halliday the bank had removed these and put in two very well-proportioned sash windows, which had indeed been in the house as it used to be, for the french windows were a Victorian alteration, only a hundred years old, or so.

"The lion," said Mrs. Halliday, "—*how* nice and dignified the windows are, Mr. Cross. Those french windows spoilt the back of the house completely as you see it from the garden—was of course US, because we go about seeking whom we may devour, or so his lordship stated though I really don't know on whose authority, and I think the lamb was Russia, or perhaps India— not Pakistan, of course, which is English—the disloyal part," and then she wondered if she had gone too far, for the Palace and anti-Palace factions were far more vehement than Guelf and Ghibelline, than Montagu and Capulet.

"I have always imagined," said Mr. Cross, waving Mrs. Halliday into a large leather-covered chair and Edith to another, "that his lordship believes in direct inspiration. But I must not take up your time, Mrs. Halliday."

"Never mind my time," said Mrs. Halliday, settling herself comfortably. "It *is* such a comfort to talk with anyone who really appreciates the Bishop. You must come and have a talk with my husband; it will do him a lot of good. And now, what I would like to do, if it is not too much, is to look at the house and see, roughly, what needs doing, so that I can tell my husband. You know he is rather an invalid now."

Mr. Cross gave just the right amount of sympathy, as from a paid servant of the Bank (who was yet, as their servant, entitled to a certain status) to the wife of the principal landowner in that part of the Rising Valley, and said he would be delighted to show Mrs. Halliday round.

"It will not take long," he said, "for we don't use the upper part. The bank did think of asking Mr. Halliday for permission to let the two top floors, but as we are moving to the new Housing Estate the whole matter will lapse. I shall be very sorry to move myself, though I only spent part of the week here," to which Mrs. Halliday said they would be sorry to lose him, but she supposed it meant promotion.

"Yes, yes," said Mr. Cross, "it does. And of course for the bank's sake I am glad."

George then earned the gratitude of his mother and Edith by asking why.

"A matter of pride—perhaps rather old-fashioned pride," said Mr. Cross. "Every clerk who is promoted to branch manager, every branch manager who is promoted to a more important branch, shows that the selection of the bank's staff is good, that the training of those who are selected is good and therefore, ten to one—I beg your pardon Mr. Halliday—or should I say Captain—did you say something?"

"Sorry, Mr. Cross," said George. "I was only thinking it's just like the army in a way. Captain it was, but that's all over till next time."

"Passing by the slight terminological inexactitude," said Mr. Cross, though lightly and kindly—

"Excuse me butting in again," said George, "but it isn't exactly a terminological inexactitude, is it? Just rather loose thinking. But you must admit I didn't say 'sort of,'" at which Mr. Cross laughed and then Mrs. Halliday laughed. And so did Edith, for everyone else was laughing, she didn't quite know why, and one might as well laugh too.

"The front room you do know, of course," said Mr. Cross, opening the door. "We had to put in a counter and a few other things, but they will all be removed at the bank's expense and everything made good. I wouldn't consent to the safe being put right up against the wall in case the panelling or the skirting board were damaged, so it won't be difficult to move. And the drawing-room we haven't touched, except for some shelves, but they are well away from the wall and we didn't touch the panelling."

Mrs. Halliday, though she had seen the drawing-room more times than she could count, found that it still took her breath away. The floor, laid by craftsmen who knew their work with narrow planks running lengthways, needed scraping and re-polishing professionally. At a pinch it could be used as it was, but Mrs. Halliday decided that the pinch should not be encouraged, for so distinguished a room deserved the very best. The Chinese wallpaper though faded was in good condition, the plastering on the ceiling and cornice showed no sign of wear. She walked to the end of the room which was a kind of apse and looked through the large bow window with its well-proportioned panes into the garden.

"The garden is beautifully kept, Mr. Cross," she said. "Is that the bank's doing too? How kind!"

"Well, not exactly," said Mr. Cross. "We did get a man in to keep the lawns and the grass borders mown, but your man— Caxon is it? oh, Caxton—thank you—said he wasn't going to see that something fellow—I think gormed was the exact word—spoiling his grass edges and he came here with several pairs of shears, or clippers, or whatever they are called, and yards of twine with a peg at each end and made them as neat as a balance-sheet."

"I do hope he wasn't a nuisance," said George, knowing how much he would have resented his landlord's man coming uninvited to improve what was for the present the bank's garden.

"Not a bit," said Mr. Cross. "And he gave me a very good cure for a kind of rash I get sometimes after shaving."

"I'm sure there was something *awful* in it," said Edith. "Father's bailiff cures warts with spitting on them and a bit of a pig's eye when we kill," which piece of country lore caused George to look at her with a respect he had never felt before.

"I say, that's an awfully good cure," said Mr. Cross. "Would you mind if I used it? I don't mean for myself, but your Caxton has given me so many cures that I want to make a little pamphlet about them for the Friends of Gerard."

Mrs. Halliday said, in a detached way, that there were far too many Friends of People about and who was this one.

"Is that Gerard's Herball?" said Edith, to the surprise of all present. "I like his book. Father's got it at Holdings and he tried to grow Stinking Pisswort, but it needs a new-born pigling's blood to make it grow and Goble—that's father's bailiff—wouldn't let him have any."

"So what did your father do, Miss Graham?" said Mr. Cross.

"I think he went over to Marling Hall to see Pucken, Mr. Marling's pig-man and there was a runt in a new litter and it wasn't worth keeping so he got the blood," said Edith, as one might say one had been to the grocer and got half a pound of China tea. "But the Stinking Pisswort didn't grow. I expect he ought to have planted it at midnight."

The Graham girl was coming out with a vengeance, Mrs. Halliday thought. A young woman to be reckoned with.

"That *is* an idea," said Mr. Cross, looking at Edith with admiration. "I must tell my governor. He's awfully keen on those old customs. He says, take them by and large, there's something in them."

By this time Mrs. Halliday and George were distinctly at a loss—a thing which rarely occurred to either of these two very sane, well-balanced people. Mr. Cross was the manager of a small branch bank and a very pleasant man and he was hoping for promotion and he had struck them both as unusually quick and intelligent and what was more, very easy to talk with, and apparently well acquainted with country life. Suddenly George saw light.

"I say," he said to Mr. Cross, "I don't want to butt in, but are you any relation of the Cross who bought that new motor mangold stacker from America? He was a lord though, I think."

"Yes, that's the governor," said Mr. Cross. "He's a director of the bank and he asked them to take me on for a bit for experience. I had to do all the proper exams of course and I rather like it. One meets a lot of people that way. I have seen your mother here once or twice and Miss Graham—and you of course. I say, you weren't near Vache-en-Foin in 'forty-four, were you? Some of the Barsetshire Yeomanry were there. I was only a very young second Lieutenant then."

"*Was* I?" said George. "*Wasn't* I? And of all the stinking holes in Northern France that was the one. Nearly broke my Yeomanry's hearts."

"Lord! and I was with the guns at Vache-en-Etable a few miles down the road," said Mr. Cross. "I say, did you ever come across Dogger Musgrave? He won two months pay off me at vingt-et-un and never showed up for my I.O.U. That was just before Christmas."

"I saw him all right. Toes up, poor chap," said George. "But, I say—"

Edith, entranced by this conversation could have listened all day, but it was now a quarter past one and Mrs. Halliday mentioned the fact and said they must go home at once or her husband would worry. With promises to meet again they went away, leaving young Mr. Cross, son of a lord, seriously interested in finance, heir to a considerable amount of money, at present manager of a small branch of a country bank to get experience, probably controller in years to come of that bank's policy, rather wondering who and where he was—or in his own words, where he got off at.

Some families are good at talking when left to themselves. They may be stiff or uncommunicative in company, but as soon as they are alone every tongue is loosened. Others are excellent mixers, the life and soul of any party at which they find themselves, but when they get home they will eat their dinner with a minimum of talk (though in a perfectly friendly atmosphere) and spend the evening in quite companionable silence, reading the Times, writing letters, knitting, occasionally exchanging a few words. So were most of the Halliday family. Affectionate, nay devoted in their relationships, but as a rule quite happy to sit quiet. Mrs. Halliday, one of a large talkative family, had tried to cure in her children this family trait, but finding that as they grew older it was apt to produce a mild form of sulks, she had given it up. George and his father would discuss a point of agriculture or whether that black pigling in the last litter ought to be kept: Mrs. Halliday would ask George if he could leave her shoes to be mended as he was going into Barchester; Mr. Halliday would ask his wife if she had noticed old Throckmorton's death in the Times, showing also a certain conceit about outliving a man ten years his senior. Each would answer the other with politeness and affection, but there was not much give and take now. So different, Mrs. Halliday often felt and tried not to feel it, from the time before Sylvia was married and the children (for George and Sylvia were still children to her as all our once young still are) made meals so amusing. This question of talking at meals with the people one lives with can be very difficult. Some families only have to get together for their tongues to be loosened and are never more amused and amusing. Others, while full of mutual affection and admiration, become almost paralysed without outside help. So it had, to a

certain extent, become with the Hallidays. Before the war
George and Sylvia had twittered like sparrows at all times and
their parents had enjoyed the twittering and joined in it. Or if
Mr. and Mrs. Halliday were talking of a book, or a friend, or
some plan, George and Sylvia would eagerly take sides and
approve their parents or laugh very kindly at them. After Sylvia's
marriage some of this easy talk had been lost and then with Mr.
Halliday's decreasing health a kind of gentle depression had
fallen on the household. It was not Mr. Halliday's fault, who
never complained or cavilled, but he was now cut off from so
much that his wife and children did, accepting this uncomplain-
ingly, bearing his loneliness in silence, and his wife sometimes
wished he would explode as he used to do. George felt much the
same, was thankful to be out and about on the place and though
devoted to his parents sometimes wished he were only a hireling
who could do his work well and go back to a humble cot
where a buxom spouse and chubby toddlers would greet him and
not ask about the tractor: though in his heart he knew this
was not quite all he wanted. To this rather uncomfortable self-
consciousness Edith's visit had been a distinct help. With an
outsider there—a delightful, well-mannered, amusing outsider—
meals were much more pleasant. We are not sure whether Edith
noticed the atmosphere. Lady Graham, though a most devoted
nay besotted mother, had never allowed the talk to be dull, or the
heavy mantle of silence to fall. When James and John and
Robert were at home or on leave there was a great deal of noise
and laughter, with the friends of one or another of the family
coming in for drinks or a meal. And on the week-ends when Sir
Robert Graham came down it was said by their uncle David
Leslie that the noise reached Barchester and made the Bishop
shake in his shoes. But David was famous for saying what he
thought people would like him to say. Now with the boys away
Holdings was not as noisy as it used to be, but there was always
a feeling of life going on and Edith had never been lonely. Not
that she felt really lonely at Hatch End, but she was intelligent

enough to realise that without Sylvia and indeed without herself—
for even a quiet young guest makes a change in a family mixture—
life for George must be rather heavy going.

It was too cold to sit outside and watch the harvest moon
across the river valley, so they sat in the drawing-room and Mrs.
Halliday said it would be nice to have a fire. George lit it. It
flared and died down. Good advice flowed over George from
every side. Mrs. Halliday said she had told Hubback how to lay
a fire for at least twenty years and that was the result. First some
shavings, she said, and Caxton always had plenty, or very small
chips of pine or fir; only Hubback wouldn't go to the carpenter's
shed for them and Caxton wouldn't bring them into the drawing-
room. Meanwhile George rearranged the fire and relit it. After
a few sulks it began to crackle and then to blaze. George put dry
pine cones on it and a couple of logs and it settled down to burn
properly.

"But couldn't he leave the shavings at the back door?" said
Edith.

"You see," said Mrs. Halliday, "if he left them there, and he
might if I spoke to him myself, Hubback wouldn't bring them
into the house."

"But couldn't you *tell* him to bring them into the drawing-
room?" said Edith, who had much of the Pomfret tenacity of
purpose.

"I could, my dear. Indeed I quite often have," said Mrs.
Halliday, without complaint, merely stating an ineluctable law
of nature. "But he always manages not to hear."

"Well, then, couldn't Hubback bring them from the back
door to the drawing-room?" said Edith.

"No," said Mrs. Halliday. "You see it isn't her place to do it,"
and this she said with such simplicity that Edith could not for
the life of her tell whether her hostess believed what she said or
not. Our own opinion, for what it is worth, is that Mrs. Halliday
was feeling older and more tired than she liked to admit and was

prepared to let things pass that earlier she would have fought and conquered.

"Would you like to play chess, Mr. Halliday?" said Edith in a society voice.

"What sort of a game do you play, young lady?" said Mr. Halliday, amused by his young guest's assured manner, as of Nanny speaking to one of her charges.

Edith said her brothers had made her play, and James always beat her and she always beat Robert but she and John were pretty equal, and when James was on leave he always played with her because he liked winning.

"James is on the whole my favourite brother," she added, with her amusing air of being very grown-up and world-weary, "but Robert is very good company. He is the most poetical except me."

"I didn't know you were a poet, my dear," said Mr. Halliday, amused.

"Well, I'm not really a poet, but sometimes I make poetry," said Edith, which was a very lucky remark, setting everyone off on his or her own definition of poetry. Mr. Halliday said he liked something he could understand, but he did like Wordsworth because although one couldn't always understand him he knew about the country all right even if it wasn't Barsetshire.

"If it comes to Barsetshire, what about Barnes?" said Mrs. Halliday. "He wasn't quite Barsetshire perhaps, but near enough. My mother used to read his poems to me properly—she was a Dorset woman and knew the language. It was like enough to the Barsetshire talk as the old people here used to talk it. You remember Mrs. Hubback's grandmother, Leonard? She talked pure Barset, but she was the last."

"She was a witch of course," said Mr. Halliday, as one might say she was a good plain sewer. "Old Sir Harry Waring over at Beliers used to boast about his half gypsy keeper whose grand-mother was a witch and changed into a black hare of nights; but that was comparatively modern and I never quite believed the story that her grandson shot her with a silver button in his gun. Now old Mrs. Hubback could charm warts away and all the village girls used to go to her when they got into trouble," at which artless words his wife gave him a wifely look, but Edith had either not heard or not taken in the implications. Or it is possible that she knew what they meant but found it of no interest.

"And she used to melt the silver paper off chocolate," said George, "and drop it into water and the shape of the silver paper when it stopped fizzling was the first letter of the person you were going to marry. But as it was usually like Z, or like nothing on earth, you could always pretend it was anything," which his father said was a pretty fair description of the practical results of most fortune-telling.

"Let's do some now," said Sylvia. "I've got some silver paper on the chocolate I bought today."

"No use for you, my girl," said her brother. "You've had it," to which Sylvia replied that there was no law against marrying twice, or even oftener, and she might as well know who her other husbands would be and went away to get the silver paper.

Mrs. Halliday looked at her husband to see if he was tired, but he seemed to be enjoying the children's silly games, and then Sylvia came back with the silver paper, an iron saucepan and a pudding-basin of water. She set the saucepan on the fire, dropped a ball of silver paper into it and before it could amalgamate itself with the bottom of the saucepan (which it was longing to do), she poured it into the basin. There was a fizzle and the silver paper was quenched.

"Nothing a *bit* like a letter," said Sylvia indignantly, as she inspected it.

"Well, I should hope not," said her brother. "You don't want to have to murder Martin do you? Bigamy isn't allowed here— any more than it was in the reign of James the Second," he added, sure that his parents would take the allusion, as indeed they did. Edith we fear did not, for her generation though they profess to like Gilbert and Sullivan do not know their works inside out as we elders do, and those few younger ones who have been well brought up.

More silver paper was melted for Mr. and Mrs. Halliday.

"My dear parents," said George, "I regret to say that your respective future spouses are nameless—at least I mean initialless. One bit just looks like a lump of silver paper and the other *might* be a very small star-fish with only two legs. Edith's turn."

Edith obediently thrust her silver paper in.

"The eye of faith," said George, "can just imagine an N. It *might* of course be a Z sideways, or a W that has lost one leg."

"Or an M that lost one leg if you put it the other way up," said Sylvia.

"Well, now we all know," said George. "Do you want the nine o'clock news, father? Sorry, it's a quarter to ten. Oh, I've not had my turn" and he put the saucepan on the fire for a moment and then dropped his piece of silver paper in it.

"Absolutely a wash-out," said George, eyeing his fortune. "A bachelor life for me, unless my future wife is to be a toad, because that's about all it looks like. Do you want to play Patience, father?" for Mr. Halliday had taken to the game of late.

Mr. Halliday said he would like to, so George brought his table and Sylvia brought her cards which he began to shuffle and his wife noticed with a pang how old his hands looked—older than his face—a little tremulous, just a little more than they had been in the winter, more blotched with those strange brown marks which we have disliked in our elders, knowing that *we* should never look like that—little knowing that we ineluctably should. But it is useless to dwell on these things so she didn't; which did not for a moment prevent them from dwelling with her. While Mr. Halliday laid out his cards the others talked about the Old Manor House and that very pleasant young man who had turned out to be a son of Lord Cross. Sylvia said she thought Martin knew them through the Barsetshire Agricultural Society but she didn't think she had met him. George said he would look the name up in the Stud Book and took the last year but seven's current volume of the Peerage from the shelf where his father kept all the dictionaries and reference books.

"Yes, that's it," he said. "Cross, John Morton, third baron Cross, son of etcetera. Educated Eton and Balliol and all that. One ess, two dees" (which his audience rightly interpreted as son and daughters), "seat Cross Hall. And he seems to have some good directorships and was in the 1914 war. Sounds all right, father. The ess is John Arthur."

Not so very long ago either Mr. or Mrs. Halliday would at once have said they must ask young Mr. Cross to dinner, but no such words were spoken. Mrs. Halliday would like to have asked him, for she thought Leonard would enjoy his company, but if Leonard did not feel up to it, that was that. She did not repine, but there was a faint feeling of claustrophobia which she did not like. The insistent, tactless voice of the telephone broke into the short silence. Sylvia went to attend to it.

"Mr. Cross, mother," she mouthed, her hand over the telephone's face.

Mrs. Halliday, a little curious, went to the telephone, sat down on the comfortable low chair by it (for she refused to stand in a rather bent position while her friends maundered on, or the exchange kept her waiting) and said she was speaking.

"There ought to be listening-in things for everyone," said Sylvia, in a low voice that her mother's conversation might not be disturbed. Or amplifiers George said.

"Oh *no*," said Edith. "They have them in the Ladies' Annexe of The Club" (for by this name the County Club in Barchester was always known, though we doubt whether many of the members knew about its much older namesake in London—nor would they have taken much interest in what went on in foreign parts), "and you can't ever hear what they say," and she gave a very good imitation of the raucous gabbling which told the

world that Miss Edith Graham was waiting for Lady Graham in
the Lounge, and made George and Sylvia laugh.

"One moment, Mr. Cross," said Mrs. Halliday. "My young
people are making so much noise I can't hear you properly," at
which words George said Kamerad and threw up his hands,
though it was really Edith's fault.

"All right, mother," he said. "Carry on and we'll listen." But
listening did not afford much entertainment, for Mrs. Halliday's
part in the conversation was mostly such useful interjections as
Oh, Certainly, Yes always, Not really, Yes, of course, Yes, Yes,
after which she laid the receiver down and put one hand over the
mouthpiece.

"And now, mother, what was it all about?" said George. "Was
Cross proposing for Edith's hand?"

"Certainly not," said Mrs. Halliday, with an almost motherly
look at her son (and worse we cannot say) for being so flippant.
"Leonard, that young Mr. Cross at the Old Manor House wants
to know if we can have a drink with him tomorrow. He thought
you might like to see the house as we are having it back again."

"And don't say you have one foot in the grave, father," said
Sylvia, rubbing her cheek against the top of his head, "because
you haven't. And we all want to see all over the house frightfully."

"One moment, Mr. Cross," said Mrs. Halliday, "I must just
see what my husband is doing," and to her great credit there was
in her words not the slightest trace of impatience.

"Well, I suppose I had better go," said Mr. Halliday, of which
slight ungraciousness his wife took no notice at all and after a
few more words with Mr. Cross, put the receiver up.

"That will be very nice," she said. "I've been wanting to see
what condition the rest of the house is in for ages. About six
o'clock, he said. You haven't ever seen the upper floors, Edith."

"Oh, but Mrs. Halliday," said Edith, "I'm going back after
lunch tomorrow. And I *did* want to see the house."

"Why not?" said Mrs. Halliday calmly. "We can ring up your

mother. You can run Edith over to Holdings afterwards, George, can't you?"

George said of course he could. Mrs. Halliday and Edith had better ring her mother up now, which she did, while the family—knowing that there were not any secrets—listened with the amused, half contemptuous interest that a one-sided conversation affords us. As Edith's side was chiefly, Yes, mother, or Oh *no*, mother, or Oh *lovely*, mother, they were not much the wiser. But Edith quickly put them out of their pain by reporting that mother said that would be delightful and she had wanted to see the house for ages and would pick Edith up there.

"*Isn't* it nice of mother?" she said, as she took her seat again.

Her hostess, her hostess's husband and her hostess's daughter all agreed. Mrs. Halliday liked Lady Graham more than a little; Mr. Halliday admired her extremely as what a local magnate's wife should be (his own wife being of course, always, hors concours); Sylvia had seen a great deal of her, for the intercourse between Rushwater and Holdings was frequent and most friendly and Agnes the kindest of aunts-by-marriage. George also liked and admired her, but thought it a little unnecessary that Lady Graham should come and fetch Edith when he could perfectly well have run her home himself. At which same moment his mother said That was really the best way, because if George had taken Edith back to Holdings he would probably have been pressed to stay to supper and she knew he wanted to see that man from the West Barsetshire County Council who was coming about that bit of road that had to be widened. George had to admit to himself that his mother was perfectly correct, so he sighed as one who felt that Edith was a nice kid and not bad-looking, and obeyed as a prospective land-owner.

Mr. Halliday then said he did not know if he wished to see the house again. It was full of memories, he said.

"Oh, come off it, father," said George, though most affectionately and with suitable filial respect. "Of course it's full of memories, but they are pretty old ones now. After all we left it

more than two hundred years ago and you've never even stayed
in it. I have though. I spent a week there when I was a kid
because there were measles at School and my quarantine wasn't
up, and the old aunts were jolly good to me. Come with us,
father. You ought to see it, you know. Perhaps there's dry rot or
wet rot or something. And we might find that old photograph of
your grandmother that you lent to the aunts and they never
returned it."

"I should never have lent it. Give, but never lend," said Mr.
Halliday rather sententiously. "Besides, one gets real pleasure
from giving; more, I think, than one does from receiving," to
which his son disrespectfully replied that he quite agreed and
would his father at once give him that old Inverness cape and
deerstalker hat that had been put away for umpteen years, so
that he could pretend he was Sherlock Holmes and frighten old
Lady Norton.

Mr. Halliday tried to be offended but couldn't, and they all
fell into a great jumble of laughter, nay, giggles from the girls
(for Sylvia though mother of two and expectant mother of the
next remained a girl at heart and also, when at her old home, in
manner).

"And don't say I'll have it anyway when you're dead, father,"
said George, though most affectionately, "because give us another war and I might die first and Lord! what a mess the estate
would be in."

"I know," said Mr. Halliday. "I know, Have the Sherlock
Holmes outfit by all means, my boy. You can wear it at my
funeral," at which George looked quite aghast, as did his mother
for one millionth of a second, but she knew her husband would
never willingly snub his son. "Then you will look exactly like
Dracula," said Mr. Halliday, which unexpected remark made
everyone laugh, and Mrs. Halliday felt, as she had felt ever since
before young Mr. Leonard Halliday proposed to her, that he was
the nicest person in the world.

CHAPTER 5

Monday dawned chill and cheerless, but as every day had been like that and would be for the rest of the year, no one paid much attention to it. Sylvia went away after breakfast, sincerely sorry to leave her parents and her brother George, but eager to see Martin again and be sure that he hadn't done anything silly with his crippled foot; also to assure herself—in spite of several telephonings—that Miss Eleanor and Master George were well. As for the shadowy third (to use the words of Robert Browning, that writer of plays) it was also extremely well and lively, though for the time being not very visible to the human eye. George as usual went off to the farm. Edith packed her suitcase and then suddenly there was nothing to do, so she went in search of her hostess, running her to earth at last in the linen room, a large room on the second floor with the kitchen flue behind one wall, so that it was dry in the dampest weather and gently warm, for the old-fashioned kitchen-range was hardly ever let out, Mrs. Fothergill not holding with it unless the sweep was expected.

"Come in," said Mrs. Halliday, "and help me to go through these sheets and table-cloths. Old Mrs. Halliday, Leonard's mother, had a lot of linen and was a very good needlewoman. When she came to stay here we always went through it together. Look at this," and she shook out a damask table-cloth woven with a very fine pattern of beasts of prey chasing smaller beasts, on a background of vine leaves. Edith exclaimed in admiration.

"It is in extraordinarily good condition," said Mrs. Halliday. "My mother-in-law always had them washed at home in the old wash-house, in spring water, and laid out to bleach on the grass. Of course there were servants then. Now I hardly know what to do with them. We shall never have proper dinner parties again. Some people use them for sheets, or have them dyed for bedspreads or curtains, but I don't like the idea. Here is one pattern I am particularly fond of with a grove of trees all round it and deer in the middle. Four yards by two, at least, and some of them are larger. I do wish I could think what to do with them. It isn't good for them to lie her folded."

"Mother had some cloths like that from The Towers after old Uncle Giles died," said Edith, alluding to Lady Graham's uncle, the late Lord Pomfret. "She had some rollers made for the linen-room and the table-cloths were hung on them, like maps, and then they could be rolled up without creases."

"What a very good idea," said Mrs. Halliday. "I must ask Caxton if he can make something of the kind for me. I wonder where he is."

Edith offered to go and find him. Mrs. Halliday said that would be very kind, and if he was not about the place not to worry, as she could always find him later. But the blood of Grahams, professional soldiers from generation to generation, was up. Caxton was not in his workshop. Undaunted, Edith tracked him via the pigsties to the poultry-yard where he was making good some weak places with bits of wire netting.

"Morning, miss," said Caxton. "Waste not, want not and the Vicar's gardener was going to put these bits of wire netting on the rubbish heap. 'You let me have them' I said to him. 'Waste not, want not,' I said, so he said what about the Vicar. 'Take it from me, my lad,' I said, 'Mr. Choyce he wouldn't notice if you walked off with his trousers from under his very eyes,' I said," at which Edith nearly had the giggles at thought of Mr. Choyce being as it were debagged from trousers that came up to his armpits.

"Oh, Caxton," said Edith, "Mrs. Halliday asked me to find you. She wants to know if you could get some long rollers to hang her old cloths on. I don't mean old *cloths*," she added quickly, seeing Claxton's face darken. "I mean some beautiful real linen table-cloths that are very old and being folded is bad for them and they'll go at the creases," after which explanation she felt sillier than ever and waited for Caxton to dismiss her with ignominy. To her surprise and relief he appeared to think the matter worth considering.

"Now, miss, them sheets, I know which you mean. Old Mrs. Halliday that was the Squire's mother, she was a one for linen, she was. Went to every sale in the county when there was linen going. I can tell you where those sheets came from, miss," and he paused dramatically, so that Edith felt she must ask, in common courtesy, where it was.

"Ah, that's telling," said Caxton, to which Edith very neatly riposted that he *wasn't* telling.

"Sharp as a pig's tooth!" said Caxton admiringly, "and no man as hasn't been bitten by a pig can say fairer. Look here, miss," and baring his thin strong left arm he showed Edith two white marks. "And those I got when I was a nipper," said Caxton. "Teasing the old sow I was, and she got my arm. Father was there and he hit her over the snout and give her a kick in the arse, and there was I a-hollering and a-bellering away," and he paused.

"So what did your father do?" said Edith.

"Ah!" said Caxton, who had been deliberately working up to this dramatic point. "What did he do? He took and give me the soundest thrashing he'd given me yet. A fine old fellow he was. Now miss, let's see what Mrs. Halliday wants. I'll just smarten myself up a bit first though," so they went back to his shed where Caxton washed his hands in the same basin of water in which he had already washed them twice that morning, dried them on a piece of sacking, and putting his square paper cap on his head, announced his readiness to follow Edith.

Of all the single combats in the world, perhaps one of the most impressive is when—in the great words of a great poet—a Throne speaks to a Throne. In Mrs. Halliday Caxton recognised his feudal superior, for matriarchy has always been tacitly accepted in England and nowhere more than in the solid working class where Mum ranks a good deal higher than Dad; his whole status indeed depending on whether Mum makes the children respect him. If she does, well and good. If she does not, heaven help Dad and even more the children. Never once in all her married life had Mrs. Halliday, representing Mum, put herself in public opposition to Dad, in the person of Mr. Halliday; and we may add that never had Mrs. Halliday failed to have her way.

"Good-morning, mum," said Caxton, touching his cap of office which he never removed when on duty so to speak. "Miss Edith she said you wanted to see me about a job of work."

Mrs. Halliday said Yes, it was about those large linen tablecloths. If they were folded all the time it wouldn't do them any good and they would go along the creases, which Caxton at once understood.

"Well, mum," he said, after a silence meant to indicate weighty thought, "it's like this as I see it. If you fold the cloths they go at the folds. Don't fold them, and they won't."

Mrs. Halliday professed to be much struck by this novel idea.

"So what I'd say, mum, though mark you it's no business of mine and I never was one to speak my mind unless asked," Caxton continued unblushingly, "is, don't fold them."

Mrs. Halliday, too wary through long experience to show impatience, said there was something in what he said and could he think of any way of storing them. There was a way, Caxton said, but it wasn't for him to speak his mind unless asked to. Mrs. Halliday said she would be glad if he would speak his mind and she would consider it.

"Ah! that's just it, mum. Consider's the word," said Caxton. "Now if a man considered, that man might say, Why not have those table-cloths on a roller, being as so the roller is the same length as the width of the cloth, or say a bit longer to allow."

Mrs. Halliday said that was a good idea.

"Ah," said Caxton with deep satisfaction, a foretaste of triumph in his voice, "but saying that was done, you'd have to unroll that cloth whenever you wanted her and roll her up again when you didn't, and rolling things straight takes a power of doing. Get one half inch out of the straight at the beginning and you'll be a foot out when you get to the end," which though not quite clear to his hearers did give them a general feeling of lopsidedness.

Edith, feeling she could not stand by inactive while the battle raged, asked Caxton what he would do if they were his sheets.

"Well miss, if they were mine, I'll tell you what I'd do," he said. "You see that end wall, ladies. Well, that wall she's a bit over ten foot height. I wouldn't like to say to an inch, but say ten foot six."

Mrs. Halliday and Edith, assuming an interest that they could not yet feel, produced a kind of noise of satisfaction.

"Well then," said Caxton, taking from his apron pocket something like a large watch case, "let's get her measure," and pulling out the steel tape he laid it along the wall. "Ten four and a half. My eye's out. Not what it used to be. How wide would you say that largest cloth was, mum?"

Mrs. Halliday said she knew the width and it was about eight feet.

"Very well, mum, there we are then," said Caxton. "I'll put you up a nice roller, about nine foot wide and I'll hang it so as you can pull it up and down easy. Now, suppose you want to hang them cloths so as they won't get creased, you lower that roller till she's about four feet from the ground and you lay one end of that cloth over the roller, if you get me—" a threatening pause made Mrs. Halliday and Edith hasten to say they quite understood "—and then you pull her up a bit and she rises and you ease her a bit over the roller and when she goes a bit higher again one of you goes behind and pulls her over, very gentle-like, and you pull and you ease till she's hanging from the top and not a crease in her. And there she stays till the Judgment Day; unless of course you wanted her down. And similar if you want to let her down, you let her down gentle and put an old sheet underneath the way she won't touch the floor. Leave it to me, mum."

Mrs. Halliday, sturdily keeping up the majesty of the British Raj, said that sounded very nice; but it was obvious that she did not understand it in the least, largely because of the number of females who appeared to be involved. Edith, however, being used to elder brothers who had forced her to be the not unwilling spectator of their various essays in carpentering and even down at the forge, saw what Caxton meant and re-explained it to Mrs. Halliday, who felt just as confused as she had before the explanation but was too cowardly to say so. Caxton went off to his dinner which usually took place about noon in his shed and during which no one was allowed to disturb him, while Mrs. Halliday, rather battered, returned to her desk and her eternal papers and letters, so that Edith was again at a loose end. Her packing was done, Mr. Halliday was taking a long morning in bed as he often did, Hubback was busy upstairs and old Mrs. Fothergill, in what was even now called the still room, was making jam. A hard world, Edith felt, and being a poet she tried to make a poem about it all, sitting on the back doorstep where there was sun without wind and one of the stable cat's kittens to keep her company. The difficulty was Hatch House. The only rhyme to house appeared to be mouse. Of course if one said howse there would be bows, cows, pows if one felt Scotch, rows only that kind of row wasn't very poetical, sows—and here she paused. George liked pigs. Hurriedly she ran through the rest vows, wows which wasn't a word, yowes only that was Sctoch and one was not quite sure whether it rhymed with cows or not—and that was all.

George Halliday came round the corner and saw Cinderella on the doorstep, turned out by her cruel stepmother.

"What's up?" he said. "Lord! there's a wind up in the top field."

"I was trying to make a poem about Hatch House, but there weren't enough rhymes," Edith said rather grandly.

"Good lord! my girl, I thought you were a poet," said George. "Plenty of rhymes. Bows—dogs say bow-wow; cows, sows, vows—dozens."

"Yes, I know," said Edith, "but you see it isn't really hows, it's howsss."

George said that needed a power of thinking and sat down on the doorstep beside her, feeling to her much larger in his farm clothes than he did in his ordinary clothes.

"I do wish it wasn't over," said Edith. "I *have* enjoyed it so much."

"So did we," said George, wiping his face and neck with a large red handkerchief with white spots. "Pff, it's hot up there. Why don't you come up to the Knob? We've time before lunch," so Edith put the kitten down and they went up the track under the steep escarpment of Freshdown, once Frey's Down, and paused in the shelter of Bolder's Knob, where no tree has ever grown since St. Ewold, in an access of slum clearance, had caused the sacred oak-grove to be cut down.

George looked abroad over the land and wondered, as he had often wondered before, how he would get on when his father was dead. Gone he did not say, for gone might mean a journey to London, a trip to Paris; and he had no feeling about the word as a word. One had said it often enough in the war—though even then one had been apt to use the current euphemisms— one's friends had had it, they had stopped one, there were a hundred ways of avoiding it.

"George," said Edith, "when Mr. Halliday—when your father dies—will you be able to keep the farm on?"

Half of George was outraged that a gently nurtured girl and

the daughter of a neighbour to boot should ask such a question. But Edith was very young, said his other half, and what was more, very sensible. It was no good trying to forget death. It had to come and that was that.

"Father has made all the plans he can," Edith continued. "Of course Holdings will go to James, unless there was another war and he got killed. If he wasn't married with a son John would have it. Father says it's high time the boys thought of getting married, only Robert really isn't old enough and the Brigade of Guards doesn't encourage early marriage," which she said with so absurdly grown-up a voice that George laughed out loud. There was no laugh from Edith, who was usually ready to join him. He looked down and saw nothing but the top of her head.

"Anything wrong?" he said kindly.

"Oh no," said Edith, but still looking down. "I was only thinking about people being killed. It must be dull not to have brothers, but it's better for your mother perhaps."

George asked what on earth she meant.

"Oh, you might all get killed one after another," Edith said. "If one had only one brother and he was killed it would all be over. But with three—" and she left the sentence unfinished.

George felt extremely uncomfortable. There was little that he did not know about war, having been through the last years with the Barsetshire Yeomanry, but he had never thought much about the families of the killed, and for the first time he tried to imagine his father if there were another war and he were killed, as would be both probable and reasonable. He did not like the thought at all. Then he thought of Lady Graham with her three sons, all professional soldiers or about to be so. Might that be worse? Niobe and her children, he thought, remnants of education floating into his mind.

"Then I suppose Emmy's eldest would have it," said Edith, pursuing the subject of Holdings. "She's the eldest and hers is a boy."

"Do you know," said George, relighting his pipe for the

severalth time (and if that is not a word, it ought to be), "I haven't the faintest idea what would happen if I died before father, I haven't any children—"

"Of course you haven't. You aren't married," said Edith. "And illegitimate sons don't count."

"I say, Edith, look here!" said George outraged. "You don't think—"

"Oh no," said Edith. "Now, we Grahams are all *awfully* illegitimate. I don't mean us specially," she went on, rather to George's relief who wondered what the girl would say next. "I mean father's great-grandfather started it. There are quite a lot of Raghams in East Barsetshire."

"Raggums?" said George, and then as light broke on him, "a rather gypsy lot? Mr. Gresham told me he had a bit of trouble with them sometimes, but he paid a kind of Danegeld and then they stole other people's hens and things. But why Raggums? Because they were ragged?"

"Oh no; anag:" said Edith calmly. "Like the Times Cross Word puzzle. You know. Great-grandfather must have thought a lot before he found it. We've got an old box of ivory letters—I mean the letters of the alphabet on little ivory squares—and father says his father told him that *his* father used to play with them in the evening, making names for his family. Graham *is* an awkward name," which cool treatment of the question quite flabbergasted George.

"But of course we shouldn't *think* of it now," said Edith. "All Emmy's children are legitimate and so are Clarissa's; at least this one is and the next one will be. And so will all mine."

A thousand repartees flashed into George's mind, one being How do you know you will have any. But this was not the way to talk to a young female guest, so he said it was lucky his people had been fairly respectable as one couldn't make an anagram out of Halliday. They then tried to make some, but each was sillier than the last, so they came down the hill again with a great deal of foolish, happy laughter. Lunch was peaceful and then George went back to the farm while Edith talked with Mr. Halliday, or rather let his talk flow over her and Mrs. Halliday dealt with her endless correspondence, for her husband left almost everything to her now, except such farm business as George dealt with. Presently Mr. Halliday went to his study to be quiet before the outing and Edith was alone in the drawing-room. The brief hour of medium weather (for no one could call it good weather) was over and a cold wind was battering a cold rain against the panes. Edith turned on the wireless, though very low lest anyone should be disturbed, and curled up in a chair close to it. A woman with a husky voice was singing popular songs of the melancholy love type. A song about These Foolish Things which panders to all one's lowest and most penny-novelette feelings and yet has a horrid way of making one's eyes a little dim and giving one the gobbles in one's throat. And then in an even huskier voice she sang a song of incredible silliness, both in words and sentiment, about sitting at the window and looking at the rain and how tomorrow it would probably pour again hi-lilly, hi-lilly, hi-low—or words much to that effect, by the end of which Edith found herself crying; though why she had not the faintest idea. And neither have we as yet, for so far in her life there has been so little to cry about, nor was she a crier. Her sister Emmy could bellow like a bull, drown the stage with tears, use three handkerchiefs and then forget all about it. Clarissa had cried her heart out when the beloved grandmother Lady Emily Leslie died, her pretty, insolent face pale and blotched with tears, but was otherwise restrained, and also very happy with Charles Belton. Edith had been the fat, jolly, rather spoilt youngest and a true Pomfret in her happy insouciance. But one does not remain young and uncaring for ever. At least some people do, but though one envies their tranquility one would not give up one's own storms and strains.

Then the music became rather less sad and less husky and Edith heard Hector Woollff's orchestra the Happy Hectorians and then a talk on Chryzomes and Epizomes by Professor

Spatch and a relay from Zdbrosz on How to Fake Genuine Antiques by Prsz (who apparently had no vowels nor any other name). But none of these could deaden a feeling that she could not explain of unhappy happiness; or happy unhappiness, and before she realised how time had passed it was tea-time and George coming in all washed and clean in ordinary clothes. And at the same moment life became quite ordinary again, with a visit to the Old Manor House at cocktail time.

To drive sixty or seventy miles to lunch, though tiring to some, is not difficult. You know how long it takes and arrange accordingly, allowing extra time of course if it is market day in Barchester. To drive a short half mile is extraordinarily difficult. From Hatch House to the Old Manor House for instance should be easy enough. Down the short drive, pause at the gate for possible traffic along the narrow road, across the road, down a little slope and over the long causeway and bridge to the other side of the Rising, to the left up the village street and there you are.

But it is rather like Snakes and Ladders, that delightful game of our golden youth. A snake at the gate means that a farm wagon overloaded with hay or mangolds will cross your path; a ladder may get you safely into the road, but a snake as you turn to the left onto the causeway may mean a drove of cows who simply could not care less, sauntering aimlessly back to be milked, and there is nothing for it but to wait till Jimmy Panter, or some other very young cowherd, has driven them past with shrill, hearty Saxon objurgations. Across the causeway and the bridge should be a ladder, but if Packer's Universal Royal Derby, on its way from one flower show to another, happens to be crossing the bridge (which has a notice, to which no one has ever paid the faintest attention, that it will not stand more than a certain weight) you must pull up on your haunches and let it go by. And should you get safely to the further end it is quite possible that Vidler's van will block the way because the pro-

prietor is having a second beer with Mr. Geo. Panter at the
Mellings Arms, thus holding up the traffic indefinitely.

However Fate today was kind, or at any rate had taken herself
and her obstructive ways to Greshamsbury where there were two
weddings and anyone who had a garden had opened it for one of
the many deserving charities, namely St. Aella's Home for
Stiff-necked Clergy, and the crush was enormous. They crossed
the bridge without any difficulty and only had to wait for a very
short time outside the Mellings Arms, where stood Pilward and
Sons' Entire's huge dray, with its grey horses groomed to the last
glossy inch, its spotless red and black paintwork, the shining
brasses of the harness, and the draymen in scarlet linen coats and
black leggings who were delivering casks and bottles. However
this did not take long. The driver blew a hunting-horn from
which depended the banner of Pilward and Sons and the equipage went away at a smart pace, followed by all the naughty little
boys of the village.

It was an old custom in West Barsetshire that if there were not
enough garden behind, the better-to-do citizens in a village or
small town would annex a field opposite their house and make a
garden of part of it. So it was with the Old Manor House and
about half an acre on the other side of the road had been made
into a very charming garden, though now sadly in need of care.
A semicircle had been taken from this field, an elegant light
railing on a low stone wall put round it, and an equally elegant
iron grille or gate at the tip (if a semicircle can have a tip), thus
making a safe place for visiting cars. The Southbridge United
Viator Passenger Company had at one time tried to grab this
half-circle for a stopping place, but owing to the public spirited
action of Mr. Halliday and Sir Robert Graham, this had been
squashed. No power on earth, legal or otherwise, can of course
prevent the inconsiderate rudeness of motorists who look upon
the whole world as their parking ground, but they had mostly
rushed through the village before they noticed it. And the

parking of cars outside other people's houses without excuse or apology is just one of the Rudenesses that have come to stay.

As Squire and Lord of the Manor, Mr. Halliday had every right to park his car in the half-circle and did so. A small boy who was building a castle with some broken tiles looked up and stared at them.

"Hullo, Jimmy," said Mrs. Halliday, recognising a scion of Panter family. "Don't let the other boys touch the car and I'll let you blow the horn when I come back."

"Okay, miss," said Jimmy, with an engaging if slightly tooth-less grin. "I'll stone 'em. Widdy widdy wen—*I'll* stone 'em."

"Good God!" said Mr. Halliday.

His wife, unused to such emotion from her husband, looked anxiously at him, fearing that he might be in pain; also that Master Panter might, as indeed he promptly did, appropriate the words.

"Did you hear Jimmy?" said Mr. Halliday with the reverent voice he kept for the cathedral, even when the Bishop was in it. "He's talking Dickens. Pure Dickens. But that boy has never been to Rochester—he's never been outside Hatch End except to Barchester once or twice and I doubt whether he can read anything except Westerns. I say, Jimmy! What's that you're saying about Widdy Wen?"

"You always says that, sir," said Jimmy, whose father had threatened him with appalling penalties if he cheeked the Squire. "You says that when you're going to throw a stone at any one."

"I wonder what it means," said Mrs. Halliday. "You might get Lord Stoke onto it, Leonard," for Lord Stoke, in spite of his age and deafness, was perhaps the keenest antiquarian in the county and certainly the oldest. "There's Mr. Cross," and she gently directed her husband's steps across the road to where Mr. Cross was standing in the doorway of the Old Manor House. As it was not an official bank day he was in grey flannels and looked very personable.

"Welcome to your own house, sir," he said. "Hullo, Halliday."

"Lady Graham is coming to collect Edith, isn't she?" said Mrs. Halliday. "Will it be all right if we leave her luggage in the car?" for alas, the housing estate was having the usual disastrous effect upon its surroundings; and where poaching had been the most serious crime there were now a good many cases of thieving and breaking in, though so far no violence.

Mr. Halliday said he had left Jimmy Panter in charge.

"You couldn't do better," said Mr. Cross. "He must be related to one of Sherlock Holmes's Street Arabs. He's got more brains in his little finger than the whole village put together. Where does he get it from?"

"I couldn't say," said Mr. Halliday. "They're a good lot the Panters. I shouldn't wonder if there's some outside blood in them. The Hubbacks have a good bit of gypsy and his mother was a Hubback. It's very good of you to ask us here, Cross. I've hardly been in the house since my old aunts died. Your people wanted it and it suited me to let at the time. That floor's in very good condition," he added, looking at the black and white paving of the hall.

Mr. Cross said his housekeeper washed it every week and he saw that she *did* wash it and that she rubbed it well with a dry cloth afterwards. There was nothing, he said, like leaving those old flags wet for making them come loose and then they were bound to get chipped somewhere. There was, he added, one stone a bit chipped at the corner, but he didn't think he or Dorothy had done it.

"That's *my* chip," said Mr. Halliday, with the pride of one who has shot his first rabbit. "I was a lad then and someone had given me one of those spud-walking sticks—*you* know what I mean, Cross," he said, rather meanly excluding his wife, his son and his guest, who might all be expected to know about such things. "And I dug up everything I could lay hands on, at least not exactly that but you see what I mean. I was showing Aunt Jessie how you do it and I hit the pavement a bit too hard and a bit of stone flew up. Aunt Jessie said she'd mend it with seccotine, but it never stuck and finally it got lost. Swept up I expect."

Mr. Cross said By Jove, and Mrs. Halliday thought well of a young man who could listen with apparent attention to her dear husband's uninteresting and pointless story and then make so sensible a comment. Mr. Cross asked if they would have sherry now, or see the upper stories. Mrs. Halliday, feeling that it would be easier to bring her husband down again if he looked tired before sherry than after sherry, said upstairs please.

Barsetshire is full of beautiful houses—not but what it can also proudly boast several of the most hideous in England, notably Gatherum Castle and Beliers Priory. Many of them are now well-known and open to Members of the National Trust and other worthy bodies on certain days. But there still are, and we hope always will be, modest houses distinguished by their proportions, their workmanship, their structure (often stone, or that charming combination of stone and brick, or with an enchanting homely Caldecott beauty of mellow red brick alone) and their setting. The Old Manor House, of the local stone which goes gently grey with age and acquires various delicate golden tints from lichenous growths, had all these graceful charms and a handsome staircase as well, with wide, low steps and a little landing at the half turn of each flight.

"I get Dorothy to keep the stairs polished," said Mr. Cross, "but not too much. I had to ration her on polish, or we'd all have broken our legs."

Mrs. Halliday said she thought servants ate polish; nothing else could explain it. She paused on the little landing to look out over the garden. It was in a neat and flourishing condition and beyond it fields sloped upwards to the line of down that separated Hatch End and Little Misfit.

"Some people would hang framed colour-prints out of old herbals and things on the wall," said Mr. Cross, "one in each panel," which made Mrs. Halliday laugh, and she looked lovingly at the white panelled walls, with no frippery of carving, but good simple proportions; no nonsense about exotic woods, but what we can (in the absence of any special knowledge of the subject) only call carpenter's wood, painted white.

"I'm glad your bank left it white," said Mr. Halliday. "All this nonsense about wood being pickled!"

"As a matter of fact, sir," said Mr. Cross, "the bank did want to scrape or pickle the white paint, so I got father onto it and he rubbed it into them that it was deal. So as they thought deal sounded cheap, they left it as it was," at which everyone laughed and Mrs. Halliday felt—a little snobbishly, but we all have our snobbism even if it is having been to what are known as World Premières more often than other people—that it was nice to meet a young man so obviously one's own sort.

On the first floor was a landing running from the back to the front of the house with bedrooms to right and left; always a very charming effect though not altogether practical in England owing to cold weather on about three hundred and sixty days out of the year.

"All this and the rest of the house is much as the last tenants—relations of yours of course, sir—left it," said Mr. Cross. "I have a bed in one room in case I want to spend the night here. Do come in," and he opened a door near the head of the stairs.

"Dear me, I had quite forgotten how charming these rooms were," said Mr. Halliday. "This is the room that old Aunt Sylvia used to have. And the same Chinese wall paper. Well, well."

Mr. Cross did not feel quite sure whether the "well" was approval, disapproval, or merely a tribute to time past, so he said the paper was a bit worn in places but so lovely that it would be a shame to change it.

"It's a pity it's so bad in that corner," he said. "It looks as if damp had got in, but I had our builder here for some small repairs and he says there isn't a sign of damp anywhere. If it was some houses it might be creepers, or ivy; but none of these walls have any."

"It's very simple," said Mr. Halliday, who had been looking amused. "That's where old Aunt Sylvia had her washing-stand. I remember it quite well. I was hardly ever upstairs in the house because the old ladies didn't hold with boys about, but after Aunt Jessie died Aunt Sylvia rather liked to see me. Old fashioned washing-stand, you know, with fat mahogany legs and a grey marble slab and a huge jug and basin and a small jug and basin and all sorts of other odds and ends. And a bit of muslin drawing-pinned onto the wall to keep the splashes off. That wall must have been wringing wet. Aunt Sylvia did pretty well all her washing in the basin because baths were unladylike. Well, well. I wonder what happened to the washing-stand," and they went on to look at the other rooms; all well-proportioned and no feeling of damp. Only a feeling of not-being-lived-in; not unreasonable under the circumstances.

"By the way," said Mr. Cross, "you know the bank put in a bathroom. They did ask your permission."

"Which," said Mr. Halliday, "I was delighted to give. I wanted to put one in for the aunts, but they refused. Said they'd never had a bath except in their own room and didn't want to change," and while he spoke Mr. Cross led them across the landing into a small room where a shining white bath with shining taps, a shower above it, pink plastic curtains round it and white tiles in the corner where it lived, made a pleasant effect.

"Now, let me see, this was the Small Pink Dressing Room," said Mr. Halliday, "and as far as I remember it was the cat's bedroom. My aunts had a favourite cat and he had a bedroom to himself. This is an improvement."

"I'm glad you think so, sir," said Mr. Cross. "The bank did ask your permission, but I was afraid it might be a bit of a shock. The door into the bedroom had been boarded up, but we took that down," and he opened it for his guests to pass.

"Better than Vache-en-Foin, Halliday," said Mr. Cross, while Mr. and Mrs. Halliday looked round what had been Aunt

Jessie's bedroom. "Did you ever have a bath in old Madame Poirot's kitchen?"

"Did I *not*," said George, "and all those nice fat girls coming in with jugs of hot water one after the other and giggling and there one was, sitting in the bath all hunched up, trying to look respectable. And do you remember——"

"They're off," said Edith Graham to herself and while the Hallidays were arguing in a friendly way as to whether Aunt Sylvia without her false fringe or Aunt Jessie without her false teeth looked the more revolting in bed, she went into the next room and amused herself by looking into the drawers of a massive dressing table. Beyond yellowing newspaper there was nothing to see, but one drawer stuck a little and as she tugged and shook, it suddenly came out at her and then wouldn't go back in spite of pushings and shakings.

"All right, come *right* out then," said Edith and with a final tug brought it out of its sockets (or whatever the right expression is) and so into her hands, almost knocking her over. She looked into the toothless gap—for what the technical name is of the hole a drawer goes into we do not know—and seeing some odds and ends at the back she reached in and pulled them out. They consisted of some bits of paper with curious marks of scorching on them, some rather unpleasant grey hair-combings and a very faded photograph with one corner doubled over and on the verge of coming off. So she put the drawer back again, though not without difficulty, for it was obdurate and like Browning's villa-gate practically ground its teeth at her efforts till suddenly it went in with a bang.

"And you can jolly well stay there," said Edith vengefully, at which moment the Hallidays and Mr. Cross, in the course of their progress, came into the room.

"I'm so sorry, Mr. Cross," said Edith. "I was looking into the drawers and one came out at me and wouldn't go back till it suddenly did," which made everything quite clear. "And there was a photograph there, Mrs. Halliday," and she handed it to her.

"You will know what it is, Leonard," she said, handing it to her husband. "It looks rather like old Aunt Sylvia, but I don't think it is."

"Quite right, my dear," said Mr. Halliday. "It isn't. It is my grandmother. Aunt Sylvia was like her. By Jove! it's the photograph that I lent to the aunts and they never returned it."

"I expect there are *lots* of secret things in the house," said Edith. "I'd like to look in all the drawers and everywhere. There were these bits of paper too, half burnt. Do you suppose anyone had been burning a will?" But Mrs. Halliday after looking at them laughed and said they were bits of paper that one of the aunts had tried her curling tongs on, and she remembered when she was a little girl seeing her mother heating the tongs on a little methylated spirit stove, then twiddling them round by one leg to cool them, then trying them on a piece of paper and finally nipping a bit of her fringe and twiddling the tongs round on it. And once, she said, the tongs had been a little too hot and some of her mother's fringe had fallen off and smelt horrid.

Edith asked again if there were any secret drawers and Mr. Cross said he was afraid there weren't, and why that one chest of drawers had been left in the house he did not know, but if they would like to look at the top floor, they were welcome. So they all went up another flight of less elegant stairs to the top floor where there were several more bedrooms than on the lower floor because of all being smaller; except at the back where one room ran nearly the whole width of the house, its three windows looking over the downs.

"The old nursery," said Mr. Halliday. "It's a long time since it was a nursery, but the windows show you," and sure enough there were two bars across each window to stop anyone of tender years deliberately killing itself while Nurse's attention was otherwise engaged.

"By the way," said Mr. Cross, "I got the bank to put a bath on this floor too while they were about it. Ploughing-in Excess Profits I think it's called. So if anyone wanted to live here everything's handy," and then they all went downstairs again and looked at the drawing-room. Mr. Halliday said it was a pleasure to see the room empty. The aunts had it as full of furniture as a bargain basement and none of it good. And it was indeed a handsome and peaceful room with the bow or apse at the garden end and two handsome sash windows onto the road and the plaster-work round the ceiling. Nothing elaborate; simply the sort of decoration a gentleman's house ought to have. At this moment the front door bell sounded, away in the servants' quarters below.

"I expect that is Lady Graham," said Mrs. Halliday to their host who got up and went into the hall in time to open the door before Dorothy could get there. He had seen Lady Graham more than once at parties, at the Deanery, or at the Fieldings' in the Close, and felt a deep though respectful admiration for her, but had never really made her acquaintance, so he introduced himself and said how glad he was she could come.

"So am I," said Lady Graham. "I have always admired this house so much. My husband's people knew the Miss Hallidays— at least they liked to be called the Misses Halliday I think—but I never met them. And now they are dead," which words she spoke with a sweet muted voice as though the corpses were lying upstairs.

"Yes, they died some time ago," said Mr. Cross cheerfully and then blamed himself for being or sounding cheerful. Possibly, nay probably, those old Miss Hallidays had been friends of Lady Graham—much older friends of course—and she was still feeling their loss. And then realising that Lady Graham was still standing in the open door as if she had come to beg for a charity, he asked her to come in, and shut the door with a bang that echoed through the house.

"I *am* so sorry," he said. "The door slipped through my fingers."

Lady Graham, whose nervous system was as near non-existent

as makes no odds, except where her husband and children were concerned, smiled at him like a Madonna (or so he felt) and asked after his father.

Mr. Cross, recalled to earth, said he was very well, at least he was very well when he last telephoned.

"I suppose he is mostly too busy to write," said Lady Graham. "My husband hardly ever writes, but he telephones quite often, which is *much* more expensive," but whether her ladyship said this in praise or in blame of her husband, he was not sure. "Do tell me, *have* your cellars been flooded since you were here?"

Mr. Cross said not so far as he knew, but he had not been there very long and was not there all the time.

"You mean," said her ladyship, half sitting on a low oak chest that stood against the wall, "you travel a good deal? My husband is always travelling—on missions of course."

Mr. Cross, already strongly affected by the sight of Beauty in Distress (which was, for no reason, the effect Lady Graham had on him) and also left unprotected by a husband, asked if Sir Robert would be long away and what kind of mission.

"Not missionary work of course," said Lady Graham, "only going abroad to see people when really it would be *much* cheaper to write as in any case he nearly always has to have an interpreter. Of course his French is perfect—he was at Saumur for a time as you must know—and so is his German, but Mixo-Lydian he has *never* been able to learn. How is your father?"

"Oh—quite well thank you," said Mr. Cross. "He has been abroad but now he is back. He has to go on business sometimes, but he doesn't much care for it. He likes Barsetshire best."

"I know," said Lady Graham sympathetically. "*All* those places abroad. I am longing to see your house. Is Edith here yet?"

"Oh yes, of course," said Mr. Cross, "in the drawing-room. We have just been over the house. Do come in" and he escorted her ladyship to the drawing-room where Mr. Halliday was giving a vivid account of how his Aunt Jessie had a very cheap wig and when you stood by her bed and looked down on her you could see the canvas parting, which made Edith laugh.

"Darling Edith," said her mother coming in. "I am late. It was Goble's fault. How are you Mrs. Halliday? And how delightful that you could come, Mr. Halliday. I had a feeling that you would *never* see the house and I do so want you to," which confused Mr. Halliday dreadfully, for after all the house was his, and even if it was let to the bank it was not let to Lady Graham, as her speech would appear to indicate.

Nearly all of us recognise in ourselves as we grow older the characteristics that have least pleased us in our parents. A father's habit of saying as he sat down to dinner, "Well, what have I done today?" and then retailing the day's occurrences at extreme and tedious length. A mother's way of insisting that everyone should take a sprightly part in the conversation whether they had anything to say or not, which they often hadn't, and recount the uninteresting minutiae of their daily round. A daughter who *had* to tell the table how Ruby Bunter had cheeked Miss Podsnap and been given an Order Mark. A son who was stage-struck and took offence if one did not know the names and present rôles of a number of unknown players. All these have been our crosses and sent to try us.

Those, and there were very few now of her generation, who had known Lady Emily Leslie well, were more and more conscious of Agnes Graham's resemblance to her mother. Not that she was a shadow of a shade, for her ladyship, under her appearance of vague sweetness, had a marked character of her own; but increasingly did she wish to intromit, as the old Scotch agent at Rushwater used to say, in other people's affairs and most people were so fond of her that they took it with great good-humour; and it was always done with a sincere desire for the welfare of whoever she was meddling with at the moment.

So they all went into the back room, overlooking the garden, where Mr. Cross had his own sitting-room. Dorothy brought in sherry with such trepidation at the sight of Lady Graham who was a real lady, that she put the tray down with a bang and some sherry sloshed over.

"Ow!" said Dorothy. "And I'd arranged it all ever so nice. I'll get a clorth."

"They *will* fill the decanter too full," said Lady Graham settling herself, though quite unconsciously, in the most comfortable chair. "I remember once when the Duchess of Omnium— or was it Lady Hartletop—no, it *must* have been the Duchess because I remember we were talking about weevils—came to see darling Mamma at Rushwater—now, what on *earth* was I going to say?" But as no one (very naturally) knew, nor was anyone equal to following her ladyship's train of thought, there was a silence.

"And what did you do about the weevils, Lady Graham," said Mr. Cross, to whom Mrs. Halliday at once gave a good mark in her mind for his presence of mind in emergency.

"I think," said Lady Graham, "that darling Papa—because this was of course *years* ago before any of us were born—"

"But you said you remembered the conversation," said Mr. Cross, enchanted by his guest.

"Of course I do," said Lady Graham. "I only meant a good *many* people weren't born then; like Edith," she added, casting an affectionate glance on her youngest. "And of course that makes it all much more difficult for them to understand anything," and her ladyship looked round with a smile of satisfaction at having made everything clear.

"I've brought a clorth, sir," said Dorothy, bursting back into the room, "and please will you be wanting me any more because I've got my washing out and it looks as if it might come up nasty any moment now. I did put the wireless on this morning and it said there was to be scattered showers in places. I'll just wipe up a bit," and in token of good will she wiped round the edge of the tray, leaving decanter and glasses sitting in a puddle.

"That's all right, Dorothy," said Mr. Cross, taking the cloth from her. "You run along home. I'll see to this."

"Thanks ever so, sir," said Dorothy, who managed to combine the old words of feudal allegiance with the modern sloppiness of speech. "I'll be along tomorrow as usual. Ta-ta, sir," and she went out of the room, shutting the door so heartily that it sprang open on the rebound.

"*Dreadful* woman," said Mr. Cross, quite unmoved. "If you'll shut that door, Halliday, I'll do my best with the cloth. I haven't called it a clorth yet but I expect I soon will," and he wiped the tray with speed and skill, while George, after one or two ineffectual bangs, got the door to stay shut and managed to muzzle it for the time being.

"The locks in this house are quite dreadful—always were," said Mr. Halliday. "There is only one man left in West Barsetshire," he continued with gloomy satisfaction, "who can call himself a locksmith. All the others want to take your whole lock off and put a new one on. Bah!" which expletive, more often written than spoken, gave his audience great pleasure. "And he's nearly ninety and won't last long and then there won't be any one left."

"I should hate to disappoint you, sir," said Mr. Cross, "but there's a man over at Hogglestock who isn't bad. He is in Adams's big works—"

"Adams that married Marling's daughter?" said Mr. Halliday, who knew Barsetshire families high and low as well as any man in the county, though he had been heard to confess that some of those half gypsy people over Beliers way had got him beat. "He's done well, Adams has."

"Yes, indeed he has, sir," said Mr. Cross, which was really very nice of him, considering that Mr. Halliday's words had been an entirely irrelevant and valueless interruption. "And by the way, sir, if you need a man for locks at any time I'll give you his name. His father was a master locksmith and he took up the trade, but it doesn't pay now. Adams took him on—I rather think his father and Adam's father knew one another—and he's on precision work now. But his heart's in the locksmith's trade," and the two men had a short but delightful talk about the vanishing of the real tradesman who knew and loved his work.

"There is one thing I never showed you, Mrs. Halliday," said Mr. Cross, deserting Mr. Halliday; for he took his duties as a host seriously. "The roof. Have you ever been up there? There's a wonderful view up the Rising valley and it's absolutely safe, with a parapet in case of fire," but we fear that these great words were lost on his hearer. "Would you care to see it? And of course anyone else who would like to come."

Mrs. Halliday said she had no head for heights and would fall over the parapet at once but perhaps Edith would like to come, and she was sure George would.

"You will come, won't you, Lady Graham?" said Mr. Cross.

"It is most thoughtful of you, Mr. Cross," said Lady Graham, making what her brother David Leslie had irreverently called doves' eyes at her host, "but I think I will rest a little. Perhaps when you come back we could look at the basement if Dorothy won't mind. I am always *so* much interested in basements," and whether this was true or not, we cannot say, though we think it was a good deal her ladyship's general wish to give pleasure: as well as her atavistic wish to inspect every hole and corner of everyone's house; though not on the roof.

So for the second time Mr. Cross took visitors up the staircase and this time straight up to the top floor. He and George Halliday almost at once fell into what Edith's Leslie cousins irreverently called Old Bill in the Dugout conversation, by which they meant their elders going back to old war memories; but these memories were of a later war than the war we knew some forty years ago; a war longer, more terrible, more full of future menace to humanity, yet somehow far duller than its predecessor and not even ending in a blaze of glory and hope. Edith, who was used to brothers, did not find this unusual, but she did wonder—being an omnivorous reader and well up in her classics—whether Becky Sharp would have allowed two young officers to be so dull when she was with them and came regretfully to the conclusion that Becky would not; but then she was not Becky, her father had not been a poor, unsuccessful artist nor her mother a dancer who had to support her husband and her child, nor was she herself sandy-haired and extremely clever, nor the sort of person that everyone fell in love with, all of which reflections, so quickly do our minds work, were dealt with while they went up the two flights of stairs to the nursery floor, where Edith forgot to reflect. For Mr. Cross took them into a kind of long narrow housemaid's cupboard between two bed-rooms, lighted by a window at its far end. On one side of it were slatted shelves, evidently meant for linen. In the ceiling was a square trap-door and along the ceiling a step ladder was moored.

"I got the bank to put this in," said Mr. Cross. "At least I got my governor to tell the lawyers to tell the bank they jolly well must" and Edith noted with slightly priggish approval his use of the rather outmoded word governor. "A child can lower it and the trap-door goes up like a baby."

"As far as I remember when I used to stay with the aunts," said George, "there was a kind of garden ladder that lived here and you stuck it up against the trap-door and then you went up and tried to unbolt it. If you were lucky and had taken up some oil you got it to open. If not, not. And when it opened it fell right back into the loft and it was a dickens of a job to get it back again as you came down. To stand on a ladder with both hands above your head trying to fit a horizontal door into a hole and bolt it with rusty bolts isn't every man's idea of clean fun."

"If one weren't quite sick of the expression," said Mr. Cross, "I would say that you were telling *me*. I went up there when the bank took over—I've always liked exploring—and got such a whack on my head that I've never got over it. So I got them to have this put up. Will you come up, Miss Graham?"

Faintly startled by this very proper mode of address, Edith said she would love to. Mr. Cross let the ladder down, went up it, unbolted the trap-door and pushed one side of it up. It rose, described an arc in its progress and came to rest against a beam.

"That's all right," said Mr. Cross. "Now if you'll come up, Miss Graham, Halliday can come up behind you and I'll give you a hand," all of which George thought an unnecessary amount of fuss as Edith was quite capable of negotiating any amount of ladders, but it wasn't his business, so he followed Edith and all three stood in a large attic, high in the middle, with roofs sloping to the ground on every side, and at every angle. A very faint musty smell reminded George that his old aunts used to have the apples stored up here and how often he had stolen them.

"I'm sorry about the dirt," said Mr. Cross, banging some of the dust and cobwebs out of his clothes. "You'd better shut that trap, Halliday. There's no sense in falling down a ladder," and though George thought Cross was being a bit fussy, he obeyed. "Now, Miss Graham, I want to show you something," and he took her, carefully, for the huge joists were only boarded over in places, to the front of the house where there was a wooden door. This he opened and stood aside for Edith to walk out onto a leaded path or sentinel's walk, about eighteen inches wide, which ran all round the house behind a parapet, with holes in the wall at intervals for the rain water to run away down the handsome old lead pipes with their decorated heads—and here again we do not know what the correct term is.

"I shall be awfully sorry to leave this place," said Mr. Cross, looking away over the Rising Valley. "But when I've finished here father wants me to go into one of the London offices. Of course I'll get home for weekends, but one misses an awful lot. I'll probably have to go abroad too. Father has too many irons in the fire. If he hadn't, he is really the one who ought to go. He's got a terrific bump of finance or whatever one calls it."

"But if you and he both want to do the other one's job, why can't you change?" said Edith.

Mr. Cross did not answer and Edith wondered vaguely if she had said something she oughtn't to say. George was examining one of the slates—though slates is hardly the word for those beautiful layers of split stone which adorn so many Barsetshire roofs and take a colouring from wind and sun and rain and lichen as the years pass—noticing a crack in it that ought to be seen to: half his mind on the job as a good land owning farmer's should be, the other half wondering vaguely what Edith and that young Cross had found to talk about. And that bit of lead guttering needed attention too. A saying came into his mind. The arch never rests; but no more, he thought—thinking was less the word than a passage allowing fancies and ideas to drift through his mind like wandering clouds—does any part of a house. So long as the Old Manor House remained in the family, so long would it insatiably require sustenance of its walls, roofs, chimneys, floors, foundations: and so would Hatch House. And where the money was to come from he did not know. Something would have to be sold. His father had done what he could and so long as his father lived they must all pretend that things were going well. Sylvia was safe with Martin Leslie, his mother was provided for and the farm was doing well; and then he gave himself a mental and moral shake and continued his peregrination of the roof till he came round again to where Edith and Mr. Cross were deep in conversation. So eager were their looks and speech, though George could not yet hear what they were saying, that he almost felt like an eavesdropper as he came up behind them.

"Oh, George!" said Edith as she caught sight of him, "isn't it lovely! Mr. Cross's father is starting pigs and I said he had better come over and see Goble. Goble knows more about pigs than anyone in Barsetshire, except old Mr. Marling's man Pucken. Lord Bond's man is absolutely nowhere. You must come too."

"Look here, Miss Graham," said Mr. Cross, "If we are to have a deal in pigs you can't go on Mister-ing me."

"But I've only Mistered you since after church on Sunday," said Edith, giving him an upward look from downcast eyes—a form of address which can be very attractive if well done.

"Besides you Miss-ed me. And besides I don't know your name."

"Then you ought to," said George Halliday. "Didn't I get that great Peerage that weighs nearly a ton out yesterday so that we could vet him? John Arthur, my girl."

"Isn't it awful," said Mr. Cross. "I mean the Arthur part." But Edith said it was quite a nice name and anyway Edith was just as bad and she supposed they were both Anglo-Saxons or something, all of which led to a delightful conversation about the Bonds over at Staple Park, Lord Bond's only known ancestor having been a Yorkshire manufacturer of woollen goods called Jedediah who had come south with his large fortune and called his eldest son Ivanhoe; since when the reigning Bonds— Athelstane, Ethelwulf, Alured and the present peer Cedric Weyland—had all borne the names of their possible Saxon progenitors; though the present baron and his wife was determinedly breaking the chain, with each new baby.

"Lovely, lovely valley," said Edith, aloud to herself, looking up the Rising to where the spire of Barchester cathedral lifted its white elegance to heaven.

"You write poetry, don't you?" said Mr. Cross.

"Sometimes," said Edith, still looking up the valley. "I mean I did when I was young. But one grows out of things. Mother will be wanting me, I expect. Shall we go down?" Mr. Cross felt he had been given his congé, so he followed her to the trap-door. George went down first. Edith came next and Mr. Cross made the trap-door fast and followed them down to the sitting-room where Lady Graham and Mrs. Halliday were talking Women's Institute while Mr. Halliday sat resting and, if the truth must be told, in a light slumber, which he really needed.

"I am *so* sorry, Mr. Cross that we shall not have time to see the basement," said Lady Graham, "which I did particularly want to see."

Mr. Cross said he was afraid they had stayed too long on the roof.

"Not that, dear boy," said her ladyship, who had known his parents vaguely and liked this well-mannered personable young man. "I am sure you would have helped me to look at everything, but Robert is coming down tonight and he can so seldom get away that I must be there. Of course you will *quite* understood. Good-bye, Mrs. Halliday. You will all come over to lunch one day perhaps? I shall ring you up when Robert is here as he does so want to talk to your husband. Your darling Sylvia is so beloved at Rushwater and I am sure darling Mamma is pleased. She did so love to see children about the house. Darling Edith, we must go" so Mr. Cross took them across the road to where the Holdings car was drawn up by the Hatch House car.

"Please Mr. Cross, there hasn't been no one after the cars," said Jimmy Panter who was doing gymnastics on the railings. "I'd have given them widdy wen if they did."

"All right, Jimmy," said Mr. Cross. "Just have a look up the street. Lady Graham wants to drive back to Holdings," and Jimmy at once became an A.A. man, with a windmill of arms directing the course of the car. Lady Graham smiled at Mr. Cross, Edith waved her hand. Mr. Cross gave Jimmy a shilling and went back to the house. As he went up the lovely front-door steps he asked himself why he had tipped Jimmy so lavishly, in a way calculated to spoil the market: but there was no answer. The Hallidays were already on the doorstep, so he helped Mr. Halliday into his car.

"It was so kind of you to let us see everything," said Mrs. Halliday. "Will you come to supper—I really can't call it dinner now—one evening this week? Rather dull, I'm afraid, but we should like to see you," and Mr. Cross said he would like it of all things and the car went away.

The air was chill—as when was it not in that horrible summer? A chill wind came from the downs and the front door slammed in its temporary owner's face. He felt for his latch key and remembered he had left it on its chain in his bedroom. Very crossly he went round to the back, came in by the kitchen and so into the house. Dorothy had gone. On the table she had left a tray containing some slices of ham in a cold perspiration, a lettuce, some slices of cold potato and a bottle of beer which had been opened and not properly screwed up again. Mr. Cross looked at them all with intense distaste, lighted the gas fire, unlocked a cupboard and took out a bottle of burgundy which somehow made everything look even nastier. Very crossly he turned off the fire, went to the garage, got into his car and drove straight into Barchester to the White Hart where, being Monday, and leftovers, the meal was almost as nasty as the supper he would have had at home. There was nothing to do in Barchester, so he drove home again and put the car away. The sitting-room with the untouched supper on it looked more depressing than ever. The telephone rang.

"Oh, Mr. Cross, this is Lady Graham," said her ladyship's cooing voice, "we are so disappointed. Robert is down just for the night and he wanted so much to meet you and I said I would ask you to supper, but when I rang up there was no answer. And *did* I leave a scarf anywhere, a kind of pinky-mauve scarf? I *am* so sorry to bother you."

Mr. Cross said, in a polite dégagé way, that he was frightfully sorry he had been out when Lady Graham rang up and if she would wait he would look for the scarf. By the special mercy of Providence, who certainly must have been thinking of something else or she would not have been so agreeable, the scarf was on the seat of the chair where her ladyship had been sitting

"Can I bring it over now, Lady Graham?" he said. "I could be with you quite soon."

"How good of you, dear boy," said Lady Graham, "but you mustn't. You have seen quite enough of us for today. Goble has to be in Hatch Ford tomorrow and he will call for it. It was *such* a charming visit and Robert is so sorry he was not down in time. You must ask us again and you must come to see us. We *never* see you. We will make a plan" and that was the end.

Black fury descended upon Mr. Cross. Everything had gone

wrong. For twopence he would have thrown his horrid supper through the window. But instead of doing that he went to the kitchen with his bottle of Burgundy, poured most of it into a saucepan, added various odds and ends such as cloves, sugar, and cinnamon from the kitchen cupboard, and did what Dorothy called hotting it up. The resulting mixture he strained into a Thermos flask and took it upstairs. He then turned on the hot water in his bath and had a private orgy of sitting in almost boiling water, drinking mulled wine, and reading one of Mrs. Morland's Madame Koska thrillers, after which he went to bed and slept extremely well.

CHAPTER 6

On the whole Edith Graham was glad to be home. She had enjoyed her visit to Hatch House very much. Mrs. Halliday had surrounded her with a kindness none the less motherly for being rather abstracted; which was exactly what she had at home and was used to. Mr. Halliday had been very nice and told her lots of interesting things and shown her an old, cracked and entirely illegible bit of parchment on which the name of Holdings occurred. Sylvia had been so kind and George was very nice and understanding and Mr. Cross at the Old Manor House had been rather dashing and the walks to Bolder's Knob had been great fun. But home was home and later the boys were all coming down together, which did not often happen owing to the variety of their military occupations. And what was more, Uncle David, Lady Graham's younger brother, with his delightful wife Rose, were coming to see them on one of their brief visits from America where they mostly lived. So that even if the weather was beastly, which of late years it ever was, is and apparently (in future years) ever shall be, there would be a great family circle, which suited Edith down to the ground. And perhaps that nice Mrs. Morland who wrote such interesting books would come to lunch or tea one day. So Edith returned to her small county and local duties, for she had a proper country feeling about not giving up a job one had taken on. There is of course a feeling, just as important, that you should not go on

doing a job when you are obviously, by age, ill-health, or slight
dottiness, incapable of attending meetings regularly or remembering people's names and faces, though this feeling Victoria,
Lady Norton, unfortunately did not possess. George Halliday
was busy on the farm and would be going up to Scotland later
for a well-earned holiday, taking his guns with him to shoot
whatever is shootable at that season. So the life at Holdings—as
so often—folded in upon itself, except for Mr. Cross who had
been over twice and played tennis well.

A week or so later the Vicar rang up to ask if he could come
and see Lady Graham. Most of us would at once have had a
(quite unnecessary) attack of conscience and wondered if we had
been accused of brawling in church or coveting our neighbour's
maidservant (a sin which has now, by force of circumstances,
become Common Usage), but to Lady Graham's admirably
balanced mind it was clear that the Vicar wanted to see her, or
otherwise he would not have telephoned, so she asked him to
lunch.

"How good of you to come, Mr. Choyce," she said when he
arrived, a little early for fear of being late. "Robert left all sorts of
messages for you. You know he will be retiring almost at once
and then we can talk about all *sorts* of things," which rather
addled Mr. Choyce's mind, making him feel that Sir Robert
might have objected to the patch on the carpet of the aisle, or the
re-whitewashing of that bit of wall. "We are not a party. Only
my brother David whom you know and his wife and the Pomfrets and our boys of course, only they all went over to Rushwater to look at the new bull and may be a little late. But they
promised to be punctual and as we know, the readiness is all,"
which last words her ladyship spoke with such reverence that it
was clear to the Vicar that she took them for Holy Writ. But he
could not find it in his heart to undeceive her, the more so as he
was not quite sure which of Shakespeare's plays it came from. So
he said how nice that would be and they had not seen David for
quite a long time now that he lived so much in America.

"I know, I know," said Lady Graham sympathetically. "It is the distance. Of course they do fly, which is faster than a ship, but you lose the time, or gain it, whichever you go by. Though I have often wondered how they manage that exactly," said her ladyship, "because when I went to America we had to alter the clocks an hour every day I think it was and in an aeroplane you would have to be altering the clock all the time and *so* confusing to get out and find it was still the same time—I mean the same time had been going on in England all the time you were away, so what *can* have happened to the extra hours?"

Mr. Choyce said he did so sympathise and he couldn't think why all the trains didn't run into each other on the days when they altered the clocks, but he supposed someone arranged those things.

"My husband is a Director of this line," said Lady Graham, "but then he has a very good secretary."

"I wish I had," said Mr. Choyce. "Not that I could afford one and there wouldn't be enough for her to do, but it would be so nice to have someone to help one with letters. Which reminds me that I do want to ask Sir Robert about the lessons."

"Do you mean the teacher at the Infant School?" said Lady Graham. "I remember that she got a picture by Mr. Scatcherd in the raffle at the Bring and Buy Sale we had just when peace broke out. Rather a trying woman."

"But not so trying as she was, I assure you," said Mr. Choyce. "She has even made those Vidler children—not the fish, the odd job one—come to Sunday School. So I told them that if they were good I would let them scrape some of the moss off the graves in that corner where the big sycamore drips over everything and they were delighted. Indeed I found Percy Vidler teaching his younger illegitimate brother and that little girl of young Mrs. Hubback's—the one that is rather spastic—to read off Jno.—I mean John—Vidler's tombstone, the Vidler who was struck by lightning under a tree while—"

"How wonderful of you, Mr. Choyce," said Lady Graham,

tactfully cutting short any further relation of the circumstances under which Jno. Vidler and a foreigner (for so did the older people still very rightly call anyone who lived more than two miles away) were blasted by heavenly vengeance. "No, I meant The Lessons. In church on Sunday. Mrs. Halliday tells me that her husband does not feel up to them," and her doves' eyes became misty, though we think this was more because she heard herself saying the words than because she felt deeply grieved: for one's own voice speaking, if one listens to it, can be very interesting.

"Young Halliday deputised very well," said Mr. Choyce.

"Such a nice boy," said Lady Graham. "And if there was any difficulty—I mean a farmer's Sunday isn't really his own and if it were a case of a cow—"

Mr. Choyce, interrupting what her ladyship was only too obviously about to say, said it had also occurred to him that young Halliday might not always be free. There were, he said, men of riper years who, he felt, might be considered.

"I know *exactly* whom you mean," said Lady Graham, her eyes almost as shining as her mother's used to be at the thought of doing some useful meddling. "You mean that nice young Mr. Cross at the bank, only he will come into the title when his father dies and be in East Barsetshire. But of course no one knows when Lord Cross will die. One never does," said her ladyship in a voice of beautiful muted resignation to the unfathomable ways of Providence.

"No, it wasn't exactly that," said Mr. Choyce. "It was—if I am not asking too much—that I wondered—only just wondered of course, if Sir Robert would perhaps read them. Only if he is here, of course."

"You are always so thoughtful, Mr. Choyce," said Lady Graham. "I think Robert would do beautifully. He has a splendid voice. When he is addressing a meeting he always looks first to see if there are microphones and if there are he says 'Take the damned things away,' which I *know* you will understand. His old friends still call him Barking Bob, because he could make more noise on parade when he was a second lieutenant than any other officer in the Brigade."

"Dear me, how very interesting," said Mr. Choyce. "Of course we should hardly need so loud a voice at the lectern. As for microphones in churches, I can assure you, Lady Graham, that they are works of supererogation."

"And we all know what *they* are," said Lady Graham sympathetically, though we think that this was more in the nature of encouragement to the Vicar than any firm convictions as to what the word meant.

"Yes, indeed," said Mr. Choyce, "they cannot be used—I alter the word slightly—without arrogancy and impiety."

"That is *exactly* what I feel," said Lady Graham, "and when I am in a church, or an abbey, and I hear the words coming out of a box at the back of my neck instead of out of the clergyman's mouth, I can hardly bear it. Last week, when I went to Evensong at the cathedral because the Bishop was preaching and one must be civil occasionally, though it was the *office* I was thinking of, not the man," said her ladyship in a rather learned voice, "I couldn't help looking at the Bishop's face because I was quite near the pulpit and by the time the words came into the back of my neck he was a word ahead of what he was saying, so his mouth was quite the wrong shape for the word we heard."

"Admirably put," said Mr. Choyce. "And why," he continued, with growing fervour, "did people crowd the whole nave of St. Paul's to hear Dr. Donne speak? Because they could *hear* him. And they stood all the time; simply because they could hear every word."

"And loudspeakers at stations," said her ladyship, with a warmth she rarely showed. "Not one word can you hear, not even if the engine stops letting off steam, though I daresay that is the engine-driver's doing quite as much as the engine's."

Mr. Choyce said What were we coming to.

Lady Graham, taking his words at their face value, said she

did not know, but it was almost lunch time and David ought to be here at any minute and she thought that was the Pomfrets' car. And so it was, with the whole Pomfret family, including Lord Mellings, Lady Emily Foster and the Honourable Giles Foster all of whom the Vicar knew quite well, and with them a quiet middle-aged woman known affectionately to all the Pomfrets and Leslies as Merry; once secretary and friend to old Lady Pomfret, the present lord's cousin by marriage; then secretary and more than friend to Lady Emily Leslie, Agnes Graham's beloved mother; and now again at the Towers, serving the family to whom her life had been devoted. Between her and Lady Graham there was a special bond though neither spoke of it, for at Holdings Lady Emily had spent the last years of her life, with Miss Merriman as her faithful secretary-guardian-friend. But even Lady Emily had never managed to encroach upon Miss Merriman's inviolable privacy of thought.

"Dear Ludo," said his cousin affectionately. "You are almost too tall for me to kiss now."

"Not a bit, Cousin Agnes," said Lord Mellings and stooping to her he gave her a kiss and a hug.

"You are just like Uncle Giles," said Lady Graham, alluding to the late Lord Pomfret who was as tall as Lord Mellings, twice as broad and heavy and had—in all her remembrances of him—a large bald head, bushy eyebrows, a heavy moustache of a pale sandy colour and small angry eyes. "And dear Emily and you too, dear Giles," said Agnes, softly embracing the young Fosters.

"I say, Aunt Agnes," said Giles, "can I fish by the hatches after lunch? I've brought my fishing-rod."

"And can I ride on the boar?" said Emily. "I nearly rode on Lord Bond's boar, but he said to get off. I had my school knickers on, so it wouldn't have mattered a bit if I fell off. Oh *can* I, Cousin Agnes?"

"I shouldn't think so," said Agnes calmly. "But you must ask Goble. I never interfere with his pigs."

Giles was heard to say rebelliously that they were Uncle Robert's pigs.

"Of course they aren't, you idiot," said his sister Emily. "No one's animals are their own. They belong to the people that look after them. You know father has to ask Peters when he wants to ride. O.U.T. spells Out," which last remark must appear irrelevant to our reader, but it was the remains of a nursery game in which a rhyme was recited, the reciter saying one word and pointing a finger at each player in turn, the one who got the word Out having to leave the circle till at last only one was left.

Lady Pomfret did not say anything, indeed she barely paused in her talk with Lady Graham, but Emily and Giles saw her face and said no more for the moment. There was a knock at the door.

"*How* often I have told Odeena not to knock I cannot say," said Lady Graham. "Come in, Odeena. What is it?"

"Please marmalady—" said Odeena who, being under strict instructions from cook not to say mum like as if her ladyship was quite common, naturally said it repeatedly from sheer nervousness but tacked my lady onto it whenever she remembered, "please cook says is she to wait?"

Lord Pomfret thought his cousin Agnes must be very short-handed if cook had to wait as well as cook the lunch, but it became clear to him almost at once that it was a question of waiting for other guests. Even as he came to this conclusion there was a roaring, ripping noise outside. The younger members of the party rushed to the window and were rewarded by seeing a very large white sports car in the very middle of which, rather like the conning-tower of a submarine, was a little enclosure in which Uncle David was sitting, driven by Aunt Rose whose driving was second only to Lady Cora Waring's. Rose Leslie got out with a fine display of her perfect legs in the latest U.S.A. nylon stockings and gave a few touches to her face while David, rather more slowly and less showily, followed her example. A rush of the younger children to greet their Uncle—for

so they all called him whether nephews and nieces or cousins—
then took place and he was escorted into the house by a crowd
almost as riotously cheerful as the supers in Titian's Bacchus and
Ariadne. Not that they wished to neglect their Aunt Rose, but
David—perhaps rather unfortunately for himself in some ways—
could not, in spite of receding front hair and a decided tendency to
put on weight, help exercising his old charm, even though he knew
and everyone else knew exactly what he was really like.

"Darling David," said Lady Graham, just not letting her soft
cheek touch his, "and darling Rose! And how are the children?
Darling Dodo and Henry, they are so adorable."

"They are very well," said Rose. "We have left them with
Hermione at Tadcaster."

"I am sure you know Rose's sister," said Lady Graham to the
Vicar, not wishing him to feel out of things. "Hermione, who
married Lord Tadpole. They have a charming old house near
Tadcaster. Tadpole knows absolutely *everything* about shire
horses and is a churchwarden. And that reminds me, Rose, that
we must have a really good talk with Mr. Choyce after lunch,
because he thinks Robert ought to read the lessons on Sunday.
Mr. Halliday is not in a fit condition to read them, which is so
sad," and her ladyship looked at Mr. Choyce rather like a
repentant Magdalen in an Old Master, but not showing the
whites of her eyes so much.

"Tadpole could tell you *all* about it," said Rose. "And what is
more he does. I absolutely adore him and he is an angel and so
sweet to Hermione and worships the ground she treads on—but
he never forgets to see whether it is wheat or oats or pasture.
Quite, quite estate-minded. Not like Robert. We had dinner
with Robert last night, Agnes, and he was in very good form and
is looking forward so much to having a real holiday here."

"Yes, it will be delightful," said Lady Graham, "and I shall ask
him to tell Emily that she simply *cannot* ride on the boar. She
pays no attention to Goble and I feel she is really rather too old
to ride *astride* on him."

"Darling Agnes," said her brother David, "you are quite divine and the one thing unchanged in a changing world. It would *have* to be side-saddle. Europa is always side-saddle in pictures and holding on by one horn."

"But the boar doesn't have *horns*, David," said his sister, "and I don't think holding on by his tusks would be any good because they bend the wrong way. I mean one could not get a safe grip on them."

"Bless your heart, Agnes," said David, "you are the nicest woman I know. Where are your boys?"

"They all went over to Rushwater to look at Martin's new bull in the Old Ford," said Lady Graham, which caused the Honourable Giles Foster to say to his cousin Edith that a bull in a Ford must be an Irish cousin of a dog in the manger; which rather elaborate joke made no impression on her at all.

"Quite right. *Not* funny," said Giles, at which Edith, such is the contrariness of women, did laugh.

"Please my lady," said Odeena, re-materialising and for once remembering cook's awful warnings, "cook says will you wait for the young gentlemen because there's a ever so nice soufflé to follow and she doesn't want to be kept waiting or it's sure to go down."

Giles said he betted it *would* go down if he got near it and was looked at by his mother.

"It's no use waiting for those bad boys," said Agnes to her brother. "We will go straight in, Odeena. You must sit next to Sally, David and tell her *all* about Rushwater Churchill," for David knew a good deal about beef-breeding in the Argentine and it was he who had negotiated the sale of the best bull ever bred at Rushwater; which bull, born on the day when Peace broke out, was—to do homage to our Great Prime Minister— called after him, Rushwater Churchill, breaking the long tradition of a name beginning with R, never interrupted since old Mr. Leslie's father had bred the first great prize winner, Rushwater Ramper.

Even the large round table at Holdings was not large enough for today's party, which with the three Graham boys when they turned up would be a round baker's dozen or more—we have tried to count them but it has come out differently each time— so the elder people sat together at one table, with Edith at the other in charge of her cousins Ludovic, Emily and Giles. To them were very shortly added Lieutenant James Graham and his two brothers, also in or about to be in the Brigade of Guards, very noisily back from Rushwater and full of their exploits which had included trying to ride the new bull-calf whose horns were not yet dangerous though he looked rather like an outsize furniture van on four stubby pillars.

"I say, Ludo, is it true that you know Jessica Dean?" said Lieutenant James Graham. "Some of the fellows said they'd met you in her flat. What's she like?"

"She's awfully like herself and awfully like everyone," said Ludovic, which was not a bad description of that child of peculiarly normal parents, born apparently in the coulisses and a rogue and vagabond by nature as well as one of our most brilliant and hard-working stars.

"How on earth did you get to know her?" said his cousin, apparently hoping for some Open Sesame that could be bought for sixpence or swapped for a fishing-rod in fairly good condition and half a bottle of whiskey.

"It was Mrs. Merton," said Ludovic. "I mean she's Lady Merton now. She was awfully nice and asked us all to dinner and the Clovers were there and then there was a Coronation do at Northbridge and Aubrey said I would do for the young man in a short play he and Jessica were doing—so I acted with him and he said to come to the theatre or their flat whenever I liked, but of course Sandhurst keeps a fellow pretty busy."

"And you are telling *me*, my lad," said his cousin James. "Just you wait till you're in the Brigade. My boots! you'll know what life is then."

"That's a new one," said Ludovic, frankly envious. "Can I have it?"

"My boots, do you mean?" said James Graham. "Of course you can. Only don't swank that I gave it you."

"All right. I'll fight you when we get outside," said Ludovic, by which remark, spoken as easily as if he had said I haven't any change but I'll get some at the post-office, made a strong impression on his older cousin, who might later be his superior officer, and caused him to reflect that Ludo had come on. And then Lord Mellings asked him various questions about his duties and he was able to be the elder cousin again, patronising the younger cousin. Obviously Ludo was a person to be reckoned with, and Lieutenant Graham was about to pursue the subject when his cousin turned to Edith and asked her how life was, leaving James distinctly surprised at Ludo's cool way of going on.

"And tell me about life," said Ludovic to Edith.

"Living, and partly living," said Edith. "I read that bit in a book," she added, seeing her cousin rather surprised.

"I know you did," said Ludovic. "I've read the book too. I didn't understand a lot of it but I liked that bit. What else do you read?"

"Oh, everything," said Edith. "I used to be a poet and I read a lot of poetry. But I think I'm not a poet now. Real poets get published."

"And won't anyone publish you?" said her cousin, amused.

"I haven't tried," said Edith, "but I don't suppose they would. And my poems are mostly what is called extempoor. I don't write them."

"It is usually called ex*tem*pory," said Lord Mellings, obeying the instinct, a strongly ingrained piece of atavism in many of us, that makes us say aloud in a horrid voice "*Con*troversy, you fool!" when some golden-voiced speaker of the wahless has said con*tro*versy. Perhaps it is becoming standard English now. "Do let me hear one," he added quickly, not wishing to appear too pedantic or to hurt Edith. To his surprise his cousin blushed deeply—though very becomingly—and looked confused.

"If you'd rather not—" he said, wondering if she was shy of her own poems and not wanting to press her.

"It's not that," said Edith. "It was me being so beastly at the Mertons' that evening. I feel *horrible*."

"Do you mean when you were staying with us at the Towers last year and we all went to dinner with the Mertons?" he said. "The night Aubrey Clover invented that pretty song about 'Though I am not twenty, sweet'?"

"Yes," said Edith, still pink in the face and her eyes averted. "I am so *awfully* sorry, Ludo."

"That's all right," said Lord Mellings, "but what are you sorry about?"

"Don't you remember, Ludo?" said Edith. "That stupid poem I made when we all had two helpings of the soufflé."

"Oh *that*?" said Lord Mellings, which words always express contempt for and want of interest in a subject. "You mean the one about 'Darling old Mellings, Is covered with swellings'— how did it go on?"

"'Because he did eat, Too much of the sweet,'" said Edith, and looked up at her cousin's face quite piteously. "I'm so *awfully* sorry, Ludo. I've never got over it," which she said with so grown-up a voice that her cousin couldn't help laughing.

"Look here, old girl," he said. "I may have been silly enough to mind then—just for a moment—but I promise you I'd clean forgotten it. You mustn't brood. It doesn't help."

"Do *you* brood, Ludo?" said Edith.

"Like one o'clock," said her cousin. "There are two kinds of Fosters. One is like Giles and Emily. They are called extroverts and so long as they have plenty to do and plenty to eat and plenty of work and fun they don't care a hoot about anything and they usually get on pretty well. The other ones are called introverts— that's father and me; or I, I should say," he corrected himself, at which Edith laughed and looked relieved, for his exordium had rather frightened her. "And they are always wondering if they have said the right thing and if they have annoyed or offended anyone. And if they do make a success of anything they are frightfully pleased just for a moment and then the horrid feeling of you being wrong just because it's you comes back again. It's hell."

Edith, unused to such serious talk, looked rather frightened again.

"Sorry, old thing," said her cousin. "Hell was pure showing-off. Look here, you are absolutely all right. And if I see you going wrong I'll tell you at once."

"Truth-and-honour?" said Edith, in an old schoolroom phrase.

"Truth-and-honour of the Brigade," said Ludovic seriously, just to see how Edith would take it. Like Maud, she took it sedately, though tall and stately she was not, but a very nice girl just grown-up and perhaps—for we do not like to criticise Lady Graham—a little too much kept at home. But it is notoriously difficult not to spoil one's youngest, of whatever sex.

Then the Graham boys, who had been arguing violently with Emily and Giles about how to tame a badger if you could catch one, became so noisy that their mother looked in their direction.

"Pipe down, Emily," said James Graham. "No, Giles, you can't ride the boar, nor can Emily. Ask Goble if you like. He'll say the same."

Emily was heard to say What a boar.

"And that's enough, Emily," said James, rather to her annoyance treating her as a mere schoolgirl, as indeed she was. "I'm not going to have anyone gored while father's away."

"Then can I ride the boar when Uncle Robert comes back?" said Giles, a permanent optimist who will probably bang through the world on his good looks and vitality, to which his cousin James replied that he could ask Uncle Robert himself and Giles subsided.

It must be said to the credit of the young table that though they were all talking and some of them indulging in that unnecessary bickering so extremely boring to others, they had managed not to annoy the grown-ups who were having a conversation of their own, probably just as dull in the perfect witness of all-judging Jove, but more interesting to us. Lady Graham had put Mr. Choyce next to her, partly because she knew it would make him feel safer and partly because he would have Miss Merriman on his other side, an old friend of the years that she with Lady Emily had lived at Holdings. For the moment Miss Merriman was engaged with David, and Lord Pomfret on Lady Graham's other side talking to Rose Leslie, so Lady Graham had the Vicar to herself.

"Now, we will have a cosy talk about Church Matters," said her ladyship, casting such a look of such adoring yet intimate piety at her neighbour as seriously disturbed him, used though he was to her ways. "About those Lessons. I shall speak to Robert about them the very next time he is here."

"That will be most kind, Lady Graham," said Mr. Choyce. "And if I may ask you one more question—" and his voice trailed off, for what he wanted to say was a little difficult.

"Oh yes, *do*," said Lady Graham. "Darling mamma loved asking questions. I remember once at Rushwater, before I was married, old Lady de Courcy came to dinner and darling mamma asked her if George de Courcy was out of prison yet. It wasn't anything very serious he was in prison for, something to do with money matters I think, which of course *no* one can be expected to understand and poor George was quite the most stupid of the family, but Lady de Courcy was so unpleasant that darling papa told Gudgeon—you *must* remember our old butler Gudgeon?"—Mr. Choyce said he did not remember him because he had unfortunately never seen him but he had often heard Lady Emily speak of him and her description was most vivid—"well then, dear Mr. Choyce, you will quite understand me when I tell you that papa ordered Gudgeon to sound the gong, which made a really deafening noise. So Gudgeon, who was a wonderful servant and we all adored him, sounded it very loudly and Lady de Courcy went on speaking all the time exactly like the French Revolution, but none of us could hear what she said though we were all longing to know if George would be free soon, because he used to make skipjacks for us—you know, with the breastbone of a chicken and some twine and some cobbler's wax."

Although her ladyship had evidently come to the end of what she was saying Mr. Choyce was still far from understanding what it was all about, but did not like to say so owing to the reverent adoration he had for her. With the courage a Christian should always show when faced with the Hill Difficulty, he returned to the earlier stage of this conversation and said if it were not presumptuous there was one further request he had to make and before her ladyship could again side-track him, he spoke.

"You know," he said in a low voice, "that Mr. Halliday does not feel equal to reading the lessons which is a great grief to me—"

"And to us all," said Lady Graham, laying a hand upon his clerical coat sleeve and speaking in a muted voice.

"And indeed to us all," said Mr. Choyce. "But I am afraid matters are worse than we knew. I had a letter from him today about resigning his position as churchwarden. He says he cannot conscientiously hold a position if he cannot do the work."

"But of *course* he can't," said Lady Graham. "I have not the least idea what it is, but if he could do it he certainly would. Poor Mrs. Halliday. We must have a *real* talk about it later, Mr. Choyce. I see the soufflé and no one can hear themselves speak when these children are in the room," and indeed a noise as of the Thracian women, strongly supported by the Thracian men, preparing to tear Orpheus to pieces rose from the younger members, the elder of whom were quite old enough to know better. "After lunch when the young people have gone to see the pigs."

Mr. Choyce thanked her, for he knew by long experience that her ladyship, infinite as was her variety of mood and intention, always came back to the subject in hand, though often by devious ways and in her own time, so he turned to Miss Merriman whom he felt, for he was a courteous gentleman, he had too long neglected to address. There were many old friends in the neighbourhood and in the village that Miss Merriman had seen much of during the years that she lived at Holdings and she enjoyed being brought up to date with their births, deaths and marriages. To her Mr. Choyce also confided a little of his difficulty about Mr. Halliday's wishing to resign his church work. She listened with her usual calm and admirable common-sense, sympathised, and said Lord Pomfret had had much the same difficulty a year or so previously, only in his case it had been a churchwarden who had to be asked to resign, a far more difficult and unpleasant business than a voluntary resignation because of ill-health.

"Not anything truly serious, I hope," said Mr. Choyce. "A brother parson of mine up in the north found that his church-warden—it was in a very squalid part down by the docks—was living on immoral earnings. The difficulty was that he was really helping these unfortunate women, who if they had declared all they earned would have been assessed at a fairly high rate for Income Tax, which seems very unfair. So he took care of their money for them and paid them very good interest—in cash of course. Apart from a tenth which he took for the church—and I can assure you it was sadly in need of repair after the bombing—he was merely a steward for them as it were."

Miss Merriman who had listened with interest to this story and rather wondered who was in the right, if anyone, said the case over at Pomfret Towers had been a really serious one. The churchwarden in question had been habitually shooting foxes over a number of years. Mr. Choyce, though not a sportsman himself, was deeply moved. And what made it even worse, Miss Merriman continued, was that he was not the Vicar's warden, but the people's warden, elected by the Vestry, which had led to considerable feeling. Mr. Choyce said he should think so and what a story George Eliot would have made out of it, which effectually put an end to that particular subject. But Miss Merriman, who did not speak without thinking, suggested to Mr. Choyce that Lord Pomfret, if Mr. Choyce cared to talk with him later, might give him some useful hints.

Cook, even better than her word, produced a second soufflé which was dealt with most efficiently by the younger table and then the party began to disperse, some to the farm, some to sit in the Saloon, the large beautiful eighteenth century room with its four long windows looking over the garden to where the Rising winds among the rushes. It had been shut up all through the war and then re-furnished by Lady Graham with some old furniture and family portraits and her second daughter Clarissa, now Mrs. Charles Belton, had with her own peculiar gift touched up the gold on the carved pilasters and plaster swags. Long curtains of faded rose-colour made from some old brocade found at Pomfret Towers had helped to set it off and in the large marble fireplace a wood fire had burned and smouldered ceaselessly through that unsummerish summer. All the young Leslies and Grahams went off to the farm or to the river and the grown-ups were left alone which was the best thing that could have happened to them, for much as we love our young, the young in a loomp (as Lord Tennyson almost wrote) are bad. Taken singly what darlings, how funny, how kind, how touchingly interested in hearing about past days, how splendidly uninterested when they stop feeling interested. Taken in lumps how noisy, uneducated, self-opinionated and incredibly boring. It must however be said in our favour that they judge us less hardly than we judge them, because they have next to no standards and so cannot make comparisons. But bless them all and may we have small doses of them frequently.

"Will you do the talking or shall we both?" said Lord Mellings, who was to be taken to visit the pigs by his cousin Edith. "I really don't know the right things to say about pigs. If it was horses mother knows everything about them. I'm not much good."

"Well, I don't really know much," said Edith. "Emmy did. Goble used to say now she was a young lady as *could* make a silk purse out of a sow's ear and she asked him to save an ear for her if any of the sows died and he was furious. You're looking very large Ludo. You aren't still growing are you?" she added anxiously.

Lord Mellings said he had stopped for the present and hoped he wouldn't go on again as his allowance wouldn't run to any more new suits and if he grew out of his old ones they would be wasted because they would be too long and thin for Giles. Edith said the one nice thing about being the unmarried daughter was that one didn't have to wear other people's clothes.

"Clarissa used to have Emmy's old frocks when they were little girls," said Edith, "and Nurse told me they squabbled over them dreadfully. But I'm an only, so I get everything new."

"It's rather lonely, To be an only," said her cousin. "Or is it?"

"But you are talking in poetry, Ludo," said Edith. "Are *you* a poet?"

Lord Mellings laughed and said he was a doggerel bard, but Edith's education had been rather neglected and though she had loved Gilbert and Sullivan whenever taken to one of those enchanting works, she had never read and probably never heard of the Bab Ballads.

"You are an extraordinary nice girl, Edith," said her cousin, "but terribly uneducated."

"How couldn't I be?" said Edith. "I don't call school education. I call it a dull tunnel that you've got to go through to get out at the other end."

"And what do you do when you get there," said her cousin.

"I don't know," said Edith, in a small desolate voice. "Emmy always loved pigs and cows and Clarissa is so lovely and she can sew so beautifully and paint things. I'm just the runt."

Lord Mellings was not often swift of speech, but when he saw his cousin Edith so suddenly and, he thought, so unjustifiably cast down, he flew to her rescue with the comforting words, "Don't be a juggins."

These beautiful words suddenly opened a window in Edith's mind. Never had she thought of herself as a juggins. Often in her poetic musings she had pretended to be a princess in a tower, or a goose-girl who was really a princess, or a king's daughter with a wicked stepmother, but never had the word juggins come into her life.

"Cousin Agnes is awfully nice," said Lord Mellings, "and so is Cousin Robert and so are you and Clarissa and Emmy and the boys. Goodness! you've got everything. Holdings and the farm, and Cousin Robert doesn't have to keep on wondering if he can afford to live in his own house as father does. You must think again, Edith. Pull yourself together."

"It's awfully good of you, Ludo," said Edith, at once like a true woman licking the hand that chastised her. "I didn't think anyone minded about me not being frightfully good at things."

"I'm not good at them myself," said Lord Mellings.

"But you *are*, Ludo," said Edith. "You are going to be a soldier and you acted with Aubrey Clover and Jessica Dean."

"They made me act," said Lord Mellings. "Look here, Edith, just cheer up. I expect you're a bit lonely here, that's all."

"Lonely?" said Edith, immensely surprised.

"Well, here you are with the boys away and Emmy and Clarissa married and Uncle Robert only down for a week-end, and no one to talk to," said Lord Mellings. "Cousin Agnes is frightfully kind, but you need some friends of your own age. That's one of the things about Eton and Sandhurst, or any school and college come to that. You find lots of fellows and if you don't like some of them you do like others. But if you don't like old Lady Norton you've got to find someone else to like. Who is there here?"

Edith was rather hurt by her cousin's summing up of her life

and said there were the Hallidays and she had a very nice
week-end with them. Her cousin said he was sure she did, but
they were all pretty old.

"Well, Mr. and Mrs. Halliday are," said Edith, "and so are all
the servants, but George isn't. He's *very* nice, Ludo. He was in
a lot of the war with the Barsetshire Yeomanry. He was a
Captain."

"Good fellow," said Lord Mellings. "I wish I'd been old
enough. But I daresay there'll be another war," he added hopefully. "George must be twice my age."

"He *isn't*," said Edith indignantly. "He's—I don't know how
old he is."

"Must be all of thirty," said Lord Mellings. "All the young old
soldiers are thirty now. And probably more. Twice your age."

"He's *not*," said Edith indignantly. "He's not half old enough
for that, so there!" and she pouted, an art now almost forgotten,
but the Leslie and Pomfret background must be taken into
consideration. "And there is Mr. Cross at the bank who is *very*
nice and took us all over the house and is coming to play tennis
this afternoon, and he was in the war with George," said Edith.
"And his father is Lord Cross. I think it's rather dull to have the
same name as your father if he's a lord."

Lord Mellings said it rather depended on the person's own
dullness. Nothing could be duller than young Lord Norton
whose family name was also Norton, but Lord Bond over at
Staple Park was awfully nice and kind and his children were all
Bonds and seemed very nice too. Edith said, rather wistfully,
that it must be rather fun to get about in the county and see
people, but mother didn't like her to go about alone.

"Do you always do what Aunt Agnes says?" said Lord Mellings and Edith, surprised at such a question, said Of course and
what about the pigs.

During this talk they had been walking slowly and with no
particular objective, but now they turned their steps towards the
farmyard which was separated from the garden by a lane which

the farm carts and the tradesmen used. Just as they were about to cross the lane a small but dashing grey sports car came round the bend and pulled up when it saw them.

"Oh, it's you," said Edith, recognising Mr. Cross. "You've got into the back drive but it doesn't matter. This is my cousin Ludovic, his father's Lord Pomfret. This is Mr. Cross, Ludo, who let mother and me see the Old Manor House."

Mr. Cross got out of his car and shook hands.

"I think our progenitors meet in the House," he said to Lord Mellings, "that is if yours ever goes there. Mine says it would be hell unless you thought of it as a club, so he does. But a respectable hell, I gather."

"Father says he'd like to get letters patent to have himself un-earled," said Lord Mellings, "but he doesn't know if it would work."

"Tell him from me," said Mr. Cross, "that a title is the only way to get servants now, unless you're a film star. It just shows how snobbish servants are. By the way, who do you think father's got for a butler now—or ought I to say whom?" he enquired, rather of himself than of the others.

Lord Mellings said was it the Chancellor of the Exchequer, at which Mr. Cross let out a sympathetic guffaw and Edith wondered what it was all about, her wonder being so apparent that Mr. Cross was smitten with remorse and said the present Chancellor of the Exchequer was called Butler. "It's Peters!" Mr. Cross added triumphantly to Lord Mellings.

Lord Mellings said he was so sorry but he couldn't do it.

"Oh! Mr. Cross," said Edith, "not the one who used to be at the Towers? Merry used to tell me about him. He was the butler when she was with old Aunt Edith, Ludo's aunt."

"Well, she wasn't exactly my aunt," said Lord Mellings, "she was father's second-cousin-by-marriage or something and I never saw Peters—at least I suppose I did when I was about two, but I can't remember. He must be frightfully old now."

"He said fifty-seven when father asked him," said Mr. Cross, "and he's extremely spry—if you can call it spry to go about like a theatrical ghost. That would have made him—" but to discuss the age of someone when you have not the faintest notion when he was born and have not seen him for some fifteen or sixteen years is bricks without straw; nor could anyone be certain if Peters had given his right age, for some employers prefer un-skilled youth to skilled and perhaps rather overbearing age; or the other way round.

"I'll tell you what," said Mr. Cross, "couldn't you come over and see him? I know he'd be frightfully pleased to meet you. He is always talking about your father and the glories of the Tow-ers," and as neither of his hearers had more than a very slight acquaintance with Mrs. Samuel Adams Mr. Cross's opening words passed un-noticed.

"The best thing," said Edith, suddenly remembering that she represented the house of Graham for the moment, "would be if you would come and look at the pigs, Mr. Cross, and then come back to tea. Mother would *love* to hear about Peters and so would Miss Merriman—she was old Aunt Edith that I'm called after's secretary then, before Aunt Edith died."

"Oh, thanks most awfully, I'd love to," said Mr. Cross. "Can I leave the car here?"

"No, you can't," said Edith, "because it's really only the farm lane and if anything does come through you'd have to put your car right into the ditch. It's just wide enough to hold the pig-van, only if it's been raining a lot we have to put some plants over the ditch at the turn, or it goes in on one wheel, just as it did on the day the Barsetshire Agricultural had its meeting at Rising Castle. Lord Stoke *will* not have his roads widened on the estate. He says they were good enough for his father and they are good enough for him," at which Mr. Cross laughed and said he liked Lord Stoke immensely. And though he did not say so, he liked that pretty, perky (his word, not ours) Graham girl im-mensely. And, come to that, he thought Lord Pomfret's tall boy a distinctly decent chap.

"If you drive on just round that bend you'll find plenty of room to park," said Edith.

So Mr. Cross drove slowly on and by the time they had caught up with him he had turned his car and parked it with its tail to the farmyard wall, out of everyone's way.

"I shall introduce you to our bailiff, Goble," said Edith to Mr. Cross with a sudden Lady-of-the-Manor air which amused him. "He is the best pig man in West Barsetshire. I don't know about East Barsetshire."

"You wouldn't," said Mr. Cross cheerfully. "It is inhabited by Yahoos and Cocqcigrues."

"I know Yahoos *very* well," said Edith. "In fact since I was quite small, because I could read when I was five," to which her cousin Mellings said not to be a prig.

"I'm *not* a prig, Ludo," said Edith indignantly. "I just happened to be able to read; so I did read. Everything."

"Have you ever read the Bible?" said Lord Mellings.

"Of *course*," said Edith indignantly. "Heaps of it. Not all the begot bits and the dull bits."

"All right, my girl, you have *not* read it," said Lord Mellings. "I did, when I had that go of rheumatic fever at my prep. school. I suppose they call it something else now and give you P and O or something of the sort that only has initials and don't let you read because it might affect your eyes."

"Did it affect them?" said Mr. Cross.

"No, sir," said Lord Mellings, but so skillfully that Mr. Cross was not quite sure whether this lanky young man was addressing him with quite unnecessary respect, or as one rather old fashioned gentleman to another.

"Then, sir, I withdraw the question," said Mr. Cross, at which Lord Mellings burst into a quite young laugh, so Mr. Cross and Edith laughed too.

"Now," said Edith, "we will go and see the pigs and I will introduce you to Goble. He is a dear, but he has been rather above himself ever since his best sow got the Omnium Cup at

the Barsetshire Agricultural last year." So they went across the
yard and through the great barn on the opposite side, full of
warm comfortable smells of straw and sacks, to where lay what
we might almost call a pig-colony of neat brick-paved sties and
above each sty the name of its present owner. Leaning on the
door of one of the sties was the bailiff, Goble, in his Sunday
blacks, contemplating what we can only call a spate of piglets, so
did they perpetually move and push and shove and nose each
other out of the way the better to get at an immense matron
lying on her side half asleep among them.

"Hullo, Goble," said Edith. "I've brought Lord Mellings to
see Holdings Hangover. And this is Mr. Cross. His father lives
in East Barsetshire. He's Lord Cross."

Goble touched his Sunday bowler and said he didn't know
much about those parts, rather letting Mr. Cross infer that East
Barsetshire was probably a Terra Incognita, inhabited by An-
thropophagi and men whose heads Did grow beneath their
shoulders.

"Good-afternoon," said Mr. Cross. "She's a fine sow. And
that's a handsome fellow you've got next door. He must be about
fifty score. Is he a Porkminster?"

"That's right, sir," said Goble, concealing very well his surprise in finding the young gent (for so in his mind he had called
Mr. Cross) so knowledgeable about pigs. "White Porkminster
he is, sir. Holdings Hangover. Second prize last year at the
Barsetshire Agricultural. It did ought to have been a first, but
Mr. Gresham he thought different. It's a free country they say,
but there's a sight too much freedom sometimes to my way of
thinking."

"Oh Mr. Gresham isn't a bad sort when you know him," said
Mr. Cross, "but he's got a bee in his bonnet about White
Porkminsters. His line is Norfolk Nobblers."

"Norfolk Nobblers. Ar," said Goble, "a Norfolk Nobbler he
may run to weight, he may do for curing, he might pass for pork
if so be no one was too particular, but you'll never get good bacon

from a Nobbler, not if you was to cross them with the Lord Mayor himself. I've been minding pigs, sir, father and son, ever since there was pigs in West Barsetshire and when I say Norfolk Nobblers are a mucky lot, sir, I say what I mean, be the other who he may. And what's more, I mean what I say."

"Oh, I say Goble," said Lord Mellings, "I've got a message for you from my uncle Roddy Wicklow—father's agent, you know. He wants to know if you could come over some time. He's putting up some sties for the new cottages and he'd like to have a talk with you."

"Now, Mr. Wicklow, that is a man as I would call—well, I don't exactly know what I'd call that man," said Goble, thoughtfully scratching the sow's back with his stick. "He's a man, my lord, as takes a power of knowing, but when you know him, well, you know him; and I can't say fairer."

Murmurs, as from a Shakespeare crowd, of "No, one can't," "That's perfectly right," Uncle Roddy must have been born in a pig-sty" rose from his audience.

"Well, my lord, you tell Mr. Wicklow I've got to go over to Nutfield on Tuesday next week about a boar and I'll come up to the estate office any time he chooses to name. And talking of boars, my lord, just come and have a look at his lordship here—not meaning any offence, my lord" and he led them to a kind of luxury sty where an immense double-cube was lying half asleep. It opened one small, red, malevolent eye, looked at them with disgust and shut it again.

"That's Him, my lord," he said reverently. "Holdings Blunderbore. If he doesn't get a First at next year's Barsetshire Agricultural, my name's Old Gunder."

"Who on earth is Old Gunder?" said Mr. Cross.

"That's what Mr. Wickham asked, him as is Mr. Merton's agent over at Southbridge, sir. Sir Noel I should say, but there's too much of this baro-nighting. It fair gets a man mixed."

"But Mr. Merton—I mean Sir Noel—isn't a baronet, he's only a knight," said Edith, "and he's awfully nice."

"So is Lady Merton," said Lord Mellings, loyally supporting his cousin Edith and also, we may say, the Mertons through whose hospitality he had met the Aubrey Clovers.

Goble said nice was as nice did, and anyway it was Mr. Wickham as had asked who Old Gunder was. Well, he continued, Old Gunder it always had been and that was that and Mr. Wickham had gone on about Gundric's Fossway till a man didn't know if he was setting on his head or his heels, so Edith thanked him very nicely for letting them look at the pigs and took her party away.

"There is nothing I like so much as talking with my father's tenants," said Mr. Cross, "but Lord! how they do go on. I daresay Old Gunder *is* Gundric but as no one knows who Gundric was that doesn't get us much farther. Barsetshire is full of things of that sort."

Edith said they had better get back as the boys wanted to play tennis and had Mr. Cross brought his racquet, which he had and apologised for not having proper tennis things but it really wasn't worthwhile when one played so little, at which moment there was a great irruption of Grahams into the yard, accompanied by Giles Foster and by their Leslie cousins who had all three come over in a very battered Ford which they had bought with their united savings and were finding more expensive in the way of repairs than they had bargained for.

"I say, Goble," said Giles, "can I ride the boar?"

"Now, Mr. Giles, that's what you can't do," said Goble, "and well you know it."

"Oh, I say, Goble!" said Giles reproachfully. "Major did ride one of your boars once."

"And a good hiding he got for it," said Goble.

"Richly deserved," said Major rather sententiously. "All right. If we can't ride the boar we'll go on the river."

"We can't all go on the river," said Minor. "Let's toss up for who has the punt and who has the canoe," which led to a very inconclusive argument as to how you could get ten people, if you included Edith and Emily, into a small punt and a canoe: which was impossible, or at any rate uncomfortable and slightly dangerous if one went too near the left bank at that muddy bend.

Edith, who did not care particularly for boats, suggested to her favourite Leslie cousin, Minor, that some of them should go to the Vicarage and Minor could climb the monkey-puzzle.

"Good girl, Edith!" said Minor. I had a go at the Mertons' monkey-puzzle last summer and got into a frightful mess. I took all the skin off my knee and I got a great scratch on my arm and a nasty tear in my shirt. I don't know what happened to my trousers but Nanny Twicker—that's the Mertons' old Nanny—said they weren't hardly decent and made me take them off and sit in her dressing-gown while she mended them. Oh Lord! it's beginning to rain again!"

And so it was and they all went back rather disconsolately to Holdings. But there was a fire in the Saloon, where there were also a piano and a gramophone and a wireless, and as nearly everyone had the splendid indifferences of our modern young to mixed noises, joy was unconfined. The boys rolled up the carpet and laid it neatly on one side, everyone took it in turns to look after the gramophone and what with the good wood fire and singing and dancing and a great deal of foolish happy laughter, the grey afternoon passed very pleasantly.

Those who knew Rushwater in its earlier days will perhaps remember Lady Emily Leslie's French maid Conque, who now lived with a Rushwater ex-housekeeper on an annuity left to her by her late mistress, quarrelling with her landlady quite frightfully. Once a year it was Lady Graham's kind habit to invite Conque—better known in the kitchen as Miss Conk—to spend a week or ten days at Holdings, for which period Cook was able to tolerate her,—but not a day longer, said Cook, for there were some people whose names she did not wish to mention who would make the milk turn in the fridge—on which visits Conque was always given the bedroom she used to occupy when Lady Emily was living at Holdings and was on the whole no pleasure to anyone. But duty to old servants is a form of chains and slavery that must be endured in common decency. Soon there will not be a single old servant left and then we shall probably mourn what we dreaded and on the whole disliked. As there was not now a housekeeper's room at Holdings, a corner of the large kitchen had been partly partitioned from the rest. Here Conque was usually to be found, and hither Edith went with David in tow, just as Clarissa used to follow or accompany him when she was Edith's age.

"I've brought Uncle David to see you, Conque," said Edith and stood aside to let David pass, who heartily embraced his mother's old maid and then felt with considerable satisfaction that *that* was over. Edith looked with satisfaction at her work and went away.

"Mais, asseyez vous donc, monsieur David," said Conque, who had not troubled to get up.

Against his own will David sat down on an obvious kitchen chair with a hard wooden seat and asked Conque how she was.

"Bad," said Conque. "Depuis qu'on m'a opérée, monsieur David—"

"Je sais, je sais, ma pauvre Conque," said David. "Vous êtes toujours fatiguée; c'est comme un énorme poids qui vous pèse sur l'estomac; vous avez des maux de tête affreux, mais affreux; la migraine ne vous quitte pas; il y a une jambe qui est quasi engourdie de sorte que vous trébuchez à chaque pas; la nourriture vous répugne; vous ne dormez pas et pour peu que vous dormiez vous avez des cauchemares où miladi vous appelle et vous ne pouvez pas lui repondre. Et le révérend père Ossquince ne vous comprend pas, étant anglais, de sorte qu'on ne sait pas si le bon Dieu vous a pardonnée ou non."

"Quant à ça, monsieur David," said Conque, suddenly very much alert, "j'ai tout réglé avec le bon Dieu. Il connait la valeur d'une bonne femme de chambre lui, allez. Sinon, à quoi serait-il bon?"

"Well, don't say that to Father Hoskins," said David, slightly alarmed at the spirit he had conjured up. "How Edith has grown. She is a very charming young person. We must find a husband for her, Conque."

"Osbond!" said Conque. "Et où trouverait-on des Osbond ici? Who can she see, my poor young lady? There is yong M. Halliday. When I say yong it is because his father is old, but he is not young. There is no yong man here. In France—"

"Yes, Conque, we all know about France," said David. "She would be married straight out of the convent to a very rich old nobleman, but as she has never been in a convent she can't very well marry out of one. What about that young Cross? He seems a nice fellow."

"Il sera baron après la mort de son père," said Conque. "C'est déjà quelquechose. Ils ont tous les deux le goût de la campagne."

"Well Conque, you are a woman of the world," said David. "You have lived long with her ladyship and made your observations of human nature. But one never knows. Their children might be idiots or hydrocephalous."

"As for that word, I do not know him," said Conque. "Les enfants, ça vient du bon Dieu."

"Or a gooseberry bush," said David, piously relying on Conque's almost total ignorance of the English language after some forty years' residence in England.

"Ecoutez, monsieur David, que je vous dise" said Conque, bending forward mysteriously. "Il y a un moyen de tout arranger."

"Go ahead then," said David who, as always, was already beginning to be tired of the occupation of the moment.

"Le jeune baron," said Conque.

"What baron?" said David. "All the lords round here are married like Bond and Lufton, or about a hundred like Lord Stoke."

"Mais, son cousin, n'est-ce-pas?" said Conque, raising her eyes to heaven to witness the stupidity of men. "Milord Mellings."

"My hat!" said David and sat stunned.

"Enfin, un marriage entre cousins c'est pas défendu ici," said

Conque. "Ils sont à peu pres du même âge. Ils auront quelques sous. Ils feront de beaux enfants. Et dire que miladi ne pourra pas voir ses arrière-petits fils!" and Conque wiped her eyes.

"Now, look here Conque, let's get this right," said David, who although he spoke French well for ordinary circumstances did not feel equal to unravelling the laws of God and man about marriage. "Old Lord Pomfret was Mamma's brother. But he hadn't any children alive. This Lord Pomfret's father was a very distant cousin of old Lord Pomfret. There's practically no relationship at all. Lord! to think I never thought of that! Now, look here, Conque, not one word of this to anyone. Not even to Father Hoskins."

"Ce n'est pas au père Ossquince que je débiterais des affaires de famille," said Conque scornfully. "Il peut bien se contenter de mes petits péchés. Et s'il n'en est pas content, je saurai bien lui en fabriquer d'autres, allez!"

"Well, Conque, you are a clever woman," said David getting up. "But don't say a word. Honour among thieves."

"Ce serai drôle, enfin, l'honneur entre les tamis, monsieur David," said Conque, "mais si vous le désirez . . ."

"There's a dear old Conque," said David and with a hearty kiss he left her, relieved to have done his duty and much interested in Conque's proposals. No business of his to match-make, but certainly Conque had an idea. Still, Edith was young and there was plenty of time. Girls now were still girls at thirty and more. Ludo though the same age in years as Edith was much younger in some ways because he was a man. On the other hand he seemed to have come on a lot and developed plenty of horse-sense. He tried to remember how old his sister Agnes was when she married Robert Graham. It was her first season, so probably she was about the age Edith was now. And look at Agnes, the adored and adoring mother of three fine sons and three good-looking daughters, two of them happily if not excit-ingly married. On the other hand Robert had been a good deal older than Agnes and indeed still was. Well, thank goodness his own children, Dorothy (after his wife's masterful and deceased mother Lady Dorothy Bingham) and Henry (after old Mr. Leslie), would not be old enough to give him trouble for a long time. So he went back to the drawing-room where Lady Graham with the Pomfrets and Miss Merriman and his wife Rose were talking family talk very comfortably. Mr. Choyce was also there, not altogether of his own wish for he felt he might be an outsider, but Miss Merriman had suggested that he should have a word with Lord Pomfret about the business of the churchwarden, and if he left the party he would be but a Hireling Shepherd, forgetting his flock while he toyed with—but at that moment a large picture with that name, by a member of the Pre-Raphaelite Brotherhood, of a pleasant if blowsy shepherdess sitting in a meadow whose every blade of grass and petal of flower was clearly painted, on the verge of succumbing to the importunities of a farm labourer (also red in the face with what one regretfully had to consider to be concupiscence, though it was not a word one had ever said aloud) came very vividly to his mind and confused him a good deal. However as the others were talking busily he had time to reflect that they were in a drawing-room and not at all red in the face and perhaps no one had noticed. As indeed they had not.

"How long will you and David be in England?" said Lady Graham to Rose Leslie, to which Rose replied that they were flying back in about a fortnight with the children and how lucky it was that they had an aunt to go to in England as Dodo was seven years old now and Henry six and Dodo had begun to be unhappy when her parents went away. But luckily in America Martin's mother would always have them to stay with her, which was almost like being at home.

"Oh dear, how *old* it all makes one feel," said Lady Graham, for Martin's mother had married an American so many, many years ago, after Martin's father had been killed towards the end of the 1914 war, and had become entirely American. "Darling mamma, I believe she was always thinking of Martin's father.

You know she was talking to Martin when she died and she thought he was his own father coming back to her from the moors when they used to go to Scotland."

"Listen, Agnes," said Rose, "I want to ask you something."

"Do," said Lady Graham, looking at her sister-in-law with interest. "But if it is anything important you had better wait till Robert comes down. He is much less busy now. It is really ridiculous to think that he will be retired so soon."

"Never mind about that for the moment," said Rose. "David and I are flying back in about a fortnight. Will you let Edith come with us and stay a couple of months, or longer if she likes? We don't think she is seeing enough life. Not your fault, darling, but it *is* like that in England now so often. Half your young people live in digs in town and have jobs and think they are seeing life. Take it from me they are *not*. But Edith isn't seeing it either. Has she had any love affairs? Oh, I don't mean affairs in that sense. I mean has she fallen in love with the second footman or the local scoutmaster, or the vicar?"

"Of course we have never had a footman," said Lady Graham. "Nor did darling mamma. We had Gudgeon, our old butler at home, and there was Walter who was under him, but not really a footman. I don't think they had footmen after the first war. Before that they did, with yellow and black striped waistcoats I cannot think why like wasps."

"Then I take it that Edith has no young men to break her heart about?" said Rose. "That's all right. Now, Agnes, just listen. When will Robert be down next?"

Lady Graham said the following weekend for certain.

"Then just listen to me," said Rose. "When Robert comes down, tell him that Edith is going to America with us and we'll take great care of her and send her back safe and sound and with a bit of world-sense."

"I suppose I have kept her too much at home," said Lady Graham placidly. "I was very happy at home with darling mamma till I married. Did I ever tell you how Robert proposed to me?"

"I'll say you did," said Rose very firmly. "I sometimes say it aloud in my sleep," and then she felt sorry, fearing she might have hurt her gentle sister-in-law, but her words had rebounded from Agnes leaving no mark at all. Like the rhyme about "Feather-bed 'twixt castle wall And heavy brunt of cannon ball," Rose thought, those lines from we know not where suddenly coming into her mind.

"Then that's settled," said Rose.

"I must see about her passport and some clothes," said Agnes, but Rose said Certainly not. All Agnes had to do was to see about the passport and deliver her daughter at Porridge's where she and David were staying the night before they sailed and she, Rose, would see about the reservations and would supervise Edith's trousseau in New York where they really understood clothes and Agnes must not bother about dollars because David was making enormous amounts of money somehow or other.

"Then you had better tell her about it yourself, Rose darling," said Lady Graham. "I daresay I shall hardly know her when she comes back. I know when that dreadful Hermione Rivers went to America to give talks—though goodness knows she talked more than enough here and Robert said he would not have her in the house again—she came back looking quite peculiar."

"She always does. Dreadful woman," said Rose, quite without heat. "You know what happened to poor George?"

"*Not* a stroke?" said Lady Graham. "His father died of one. At least he began dying with the first, but couldn't really manage it till the third, which was so distressing."

"Worse than that," said Rose. "When Hermione came back she was going to write a book about a woman who has a terrific affair with an English boy who is cow-punching on a dude ranch in Texas and then sees the light and comes back to her husband."

Lady Graham said placidly that she was sure Hermione could do it, because it was just the same as all her other books so everyone would read it. "Look at that nice Mrs. Morland," she said. "She tells everyone that she writes the same book every year and it is quite true and as everyone reads her book every year that is very nice. I want to get her to come to lunch before you go. Could you come down if I did?" but Rose could not promise.

"And now do listen for one moment, Agnes," she said, "because I haven't finished about Hermione."

"I know exactly what Hermione did," said Agnes, who had, in the loving words of her brother David, the occasional flashes of genius vouchsafed to idiots. "She wanted to try it out on George. But dear George always sleeps in the Little Tulip Room now. He showed it to me when I went to lunch with him because I was staying quite near, and I thought he had made it extremely comfortable."

"So all that happened," said Rose, quite unperturbed by her sister-in-law's second-sight, "was that she went straight into George's old bedroom and all the lights fused and as she didn't know where George was she had to get back to her own room and couldn't put it down in a note book or whatever authors do because everything was dark. There were some matches on the mantelpiece but as there weren't any candles, that was that."

"It was just the same at the Towers when darling mamma was a girl," said Agnes. "Oil lamps everywhere and candlesticks for everyone to take up to bed. I wonder where all the children are. I expect they are in the Saloon."

Rose, who had thought much the same, considering the noise that had been coming from that direction, agreed.

"Then we will have tea in the dining-room," said Lady Graham. "And I must not forget that Mr. Choyce wants to talk to Gillie about churchwardens." Rose said she would go and have a word with Conque and tell Aggie about tea in the dining-room and went away.

"And now, Mr. Choyce," said Lady Graham, interrupting with gentle ruthlessness his gossip with Miss Merriman, "you must come and talk to Gillie. He is simply longing to talk about churchwardens" and having thoroughly embarrassed both gentlemen by this explanation she settled herself with Miss Merriman.

Regarded as a helpful discussion of churchwardens the conversation could not be regarded as a complete success. Lord Pomfret certainly did not wish to bring up the subject unless pressed. Mr. Choyce did not wish to press his private worries upon Lord Pomfret unless requested to do so. However the question of tithes made a good stop-gap and both gentlemen much enjoyed it, especially when it transpired that Mr. Choyce's father had been an invalid and in his later years had always wintered in Florence where he had met and cordially disliked Lord Pomfret's father. And as Major Foster had been an unloving father and not particularly kind to his wife, Lord Pomfret had no filial feelings about him except of relief when he had died. Not that Gillie Foster, as he was then, wished to be any nearer the Pomfret earldom, but he was willing to pay that price, and had given full value for his position and his responsibilities ever since.

"I wonder if I might consult you—I might even say trouble you—about a small matter," said Mr. Choyce.

Lord Pomfret, one of whose many duties in the station to which it had pleased the death of his predecessor to call him was to listen to people, said in his courteous tired voice that he would gladly hear what Mr. Choyce had to say and would do anything in his power.

"It is about churchwardens," said Mr. Choyce. "I understand from Miss Merriman that you have had considerable trouble with one."

"Yes. A very unpleasant affair," said Lord Pomfret. "This man—I need not mention his name for you will doubtless have heard it—had been shooting foxes for a long time. It was well known, but a difficult thing to bring forward or to prove. In fact there *was* no proof except that everyone knew it."

Mr. Choyce said of course the name must not be brought in, though secretly he was determined to find out who it was and perhaps contribute a short article to the Church Times on the subject, not mentioning names or places, and with a reference to the Song of Solomon, Chapter Two, Verse Fifteen. And it must, he continued, have been extremely awkward for everyone. Luckily, Lord Pomfret said, the person in question was the choice of the Vestry, so the Vicar was not dragged in more than was necessary. Mr. Choyce said it would indeed have been unfortunate for the Vicar had he had to have been dragged in and then wondered if he had said more than he meant. However, Lord Pomfret continued, the man resigned so no further steps had to be taken. Mr. Choyce said might he enquire whether Lord Pomfret knew the Archdeacon's Registrar who was a recent appointment, not personally known to him. Lord Pomfret said he had met him somewhere and couldn't remember his name. Mr. Choyce thanked him profusely. The momentous interview came to an end and tea was announced in the dining-room where, with extra chairs brought in by the boys and a certain amount of squeezing, everybody was seated. There was no formal arrangement. The young people by natural gravitation sat more or less together, but some preferred the grown ups, and some grown ups were happy to sit with the children, the Vicar being one.

It has been noticed that people who are not parents often have a peculiar fondness for children. This is sometimes attributed to a very beautiful nostalgia for a gift denied to them—dream-children, flowers that have only bloomed in imagination—but we think it is rather because they have not the faintest idea how dreadful children are. Even schoolmasters, those incorrigible and visionary optimists, often live and die under the illusion that children are plants, some frail, some sturdy, to be fostered, guided and helped, full of fine thoughts and impulses, only needing a firm guiding hand to become human. Parents know better. Though Mr. Choyce had dealt with his industrial parish faithfully and well he had never had to suffer the joyous patter of little feet far too early in the morning, or The infant crying in the night (blast it), An infant crying for the light (you know *perfectly* well you don't need it: go to SLEEP), And with no language but

a cry (Listen: if you say you want a drink of water *once* more I'll
SMACK you).

"I hope you had a nice afternoon, Mr. Choyce," said Edith,
feeling responsible as deputy-hostess for her guest's entertainment. "We went to see the pigs and then it rained so we couldn't
play tennis or go on the river, so we had the wireless and the
gramophone in the Saloon."

"I shouldn't think the wireless was much help today," said the
Vicar, who always got on very well with Edith. "They were doing
that Symphony for two orchestras and a military band and the
chimes of Big Ben by Hvord Krogsbrog, weren't they? I can't
think why a Swede wants Big Ben."

"Oh, *that*," said Edith, which simple words convey eternal con-
demnation. "Anyway it only lasts for half an hour and then there
was some *proper* music, Schubert, so we invented a dance for a bit
of it and then we had the gramophone. Minor is awfully good."

"Now, who is Minor?" said Mr. Choyce. "Your cousins are a
bit mixing for outsiders, you know."

"Oh, he's really John Leslie," said Edith, "but Uncle John is
John too, so we always call Minor Minor because he's the
middle one. I say, Mr. Choyce, I had such a lovely time with the
Hallidays. They are so kind. If only Mr. Halliday weren't so ill it
would be perfect. He said he couldn't go on being a churchwarden because you oughtn't to say you'll do things you can't do."

Mr. Choyce said he was extremely sorry to hear it.

"I had a talk with George about it on the telephone this
morning," said Edith, rather importantly, "and he says his father
is going to write to you and say how sorry he is but he can't be a
churchwarden any more. I expect you'll get the letter tomorrow
morning, only one never knows if they'll remember to post
letters before three o'clock in that little letter-box outside Hatch
House. I'm so sorry about him."

"So am I," said Mr. Choyce. "And we can't elect a new Vicar's
Warden till the Easter Vestry."

"Then what do you do?" said Edith. "You can't *make* Mr.

Halliday not resign. Unless perhaps you got a certificate or something from Dr. Ford. He's awfully nice about helping people."

"It's a rather complicated business," said Mr. Choyce, amused
by Edith's parochial conversation. "If Mr. Halliday isn't well
enough, he must resign. We can't have him tiring himself. As he
is Vicar's Warden I can appoint someone un-officially to take his
duties till next Easter, and then we have a proper election."

"I say, *do* have father," said Edith. "He'd love it."

"There is nothing I should like better," said Mr. Choyce. "But
as Sir Robert is hardly ever here it might be difficult for him" and
we think it shows how very nice Mr. Choyce was to think of the
difficulty for Sir Robert rather than of the difficulty for himself.

"But father retires this month," said Edith. "Didn't you know
that?"

A great surge of hope rose in Mr. Choyce's breast, but he only
said to Edith that it would be very pleasant to see more of Sir
Robert.

"But what is not so pleasant for me," said Edith, "is that I am
going to America with Uncle David and Aunt Rose, just when
father will be here."

"Ungrateful girl!" said Mr. Choyce, who was very fond of
Edith. "All this and America too. You won't be in America for
ever and when you come back your father will have settled into
his duties here."

"And he reads aloud *beautifully*," said Edith, forgetting her
own woes. "He used to read Tom Sawyer and Huckleberry Finn
aloud to us when we were small and we adored it. He did all the
different voices."

"That is partly why we want him," said Mr. Choyce, wondering at the back of his mind whether Sir Robert would want to
read the Scriptures in character as it were.

"Of course he won't be able to spare a *lot* of time," said Edith
importantly, "because he has so many county things to do. He
is going to stand for all sorts of councils and be on committees
and all the things he couldn't do when he was in London. But he

is highly conscientious," she added, with the amusing grown-up air of a youngest child who has always lived among her elders. Then Mr. Choyce went away to take the Evening Service, and the rest of the party began to think of leaving, David and Rose Leslie being the first to go.

"I do wish you weren't going, Aunt Rose," said Edith.

> "'You are the Rose
> That always goes.
> Ah, do not go
> We miss you so.'"

"If you can do that in the States they'll pay you a hundred dollars a minute anywhere," said her Uncle David. "Won't they, Rose?" at which words his wife made a face of not approving his silliness.

Edith said with considerable dignity that she was only an amateur and could not take money, and then became a not-so-old young lady, hugged her uncle and aunt fondly, and came out onto the doorstep to see them off. The rain was coming down as if it had just had the very original idea of raining, the sky was one horrible slate-colour, a chill wind blew.

"'In August
Away I must' and at every other season of English weather too," said David, and with a last and very loving embrace of his sister Agnes he got into the car and drove away. The Leslie boys then suggested that their Graham cousins should all get into their old Ford and go to the Barchester Odeon on the way home; but as the last bus left Barchester at six o'clock on Sundays the Graham boys would not have got home unless their Leslie cousins drove them back which would have made them very late and Leslie Major and Mother would worry, so this plan was rejected. The Leslies thanked their Aunt Agnes with many hugs, embraced their cousin Edith with equal fervour and want of interest and were just going off to their car which they had left at the farm when Mr. Cross spoke up.

"And whatever you do, *don't* break down in the back drive," said Mr. Cross, "because you'll never get going again and I shan't be able to get past you" which advice was received with derision. The Pomfrets also took their leave, but not before they, Miss Merriman and Lady Graham had settled with Mr. Cross a day when they would come over to see Peters, the Pomfret Towers ex-butler, bringing Edith with them.

"Won't you come too, dear Ludo?" said his cousin Agnes.

Lord Mellings said he would like it very much and both Lord and Lady Pomfret sent messages of kind remembrance to Peters. Then they drove away in the cold rain and only Mr. Cross was left.

"Why not stay to supper, Mr. Cross?" said Lady Graham. "It is only Edith and myself, but it will be hot. My cook does not approve of cold Sunday supper. Nor does Robert. You must meet him when he comes down. He will be here a great deal more now, which is delightful," and of course Mr. Cross said he would love to stay and hoped so much to see Sir Robert later.

"I must go and have a word with Conque before supper, or she will be offended," said Lady Graham. "Faithful old servants are such a trial. By the way, Mr. Cross, do you speak French?"

Mr. Cross said he could get along all right. Not educated French, but he had picked up a lot in France when he and that nice fellow George Halliday were at Vache-en-Etable.

"But, my dear Mr. Cross, that is Conque's home!" said Lady Graham. "She went back once after the war, but there was a terrible family scene about a field of mangolds that had to be divided between eighteen legatees and she never went there again. And she is *quite* used to our kind of French. Robert, as you perhaps know, was at Saumur for a time and studied French seriously. That is why he was so much with the French during the war and is sent on so many missions where French is needed. But Conque does not like it. Robert speaks very beautifully, like a literary Academician, and he even says 'Certes,' and Conque says he is too polite and that a real gentleman should have a certain want of respect for his servants because then they know

he likes them. I will take you to the kitchen." Which she did,
while Edith tidied the Saloon and put the gramophone records
away. The sky was dark, the rain pelting, so she drew the curtain
and turned on the lights. The fire was still alive in the handsome
polished steel grate below the handsome marble mantelpiece.
The carpet was rolled up where the boys had left it. She gave it
a tug, but it was to large and heavy for her to shift it, let alone
unrolling and spreading it. Her mother and Mr. Cross came in.

"Mr. Cross has been the *greatest* success with Conque, darling," said Lady Graham. "His French is *perfect*. Just right for
Conque. Don't try to move the carpet, Mr. Cross, it is far too
heavy. The boys can do it when they come back."

"Do let me do it now," said Mr. Cross. "I was a boy myself
before the war. And won't you say John?" and he began to pull
and unroll the carpet while he spoke.

"Of course I will," said Agnes. "My elder brother is John and
his second boy is John after him and so is my second boy. It is
quite confusing, but somehow we always know which is which."

"I am John Arthur," said Mr. Cross. "If you find Arthur easier,
pray use it. Some people call me John-Arthur all in one word."

"Then let us say John-Arthur," said her ladyship, with the air
of one giving the accolade, from which moment Mr. Cross was
spiritually at her feet. Edith was used to her mother's effect upon
young men and admired without envying. But somehow she felt
very, very slightly out of things.

CHAPTER 7

On the appointed day Lady Graham and her daughter drove over to Cross Hall. When we say drove, it was Edith who did the driving, for Lady Graham had always refused to learn on the excellent grounds that if you knew you couldn't do a thing well yourself it was better to get someone else to do it for you. This might well have resulted in no one being found to drive, but not even Providence could resist one so appealingly helpless (and so very well able to look after herself and everyone round her), and if Edith was not available there were various nice, dull, no-so-young women who liked to make some extra money and knew their way about the country. For this visit however Edith was available and took her mother past the horrible Housing Estate, over the downs and away to foreign parts beyond Boxall Hill, between which and Mr. Gresham's seat Cross Hall was situated. It was a nice, middle-sized unostentatious mansion, of a good period and a pleasant red-brown brick with well proportioned windows except on the top floor, where the rooms were suddenly so low that one could barely brush one's hair safely and the sash windows, rather wider than they were high, needed a great deal of jerking to be opened or shut. As none of these rooms had fireplaces, having been intended for servants, they were mostly not used except for storing things that no one would ever be likely to want, such as a quantity of enlarged photographs of school groups, a dress stand, a great many pairs of boot trees made for the riding boots that had long ago been given away or perished of decay, a parrot cage and a quantity of towel horses. But lucky is the house that has storage room and there is always the beautiful hope that quantities of priceless lace, or a cache of spade guineas, or a diamond necklace concealed in a pot labelled SPIR: MENTH: PIP or words to that effect, may turn up.

Mr. Cross, who was digging up dandelions on the lawn with a spud, came up to the car and courteously helped them out, which really makes the getting out more difficult, for there are only two ways of getting out of an ordinary small car: the one, to slide your legs out first and somehow get your skirt and the rest of you to follow rather like coming down a fire escape, the other to get out with your back to the audience and not care what it looks like. We need hardly say however that Lady Graham managed to glide out, as it were, accepting Mr. Cross's proffered hand as a kind of banister. Edith got out quite quickly by herself.

"I expect father is in the library," said Mr. Cross, and took them along a passage to a large room with large windows and every inch of wall space filled with large bookcases of an old fashioned kind with trimmings of faded red leather stamped with faded gold above every shelf, and a section with a gilded grill in front of it.

"This *is* father," said Mr. Cross. "Father, here's Lady Graham."

"I have been longing to meet you, Lord Cross," said Lady Graham, pressing his hand and looking up at him (for like his son he was fairly tall) with yearning eyes. "My husband says he used to meet you at the Omniums years ago. Before we were married that was."

"Then it cannot have been such a great number of years ago," said Lord Cross gallantly.

"And this is my youngest girl, Edith," said Lady Graham. "It is so kind of you to invite us, Lord Cross. Do you know, I have never been here before. My darling mother—you will remember her, Lady Emily Leslie—used to come to parties here when she was a young married woman and said there was such a delightful little boy who fell in love with her and called her Princess. He wore a kilt and had curls."

"All right, father, your sins have found you out," said Mr. Cross.

"Yes, I am afraid it was I," said Lord Cross. He turned to a bookcase and took out a large album which he laid on the table and opened.

"Here I am," he said. "No—that is the one where I got behind my nurse and only my leg shows. This is it," and he showed them a faded photograph of a small boy with far too long and curly hair in very correct riding attire of the period on a stout pony with his legs sticking almost straight out sideways, a groom at the pony's head and what was undoubtedly Nurse, in a straw boater, a long skirt and a jacket that well defined her figure, standing by with marked scorn of the groom and general disapproval of everything.

"But you are not wearing your kilt," said Lady Graham.

"That was for parties," said Lord Cross. "How I hated it. No one else wore one and I was miserable."

"Father," said Mr. Cross, who had been hovering with a look of suppressed anxiety during this conversation, "Peters! You see I was on the front lawn so I brought Lady Graham in."

"Oh dear, that's bad," said Lord Cross, growing visibly pale. "You see," he added to Lady Graham, "the plan was that when you rang Peters would open the door and pretend you were just ordinary visitors that he did not know and then you would say 'Why it is *Peters*, isn't it?' and then he could unbend—if you see what I mean," he added anxiously.

"That is too annoying," said Lady Graham placidly. "If only Robert were here he would have known *exactly* what to do."

"Look here, father," said Mr. Cross. "Couldn't we pretend that Lady Graham specially wanted to see Peters *alone* and take her to his pantry—that is if you wouldn't mind," he added to Lady Graham, fearful lest the goddess should frown.

"Now that is a *very* good idea," said Lady Graham, enchanted
at the idea of seeing other people's servants' quarters, just as her
mother would have been. "But I have another idea, Lord Cross"
and as she said these words her host saw in his mind's eye the
clearest vision of Lady Graham's mother repeated in her daughter. Not the same beauty, not the same fire, but a lovely echo of
the beauty and the warmth: and the same unquenched love of
meddling. "We could *all* go to the pantry and surprise Peters."

We are of the opinion that Lord Cross would not have
listened for a second to so subversive a suggestion from anyone
else, but there were very few people who could resist Lady
Graham's persuasion, though her brother David said it was
exactly like treacle pouring slowly out of a tin and covering
everything. But brothers, however fond, are notoriously unaf-
fected by their sisters' charm, even if they recognise it: omitting
of course the Ptolemies and numerous other historical and
mythological characters whom Lady Graham did not resemble
in the least. So the whole party went through the green baize
door to the servants' quarters where Peters in his pantry was
coldly surveying the silver, cleaned by a kind of pantry-boy, who
was hoping one day to graduate to higher things.

Lord Cross, a little nervous of his reception but cheered by
the reinforcements behind him, pushed back the half-opened
door.

"A visitor for you, Peters," he said.

It is the mark of a good butler never to let anything surprise
him and we do not think Peters had ever been surprised in his
life; not even when the present Lord Pomfret's unpleasant father
had had his last and flaming row with the old Earl and thrown
a volume of the Peerage through the window; not when Lady
Emily Leslie on one of her visits had insisted on pouring her
champagne over the savoury because it tasted of anchovy (which
was quite as reasonable as many other of her ladyship's diviga-
tions); not even when the present Earl had proposed to the

estate agent's sister in the estate room after tea and been accepted by her. But this was a staggerer.

"It was too sad, Peters," said Lady Graham, "that Mr. Cross saw us coming and opened the front door himself. I had been looking forward to seeing you all through the drive. Oh dear, those days at The Towers" and she held out her hand.

Everyone stood aghast, waiting for the thunder to break and the pantry-boy breathed hard and loudly through his mouth. His superior, an eye like Mars to threaten and command, holding Jove's thunderbolts to launch at will, was actually offering to shake hands with a guest.

"Really, my lady," said Peters, quite truly overcome by emotion, "it's a pleasure—it's an honourable pleasure I might say. I've not been so gratified, my lady, not since his present lordship became engaged" and putting aside his rank and dignity, forgetting the green baize apron he was wearing, he grasped Lady Graham's hand in his. The pantry-boy waited for immediate vengeance to fall from heaven, but it did not come, so he composed mentally the tale he would tell his mother about it when he went home that night, for he was a local boy and did not sleep in the house. And we may say that when he did relate the soul-stirring experiences of the day his mother said not to tell such a pack of stories and his father clipped him one over the ear and it is quite possible that this reception taught him the great lesson that Whatever happens in the Pantry does not go outside the Pantry.

"Oh, dear, Peters! it is like old days to see you again and looking so well," said Lady Graham. "And you are comfortable here?"

"That, my lady," said Peters, with great presence of mind, "it is not for me to say. I have endeavoured to give satisfaction. It is not always easy. Not that his lordship is anything but very kind and studies my convenience, but I have been used to entertaining on a different scale. Now, at the Towers, as your ladyship will remember, we was often twenty or twenty four to dinner," said Peters, his enthusiasm getting the upper hand of his grammar, "and three or four footmen in the hunting season. And in the Room we was always equal numbers, my lady. Lord Pomfret— I relude to his deceased lordship—was most particular about that. I remember once, my lady, when we was a lady short in the Room the housekeeper asked me to tell his lordship and he went into such rage I've never seen the like. Not even when the fox ran to earth the other side of the Barchester road and one of the men as was digging him out put a pickaxe through the drain."

"Now I wonder who it was that didn't bring a maid," said Lady Graham."Don't tell me, Peters. I know. It was Mrs. George."

"Got it in one, my lady," said Peters, quite forgetting his dignity in the joy of family gossip. "The Honourable Mrs. George Rivers it was and his lordship said a lady as didn't bring a maid with her—unless of course it was a young unmarried lady and the housemaids were always ready to oblige—she didn't have no need to come at all."

"Well, it is all very different now, Peters," said Lady Graham, but she did not go on, for a terrifying clangour broke out in the passage.

"It's only the front door bell," said Mr. Cross. "One never knows if it is going to ring or not" and he hastily shepherded his father and the guests back to the library, before Peters announced "Lord and Lady Pomfret. Miss Merriman. Lord Mellings."

When young Mr. Cross and his father, who were on very good and friendly terms, compared notes afterwards, they found they both felt that the house belonged to the Pomfrets and Grahams and they themselves were welcome guests, so did the cousins coalesce. Not that anyone was being in the least discourteous, but the tribal sense was very strong and by the mysterious law which makes people who see each other every day have far more and far more interesting subjects to talk about than friends who meet every two years or so, a kind of invisible Pomfret-Graham

Maginot Line appeared, on or around which outsiders might prowl, but could not enter. Only Miss Merriman, watching it all, a little aloof as she so often was, saw their host deserted; so faithful to her life work of protecting the landed gentry, she spoke to him. What they found to talk about we do not know, but Lord Cross, who had a very good brain and was no fool in business or personal relations, appeared to be enjoying himself.

Then Peters announced lunch, which very simple but very good meal was accompanied by some good claret. The elders were soon deep in county gossip, bartering the draining of a piece of low lying land near Greshamsbury (Lord Cross) with the discovery in one of the old nurseries at Pomfret Towers, now being remodelled by the Adams-Macfadyen-Pilward combine, of a zoetrope or wheel of life together with the pictures required for the same (Lord Pomfret). As many of those present had never seen or even heard of that pleasant toy, several people tried to explain it; but no one listened to them, for few things are so exhausting as trying to understand explanations when you are not interested in them and do not wish to hear them.

"I hope you got back quite safely the other day," said Edith in her society voice to Mr. Cross. "We nearly got lost on the way here, at least I did, because mother can't drive, because of that new by-pass near Boxall Hill."

"I know," said Mr. Cross sympathetically. "I've only just got used to it myself. But it's nothing to the roundabout in the Horrible Housing Estate. Every time I go to the bank I go round about three times before I can find the right turning. Still, that won't be for much longer."

"Do you mean you are going to London?" said Edith. "You did say you might."

Mr. Cross said he expected to, but he would be coming down for weekends like anything and probably going to business on Friday in plus fours with a little handbag, so that he could catch the fast train the moment he got away from work. Edith, whose sense of humor was not very deep, suddenly laughed out loud.

"That *was* a nice noise," said Mr. Cross approvingly. "Do it again."

"I can't laugh on purpose," said Edith, "but if you say something funny I will, with pleasure," which words, spoken in what her Uncle David called her Society Voice, made Mr. Cross laugh in his turn.

"And how is that nice fellow Halliday?" said Mr. Cross.

"Quite well thank you so far as I know," said Edith. "But his father isn't at all well and wants to give up being a churchwarden because he can't be an invalid and do the work at the same time. Mr. Choyce was wondering whom he can ask to take his place. It is all very complicated. There don't seem to be enough men about. Only boys or young men," she added with a slight extra touch of grown-upness.

Mr. Cross said that the words young men seemed to cover a large variety of ages now.

"Would you be one?" said Edith, to which Mr. Cross replied Certainly, if she wished it, but considering his war service he might find it difficult."

"Oh, I didn't mean to be *impertinent*," said Edith. "I only wondered—"

"My *dear* Miss Graham—" Mr. Cross said.

"Surely we don't do Misters and Misses, John-Arthur," said Edith, looking right into Mr. Cross's eyes. "I thought we were all Christian names."

"Your word is law—Edith," said Mr. Cross and raising the remains of his claret to his lips he looked at her and drank.

As she was sitting with her back to the light the sudden beetroot-red of her face passed unnoticed except, we think, by Miss Merriman. Luckily Lord Pomfret was on her other side and she turned to him to tell him how she was going to America. Then conversation became general and mostly about Pomfret Towers, for everyone present was interested in their fate, as landowner or connected with the land. Lord Cross made no bones about his envy of Lord Pomfret, though he admitted generously that his estate was little more than a park and a few fields and his house not large enough to divide.

"But if you need dormitories for your tenants, Pomfret," said Lord Cross, "I am more than willing to let my top floor for a good rent, only your lot will have to put in heating and plumbing and repair the roof. I think most of the floors upstairs need repairing too, but I really daren't look at the joists. They are probably riddled with death watch beetle and dry rot."

So the mild county talk went on and the meal came to an end. The party drifted back to the library, all but Miss Merriman who lingered for a word with Peters. For in the old days at Pomfret Towers there was very little that was not known to his lordship's butler and her ladyship's secretary, and though there was nothing like a secret between them, each had seen a good deal behind the scenes.

"I am very glad, Peters, to find you here," said Miss Merriman. "How do you think Lord Pomfret is looking?"

"His lordship is a trifle thin, miss," said Peters, "but that is hardly to be surprised at considering the way things have changed. Ah, when his late lordship was alive, miss, and there was always twelve in the Hall, and sometimes up to twenty in the Room during the shooting season, those were the days. Dear me, miss, what we have seen. There was that day, miss, when the Honourable Mrs. George Rivers's son, Mr. Julian Rivers, wanted to paint those pictures of his in the North Attic and his Lordship wouldn't hear of it."

"Yes, I remember," said Miss Merriman. "And I told him he could use the old racket-court as a studio and I would have a good oil stove put there and he was not at all grateful."

"And the day Mr. Barton, the brother of Miss Barton that married Mr. Wicklow, the present Lady Pomfret's brother, miss," said Peters, "pushed Mr. Julian Rivers off the car as was taking some of the guests to Nutfield on the Monday. We all saw it, miss, and one of the footmen so far forgot himself as to try to wink at me. But I soon stopped *that*, miss."

"And how did you stop it, Peters?" said Miss Merriman.

"I gave the young footman a Look, miss," said Peters. "Miss Edith is a very handsome young lady, miss, if I may venture to say so."

Miss Merriman agreed.

"Mr. Cross is a very pleasant young gentleman too, miss," said Peters. "But of course you never know."

Miss Merriman said No indeed and then she shook hands warmly with Peters and followed the others into the library. Mr. Cross presently suggested a walk round the garden. The elders refused with one voice. Edith and Lord Mellings expressed approval so they went out.

"I say, you'd better take a coat or a cardigan or something," said Mr. Cross to Edith. "It's horribly cold out there, but I do want to show you the grotto. Or take this" and as they were passing through the hall he took a loose woollen coat off a hook. "It's my younger sister's," he said, "but she's in France with some friends and she says it's too cold to bathe and too windy to play tennis and there's been a landslide and the road is blocked. Joy, joy! How glad I am I live in England. There's really nothing to see in the garden now, but I thought you would like to see the Grotto."

"Is there a hermit?" Lord Mellings asked.

"Not now," said Mr. Cross regretfully. "There used to be about a hundred and fifty years ago. The man who built this house was a professional eccentric and built a Folly, but it fell down. The Grotto isn't bad," and he took them by winding paths up the slopes on the north side of the house. When they had got to about the level of the housetop he turned aside into a little wood and so to a clearing in the middle of which was a kind of Gothic-rococo temple, built on low stone arches. From the middlemost of these issued a little stream which ran brawling down the hillside and was lost to sight among trees.

"Oh!" said Edith.

"Jolly, isn't it," said Mr. Cross. "The stream runs away into the river a bit lower down. You crossed it on the way here, but it's so small you wouldn't have noticed it. It's called Gunbrook here. Probably the same name you find in Gundric's Fossway. But no one really knows anything about it."

"That looks like a bit of Barton," said Lord Mellings who had been inspecting the temple.

"Quite right," said Mr. Cross, looking at Lord Mellings with interest. "How on earth did you know that?"

"Oh, I like that landscape-garden period," said Lord Mellings. "There's a good book about Barton in the old library at the Towers with coloured engravings. I'm sure I've seen one of your temple. He was some kind of ancestor of Mr. Barton at Nutfield— the architect you know—whose daughter married my mother's brother, Roddy Wicklow. He is our agent."

"That's one thing I do like about these parts," said Mr. Cross. "One knows who everyone is."

"Only with one's own friends," said Edith. "All the people in Hatch End are each other's uncles or nieces, most confusing."

"Well, come to that," said Mr. Cross, "lots of us are too. Look at your family. I never felt so addled in my life as with all those nice young men and not having the faintest idea who was who."

"And the Dean," said Lord Mellings. "I forget how many children he had but anyway one is Octavia that married the parson with one arm over at Beliers, and they all have huge families and when they come to stay at the Deanery it's like 'This man's father is my father's son.'"

"Lord! I'd forgotten that one," said Mr. Cross. "It's a man looking at a portrait, isn't it, and he says 'Brothers and sisters have I none, yet this man's father is my father's son.' It came up at one of our Directors' Meetings the other day—I really can't think why—and the business was held up for nearly twenty minutes while they argued."

"But it's quite easy," said Edith, rather perkily. "It was himself."

"Oh, come off it, Edith," said her cousin Mellings with a sad lack of chivalry. "His father couldn't be his son—I mean his own son—I mean—No. Listen. It's his father."

"But his father's father would have been his grandfather—I mean the man's grandfather, not the father's," said Mr. Cross. "Wait a minute. I've got it. No, I haven't. Yes, I have. It's a portrait of his own son. Then this man's father would be himself and he would be his father's son."

"It all depends," said Lord Mellings. "You don't know West Barsetshire."

"We've just as high an illegitimate rate as you have," said Mr. Cross rather arrogantly.

"We haven't any illegits. in the *family* as far as I know," said Lord Mellings apologetically, "but our Italian cousins the Strelsas—they are descended from Eustace Pomfret who had to leave England in 1688 and settled in Rome—are simply *bursting* with them."

"Oh, well, come to family we are all painfully respectable," said Mr. Cross.

"So are the Grahams," said Edith, not wishing to be left behind in self-abnegation. "I mean now. We usen't to be of course. But I shall *not* have illegitimate children," to which her cousin Mellings, coarsened doubtless by his preparation for army life, said Wait and See.

"But what I *do* want you to see," said Mr. Cross, thinking this conversation had gone on long enough, "is the inside of the Grotto," and he took a large key out of his pocket. "We have to keep it locked, or trippers come up here and carve their names. Beasts!"

"I'd like to carve my name all over *them*," said Lord Mellings with a violence that surprised his cousin Edith. "The day our chapel and the big rooms were open to the public for something-or-other, I found a fellow trying to chip a bit off the chapel carvings."

"And what did you do?" said Mr. Cross, hoping that his young lordship had at least tapped the offender's claret.

"You can't have a fight in a consecrated building unfortunately," said Lord Mellings. "There's nothing you can do. And they can be much ruder than you can now. We've lost the knack and they know everybody will be on their side, the beak included—except Sir Edmund Pridham," he added. "I told Uncle Roddy, that's father's agent, and he said he'd see about it and he took the man out by his coat collar. No one ever argues with Uncle Roddy," he added with a tinge of envy.

Mr. Cross said that was a thing he had often heard of and read of in books but didn't know it really happened and then he unlocked the door of the Grotto and took them in. It was octagonal, with eight windows of thick green glass and in the middle was a basin on a pedestal and in the basin a small lead figure of a child holding a graceful water-pot on its shoulder. From the water-pot a delicate thread of water rose into the air and descended into the basin, whence the water ran away to rejoin the little stream.

"Oh!" said Edith, much as Man Friday said it for the Unknown God.

"I used to worship it when I was small," said Mr. Cross, "and put flowers round it, but Nurse said not to be silly and clear up all that mess, which is just what a nurse *would* say. And now I'll lock up. It's too cold for you here Edith," and indeed the stone room and the water with its cool stream were enough to chill the boldest heart in the middle of an English summer.

"To go back to George Halliday?" said Mr. Cross. "I rang him up, but he was turmut-hoeing or dealing with the bots or the warble-fly or something. Banking, alas, does not include these agricultural terms."

Edith said George was nearly always out on the farm.

"It's very sad," she said, "for Mr. Halliday because he has always done things and it must be dreadful to have to sit at home and see people do things differently from your own way."

"I suppose," said Mr. Cross, "that is one of the drawbacks to a farmer's life. As far as I can make out from my governor and his friends the minute they resign from their boards and things they do something else. Father is so agricultural now that it is quite a menace and grumbles when he has to go to London for the one or two boards he still sits on. I am going to resign with a Bang when I resign and be a whole-time countryman and get onto the local councils and then stand for the East Barsetshire County Council," to which Lord Mellings replied what would he do when he finally had to resign from them as well.

"Oh Lord! I hadn't thought of that one," said Mr. Cross. "That's where good old atavism comes in and I expect I'll be just as bad as all the other old fellows who stick on committees long after they ought to be dead. Let's go back."

So they walked back in a very friendly way and then the men—after the custom of men—began to talk mannishly, so that Edith felt she might as well not be there. Not with self-pity, but with the very practical Graham side of her nature, and her reflections led her to consider her cousin Ludo and to realise for the first time that he had stopped being a boy and was a man. A very young man, but a man for a' that and likely to be more so and suddenly she laughed.

"What's up, Edith?" said Lord Mellings.

"Only a silly thought," said Edith.

"I'd love to hear your silly thought," said Mr. Cross.

"Oh, it was too, too silly John-Arthur," said Edith, just as her sister Clarissa might have said it in earlier years.

"Fire away, Swan-neck," said Lord Mellings, using an old schoolroom nickname from English history.

"Well, something made me think of that Burns poem about A man's a man for a' that," said Edith, "and we had a holiday governess once and she would read poetry aloud to us and she read some Burns which was very shame-making."

"Your vocabulary is quite out of date," said her cousin loftily.

"And yours is very stuck-up and affected," said Edith, quite without rancour and suddenly a school girl again. "Now I shall not tell you what made me laugh" upon which Lord Mellings went down on one knee, put one hand on his heart and raised his other hand to heaven and Mr. Cross laughed. But a very nice, sympathetic laugh.

"Kamerad," said Lord Mellings.

"Oh, all right," said Edith relenting. "Only get up, Ludo, or you'll get your trouser-knee green and you know what Nurse is."

"Indeed I do," said Lord Mellings, rearing up his spiral form (as Harriette Wilson wrote of Sir Charles Bampyfylde, one of her many temporary protectors). "Every time I see her I have a nasty feeling that my nails are dirty or my hair needs cutting. But do not try to chide me, sweet coz. What made you laugh?"

"Oh, it was only Miss Hook, the holiday governess, and she read it as if it was that A man was a man for a *that*—and we wondered how a person could be like a that—or indeed what exactly a that is," and both her companions laughed appreciatively and they went down to the house where the elders were talking county talk very happily and wondering whether Lady Silverbridge or Lady Cora Waring would come in first for the Baby Stakes, for both these ladies were contemplating an addition to the nursery.

"It's the one thing father has against me," said Mr. Cross, "that I am not increasing the population. My married sisters are quite good at it."

"But you can't have children if you aren't married," said Edith.

Mr. Cross said, rather coarsely, Oh, couldn't he.

"You know *exactly* what I mean, John-Arthur," said Edith with dignity.

"It isn't done now," said Lord Mellings, casting an almost chilly look on his host. "Not in one's own part of the county at any rate," which kind and cousinly intervention somehow caused Mr. Cross to look slightly askance at his fellow-man.

"Well, if *I* have illegitimate children I shall have them in Loamshire, or the Yorkshire Wolds," said Edith with a businesslike voice. "But *not* in Barsetshire. One doesn't."

There was a brief silence as they walked on.

"Come to think of it one *doesn't*," said Mr. Cross. "My great-grandfather was a bit of a boy, but his are all in the Potteries, I really don't know why. They are called Bantam," which sounded so silly that Edith and Lord Mellings had the giggles and Mr. Cross, also laughing, said it was their mother's name he believed, and so they came to the house and found tea going on in the library.

"I don't use the drawing-room except when my married daughters are here," said Lord Cross. "J-A will do as he likes when I am dead."

"Dear Mr. Cross, I *am* so glad you speak of being dead," said Lady Graham, "because" she continued, regardless of or ignoring the amusement of the young people, "it is so silly to say things like joining the majority, or passing over. After all dead is dead."

"Stone dead has no fellow," said Lord Mellings aloud to himself and then wondered if it was really a quotation or if he had invented it.

"Quite right, Lady Graham," said Lord Cross. "It reminds me of a very silly play called the Blue Bird by Maeterlinck, or Marterlinck or however it's pronounced, when someone says There Are No Dead."

"Well, there jolly well are, father," said Mr. Cross, "and I saw plenty of them in the war, poor b—I mean fellows. There wouldn't be room to move if they were all alive."

Then Lady Graham said they must be going. Lord Cross apologised, quite unnecessarily, for a bachelor entertainment, or a widower's he should say, at which Lady Graham's still lovely eyes dimmed in sympathy. But Lady Cross had been dead now for some dozen years and her husband, though he had not forgotten her, had long ago accommodated himself to things and led a useful and quite contented life.

Peters was waiting in the hall and opened the front door for them to pass. Lady Graham and Edith shook hands with him,

as did the Pomfrets and Lord Mellings. Miss Merriman, who
had come last, stopped for a moment to say how pleased they
would be to see him at the Towers if he was ever that way and
she hoped all was going very well with him.

"Thank you, miss, I have no complaints," said Peters, which
exordium from an old servant is well recognised as the prelude to
complaining at considerable length. "But this house needs a
Lady, miss. His Lordship is most considerate and when his
married daughters come here they are all one could wish and
young Mr. Cross gives very little trouble. But sometimes, miss,
when I am in my pantry after dinner, going through the silver, I
think of Old Days, miss and Life at the Towers when his former
Lordship and her former Ladyship were alive. They Kept Their
Place, miss, same as I have always done. And that, miss, is what
I *do* miss."

Miss Merriman could not well comment on this but she
rather sympathised with Peters. If your own private world
crumbles, as it had with nearly every landowner in England, you
involve yourself in your own virtue (we translate by sound rather
than by sense, though one can give almost any word or phrase of
Horace a round dozen of meanings, so different is the Roman
genius from ours) and try to bear up impavidly among its ruins.
But when the whole world is crumbling it is daily more difficult
to remain just and tenacious of your proposition (as Miss Lydia
Keith rendered it, a long time ago) and very often small thanks
you get for doing it. Yet hundreds and thousands of people are
doing it all over our country (as for other countries they will, in
Mrs. Gamp's great words, please themselves) and not asking
reward or payment. Simply to be allowed to try to go on living
decently and with an occasional treat.

As it was still horribly light and would continue to be so for
hours, Lady Graham suggested that instead of going straight
home they should cross the Rising a little higher up and see how
Mr. Halliday was. So Edith drove by the river and across the
lovely one-arch bridge at Starveacres Hatches, with its perfectly

plain and exquisitely distanced white railings and the long green
water-weeds trailing like river-maidens' hair on the water below
and so along the further bank to Hatch House.

"I have hardly ever come this way," said Lady Graham. "How
very pretty it is," as indeed it was, with scattered cottages along
the road of incredible Morlandesqueness and cows grouping
themselves in the water-meadows.

"I'll drive in by the farm entrance," said Edith. "It's easier that
way," and accordingly she turned left up a lane, a few yards up
the hill, and then through an open gate to the right and so round
to the back of the house. Hubback who, in her own words, was
getting the clorths off the line, welcomed them and said Mr. and
Mrs. Halliday were just going to have tea and please to go round
to the front and she'd open the door.

"Oh, that's all right," said Edith. "We'll come through the
kitchen," but her mother, whose social sense was extremely
sound, thanked Hubback and walked towards the door in the
kitchen yard that led to the front garden.

"But mother," said Edith, following Lady Graham in as near
a mood to sulks as was possible to her, "it's much quicker by the
kitchen."

"I know, darling," said Lady Graham, "but this time it wouldn't
do. You can go alone, but if you are with me we go to the front
door."

"Oh, mother, how silly," said Edith; not rudely but as one
who tells a disobedient child for the tenth time to do something
it knows it ought to have done but hasn't done.

"Not silly, Edith," said her mother, "but just one of the things
one has to do."

"But Lord Stoke came to the kitchen door at Holdings," said
Edith.

"Lord Stoke is a baron and very old," said Lady Graham,
stopping at the green door in the wall, "and he has worked for
the county all his life. And he is a bachelor, so he is allowed to be
peculiar. They mostly are," by which we think her ladyship

meant that not getting married was in itself so marked an eccentricity that in its light all other eccentricities were as nothing. "And darling mamma could do it because she was such a Person that if she had walked down Barchester High Street on stilts everyone would have thought it quite reasonable," and then she lifted the latch and walked into the front garden. Edith followed her and shut the door carefully, remembering that the latch was old and did not always fall into place of itself. Mrs. Halliday who was, as she so often was, on her knees before a flower bed, heard them and stood up, a tin in one hand, and said how nice to see them.

"It is snails just now," she said. "Those horrid little ones with black and white shells only rather whiter than black. We are having a perfect plague of them. Do come in. Leonard will love to see you. George is somewhere on the farm but he will be back for tea. Come in," and she put a bit of tile over the snail pot adding, "They all get out again if you don't."

"I *know*," said Lady Graham sympathetically. "Like Egypt in Israel," at which Mrs. Halliday looked a little lost.

"Mother means the plagues of locusts and things," said Edith to Mrs. Halliday. "What a pity these aren't eating snails."

"George and Sylvia did eat some once, when they were small," said Mrs. Halliday. "I don't think it did them any harm, but they were very sick and nurse gave them Syrup of Figs which of course made them much sicker."

"*Dreadful* stuff," said Lady Graham sympathetically, "but we used to have Scott's Emulsion in the winter when we were small, which was much worse."

"Leonard always says he had brimstone and treacle at his prep. school," said Mrs. Halliday, "but no one believes him. Come in," and she took off her apron and gardening gloves and they all went into the house, where Mr. Halliday was doing the Times Cross Word Puzzle and delighted to have an excuse to stop, for there is a most fatal attraction about that peculiar form of amusement, brought here from across the Atlantic some thirty odd years ago and still fascinating and irritating most of the Anglo-Saxon world. And here may we divagate—not that anyone has ever been able to stop us and we ourselves are powerless when the Goddess Divagation appears—to make a modest comment on the English Cross-Word which we find the best of any we have met. As for French and German ones they are still and always will be in the Kindergarten stage. Of Russia (if any) we know nothing for their alphabet is wrong all over in shape and lettering, and anyway who wants to do a Russian crossword, probably produced (as all their sports are) on a wholly professional basis and state aided? The American cross-words are usually too large and do not run true to form. But The Times, The Thunderer, somehow produces a classic almost every day. Sometimes we do the whole thing in ten minutes except for one four letter word, two letters of which we have got but cannot visualise the other two. Older readers note, nostalgically, the total disappearance of words that used to occur in every newspaper, words such as ORLOP and EME, which appeared with monotonous frequency. We think that addicts are on the whole more self-contained than they used to be. Not quite so often does an apparently harmless fellow guest during a pleasant weekend dash at one with such mysterious remarks as, "E dot, T dot dot, O or it may be A dot, D, I, dot, dot R dot L dot, the clue is Quite unusually occurring." There are fewer appeals for a Latin dictionary or The Oxford Book of English Verse. On the whole fewer tempers are lost because someone has picked up your unfinished crossword puzzle and added in a nonchalant and rather conceited way several words that had got you entirely flummoxed; or put in while your back was turned one wrong word which throws out a whole section.

"Here are Lady Graham and Edith, Leonard," said Mrs. Halliday. "We will have tea now. You will stay, won't you?" and though Lady Graham would have been just as glad to get home, she accepted because she felt that Mr. Halliday would like it and even more because it would probably be good for Mrs. Halliday to have a change.

Hubback, with a kind of surly approval, brought in the tea and laid it on the large table so that they could all sit round it comfortably. After their chill drive a fire and tea were very welcome. Edith was pleased to see Mr. Halliday's large Eddystone Lighthouse cup again and said so.

"I have had that cup for seventy years," said Mr. Halliday. "My nurse gave it to me. And she gave me one of those delightful glass bottles with a picture somehow made inside them with coloured sand."

"Darling mamma had one," said Lady Graham, "but David broke it in a fight with Giles."

"Do you mean old Uncle Giles?" said Edith, puzzled.

"No, darling," said Lady Graham. "I was forgetting the generations. He was my eldest brother who was killed in the first war—Martin's father. He was called after darling mamma's brother, our Uncle Giles, old Lord Pomfret. So long ago," and her ladyship looked into some past distance before our world was shattered for the first time, since when the devil has come among us having great wrath, from the land of Arminius, from the land of Ivan the Terrible, from the lands of the east where evil seed springs to quick growth and spreads its upas branches far and wide, from the land whose treachery to our friends and kinsmen across the Atlantic brought an Armageddon into being for our lifetime and for many more lifetimes, not unaided by the March of Science.

"I blame Ghengis Khan for a good deal," said Mr. Halliday.

Edith said did he mean Kubla Khan, because there was a lovely—

"No, my dear, I do *not*," said Mr. Halliday, almost rejuvenated by this chance of setting someone down—and then setting her right. "I mean what I say. He conquered pretty well all northern Asia and then he tried for Japan, but there were storms and he lost nearly all his ships and a lot of his men and he had to come back. If I had been there with a few British troops we'd have shown them!" which echo of "I and my Franks" made his audience feel a little gulpy (an expression which our female reader will at once understand).

Mrs. Halliday's quick look of anxiety at his excitement did not escape Lady Graham, nor did Lady Graham's look of sympathy escape Mrs. Halliday and then George Halliday came in looking, so Lady Graham thought, very handsome in his working clothes.

"My dear boy," said Lady Graham. "How very nice to see you. We have been to lunch with Lord Cross and his nice son. And that reminds me," she said, turning to Mr. Halliday, "what are you doing about the bank? I mean the Old Manor House?"

"Oh luckily there is no hurry about that," said Mrs. Halliday, but in a manner so unlike her usual calm way of speaking that Lady Graham realised it was some sort of danger signal and changing the subject she described to Mr. Halliday her visit to Cross Hall and how pleasant it was and how the butler who used to be at Pomfret Towers was now with Lord Cross and how Lord Cross had shown her some delightful old photographs of her mother. Her good angel—not that she had a bad angel, though from time to time the angel of Irresponsibility who had watched over her mother Lady Emily Leslie would pay her a visit—then told her that old photographs were exactly what Mr. Halliday would enjoy and she offered to bring some over before long and go through them with him. Mr. Halliday said, quite truly, that there were few things he enjoyed so much as old photographs, provided one knew who they were.

"I have a photograph taken after an Eights' Week ball, when I was up at Paul's," said Mr. Halliday, "and I always meant to make a key to it—"

"I *know*," said Lady Graham. "A kind of picture of the group, only just O's for their heads and then you put a number in every O and then you try to remember who they all were and make a list of the numbers and write who they were against them.

Robert has some delightful photographs of a Dining Society he belonged to at Oxford, but he has lost the key and *cannot* remember whether number seventeen was that young Lord Lundy who became Governor of New South Wales later or that very peculiar man called Frodsham-Forster who wrote a book about Titus Andronicus to prove they were all really friends of Shakespeare's."

As all those present, except Edith who was no great Shakespearean, had read Titus Andronicus and hoped never to have to see it acted, there was a noticeable pause till Mrs. Halliday, feeling responsible as hostess for the mental and moral as well as the physical comfort of her guests, asked after David Leslie and his wife, whom she knew slightly.

"Darling David," said Lady Graham. "And darling Rose too. They were so sweet and they have made a most delightful suggestion that—"

"Oh, may I tell, mother?" said Edith. "What *do* you think, Mrs. Halliday? Uncle David and Aunt Rose have invited me to go to America with them for a visit and we are going to fly and Aunt Rose says my clothes won't do at all and she is going to buy me some in New York. Isn't that *marvellous*?"

"And what is so delightful is that she will be there in the autumn and see the lovely colours," said Lady Graham. "I mean the forests all brown and red and gold, though why they say fall when they could say autumn I do not know. It sounds like the Bible."

Strangers might have begun to go mad at this point, but Mrs. Halliday was an old friend and used to her ladyship's divagations, so she merely enquired in a most matter of fact way where the Bible came in.

"Like Milton." said her ladyship. "The Fall. About Adam and Eve, though I never feel he really *understood* them. Being a man he couldn't, I suppose," at which point George Halliday saw that her ladyship would soon be out of hand and wishing to encourage her asked why.

"Well, he had *two* wives," said Lady Graham, "and besides he was blind so I expect he didn't always quite remember what he had said, because if you shut your eyes everything is quite different."

George, who was enjoying himself, said he had always wondered if you saw anything when you were blind, because when he shut his eyes, instead of seeing nothing he saw all kinds of lights and shadows moving about and sometimes on sunny days a kind of brilliant kaleidoscope.

Mr. Halliday said something about the retina of the eye but no one paid any attention.

"But of course if you were *blind*," said her ladyship, "you wouldn't even see *inside* your eye. Like being deaf."

"But if you are deaf, you often *do* hear," said Mrs. Halliday, "and that is the dreadful part. My mother had a sister who was so deaf that she had to use one of those boxes when people talked, and she said what was far worse than not hearing people talk, or music, was that she never heard silence. I mean wherever she was there were noises going on in her ears."

"How *dreadful*," said Lady Graham sympathetically. "And perhaps people who have lost their sense of smell have *terrible* smells inside them all the time," at which point Mr. Halliday began to laugh, so wholeheartedly that everyone had to laugh with him, not least her ladyship, whose charming laugh was well known to her friends, though her brother David maintained that she had no sense of humour and never knew why she laughed: in which he may have been not very far out.

"And what was it we were saying?" said Lady Graham, recovering herself, but what with Milton and blindness and deafness and people with no sense of smell, the thread—if any—of that conversation was lost.

George said he was sorry he had interrupted Edith—not that he had, but any pretext does to bring a conversation back to where you want it—and how glad he was that she was going to America and hoped that she would have a lovely time and lots of proposals and come back with ravishing new clothes so that everyone would be jealous.

Edith said of course she wouldn't have proposals, or if she did she would not accept them because she would want mother and father to see them first.

"And in any case" said Lady Graham, who felt that this conversation had gone on long enough, "Edith is too young. But I hope she will have great fun and lots of admirers. So much more amusing than a proposal. And then when a real proposal comes it will be quite different."

As no one quite knew what she meant, a kind of murmur of agreement was heard and perhaps it was lucky that Mr. Choyce came in at that moment, under the guardianship of Hubback who approved of him.

"It's the Vicar," said Hubback. "And I'll make some nice fresh tea and there's some more scones."

"Oh, pray——" said Mr. Choyce, "I am so glad to find you in, Mrs. Halliday. No, really—I have had tea; and how are you, Halliday? Well, just a cup only *pray* don't trouble to make fresh tea for me, Hubback." But Hubback, who knew how things ought to be done and was always right in her own eyes, paid no attention to her mistress or the Vicar and removing the teapot and milk jug left the room.

"How delightful to see you Mr. Choyce," said Lady Graham, who was apt to constitute herself hostess, though quite unconsciously and without the faintest wish to push, wherever there was a party. "Robert rang me up last night and said how much he was looking forward to seeing you when he comes down. He is thinking of writing his reminiscences and I am *sure* you will be a great help," and her ladyship sat back conscious, as far as her really kind nature could be conscious, of having conferred a benefit.

"Oh, mother!" said Edith, "is father really going to write his life? What fun. Will it be a *real* book like old Uncle Giles's?" for the late Lord Pomfret's one and only literary production, *A*

Landowner in Five Reigns had had, in spite of its unattractive title, one of those waves of popularity for which there is no accounting and had even been serialised in a Sunday paper and its author had got as much real pleasure from its success as he had got from anything since his only son and only child, Lord Mellings, had been killed in a frontier skirmish in India, long long ago.

Mr. Choyce said he was delighted to hear that Sir Robert meant to write his reminiscences which would surely be of the greatest interest. He himself, he said, might in a more modest way also find himself in print, for the Barsetshire Archaeological had asked him to write an article about the church at Hatch End with a note on Bolder's Knob.

"Oh, Mr. Choyce," said Edith, "did you know there is a spring of fresh water right up near the top. I didn't till Mr. Halliday told me."

Mr. Choyce said that, to his shame be it spoken, he had never heard of it.

"No need to be ashamed of what one doesn't know, Choyce," said Mr. Halliday. "I happen to know because the spring is on my land. It has been blocked for a long time, but the water's all right. In fact we are thinking of using it for the new pig-sties this son of mine is building."

"Oh, I say father," said George, "it's all your idea. I'm only doing the spade-work."

Mr. Choyce said a man could but do the work of his hands and then wondered (a) if this were a quotation from the Bible, (b) if so from which book of which Testament and (c) whether he wasn't thinking of something in the Vier Ernste Gesänge of Brahms which are, after all, the Bible. At this point he decided not to say anything more. Nor was there any need to, for once away upon the subject of the pig-sties Mr. Halliday and George could have spoken like Prince Giglio for three days and three nights without stopping; as indeed they practically did, or would have done, had not Lady Graham said to Mr. Halliday how very sorry she was to hear that he might be retiring from being a churchwarden.

"I know one ought not to discuss such things," said her ladyship, "but after all here we all are and really it is just as annoying for Mr. Choyce, because he has to find someone else," at which the Vicar became rather pink in the face and Mr. Halliday laughed, not loudly for his strength was not great, but with genuine amusement.

"I don't like giving it up, Lady Graham," he said, "but it's much worse for Choyce than it is for me because he has to find a new one. All I have to do is to sit back and twiddle my thumbs. I must say it would be pleasant if we could get it settled soon."

"I don't know if it is simony or anything," said Lady Graham, "but why don't you ask Robert, Mr. Halliday? You know he is retiring almost at once and going to stand for all sorts of county things and I am sure he would love to be the Vicar's churchwarden, which would be much more suitable than being the Vestry's warden because Mr. Choyce is an old friend and I never quite know who the Vestrymen are. How does one know them? I don't think I could *canvass* for Robert, because I am not much good at that kind of thing. Lady Fielding whose husband stood so unsuccessfully for Parliament the year Mr. Adams got in is a wonderful canvasser and of course her husband is the Chancellor of the Diocese," said her ladyship in a very learned voice. "One might ask him to dinner—and Lady Fielding of course, who is so charming and darling mamma called on her once and *would* go over the whole of that lovely house of theirs in the Close because she had always wanted to know what the servants' bedrooms were like."

Mr. Choyce, who had been watching (and almost praying) for the moment when her ladyship would stop to breathe, thanked her very much for her kind and helpful words and said canvassing would be quite unnecessary and perhaps he might come and see Sir Robert when next he was at home.

"Oh *do*, Mr. Choyce," said Lady Graham. "He will be down

in about a fortnight. Edith will have gone, which is so sad, but he is dining with my brother and his wife at Porridge's the night before they fly to America and Edith will be with them. In fact I shall be alone. I know Robert would simply *love* to be Vicar's Churchwarden and he reads aloud quite beautifully. Not that the Lessons are exactly reading aloud," said her ladyship, evidently looking upon reading aloud as an essentially mundane amusement, "but he has such a good voice and he pronounces so well. Not like that young man the Dean told me about—a Mr. Parkinson—who said Oneasyforus instead of Onesiphorus."

Mr. Choyce said one must not judge too harshly, for he knew Mr. Parkinson who was doing extremely well and undoubtedly marked for preferment and, which was almost as important, had an excellent wife who got on with everyone.

"Robert always says you ought to be married, dear Mr. Choyce," said Lady Graham, "but who is there?"

"I agree with you in toto, Lady Graham," said Mr. Choyce. "There is nothing I should like better than to be married, but I have never yet met any woman, or girl, that I could bear the idea of being married to. One never knows of course," upon which Miss Edith Graham and Mr. George Halliday had—we regret to say—a competition as to who would be the best wife for Mr. Choyce, Edith winning by a short head by proposing Conque, which made every one, even the future bridegroom, laugh so much that Mr. Halliday had to beg them to stop before he was laughing till it hurt him. His wife looked almost grey with sudden alarm, but all was well.

While this noise was going on, Lady Graham was able to ask Mrs. Halliday whether her husband had yet made any decision about the Old Manor House.

"Not yet," said Mrs. Halliday. "If George showed any signs of marrying, we would give this house to him and his wife so that he could go on farming, and Leonard and I would move to the Manor House. It would really suit us very well. It is warmer down there since the bank put in some oil heating. I cannot think how banks can afford to spend as much as they do even if they do have all our money."

"Robert says," said Lady Graham, as her ladyship must have said at least twice on three hundred and sixty-five days in every year since her marriage, "that they earn so much that they would have to pay a great deal of income tax, so they spend it instead"

"Do you mean they spend the income tax?" said Mrs. Halliday; and indeed anything to do with money is so peculiar now that her question was hardly unreasonable.

"Not exactly," said Lady Graham assuming an ease that she did not feel, so tenuous was her grasp of what was vaguely adumbrated in her mind. "But if you spend more than you really have, you have less than you would have had, and then the Government doesn't tax you so much. At least that is my view of it," which last words her ladyship spoke with a modest pride as of one who habitually frequented the realms of high finance.

"Another way," said Mrs. Halliday, returning to the Old Manor House, "would be for George and his wife to live there, I mean if he got married, and for us to stay here. Perhaps that would be better. Leonard does love the place and so long as he is happy I don't care where I live. They could have parties much better down there in that lovely drawing-room and there would be plenty of room upstairs for the babies and we might put a small lift in for the nursery meals. I have seen more households wrecked by the nursery trays than by religion or politics."

"Of course we had a nursery maid to do that at Rushwater when we were small," said Lady Graham, "but when darling mamma took us all to London we had to have a nursery footman. Those Cadogan Square houses are so high and there wasn't a lift, so the footman used to carry us upstairs. There was one delightful footman called Charles whom I was going to marry when I grew up. He sang comic songs for us sometimes and could play on the Jews' harp and always pretended to fall downstairs to amuse us after he had carried us all up."

Mrs. Halliday asked what happened to him, but Lady Graham did not know.

"It is quite extraordinary," she said, "how many people one forgets. Even people we have known quite well. There was a most delightful Austrian friend of Robert's who used to kiss one's hand so charmingly when he came to call. I never heard of him again and Robert thinks he went to South America, which would account for it. Tell me, how is your husband?"

"A little better every week and rather lower by the end of the month," said Mrs. Halliday without emotion.

"Like darling mamma," said Lady Graham, "but she had her grandchildren about her in those last years. I think Clarissa was her favourite, but how she loved them all. She always said Edith was the only Pomfret of the family. Edith is rather a spoilt youngest," said her mother impartially, "but that always happens. My brother David was just the same. I do hope Edith will marry fairly young. We thought David would *never* marry, but Rose saw to that and it has been the greatest success except that they live mostly in America. And now we must go. I shall come over again soon if I may. Luckily I shall not have to do any shopping for Edith, as Rose says she is going to get her some clothes in New York. Now we *really* must go. If I get that nice Lord Cross to come to dinner when Robert is back, would you come too? I mean just you yourself to make a four, because I know your husband won't go out in the evening," and Mrs. Halliday said provided Leonard were fairly well she would like it of all things.

"And when Edith is back from America, George must come," said Lady Graham. "We are so fond of him," and then she got up, said good-bye to the Hallidays and collected her daughter. George took them to their car and they drove away.

"Mother," said Edith, when they had crossed the bridge and got outside Hatch End on their way to Holdings, "I am quite indignant."

"Are you darling?" said her mother. "Look out, Vidler's van is

outside the Red Lion as usual. I cannot think why he is delivering fish so late."

"He isn't delivering fish, mother," said Edith as she drove
neatly past Vidler's van in the narrow uphill street. "He is
collecting the rabbits from the Mellings Arms," for Mr. Geo.
Panter, cousin to Mr. Halliday's carter, was a kind of clearing
house for poachers by special arrangement with the local con-
stabulary (whose wife was a cousin of Mrs. Panter) and supplied
among other places the Barchester black market. There was not
much traffic and they were soon at Holdings. Edith decanted
her mother at the front door and took the car round to the
garage. When she came back her mother was in the small
drawing-room.

"And what were you indignant about, darling?" said her
mother, who had an elephantine gift for not forgetting things.

"Indignant?" said Edith.

"Well, you said you were indignant, just as we came to the
Red Lion," said Lady Graham.

"*Did* I?" said Edith. "Oh, I know. About George."

Her mother asked why.

"Oh well, nothing *really*," said Edith, "but you said he must
come to dinner when I came back from America! You don't
seem to remember he is grown-up, mother! He could just as well
come while I'm away—and of course when I come back as well.
It must be *so* dull for him, mother."

"I sometimes wonder if it is rather dull here for *you*, darling,"
said Lady Graham.

Most young women, so addressed, would have told their
mothers to Come Off It. A few less nice ones might have said
their mothers *had* said it and how! Edith wondered at once, as
we alas should have done in her place, whether she had been
looking dull, or showing signs of being dullified as it were, and
felt guilty. On no reasonable grounds at all, we think, but if one
is born a self-accuser, an apologiser before apology is needed,
there is nothing for it. Even the weekly astronomical prediction

in a well-known Sunday paper that those born under Aquarius
will find this week lucky for financial transactions and may
expect a general upward trend in future planning (for they can
give the Delphic Sibyl points in doubles entendres capable of
being interpreted in nine and sixty ways, every single one of
which is wrong) do not really carry firm conviction to our
hesitating hearts.

"Of *course* not, mother!" said an indignant Edith. "Do ask
George over while I'm away, mother. He and father will get on
awfully well about County Councils and things."

"Let me see," said Lady Graham. "George must be in his
thirties by now. He is older than Sylvia, but then I don't know
how old Sylvia is. And of course he was in the last years of the
war. I must ask his mother; she will know," though we do not
think her ladyship was quite right here, for as we got older and
less wise time begins to telescope, to fold in on itself, to mean
less and less, just as we begin to realise that in the ordinary
course of nature we have less and less of it before us. We
ourselves find it more and more difficult to date our children's
births (the entering in the Family Bible no longer being a matter
of course) and often have to calculate them in a quite medieval
way from such dates as Adelina having been born the year the
spare room ceiling fell in, or Percy in nineteen-twenty because it
makes it so easy to calculate his age because it is always the same
as the date of the year—missing out the 19 of course and
subtracting twenty—except before May, up till the twenty-
ninth day of which month he is still the age of the year before.

"I know how old John-Arthur is," said Edith, "because he's in
the stud book," which statement drove Lady Graham into a
perfectly schizophrenic (if that is what we mean) condition, half
of her wanting to get the Peerage and look up that nice boy's age
at once, the other half wondering if she ought to reprove her
daughter for speaking in so raffish a way of that great bulwark of
our past (and in many cases distinctly dubious) history. "He's
fairly old too but not so much older than me as George is."

"Older than *I*, darling," said Lady Graham with the top—or automatic—layer of her mind, but the under or subconscious part was trying to remember what it was it was trying to remember. "Wait! I knew it would come back to me. It was George Rivers's brother's second wife. At least she wasn't really his wife for a long time because his wife was alive and didn't divorce him and then they had a daughter."

"*Who* had the daughter, mother?" said Edith.

"The woman George's brother was living with abroad," said Lady Graham, "and when the daughter was born she was illegitimate of course and the wife managed to get her into the Peerage with the wrong date for her birth which was shocking. However George's brother is dead and as there isn't any money and they live in Majorca it doesn't really matter."

"Oh, mother!" said Edith, who had been apparently listening to what her mother said, but really thinking her own quite irrelevant thoughts. "*Please* will you ask Mrs. Morland to tea before I go. You did promise you would ask her."

Lady Graham said of course she would and she would write to Lord Stoke because ringing up was no use now as he would insist on answering the telephone himself and was deafer than ever. And as soon as she had his lordship's answer she would write to Mrs. Morland.

"Oh *thank* you, mother," said Edith. "How lovely. And when I am in America I shall boast that I know her."

"But do Americans read her books?" said Lady Graham. "I mean they are so very *English*," to which Edith replied that Rose said all her friends in America were crazy about Mrs. Morland's books just because they *were* so very English.

Then Aggie Hubback came in with a mixture of boisterousness (natural) and terror (because she knew whatever she did would be wrong in cook's eyes and that cook always KNEW when anything had gone wrong like the evening the caramel pudding just slipped off the dish as easy as anything and threw itself onto the floor) and announced their evening meal, which it is simpler to call supper as it was usually two courses, though when Sir Robert came down cook always gave him at least three courses not to speak of game in season by courtesy of the local poacher via the Mellings Arms; so Lady Graham and her daughter talked about ordinary things while Aggie was about and then went to bed early.

CHAPTER 8

L ady Graham, whose business-like mind was often a great
surprise to people who had thought of her as a kind of
lovely piece of seaweed, drifting with the tide, rocked by the
surges, had not forgotten her plan to get Mrs. Morland to
Holdings. To this end she wrote to Lord Stoke, inviting him
to come over to lunch and to bring Mrs. Morland. She also
telephoned to Mrs. Morland to tell her what she had done.

"How good of you to let me know about your party," said
Mrs. Morland, "because I am sure Lord Stoke would have
forgotten to tell me. He is getting older. I suppose it is hardly
surprising when you consider that he has been the same age
practically ever since I have known him except for being even
deafer," which even to Agnes's tolerant mind sounded rather
disconnected, but we all know that writers are mentally arrested
and—in the great words of the convalescent soldier at Beliers
when Mrs. Morland was giving a Literary Talk to the patients—
go into a trance, sort of, when they write books. We think that
Mrs. Morland put it very well when speaking at the Annual
Lunch of the Friends of Barchester Cathedral about that enchanting writer Henry Kingsley who, we hope, will rise again
into favour before long, for his three great books and for the
impish fun in them, whether he writes of England or Australia
or the devilish ways of children. After her talk, in which she had
divagated as widely from her subject as Henry Kingsley usually

does from his, a very dull member of the audience had risen to her feet and said She could not but deplore the fact that Henry Kingsley's approach to Life was on the whole Whimsical and Life was far from that, being rather a reverent preparation for what we should find on the other side of the Great Divide. To which Mrs. Morland, hitting her hat straight as was her custom, had replied that it was a most interesting contribution to the discussion, and though she could not but acknowledge to some extent the truth of what the last speaker had said, one could not judge any writer of fiction by any given standard. Speaking as a writer of fiction herself and one who had taken to writing because she had to earn money to support and educate her four boys and thank goodness *that* was all over now except that one still had to do so much for one's grandchildren, she must say that the wind blew where it listed, adding carelessly, St. John, chapter three, verse eight, which impressed her audience deeply and made them turn their heads and look with a kind of pitying contempt at the critic. Mrs. Morland's peroration—inspired she afterwards said entirely by hatred and scorn of anyone who was silly enough to say things like that and to use expressions like Whimsical and the Great Divide—was a comparison between Henry Kingsley and that sad genius Edgar Allan Poe. Not, she said, that there was the faintest likeness between them, but of each it might be said in certain moods that All his days were trances. And all his nights were dreams, at which point her voice became so choked with emotion (as it always did when she said poetry aloud) that she had to drink quite half a tumbler of very nasty flat water which must have been sitting in the thick glass carafe for at least a week.

No one could have accused Mrs. Morland of being a dreamer, for she wrote and delivered her books with punctuality and despatch and her publisher Adrian Coates said she had never been a best seller and never would be, but he wouldn't mind having a few more steady sellers like Mrs. Morland who could be relied upon to deliver the goods, fairly neatly packed, in as good condition as her wits could compass and on the dot. Which winged words made no impression at all upon the gifted writer herself, who though she rather enjoyed her own Madame Koska thrillers and often re-read them, had no particular belief in them or herself, and only hoped to be able to go on supporting herself and helping her family and grand-family till death them did part.

Mrs. Morland then wrote to Lord Stoke and asked if he would pick her up on the way to Holdings and his lordship rang her up and said why couldn't she use the telephone and he would be over soon after twelve with the dog-cart and she was to wrap up well because this weather played Old Harry with one's sciatica and he strongly recommended her to wear a piece of red flannel on the loins, next the skin. And then he rang off, which was his custom because he could never hear what people said on the telephone, and this was often helpful to him in arguments when the opposing party had not grasped the fact that his lordship as well as being wilfully deaf was really deaf.

We cannot truthfully say that the day appointed for Lord Stokes to bring Mrs. Morland was a nice day, for there was no nice day that summer, not even during the fortnight when we were out of England; and if it couldn't be warm then, when we were far from our native land, it will obviously never try to be warm for us again. But all our readers (except the one who cannot *possibly* sit in a room with the windows *shut*, my dear, and you must let me know tomorrow morning if there was enough on your bed of course I find two blankets *ample* but some people are funny about what they have on their beds and I can easily get the eider-down out as it is only at the bottom of that big trunk in the boxroom where I keep all my woollies with moth balls) who experienced that summer—and The Sooner The Better Forgot (which quotation, used in a rude lampoon against that gifted author Miss Harriette Wilson, is still in search of its author)—will remember and understand.

It was, not to put too fine a point upon it, a quite beastly day

of grey sky, knife-blasts of wind and wild scudding rain as chill
as hail at intervals. Mrs. Morland, determined not to wear a red
flannel petticoat which would probably make her skirt too tight,
old though it was, had given a good deal of thought to what she
should wear in the dog-cart and had finally decided to put on her
winter underwear and go in her old, thick tweeds, with a heavy
tweed coat that had a removable lining of coney seal, otherwise
known as rabbit. All these she put on, and a felt hat which she
jammed well down on her head, and took her silver fox fur
which had now been sides-to-middled as it were, so that its
stomach was velvet instead of fur and it had lost nearly all its
claws, but still had both its eyes.

As punctually as the Count of Monte Cristo the hoofs (or
hooves) of Lord Stoke's strong horse were heard outside Mrs.
Morland's door. Her faithful and tyrannous servant Stoker,
fatter and more truculent year by year, but always a superb cook,
came into the drawing-room and said, "It's his lordship in the
broom," which sounded to Mrs. Morland like the title of a
folk-song (probably bawdy). "It's Albert as is driving."

Mrs. Morland asked who Albert was.

"Mr. Tony would remember Albert," said Stoker, alluding to
Mrs. Morland's youngest son, now practically a foreigner because he lived in London with his wife and his delightful though
exhausting children. "He was under the butler at Rising Castle
and he drives his lordship when it's the brougham," at which
Mrs. Morland's heart leapt in her bosom, for much as she liked
her old friend Lord Stoke and much as she was looking forward
to seeing Lady Graham she thought of the drive in a dog-cart—
and, far worse, the drive back in a dog-cart, through the Arctic
cold of a late summer day—with genuine apprehension.

Albert on the box touched his hat to Mrs. Morland. Lord
Stoke opened the door from inside and Mrs. Morland got in;
not very elegantly, for in truth there is no way of mounting a
brougham with grace, because as you step into it you have to
duck your head and you present a foolish appearance from the

back to say the least of it. In fact we cannot think of any vehicle now which one can mount with grace, the victoria, that elegant equipage, being as dead as the majestical and deeply comfortable landau. Words which to our young must mean less than nothing; no more than tilbury and dennet mean to us now though highly fashionable in their time.

"Glad to see you, Mrs. Morland," said Lord Stoke, sitting himself well back into his corner so that his guest could spread herself. "Haven't seen you since we last met. When was it?"

Mrs. Morland said she didn't know because somehow time seemed to go faster and faster the older one got and she thought Shakespeare was quite wrong about galloping withal.

"Galloping with *what*?" said Lord Stoke. "Can't hear what you say in this brougham."

"Withal," said Mrs. Morland.

"Can't hear you," said Lord Stoke, who like nearly all deaf people knew that he could hear perfectly well if people would only take the trouble to speak clearly. "Confounded rattletrap this brougham! My old father bought it for my mother. You never knew her!" he added, as if accusing Mrs. Morland of gross negligence coupled with a tendency to prevarication.

"I couldn't, Lord Stoke," said Mrs. Morland. "She died before I knew you."

"Eh?" said Lord Stoke.

Mrs. Morland repeated her remark very slowly, in capital letters.

"Of course you didn't know her," said Lord Stoke. "Been dead a matter of forty years. Never buttoned her boots or did up her shoe-laces in her life."

"It must have been rather uncomfortable," said Mrs. Morland.

"Eh? Can't hear a word in this confounded brougham," said Lord Stoke.

Mrs. Morland repeated her words, which sounded to her as

worthless as our own words do (as everyone who has heard a recording of her own voice will know).

"Uncomfortable. Why?" said his lordship.

"Don't bully me, Lord Stoke," said Mrs. Morland firmly. "I mean if she never buttoned her boots it MUST. HAVE. BEEN. VERY. UNCOMFORTABLE. THEY WOULD FLAP ABOUT."

"What the dooce are you talking about?" said Lord Stoke. "Flap about? My mother's boots never flapped about. Her maid buttoned them for her. She never put her shoes on herself in her life. Nor her boots either for that matter. Made to order they were; bespoke. And never bought anything off the peg in her life! Nor have I. My tailor comes down here to measure me. Never go to London now if I can help it. Everyone's dead. Lot of young fellers in the club that I don't know. Don't know their fathers either. Daresay they don't know them themselves," and his lordship laughed a very coarse laugh.

"Don't be so Regency, Lord Stoke," said Mrs. Morland, but Lord Stoke did not hear, or did not wish to hear, and gave it as his unasked opinion that his sister Lucasta's boy wasn't doing badly over at Staple Park and had two good sows in farrow.

"Good lad, C.W.," said his lordship.

Mrs. Morland said she had always wondered what those initials meant.

"What initials?" said Lord Stoke. "Oh, C.W., you mean. His father was a fool. Thought he was a descendant of the Saxons or something. *His* father was a fool too, so was his grandfather. All fools. One of them called his son Ivanhoe and then there was an Athelstane and an Ethelwulf. Lucasta's husband was called Alured and they called this boy Cedric Weyland. Damn fool name, but they call him C.W. Well, Bond's dead and Lucasta's a widow and a nice little jointure too. She wanted to come and live in the village but I hadn't a house empty. *I* know Lucasta. Fine woman, but managing."

"So what did she do?" said Mrs. Morland.

"Do?" said Lord Stoke. "Did what they all do. Took a house in Bath. She's got a queer leg or thinks she has. Everyone has queer legs in Bath. *I'd* have a queer leg if I went there. If you want a queer leg you had better have it at home. Know where you are, eh?"

With this and similar valuable information Lord Stoke passed the time, while Mrs. Morland was able to think, or do what passed in her mind for thinking, about the latest developments in Madame Koska's dressmaking establishment and wondering whether her public would, for a slight change, like a young male villain, beardless and good-looking, who would disguise himself as a mannequin and so get access to Madame's jealousy guarded spring model gowns.

"Well, you don't seem to have much to say," said Lord Stoke.

"I couldn't," said Mrs. Morland, "because you were doing all the saying. But I was wondering about my new book."

"You're a damned clever woman," said Lord Stoke, "but I can't read your books. Not in my line. You don't mind?"

"Not a bit," said Mrs. Morland. "They would mean absolutely nothing at all to you. But I want your advice."

"No one wants advice," said Lord Stoke. "And they wouldn't take it if they got it. Damn that feller of mine, what's he up to? I told him to go round by the lower road" and he pulled the check-string which, to the joy of the whole county (except people like Lord Aberfordbury ci-devant Sir Ogilvy Hibberd) he always had attached to his coachman-groom when being driven. The driver pulled up his horse and sat motionless on the box.

"Damn nuisance not having a footman," said Lord Stoke and held down one window and put his head out of it.

"Here! I said the lower road," said Lord Stoke, and if he did not add a good late-eighteenth or early-nineteenth century oath it was because he never swore before ladies unless he had to.

"Yes, my lord," said the coachman.

"Well, why the dickens don't you?" said Lord Stoke.

"Road up, my lord," said the coachman. "West Barsetshire County Council road repairs."

"Oh, all right, all right," said Lord Stoke and he slammed the window up (which, given enough skill and strength can be done quite as angrily and swiftly as slamming it down) and sat back in his corner till they got to the Holdings front door which in pleasant country fashion was always open, though there was an inner door which had not once been left open during that horrible summer, though never locked till late.

Lord Stoke heaved himself out and gave his hand to Mrs. Morland with the courtesy of the age of carriages. Not that this form of courtesy is of much use now, for who can hand a lady into or out of a car when she has to bend double to get in and can only get out by pushing her legs out first and getting her skirt and the rest of her out as best she can?

"Might stay on to tea," said Lord Stoke to his coachman, "or I mightn't," with which helpful instructions he went into the house and the coachman turned the horse and went happily towards the stables where there would be friends, and a good dinner presently in the kitchen where cook kept a very liberal table for visitors.

Lady Graham and Mrs. Morland had known each other off and on for a good many years with mutual respect but never with familiarity and got on excellently, each giving the other plenty of elbow room for talking (if our reader sees what we mean), each admiring in the other gifts and work out of her own sphere. Never could Mrs. Morland have run Holdings with its garden, its farm, its outlying properties, its owner Sir Robert Graham and its perpetual open house. On the other hand, had Sir Robert unfortunately died when still only Colonel Graham, leaving his wife a widow with six children, Agnes would have had the choice of marrying again (which we think would not have been difficult, nor are all stepfathers Mr. Murdstone) or being one of those depressed hangers-on of titled families, like the Bonds' old cousin the Honourable Juliana Starter, youngest of old Lord

Mickleham's eighteen children and formerly Lady-in-Waiting
to Princess Louisa Christina, daughter of Prince Louis of Co-
balt and one of the Hatz-Reinigens; or, to compare small things
with great, Miss Volumnia Dedlock: only neither of these ladies
had families to complicate their lives, not being married.

"We are only a small party," said Lady Graham to Mrs.
Morland. "I didn't ask people to lunch on purpose because of
Lord Stoke's deafness, only Lord Cross and his son, a delightful
young man and of course Edith is here. She is going to America
with my brother David and his wife. I think she will love it."

"I wonder why one always thinks other people will love
things?" said Mrs. Morland. "I am sure if some of my friends
heard I was going to hell they would say 'I am sure Laura will like
it immensely and think of all the interesting people she will
meet.' But really," said Mrs. Morland, who appeared by now to
be taking this imaginary trip to hell as a matter of course, "I
daresay one would find friends. I have found people very nice on
the whole, wherever I have been, except of course the really
horrible ones."

With this Lady Graham quite agreed, instancing various
people with whom she had got on quite well though NOT, she
said, suddenly remembering old wrongs, that dreadful little Mr.
Holt who was a garden snob and a toad-eater. And as this is one
of the very few occasions when her ladyship recorded dislike of
anyone, it is worth recording.

"I don't think I have been here since the year Peace broke
out," said Mrs. Morland, "when Lady Emily was still alive and
you had the Bring and Buy Sale though for what I do not know.
How lovely your mother was. But impossible to describe to
anyone who hadn't seen her. Those beautiful eyes like a kind
hawk's and the loveliest mouth I have ever seen."

"Darling mamma," said Lady Graham, "I don't *miss* her now,
but I often wish she were here," and she looked at Mrs. Morland, doubtful of her own power of explaining her feelings, but
thinking that someone who wrote books might understand.

"I know," said Mrs. Morland. "Rather like The Monkey's Paw," but Lady Graham had not read it and did not know what Mrs. Morland meant which was perhaps just as well, for one would not wish to think of a dearly loved mother coming to the door after dark with her human form in the shape which death had brought it to, even if not mangled by machinery.

"It is extraordinary how few people one does really miss," said Mrs. Morland. "Sometimes one says to oneself 'It *would* be nice if So-and-so were here' and it is always someone much older than oneself—one of one's parents' friends. It isn't always the people one loved best that one wants. More the people that were kind to one when one was young. I suppose one wants the safe feeling. And then they spoke the same language that we do. I don't know," and neither did Lady Graham and on the whole most of us don't.

"We can always *hope* to see them, even if one doesn't expect to," said Lady Graham, in a religious voice.

Mrs. Morland said it was not so much the fear of not seeing the people she did want to see that worried her, as the probability of seeing people she *didn't* want to see, like those dreadful Mixo-Lydians during the war and the Bishop's wife.

"And what is so dreadful," said Lady Graham, "is the people who will want to see you. I *know* that dreadful little Mr. Holt will want me to arrange for him to see the Garden of Eden on the day when visitors aren't allowed and ask if he can have a cutting from the tree of the knowledge of good and evil," at which words Mrs. Morland had to laugh and after a moment's bewilderment Lady Graham joined her.

Then Edith came in with Lord Stoke who had wanted to see the alterations Lady Graham had made in the kitchen and had been reminded by cook of the day he came in via the back door and how she would never forget it and Edith had felt that for twopence Lord Stoke would put his arm round cook's waist and kiss her.

Aggie Hubback then managed to announce Lord Cross and

his son, who had not met Mrs. Morland before and were delighted, Lord Cross in particular.

"I have so often wanted to write you, Mrs. Morland," he said, "to tell you what great pleasure my wife had from your books. She was ill for some time before she died and she must have read them all at least three times. She had a special shelf made to hold them all. But there are too many now and she is not here to read them. I used to read them aloud to her in the last few weeks of her life, when she was very weak," said Lord Cross. "She loved laughing and how she used to laugh. She meant to write to you and then it was too late."

Mrs. Morland, her kind heart sincerely touched by Lord Cross's words, tried to express her feelings but did not quite succeed and we do not think that Lord Cross thought any the less of her because his short sad tale had moved her.

"Then are you quite alone?" said Mrs. Morland.

Lord Cross said that boy of his, looking at Mr. Cross, lived at home though he mostly weren't there, and his married daughters came down with or without their children quite often. But it was not the same.

"I rather envy you," said Mrs. Morland. "You can go on loving your wife when she isn't there. I have entirely forgotten my husband. Not that he was a bad husband but he was what the French call nul. I mean as a *character*," she added, looking firmly at his lordship, "because I have four sons."

Then Aggie Hubback announced lunch, but it did not make much difference to the conversation, because there were only six people and they could talk in a general way.

"And now do tell me, Lord Cross," said Lady Graham, "is anything decided about the Old Manor House, where your nice boy was looking after the bank?"

Lord Cross said not yet. "I rather wish it were," he said, "because we—I mean the bank—feel slightly responsible. When we took it as a kind of sub-branch for local customers we did not know that the Housing Estate would develop so rapidly. Everything is drifting in that direction and we shall be doing a good deal of business. Now I hear that the owner is an invalid and I gather he would have been just as glad if we could have gone on. I think you know them."

Lady Graham said not intimately but they had been neighbours during all her married life and she and her husband liked the Hallidays very much.

"By the way, Lord Cross," she said, "did I tell you that my husband is retiring? He has been offered one or two good directorships and might travel on business. I do not quite understand it yet, but whatever he does he is sure to do very well," and Lord Cross said from what he had heard through friends on Associated Holdings Limited and the Cruscofer Export and Ullage Association, Sir Robert's name stood very high and the City would welcome him. It was curious, he said, that the first of the two interests he had mentioned should have the name of Sir Robert's estate.

Lady Graham, her brow slightly ruffled, said she didn't quite understand.

"I was alluding to Associated Holdings," said Lord Cross.

"Oh, but I never thought for a moment it was *our* Holdings," said Lady Graham. "I mean business in London is *quite* different from being here. I am not sure what Holdings really means. Robert would know. It was either someone called Holding or Holden who owned some land here, or some people say the Hol part is like Holy and there was a saint somewhere about, but I don't *think* a saint would be called Dings—except that *anything* might have happened before people could read or write. Though I must say," her ladyship added, "that quite extraordinary things happen now."

They then fell into a conversation from which it emerged that he and his wife, in search of better health for her, had once met Lady Emily Leslie at Bad Eichhorn where her ladyship was also taking the cure when she remembered. And we may add that without the invaluable Miss Merriman at her elbow she would rarely have tasted those health-giving and revolting waters.

"By the way, Lady Graham," said Lord Cross, "my elder daughter rather wants to take a house in these parts where her husband can get some fishing at weekends. I wonder if the Hallidays would consider re-letting that delightful house where we had our little branch here? My boy took me over it after the bank had done it up."

Lady Graham said she knew nothing of their plans, but she was sure that if they were going to let Lord Cross's daughter would be exactly what they would like.

"What house are you talking about?" said Lord Stoke, whose deafness was a good deal conditioned (horrible word) by his curiosity (or lack of the same) about any subject under discussion.

Lady Graham told him.

"Nice little house," said his lordship. "I went over there once to see those old women that lived there. My old mother knew them. Harridan or some such name."

"Not Harridan, Lord Stoke; Halliday," said Lady Graham. "But it has been beautifully done up since then by Lord Cross's bank."

"Bank, eh?" said Lord Stoke. "Bad plan to borrow from your bank. Now I always keep a good balance at my bank and a deposit account. That's the way to do it."

"But, Lord Stoke," said Lady Graham. "Lord Cross's bank didn't do it up. I mean it was for his son, not for him."

"Same thing," said Lord Stoke. "Qui facit per alium, y'know Cross. Shockin' the way they teach Latin at school now. Don't teach it at all. Teach them economics and birth-control and all that," and to the great admiration of his audience he added, "Bah," at which point Lady Graham, with gentle remorselessness, took charge of him and they discussed old Lady Norton, known to all her friends as the Dreadful Dowager, and how she and her daughter-in-law quarrelled.

"And how's that husband of yours?" said Lord Stoke.

"Oh, very well," said Lady Graham. "You know he is retiring.
It has been coming for some time. This is his last week at work.
He is dining with my brother David and his wife and Edith on
Friday. Then Edith goes to America with David and Rose, and
Robert will be down here on the Saturday."

"Retiring? What's he retiring for?" said Lord Stoke. "I never
retired. My old governor—*you* never knew him, Lady Graham,
wore one of those flat brown billycocks and rode to hounds—
taught me to ride, but I'm too old and heavy now. But I don't
retire. Do my riding in the brougham or the dog-cart. My old
governor never retired. He'd have gone mad with nothing to do.
Take my advice, Lady Graham, and tell Sir Robert once he lies
down in the loose box he's done for."

"Now, Lord Stoke," said Lady Graham, whose apparent
vagueness covered a good deal of inherited common-sense, "you
should not speak till you know your facts. Robert is going to be
busier than ever. Now, listen, dear Lord Stoke. He is going to try
for the West Barsetshire County Council and a lot of other
useful things and make the Conservative Association sit up and
what is more, he is going to be the Vicar's churchwarden here,"
to which his lordship's rather Regency reply was, we regret to
say, "By Gad he is, is he?" and what Mrs. Morland who had
overheard part of this conversation afterwards described as a
rather lecherous laugh. Though what Lord Stoke could have
found lecherous in being a churchwarden we do not know, nor
do we think Mrs. Morland did.

But Lord Stoke had had quite a long enough innings with
Lady Graham who turned to Lord Cross, leaving Lord Stoke to
Edith.

"You won't be alarmed if I shout at you, will you, Lord
Cross?" said Lady Graham. "When one has been talking with
Lord Stoke one gets quite deaf and doesn't know how loud one
is talking. And do tell me more about your daughter who might
take the Old Manor House. I went all over it with your boy—

John-Arthur my Edith calls him, but I am not so quick at
Christian names and after all he *is* your boy—" (which made
Lord Cross feel as if his son's paternity were questioned and he
would have laughed had not an inner voice told him that his
hostess would then (a) ask him what he was laughing at and (b)
not understand his explanation) "and I thought it quite charming and so easy to live in. I didn't see the basement but I gather
from my cook who knows the caretaker that there is oil for the
central heating and bath water and an up-to-date kitchen, and
gas water heaters in the kitchen and scullery as well, in case the
central heating breaks down. Of course I still feel that a service
lift to the nursery floor is an absolute essential. You might be able to
put one in the pantry and it could go through the dining-room
which would be most useful and save all the up-and-down stairs,
and then through that back dressing-room and come into that
other small room on the top floor which will make a delightful
little nursery pantry with a gas ring and perhaps one of those tiny
gas or electric ovens just for hotting things up or keeping them
hot," and she waited for Lord Cross's approval, looking—as his
lordship irreverently said to his son afterwards—like a hen who
has just laid an egg.

Lord Cross said it sounded delightful and he would like to
bring his daughter over one day to look at it, as the bank's lease
still had a few weeks to run. And then, via old Mr. Gresham,
M.P. for East Barsetshire who was a neighbour of Lord Cross,
they passed to Barsetshire society in general where we will leave
them and take a chair by Mrs. Morland who was getting on
extremely well with Mr. Cross. It was one of the well-known
author's endearing qualities that she was always surprised to find
that any of her friends, old or new, read her books, for she was a
modest creature and so long as she could earn her living had no
ambition to be considered literary—horrible mis-used word.

"But my sisters do really love your books, Mrs. Morland," said
Mr. Cross. "They buy every one as soon as it comes out."

"Do you mean they *each* buy one?" said Mrs. Morland.

"But of course," said Mr. Cross. "One must have a book to oneself. When my old grandfather liked a book—that was my mother's father—he used to order a copy to be sent to each of his family."

"Goodness!" said Mrs. Morland. "Though of course books were cheaper then. When I was a girl all the novels were six shillings but one only paid four and six, I cannot think why. And when I was a schoolgirl and The Hound of the Baskervilles was coming out—in the Strand Magazine I think—it cost sixpence, but you could buy it over the counter for four-pence halfpenny and my brother and I used to club together to get a copy every month. Oh dear! how good it was then."

Mr. Cross asked if she meant The Hound of the Baskervilles or Old Times in general.

"I really don't know," said Mrs. Morland. "Isn't she charming?" and she looked across at Edith who was flirting outrageously with Lord Stoke.

"Quite charming," said Mr. Cross. "I would propose to her tomorrow if it weren't for two things."

Mrs. Morland asked what they were.

"Quite simple," said Mr. Cross. "I am too old for her and she is too young for me. You know, Mrs. Morland, we young-old, or old-young whichever you like to put it, are a bit out of it sometimes. The fellows that were married, or engaged, came back—if they did come back—and settled down more or less. We others have dilly-dallied—at least quite a lot of us have including my horrible self—and shilly-shallied and taken our time and not wanted to walk out of one sort of war into another sort of war and here we are."

"But you are a mere child," said Mrs. Morland.

"Granted," said Mr. Cross. "But getting on, you know. How old are your sons, if I may ask: though of course they *cannot* be more than fourteen or fifteen at most," he added gallantly.

"If I had a fan I would rap your knuckles," said Mrs. Morland, "but a spoon would look too hoydenish and might hurt you. My boys—I have four—are from thirty-four to forty-four; but of course I always think of them as very trying and exhausting children of a larger growth."

"Exactly what I mean," said Mr. Cross. "And I am over thirty and so is that nice fellow Halliday. What have we been doing all this time?"

"From my point of view, wasting it since the peace," said Mrs. Morland, dispassionately. "There are plenty of nice girls—and nice women too—about. You young men have no spunk."

"How enchanting to hear that word," said Mr. Cross. "So Victorian."

"Very *late* Victorian," said Mrs. Morland. "I will say guts, if you prefer."

"Then I will say Kamerad," said Mr. Cross. "I say, Mrs. Morland, do you honestly think that?"

"But of course I do," said Mrs. Morland. "I am always truthful—except about being nice to people you don't like. I am exceptionally nice to them, just to show myself that it has got to behave if I tell it to—only I don't always tell it."

"I am deeply sorry that you don't like *me*, Mrs. Morland," said Mr. Cross and for a moment Mrs. Morland thought she had hurt him, but a glance re-assured her.

"Idiot!" said Mrs. Morland pleasantly. "But you know, Mr. Cross, the girls, if you can call them that, are just as bad. All getting Higher Education and jobs and sharing flats with other girls. I think it was so clever of Lady Graham to keep her girls so pure," at which word Mr. Cross had to laugh. "Of course Clarissa did go to college, because she insisted, but she has shed it beautifully. I went to tea at Harefield House School last week and she is so happy and so pretty that one nearly cries; and you know she is having a baby quite soon."

"On the other hand," said Mr. Cross, lowering his voice, "there is our charming friend on the other side of the table who hasn't wanted to be educated and yet isn't content. Probably she doesn't show it to you, but I am just near enough to her to feel it."

"What she needs," said Mrs. Morland, dispassionately, "is a good shaking. But not yet. Remember she is only half your age. What were you at that age?"

"A ghastly, pimpled gawky fool," said Mr. Cross enthusiastically, "and reading Tolstoi and Shaw and despising my parents. But I was always behind the times. Now I flatter myself that I am pretty ordinary."

"L'homme moyen sensuel," said Mrs. Morland rather showing-offishly, and then there was the sudden lull that sometimes falls on a party, so she smiled to Mr. Cross and turned to his father, leaving her last partner to talk with Edith.

"Are you getting very excited about America?" said Mr. Cross.

"Not yet," said Edith, "but I shall. Just at present it isn't true. I mean—I can't quite explain."

"I think it must be much the same as going over the top," said Mr. Cross. "I only saw the end of the war, you know, because of my comparative youth, but most of the time it wasn't real."

"Like a dream?" said Edith.

"A bit," said Mr. Cross. "Everything turning out differently from what you expected and yet you aren't surprised."

"*Just* like dreams," said Edith. "Only with dreams you do wake up. Did you ever wake up?"

"Now, that is a question that no one has ever asked me before," said Mr. Cross. "Did I wake up? Do you know, Edith, for the life of me I can't give you the answer. Perhaps I'm still asleep," and then he felt that what he was saying was in the nature of phony or whimsy and wished he hadn't said it. And yet it was true. One might wake up in France; or further up towards the Belgian frontier; or further still, one didn't know where. That way madness lay. Better not to think about it and carry on. Talk with Edith, who was such an amusing and well-bred child, for young woman one could hardly say, though she had all the arts of one.

Presently Lady Graham put the men under the guardianship of Lord Cross, whom she somehow felt could be trusted not to let Lord Stoke sit there talking for ever, and took her ladies to the little sitting-room and a good fire. And here Mrs. Morland showed the real kindness of her heart by letting Edith talk to her about her books and give her opinions on various characters and say what they ought, in her opinion, to have done. Lady Graham wondered if her youngest daughter was perhaps being a trifle boring, but as Mrs. Morland did not appear to mind she took out her embroidery and thought how nice and quiet the house would be after Edith's departure (though she would miss the darling creature), and how very nice it would be if her guests did not want to see the farm on this horrid cold windy day of late summer. And she felt delightfully sleepy and would have liked nothing more than to go to sleep till tea-time, but the telephone bell rang. Edith went to it.

"Oh mother, it's George," she said. "He says his father feels better today and would like to have a look at the pigs and may he drive him over."

"But of *course*," said Lady Graham. "Say just whenever he likes and to drive right up to the farm gate. We shall probably be there then and Goble will in any case. And my love to Mrs. Halliday of course," which message Edith delivered and then went back to her talk with Mrs. Morland.

"Oh, Mrs. Morland," she said presently. "Do people read your books in America?"

Mrs. Morland said they did and she really didn't know why, as her books were so very English, but perhaps it was because she only wrote about ordinary people and after all most people were ordinary.

"And do you have fan letters," Edith continued.

Mrs. Morland said yes, quite a number.

"And do you answer them?" said Edith.

Mrs. Morland said Of *course*. One always answered letters.

"But I thought perhaps you had a secretary to do that part," said Edith.

"I did try for a bit," said Mrs. Morland, "but she never understood what I said, so now I do them all myself on my typewriter. My typing is nearly as bad as my handwriting, but it doesn't make my arm ache so much and it is less illegible, though the spelling is shocking. I don't know why it is, as I spell very well naturally, but my typewriter has its own ideas about spelling. It loves to get words with ght wrong, so that instead of B-R-I-G-H-T it is B-R-I-H-G-T and I can do *nothing* about it."

"Are lots of your letters from America?" said Edith.

Mrs. Morland said a very large number were and she could not think why they took the trouble to write when England was so far away, but they were always so very kind.

"And do you always answer them?" said Edith.

Mrs. Morland said Always, because when people were kind enough to take the trouble to write, the very least you could do was to thank them for their kindness and why did Edith want to know.

"Well, it sounds rather silly," said Edith, going pink in the face in a very becoming way, "but may I tell people in America that I know you?" and Mrs. Morland suddenly realised that in Edith's eyes she was now not so much Mrs. Morland, an acquaintance of her mother's, as AN AUTHOR, and that Edith, perhaps a little overwhelmed by the thought of her first journey to an unknown continent, was looking for support. So she said Of course, tell *everyone* and Edith looked relieved and grateful.

As it was not raining Lady Graham said those who wished might as well go and see Goble and come back for tea, but she would certainly not go, at which moment George Halliday came in.

"Oh, how do you do, Lady Graham," he said. "Hullo, Edith.

Lady Graham, I'm awfully sorry, but father didn't feel up to it at the last moment, so mother said I'd better come alone. I hope it's all right."

"Of course, dear boy," said Lady Graham. "I am not going to the farm and I want to hear how your father is. I am so very sorry about him," and George was quite glad to remain with her, even if some of his thoughts were elsewhere.

"Now, sit down dear boy," said Lady Graham to George. "It is lovely to have you all to myself. And how is your mother?"

"Oh, she's all right, Lady Graham," said George. "A bit worried about father, but there it is. We shall have to have a nurse for him soon and he *will* so hate it. He has always been independent. It's really too much for mother, but I can't be in the house and on the farm at the same time."

"Of course you can't," said Lady Graham. "There is a very nice Sister Heath over at Northbridge who is a retired nurse and even if she isn't free she had two very nice friends called Ward and Chiffinch who have nursed lots of my friends. I know one of them nursed that dreadful Julian Rivers once when he had influenza at the Towers. Would it be any help if I wrote to her, just in case you need someone?" and George said indeed it would and how grateful his mother would be.

"You know, Lady Graham," said George Halliday, "it is all so Old at Hatch House now and I think that helps to get mother down. Our servants are old and father is old—and I'm not a youngster myself," at which Lady Graham laughed, though very kindly, and said he was only an older boy who used to be very kind and play with her boys, and she could never think of him as grown-up.

"Much too old for Edith, anyway," said George, who was sitting with his knees apart and swinging his hands between them.

"Is it that?" said Lady Graham, after what felt like a three hours' silence but was barely a few seconds.

"It's that all right," said George. "I didn't mean to mention it. Let's forget it."

"You are a dear, good, kind boy," said Lady Graham. "You will forget it."

"I won't," said George, though not at all rudely, merely stating a fact. "I don't think one does, you know, at my age."

"My dear boy, don't be ridiculous," said Lady Graham, but very kindly. "My husband is fifteen years older than I am, though no one would guess it to look at him. Or to look at me," which postscript or rider made George laugh and did him a lot of good. "Listen, George. I can't order you, but I do ask you, not to say anything that would make Edith guess before she goes. She will see a great deal more of life and young people with Rose than she ever would here and it is only fair that she should. When she comes back we will see how you feel. I shall not tell my husband and I trust you not to tell your mother. If you want to talk about your broken heart, come over here whenever you like. And then if you see someone else, nearer your age, if that is what you want, no one will know and no harm will be done. Shall we go and see the pigs? All the others are down at the sties. I must just get a coat as it is so cold and looks like rain. There are plenty in the hall and you had better take one too."

So they plowtered (delightful word, too little used, but we know it from our earliest days in one of the Caldecott picture books of the Three Jovial Huntsmen) across the garden and across the farm lane to where Goble was expounding his pig-theories to an admiring audience. And, as Goble said afterwards at the Mellings Arms (and far too often on many other days and at many other locals), it was a pleasure to talk to gentlemen as knew a pig when they saw one. Young Mr. Halliday, well he was young but that would cure itself in time (at which most of his hearers laughed in a sycophantic way, hoping that Goble would stand one more all round—which he didn't). Sir Robert *he* knew a pig, but it stood to reason as a gentleman who was in London all the time, there was things he couldn't bear in mind;

instancing the leak in the roof of what James Graham had very wittily called Queen Porkminster's Lying-in Hospital and the runt that he, Goble, had saved from destruction and brought up by hand and though any man as said that pig was a prize-winner, well that man was wrong, he was a prime baconer, he was. Which interesting anecdote led Goble to review in detail the art of curing pigs as it should be done, at home, not in the factories where you might send up a prime Porkminster and get him back in Norfolk Nobbler hams and sausages. To all which his audience, in what we can only call a cowardly and sycophantic way, responded with such comments as "Of course," "Ought to have known better," "Nothing like home-cured," which of course led Goble to a further dissertation on how to smoke hams and good wood smoke too, oak if you could get it, and none of your dirty coke.

The above is of course a long-hand transcript of his words at the Mellings Arms, but it must in fairness be said that he must have talked for at least a quarter of an hour, non-stop, to his audience at Holdings.

"Do you think he will ever stop?" said Mrs. Morland to Lord Cross.

"I'll give him another two minutes," said Lord Cross, taking a large gold half-hunter out of his pocket. "Then we close down," and to Mrs. Morland's immense admiration Lord Cross, at the expiration of the two minutes, snapped his watch to, put it back in his waistcoat pocket, and said he would like to see the sow.

In the fastnesses of Barsetshire we are glad to say that a Lord, provided he has roots in the county, is still a Lord, not only to the older generation but to a good many of the younger, and this we attribute partly to their fine distrust of outsiders. We may instance Lord Bond whose ancestors (as we have said before and we know it) were manufacturers from the north; whose own son, grandchildren and so on as long as anyone is allowed to hold his own land, are now and will be part of the county. But this they have earned by some hundred and fifty years of honourable service. So it was with Lord Cross whose peerage, though only going back to the later years of Queen Victoria, had been honestly earned by generations of squires who did hard work for tenants in village or farm, hard work on every kind of local council and speaking at Westminster, at least twice in every session, on affairs connected with the welfare of the country. As for Lord Aberfordbury, the ci-devant Sir Ogilvy Hibberd, who has done nothing for the country, the country shows its opinion of him by calling him "old Hibberd, him as got made a lord, the old—" or in other circles by ignoring him, or by the extreme politeness, described by Saint-Simon, which peers of an old creation offer to upstarts, giving them their full titles, while among their equals they were—so to speak—simply Pomfret, or Stoke and even Omnium, though most of his familiars simply said Duke. Rumour had it that the Bishop would not address the Duke of Omnium as Your Grace, because he hoped to be an Archbishop one day and a Grace himself, but this report (traceable we fear to Mr. Wickham, the Noel Mertons' agent) may be ignored, for everyone knew that his lordship would have given his second-best apron and gaiters to get the Duke and Duchess to dinner at the Palace.

So, to return to wherever we were, Goble, the great arch-pig-breeder, bowed to Lord Cross's wish and conducted his party to the lying-in sty.

"I could do with one or two of those," said Lord Stoke, poking at the piglets with his stick. "What's Sir Robert asking?"

"Well, my lord," said Goble, "what was your lordship thinking of offering. A fine litter they are."

"Good enough, good enough," said Lord Stoke, scratching the great sow's hairy back in a way that caused her to grunt and quiver (if anything so massive can quiver) with delight.

"Look here, my man," said Lord Stoke, as it were rolling up his shirt sleeves and spitting on his hands, "you know the market price last Friday as well as I do. That's what I'm paying. And no hanky panky about my fetching them. If Sir Robert wants me to buy them, he can send them over."

"I'm sure, my lord, I couldn't say without Sir Robert's word for it," said Goble. "He'll be down next Saturday for good, so her ladyship says, and then I'm sure Sir Robert will give you a ring, my lord," which base importation of a current pinchbeck phrase at once roused his lordship to violent protest.

"Give me a ring, eh?" said Lord Stoke, glaring at Goble. "If Sir Robert thinks I'm a Porkminster with a ring in my nose, he's welcome. Telephone, you mean. *I* don't know why anyone uses telephones. You can't hear what the other feller says on them. You tell Sir Robert I'll take two of those pigs at his price and he can send them over. Those two will do," and he poked with his stick at two of the grunting, squeaking herd who were crowding each other out at the dinner-table with disgusting greed.

"Very good, my lord," said Goble, who knew exactly how far he could go.

"No good sending me any others," said Lord Stoke. "Once I've seen a pigling I'd know him again in Australia. And here's something to wet the bargain," which archaism enchanted his listeners.

"Thank you, my lord," said Goble, touching his cap, and the party moved on to inspect the boar, who was lying massively asleep, his back turned to the audience. The afternoon was getting colder all the time and a slight but determined drizzle had now begun.

"I wish *I* had skin an inch thick with bristles all over it," said Mr. Cross to George Halliday. "It's worse than Vache-en-Etable. Do you remember that artillery major who wore galoshes? How I envied him."

"Major Spender?" said George. "The one that was always writing to his wife? Lord! how tired we got of hearing about the wife and the kiddies. I won twenty-five bob off him at rummy the night old what's-his-name got so roaring drunk," which of course led to one of those conversations described by Mrs.

Morland as Old-Bill-in-the-dugout, intensely interesting to the speakers and unbearably boring to everyone else.

"Well, I *did* enjoy that," said Mr. Cross when the whole evening had been relived from the moment when a young lieutenant produced six bottles of whiskey to the early morning when the card players had gone to sleep and the orderly quietly drank the seventh, held in reserve by him for himself. "One does miss the army sometimes. I mean I like my work and I'm keen to get on, but it was delightful not to have to think ahead."

"I know," said George. "So long as you did what the Major or the Colonel said and knew the Queen's Regulations—"

"King's Regulations then, my boy," said Mr. Cross.

"All right, all right," said George. "I was thinking of the Boer War, my boy, long before your time," and these two hard-working respectable young men had a short but agreeable all-in wrestling match, after which they followed the rest of the pig-party who had thanked Goble for their happy afternoon and everyone gladly went in to tea where Mr. Choyce joined them.

"Come and sit with us, Mr. Choyce," said Lady Graham. "The others can't talk anything but pig. Lord Stoke you have met before. Lord Cross, this is our vicar, Mr. Choyce. He has a wonderful burglar-alarm that plays Home Sweet Home," which recommendation of a clerical gentleman appeared to suit Lord Cross down to the ground. "Mrs. Morland this is Mr. Choyce. Do let him sit next to you." So Mrs. Morland sat between Lord Cross and the Vicar and enjoyed herself like anything, for both were pleasant and easy to talk to and when they talked to each other across her (which is the ideal way for two gentlemen to entertain a delightful woman—from their point of view at any rate) she was amused by their talk and bore no malice. For as men are well-known to be stupid, why bother?

"Excuse me," said Mr. Choyce to Mrs. Morland, "but is it you who writes those books?"

Mrs. Morland, well used to every form of illiteracy and

imbecility from her admirers, said if it was her books he meant, she was.

"May I tell you how *very* much I have enjoyed them," said Mr. Choyce. "All through the war I looked forward to the next one like anything. May I make one comment? Not adverse, but just a suggestion."

Mrs. Morland, who found an ever fresh pleasure and amusement in people's views of her books, said Please do.

"It was only a detail," said Mr. Choyce, "but in one of your books—I am ashamed to say I forget which—you put decani and cantoris on opposite sides."

"But they are, aren't they?" said Mrs. Morland.

"I do beg your pardon," said Mr. Choyce. "Of course they are, but what I was trying to express was that you put one in the place of the other."

"How *stupid* of me" said Mrs. Morland. "But then the other would be in the place of the one, so it would be all right, wouldn't it?"

"I fear I have not made myself quite clear," said Mr. Choyce. "One is on one side of the choir and the other on the other."

"But then it wouldn't really matter, would it?" said Mrs. Morland.

Mr. Choyce said it was *his* stupidity this time.

"Oh, but of *course* I see what you mean now," said Mrs. Morland. "One is always on ONE side and the other on the OTHER. But how does one know which is which, because they look exactly alike?"

Mr. Choyce said the decani side was the north, at which Mrs. Morland looked so unhappy that he said he meant on the right, and cantoris side was on the left.

"That is, of course, if you are looking *up* the church," said Mrs. Morland in a learned voice. "I don't mean up like looking at the roof, I mean looking at the east end."

Mr. Choyce, with an internal sigh of relief, said that was exactly it.

"So that if you are standing with your back to the altar, facing down the church, they would be on the wrong sides," said Mrs. Morland.

Mr. Choyce gave it up.

"Good Gad," said Lord Stoke, to the intense joy of all present. "It's half past five. We must be going. Lucasta's coming to see me at seven and I will *not* have my horse hurried."

Lady Graham rang the bell, and it is an interesting comment on Social Life in England that though several of those present were in a position to have a bell answered, it struck every heart afresh to find one more stronghold of time past.

"Ready, Mrs. Morland?" said Lord Stoke. "Can't keep the horse waiting. If you want your people to be punctual, be punctual yourself. Good-bye Lady Graham. Your man is sending me a couple of pigs. Tell Sir Robert, with my compliments, that he's got the best bailiff in the county. Good stock those Gobles. I remember your man's father. Children all over West Barsetshire and I'm not sure if there aren't some over Beliers way. Well, well, increase and multiply."

"But you haven't, Lord Stoke," said his old friend Mrs. Morland, at which Lord Stoke, after a short apoplectic glare, laughed in a way which convinced some of his young and far from innocent-minded hearers that he had bastards all over West Barsetshire. But we think they were wrong here. Then they all went to the front door and to the great delight of the younger members saw Lord Stoke hand Mrs. Morland into the brougham. George Halliday shut the door and then dashing round to the back of the brougham pretended to push it forward, ably seconded by Mr. Cross and it was more by luck than by skill that they did not fall flat on their faces as the horse went off at a good trot.

"Come back into the warm," said Lady Graham, "and have some sherry," an offer which Lord Cross and his son gladly accepted, as did Mr. Choyce and George Halliday. Edith did the pouring out and did it very prettily.

"So you are off to New York?" said Mr. Choyce.

"Isn't it lovely?" said Edith. "Aunt Rose is most *awfully* kind. Only I wish it weren't so far away. And I shall miss seeing father be a churchwarden. I *do* think it's a good plan, Mr. Choyce. I shall *swell* with pride. And I shall make a poem about it for father."

"You can't," said George Halliday. "There isn't a rhyme for churchwarden."

"Oh, *isn't* there?" said Edith.

> "Though his name may not be Gordon,
> He will be a good churchwarden.
> Round our sins he'll draw a cordon,
> Wash our sins out in the Jordan,
> But he *will* not live in Morden,

so there," and she cast a very pretty look of defiance at George.

"I say, why were you moving your fingers all the time?" said Mr. Choyce.

"I was counting the letters of the alphabet on them, of course," said Edith. "If you were a poet you would notice that the rhymes were in alphabetical order—except Gordon, of course."

Mr. Choyce said that had not occurred to him.

"And now, just to finish," said Edith, drunk as poets are with her own words,

> "It will be a happy wonder
> And make his heart rejoice,
> When he's a churchwarden under
> Darling Mr. Choyce.

I'm sorry I had to say darling," she added. "You see the line wouldn't have been long enough without it," but Mr. Choyce said nothing could have given him more pleasure and after some

more silly talk and laughter the men said good-bye and went
away.

"Do you know what I think, mother?" said Edith, who was in
her usual tidy way plumping up the cushions and generally
putting things straight.

"No, darling," said her mother. "What is it?"

"Well, it's rather difficult to explain," said Edith. "It's about
George and John-Arthur. I'd like to marry them both."

Lady Graham, long inured to eccentricities of her family, said
she was afraid the Bishop wouldn't allow it and they both
laughed.

The young men walked to their cars.

"Rum young woman, Edith is," said Mr. Cross. "But I like
her."

"Come to that so do I," said George. "She is awfully nice to
my people. It isn't every girl that bothers about that. My mother's awfully sensible. She never expects me to want to marry girls
just because they're a good sort."

"Forgive my butting in," said Mr. Cross. "But *do* you?"

"Come to that, do *you*?" said George.

They had been walking more slowly. Now they stopped.

"I see what you mean," said Mr. Cross. "Look here, Halliday.
We're not going to let a little thing like that come between us
after Vache-en-Etable."

"I should think not," said George warmly. "I say, next week
it's the anniversary of the day old Hopkins got his majority. Do
you remember the binge we had and how he nearly cried when
he thought of his wife and darling little kiddies. Look here. On
Friday Edith's going to London to her cousins before they fly to
America. Let's celebrate. I know the old waiter at the White
Hart and he'll see that we get a good meal. On me of course."

"Rot," said Mr. Cross. "Well, eats on you if you like. Drinks
on me. *And* champagne if they've anything decent."

"No good trying to compete with you bloated businessmen,"
said George. "Kamerad! I'll drink all you like to pay for. Look

here. Let's race as far as the Old Manor House and the loser stands beer at the Mellings Arms," all of which was duly carried out and though Edith's image remained—we think—in each heart, it certainly did not affect their appetites, nor their liking for one another.

The next few days were a good deal occupied with Edith's packing and the usual very boring fuss that has to be made about passport-renewal, currency and other unnecessary red tape. On Friday Goble drove Lady Graham and Edith to Barchester Central. Here Lady Graham put Edith into her carriage, kissed her very fondly and was driven home where, though the house was rather empty, there was plenty to do in the gentle fuss about Sir Robert's homecoming. Lady Graham also visited the Pomfrets and talked with Miss Merriman, was rung up by Lord Cross with an invitation to her and her husband to dine, went twice to see Mr. Halliday who was neither better nor worse and very good and patient on the whole, and made plans with her sister-in-law, Mrs. John Leslie over at Greshamsbury, for a great family reunion at Holdings.

"Oh Mary," she said, when the plans were more or less arranged, "that nice boy George Halliday asked me to tell you that he can take your boys on the cathedral roof any time they like. Either before they go back to school or at the half-term. Will you ring him up?" which Mary Leslie promised to do. And in case any of our readers are anxious about the excursion, we may say that Major and Minimus went as far as they dared, at which point they very sensibly stopped, while Minor with George did quite a nasty bit by the flying buttress, though the bit by the crocket was cut out by George because the masonry needed repairing. We may also say that Minor, exercising the charm which he—most unnecessarily his brother considered— used so lavishly, wrung from the old gardener a promise to look the other way if he, Minor, wanted to climb the tulip tree, and furthermore to see that His Lordship and the Old Cat (for such, we do not regret to say, was old Tomkins's way of alluding to his employers) were well out of the way.

Owing to the increasing horribleness of the food and service in restaurant cars since the noble Great Western Railway had to bow its head (and its engines, once clean as loving hands could make them from oil-valve to driver's cabin, now with wheels and axles and paint all oily, dirty and unloved; its carriages once spick and span with G.W.R. in heavy crotchet work on the head-mats—or whatever their right name is—now with unappetising seats and grimed windows and the brass handles tarnished and the horrible initials B.R. on what we can only call utility head-rests if that), Sir Robert refused to dine on the train, so Lady Graham always had dinner for him when he got home.

On this evening the house was warm and cook was putting her whole heart into the food which Sir Robert had never failed to praise except on the one or two occasions when something had gone wrong, at which times he used language that George Halliday—who had once been privileged to hear him—compared very favourably with the regimental sergeant-major's when inspecting equipment.

Lady Graham had asked Mr. Choyce to dinner, for her husband liked him and as churchwarden elect felt he ought to see his Vicar as soon as possible and find out exactly what his duties were.

"It will be so nice to have Robert here, dear Mr. Choyce," she said. "We do need good men in Barsetshire and I am sure Robert and Lord Cross will do a great deal. I do like that young Cross so much and if his sister comes to the Old Manor House it will be delightful. And a change for George too. He is so good with his father and running the farm. And Mrs. Halliday will like to know that the right people are in the Old Manor House. And, so Lord Cross tells me, they are only giving a short lease, so that if Mr. Halliday should die at any time, she will be able to live in whichever house she wishes."

"Do you know, Lady Graham," said Mr. Choyce, "the person

I feel most sorry for is George. He is such a good lad—man I should say, I suppose—doing his duty with no particular reward."

"No. No particular reward," said Lady Graham thoughtfully. "No. One never knows," and she fell into a muse, sitting by the fire with its leaping light on her face and Mr. Choyce thought, not for the first time, what a remarkably attractive and delightful woman she was. Exactly the sort of wife one would want the Vicar's Churchwarden to have.

"I suppose darling Edith is in America by now," said Lady Graham. "Or have they been going backwards? I mean all this curious arrangement of losing time or gaining time which I shall *never* understand," and as she spoke the sound of the car scrunching on the gravel was heard.

"That must be Robert," said Lady Graham. "No, don't move, Mr. Choyce. You stay in the warmth and I will bring Robert in."

So her ladyship went out into the hall. Aggie Hubback in a state of mild hysteria opened the inner door and Sir Robert Graham came in.

COLOPHON

This book is being reissued as part of Moyer Bell's Angela Thirkell Series.

The text of this book was set in Caslon, a typeface designed by William Caslon I (1692-1766). This face designed in 1725 has gone through many incarnations. It was the mainstay of British printers for over one hundred years and remains very popular today. The version used here is Adobe Caslon. The display faces are Adobe Caslon Outline, Calligraphic 421, and Adobe Caslon.

Composed by Alabama Book Composition, Deatsville, Alabama.

Enter Sir Robert was printed by Data Reproductions, Auburn Hills, Michigan on acid-free paper.

Moyer Bell
Kymbolde Way
Wakefield, RI 02879